The Alien Mate Index

Book 1: Abducted

Evangeline Anderson

PUBLISHED BY:

Evangeline Anderson

The Alien Mate Index

Book 1: Abducted

Copyright © 2016 by Evangeline Anderson

Author's Note

Throughout this book, you'll notice lots of sci-fi and fantasy references because, well, I'm a geek. :) I thought it would be fun to see how many of you are as geeky as I am. If you want to list the references as you see them, then send me the list at evangelineanderson28@gmail.com, I will put your name in the pot for the drawing of a gift card. This contest is good until book number 2 of Alien Mate Index, Protected comes out.

Good luck and see how many you can find! Some are hidden and there's one I bet no one will get ;)

Evangeline

Dedication

With love to all my Kindred readers. If you like *Kindred*, I think you'll love *Alien Mate Index* as well. I write these books with all of you in mind. I feel very blessed to have such awesome people to pretend with me.

Hugs and Happy Reading to you all!

Evangeline

Table of Contents

The Alien Mate Index

Book 1: Abducted

Evangeline Anderson

The Alien Mate Index

or

How I became an Alien Mail Order Bride

Part One: Through the Looking Glass
(No, seriously, I'm not kidding. I actually went through a freaking looking glass.)

Chapter One

Zoe

All the hottest mail order brides come from Russia.

Russia or somewhere over in the Ukraine. At least, that's what it looks like if you're surfing the Internet late at night and you run across one of those awful Bride sites.

All those women are tall and thin with sleek, perfect hair and sexy smiles. Oh, *and* they're all willing to travel halfway around the world to get out of the crappy place they're living and start a new life.

Of course, they might change their minds if they found out they'd have to travel halfway across the freaking *universe*. That might be a deal breaker. I know it would have been for me—if anyone had given me a choice.

I didn't get a choice though. In fact, I didn't even know I was *in* the AMI. That's the Alien Mate Index—which is the site full of women that Alien males with a taste for Earth girl coochie can choose from. Hell, I didn't even know there *was* an Alien Mate Index at all!

Until I got abducted.

Now, lest you go thinking that I'm some six-foot tall, hot, blonde supermodel, let me set the record straight. I'm not. I'm *so* not.

I'm five four in my stocking feet and I have curly auburn hair that tends to frizz on a humid day. And since I live in Florida, *every* day is a humid day.

In addition to not being tall with sleek blonde hair, I am also *not* thin. That's okay though—I'm not afraid to admit I'm plus sized. I own my curves and I love them. I spent too many years at Weight Watchers counting points until I felt like a freaking adding machine. Finally I decided, you know what? Forget it. Me getting skinny just isn't going to happen.

Now I live my life by the 80/20 rule. Eighty percent of the time I eat healthy and the other twenty percent I eat a damn donut if I want it. So what if I'm a size sixteen the rest of my life? I can deal with that as long as I don't have to live on nothing but kale and quinoa. Krispy Kreme is more my style anyway.

I guess what I'm trying to tell you is that I'm not exactly mail order bride material. I'm just an ordinary girl with a little more junk in the trunk than usual, flyaway red hair, and too many freckles. I'm *not* the kind of girl a guy would point to on a website and go— "Her—oh my God, I've got to have *her*."

At least, I didn't think so.

Again, until I got abducted.

But let me tell you about that—and you might want to take some notes. You might want to know what or *who* might be coming for you. That's because you never can tell who might be watching you, even when you're having the most boring, awful, ordinary day of your life…

"Oh my God, he's being an asshole again. I'm telling you, Leah, I can't take much more," I muttered into my phone as I sat huddled in a stall of the employee bathroom at Lauder, Lauder and Associates. I worked as a paralegal there and the lawyer I was assigned to, Dayton Lauder the third, was a real piece of work.

Dayton always spoke in this booming voice, as though he was addressing a crowd of admirers and he wanted the ones in the back to be able to hear him. Unfortunately, most days it was just him and me and I was most definitely *not* an admirer. That didn't stop him from "yell-talking"(as my friend Charlotte called it) all the time, though. I ended most work days with a pounding headache.

If poor voice modulation was the worst thing I had to put up with, I might not have minded so much. Unfortunately, Dayton had other problems that put the "yell-talking" one in the shade.

One problem was his personal hygiene—or lack thereof. When most people think of a lawyer, they imagine some sexy associate from The Good Wife with an immaculate, pressed, tailored suit, neatly clipped hair, and manicured hands.

Not Dayton Lauder the third.

As a tax lawyer, he didn't really go to court much. He just sat in his office and did paperwork, so I guess he thought it didn't matter how he came to work.

Well, it mattered to me. Or *anybody* that got too close to him.

My boss had a love affair with brown, polyester suits. I say "suits" but in fact, I was convinced he only owned one of them which he wore every single day and never cleaned. It was rumpled and wrinkled and he wore it with a stained white shirt that had dirt marks on the collar and sleeves. Every time he waved his arms—he did this a lot while he was "yell-talking"—a huge cloud of nauseating BO would waft out, nearly knocking me over if I stood too close.

He had coffee breath too—not too surprising since he had me brew him several pots a day. Of course, I'm a paralegal, *not* a freaking barista but the economy sucked and I needed the job. So I brewed the damn coffee and even fixed it just the way he liked it— three creams and four sugars.

Now, people can be socially awkward and not be horrible. But again, not my boss. He shouted at me a lot and just that morning he'd actually thrown a stapler at my head because I had stapled his papers in the *top* left hand corner instead of putting the staple right in the *middle* where he preferred it.

What an ass.

After the stapler incident, I had run to the bathroom where I was pouring out my heart to Leah, one of my two best friends.

"Oh, Zoe, I'm so sorry." Leah had a soft, sweet voice— everything about her was soft and sweet actually—that I normally found soothing. But today, I was too upset to be soothed.

"He threw a *stapler* at my freaking *head*," I emphasized.

"That's *awful*," she exclaimed. And then I heard her say, "All right, sweetheart, I'll help you find your pony in just a minute. Right now, though, Miss Heidi is in charge. Okay?"

Leah works in a private daycare center that specializes in mildly autistic children and she's better with kids than I could ever be. Talk about the patience of a saint.

"Kids sneaking into the break room again?" I asked.

She sighed. "Yes, I'm sorry. Heidi is supposed to be in charge but they always seem to want me. Makes it hard to take a break."

"I shouldn't be taking up your time then," I said. "Let me let you go."

"No—keep talking. You need to get it off your chest." Leah would make an awesome therapist, I swear, which is what she really wanted to be if she could ever get back to school.

There was a clicking on the line that I recognized.

"Oh, no. Hang on," Leah said, her soft voice suddenly filled with dread. There was a pause and I wondered if it was Gerald, her overprotective fiancée calling. Leah always claimed he had her best interest at heart but over time he had become more and more controlling until Charlotte, my other best friend, and I, were really worried about her.

A moment later, Leah came back on.

"It's just Charlotte," she said, her voice filled with relief. "Should I put her on too?"

"Of course. She must have gotten my message—I called her before I called you." I cleared my throat. "I, uh, thought it might be Gerald calling you again," I said as she merged the calls.

"Nope. He's off on a business trip this weekend." Leah's voice sounded light and happy—I wondered if she had any idea that she sounded that way when her fiancée was gone.

"Who's on a business trip? Gerald?" Charlotte's no-nonsense voice came on the line, filled with disbelief. "And he trusts you to be in the house alone all weekend?"

"Of *course* he trusts me." There was a note of defensiveness in

Leah's voice that worried me. I had never liked her fiancée and lately his nasty attitude seemed to be getting worse. But now wasn't the time to stage a "your boyfriend is a controlling asshole" intervention. Taking pity on her, I decided to turn the conversation back to my current situation.

Quickly, I outlined the situation to Charlotte. She's a nurse practitioner working for an orthopedic surgeon—he even lets her assist in some of the surgeries he does. She has the best job by far of the three of us but I can't be jealous of her for it—she really busted her ass to get where she is. Not that getting a paralegal degree is all rainbows and unicorns but it's not as complicated as what Charlotte is doing.

"Report him to Human Resources," Charlotte said at once, when I finished the near-miss-stapler-to-the-head story for the second time.

I sighed. "We've been over that—you know I can't! His uncle and father own the company. Human resources isn't going to do jack shit about it!"

"Zoe…" Leah didn't like harsh language.

"Sorry, Leah but you know it's true. I just—"

Suddenly I heard a strange gurgling coming from the stall beside me. Uh-oh—was someone in there? Specifically, was Mindy the office tattletale taking notes?

"Hang on a minute, guys," I told my friends in a low voice. "I'm not sure I'm alone in here."

"Uh-oh," Leah whispered.

I risked a glance down but didn't see any feet at the bottom of the stall. My heart, which had started to pound, slowed a little. Whew—all safe, I had the bathroom to myself to bitch!

"Everything okay?" Charlotte asked.

"Yup. All clear." I sighed again. "Look guys, I know I complain about my asshole boss—sorry Leah—all the time but this is the first time he's actually *thrown* something at me. I swear I don't know what is *wrong* with him!"

"He's a jerk," Charlotte said bluntly. "And he shouldn't get away with it."

"Right," I muttered. "And he wouldn't if I had the guts to quit. But I need this job too much—I'll lose my apartment if I walk off now."

"How about that law firm downtown?" Leah asked. "I thought you were going to put in an application there."

"I did," I said. "But they aren't hiring right now. So I don't—"

Suddenly the gurgling sound in the stall next to me started up again. Only this time it was louder—so loud in fact it sounded like the toilet was overflowing. And then I heard this weird music— kind of like a trumpet blast only louder.

"What the *Hell?*" I muttered, pushing open the door of my stall. What was going on in the stall beside me? Was someone flushing the toilet and playing a trumpet at the same time? And if so, who was doing it? As far as I knew, we didn't have any budding musicians at Lauder, Lauder and Associates. Or if we did you wouldn't know it—I swear working at that place smothered every spark of creativity. Still, I decided to check out the noise. When I bent down, I still didn't see any feet.

"Zoe? What's going on?" Charlotte asked.

"Yeah—what's that music?" Leah chimed in. Geeze, was it really so loud they could hear it on the other end of the phone?

"I don't know," I said. "But I'm going to find out."

Which was absolutely the stupidest thing I could have done. But of course, I didn't know it at the time. This being pre-abduction, as I said before.

Carefully, I tented my fingers and pushed lightly on the stall door. It swung open slowly revealing...nothing. Just a handicapped stall with railings on one side of the toilet and a sink with a mirror over it.

Wait...maybe not *nothing*.

The mirror over the sink was doing something weird. And by weird, I mean it wasn't reflecting what I expected it to be reflecting—namely my reflection. Instead, it had a swirling pattern going on—a whirling ring of colors that spun outward from a single point. It looked like one of those hypno-gifs you see sometimes where you're supposed to stare at it for two minutes and then close your eyes and look away and you'll see something you've never seen before.

Well, I *was* about to see something I'd never seen before—and it was going to change my life—only I didn't know it at the time.

Like a fool, I moved closer.

"Zoe? Zoe?" the voices of my two best friends pulled me back to reality. I looked down at the phone in my hand and realized I was just holding it limp at my side. When had I taken it away from my ear? And how had I gotten so close to the swirling mirror? I was standing right in front of it, almost close enough to touch it.

"Guys?" I started to lift the phone to my ear and that was when the swirling stopped and a face appeared.

Not *my* face—that would have been normal.

No, it was another face—an alien face—and it was staring at me, right out of the mirror.

I wanted to scream but all of the air seemed to have left my lungs somehow. What the hell was going on?

The alien face looked at me speculatively. It was male—that much was clear. Strong features and gold eyes with vertical pupils like a cat's stared back at me. He had cheekbones sharp enough to cut yourself on and a nose that looked like it had been broken at least once. A neatly clipped mustache and goatee framed sensual lips that looked cruelly amused. He had dark red skin—almost maroon—I could see a lot of that because he appeared to be wearing a black, wife-beater type t-shirt that left his muscular arms bare.

Actually, except for the cat eyes and red skin, he looked strangely human. Well, except for the horns.

Did I mention he had freaking *horns?*

Because he did—little short, sharp pointed ones, growing out either side of his forehead—right at his temples.

I stared at them, dumbfounded, unable to speak for a moment. And that's unusual for me because I'm almost always shooting off my mouth.

All I could think was, *the Devil.* Oh my God, the freaking Devil was staring at me from the mirror of the handicapped bathroom at Lauder, Lauder and Associates and I had no idea what to do.

My mind started going over all the things I'd done wrong recently. Okay, I might have fudged a little on my taxes. Using my laptop to check reports while I lay on the couch watching *Sherlock* reruns on Netflix counts as having a home office—right? And then there was the time I accidentally shoplifted a pair of socks. I forgot I had them in my hand and walked right out of the store with them. And then I was too embarrassed to bring them back so I guess I basically *stole* them but I didn't mean to so—

Suddenly, the Devil spoke, ending my train of thought as thoroughly as though it had run into the side of a mountain.

"Yes," he said in a deep, growling voice. "She is the one."

The one for what? The one to drag straight down to Hell and poke in the ass with a fiery pitchfork? Oh my God, was cheating on my taxes and shoplifting socks *that* bad?

"I...I'm sorry," I stuttered but just then another voice—a piping, high voice like a Disney animal—answered him.

"If you are certain this female is the one Your Eminence requires, then I shall begin the transport at once."

Transport? What Transport? Instinctively, I began backing away from the haunted mirror to Hell but then the swirling started again. And this time there was a wind that went with it.

A sucking, howling wind that dragged at me, pulling me towards the mirror.

"Help!" I screamed, or tried to scream, anyway. My voice was lost in the vortex as I was pulled closer and closer to the mirror.

My feet left the floor and I put out my hands, trying to stop my forward momentum. My phone clattered into the sink and I could hear Leah and Charlotte shouting on the other end of it but their voices seemed tiny and distant.

My hand connected to the mirror...and sank into it. I gasped in fear as I saw first my hand and then my whole arm swallowed up in the swirling psychedelic colors. My other hand and arm followed and suddenly the mirror was right in front of my face.

And then I felt myself getting sucked in completely. Lauder, Lauder and Associates disappeared and the last thing I heard was my two best friends frantically screaming my name.

Then...nothing.

Who knew the gateway to Hell was located in the employees' bathroom?

Chapter Two

Zoe

At first I couldn't see anything but a hazy rainbow—maybe the after effects of the psychedelic bathroom-mirror-portal-thing I'd been sucked into. Then the swirling colors faded and I found I was looking up into five faces—at least, I *thought* they were faces. They certainly weren't human faces though, that was for sure. Maybe they were demons? That would make sense although they didn't look like any demons I had ever seen. Also, the floor I was lying on was cold—like *freezing*. Wasn't Hell supposed to be hot?

I blinked groggily and had a blurred impression of dull silver metal walls surrounding me.

"Where am I? Is this Hell?" I croaked.

"The Pure One wakes," one of them announced in the high, piping tones I recognized as the Disney character voice I'd heard before. Great, I'd been dragged into the afterlife by the demon version of Bambi. Or something that *sounded* like Bambi, anyway—it sure as Hell (pardon the pun) didn't look like him. None of them did.

Ten bulging purple eyeballs on long stalks studied me with apparent interest. The eyes were connected to long, slender blue bodies that looked like some mad scientist had decided to grow three foot long earthworms and dye them indigo. They weren't completely worm-like though—they each had multiple pairs of arms with long, claw-like fingers.

Fingers that were currently reaching for me.

"No...*no!*" I gasped, trying to roll away from them. "Get *away* from me!"

"Be cautious! The Pure One is agitated!" Bambi squeaked and the worm-like demon creatures slithered hurriedly out of my way, obviously not too eager to be squished into worm pâté.

Suddenly, I saw the Devil again. He leaned over me and I froze at once, startled to see his handsome, horned face staring at me upside down.

"Be still," he commanded. "Tazaxx doesn't take damaged goods and I've already spent most of my reserves buying your ridiculously expensive hide. I can't afford another Pure One."

"Another *what?*" I demanded, trying to sit up.

"At least you look the part," he remarked, his golden eyes roving over my body. "Those curves—Gods, no wonder the Ancient Ones wanted your pitiful little planet protected. You'd have been raided eons ago if every female on your world looks like you."

"I...my...*what?*" The way he was looking at me made me feel naked. Then I looked down and realized I *was.* I was completely nude—*butt-nekked* to borrow a phrase from my very Southern grandma.

Not only was I naked, I was lying there on display like some kind of pale freckled, red-headed buffet for the Devil and all his minions to feast on. Well, if he *was* the Devil. Some of what he'd been saying had penetrated my foggy brain and I was beginning to have my doubts about that, despite the red skin, golden eyes, and horns.

I had no doubt about covering myself, though. I pulled my knees up to my chest and crossed my ankles tight. I own my curves but I'm still shy about showing them off in the nude — especially to a Devil-looking man who had just dragged my ass through a mirror and was eyeing me like I was some kind of Victoria's Secret angel sent just for him.

"There's no need to hide yourself," he remarked sarcastically. "I've already seen it all — you'll be most pleasing to Tazaxx. To any male, for that matter."

"What are you *talking* about?" I demanded, lifting my chin.

He seemed awfully tall and big but maybe that was just because I was huddled on the ground and he was looming over me.

"Are you the Devil? And is this Hell?" I asked, needing to make sure. "Because if it is, I swear I didn't mean to take those socks. If you'll just return me to my home I promise I'll dig them out of my sock drawer and take them back right away. I'll pay double what they cost — *triple* even."

The Devil frowned at me, his luscious, cruel lips twisting with the expression. Which raised yet another question — was the Devil supposed to be hot? I mean, in the sexy sense — not the actual temperature sense like all of Hell was supposed to be hot. Oh God, I was rambling, even to myself. I was in so much trouble here...

"What is she talking about?" he asked someone I couldn't see. "She's not making any sense." He stabbed a finger at one of the blue worm-like creatures. "You told me the transfer process wouldn't hurt her mental ability. I need a perfect specimen. Tazaxx won't trade for an idiot — not even a fucking gorgeous one."

"I believe, Master, that the female is referring to an Earth religion," a crisp voice that put me in mind of a proper English butler, stated. "The religion says that those who do evil are sent to a region called 'Hell' after death to pay for their sins. There they are persecuted by a fallen deity who torments them forever in a lake of fire."

"I would hardly call shoplifting socks 'evil'," I protested. "I mean, wrong, yes but evil—no. At least, not enough to get dragged down to Hell. Which I'm guessing this is *not?*" I added hopefully.

The Devil—(or not-Devil? Now I didn't know what to call him)—rumbled laughter.

"No, little Pure One, this is not your Hell. Look around—do you see any lake of fire?"

"N-no," I admitted.

"Then what would make you think this is your version of damnation?" he asked, his deep voice sounding genuinely confused.

"I believe, Master, that would be due to your...*ahem* horns," the proper butler voice said.

I looked around—where was that voice coming from? There appeared to be a tiny golden insect sitting on the not-Devil's broad shoulder. But could such a tiny thing speak?

"My horns? You have a problem with my *horns?*" The look on his chiseled features darkened—the amused expression sliding away from his handsome face. His cat-eyes glowed an even more brilliant gold for a moment and he seemed to get even bigger somehow. His skin got even redder and the scowl on his face made him look absolutely terrifying.

I gave a little squeak and scooted away from him as well as I could. Unfortunately, my bare butt seemed frozen to the cold metal floor so I didn't get too far. What I wouldn't give for some panties— even some big old cotton granny panties would do. In fact, they would be *great*—they would help me slide instead of sticking to the damn floor! Okay, my mind was going on a tangent again. This was bad. Really bad.

Calm down, Zoe, I told myself. *Keep it together, girl. It's going to be okay. This is probably just a bad dream. A really, really **vivid** nightmare and you're going to wake up any minute.*

I hoped, anyway.

"Master, I could be wrong, but if I read the elevated heart rate and respiration of the female correctly, I believe you are frightening her," the proper voice said. "Quite badly in fact."

"H-he's right," I whispered, trying to make my voice sound normal and failing abysmally. "Y-you're scaring the ever-loving crap out of me, to be honest."

"Forgive me." He straightened up a little and his eyes stopped glowing. "I thought you were making a reference to my parentage. I forgot—you know nothing of my kind, just as we know almost nothing of yours, as your world has been isolated for so long. Very well then, little Pure One. I am *not* a fallen deity. Or a deity of any kind. I'm just a half-breed smuggler who picked you from the AMI."

"The...the AMI?" I asked, feeling my heart rate start to go back to normal now that he wasn't glaring golden daggers at me.

"The AMI—The Alien Mating Index," piped up the worm creature I had dubbed Bambi. "We are an agency that specializes in finding and procuring only the most elite females. Only those that were seeded with hidden talents by the Ancient Ones are found and taken. Our database has millions of candidates on Earth alone and is growing daily as new abilities are being discovered and new and luscious females come of age to be harvested. Males come from all over the galaxy to see what we have to offer and—"

"Wait a minute, wait a minute." I said, holding up my hand. "Stop the sales pitch. Did you just say you're running some kind of an alien dating agency here? Because I don't remember signing up to be matched with any kind of alien, okay? So there must be some mistake—if you'd kindly just take me back to Earth—"

"Impossible," twittered Bambi in his high, squeaky voice. "You have been chosen as the prime candidate by his Eminence, Lord Sarden. He has commanded that you be transported and has paid your contract price in full—we never remit such a payment unless just cause is found."

"Lord Sarden?" I said, staring up at the not-Devil guy again. "Lord of what? Lord of *who?*"

He shrugged, his impossibly broad shoulders rolling with the motion.

"Don't pay any attention—that's just how the Commercians talk. Obsequious little bastards, always looking to turn a credit."

"But Master," interrupted the proper butler voice. "You *would* be Lord if you would claim your rightful place. If you would only—"

"That's enough, A.L.," Sarden snapped.

"Forgive me, Master." The golden insect on his shoulder— which looked a little like a dragonfly—fluttered its glittering wings in agitation.

"Forgiven. Just keep your mouth shut." Sarden looked back at me. "Basically what they're saying is that I paid for you and you're *not* going back."

"What?" I demanded, sitting up straighter. Forgetting I was naked, I put my hands on my hips. "You *paid* for me? You can't do that! I'm not for *sale!*"

"You most certainly are—this whole planet is. Now that the lock put on your world by the Ancient Ones is being dissolved, your entire world's female population is fair game."

"Lock? Ancient Ones?" I shook my head—I was getting more and more lost.

"The ones who seeded your planet millennia ago," Bambi said helpfully. "They traveled across the universe, planting the seeds of life on only the worlds they considered the most deserving. Their DNA lives on in many sectors but only on a few, rare, specially selected worlds has it been preserved in its purest form."

"And the 'lock' they put around your planet is what I believe you Earthlings refer to as an 'ozone layer,'" said the proper butler voice, which seemed to be coming from the golden dragonfly. "Now that much of it has been removed and your planet has begun to heat, outside investors are free to harvest Earth's females. Females such as yourself, who are most valuable because they have not bred with any of the other peoples of the known universe. This is why we dub you 'Pure Ones'—because you have only the pure blood of the Ancient Ones running through your veins."

Forget about the Ancient Ones and all the crap he was spouting about 'Pure Ones', my mind snagged on something else the butler voice had said.

"The *ozone* layer?" I stared at the not-Devil guy, aka Sarden, in mounting disbelief. "Are you saying that me being abducted is a result of the hole in the ozone layer? I got snatched because of *Global Warming?*"

He shrugged again. "If that is what you call it."

I wanted to laugh but I clamped down on it, knowing what came out of me would be more like a scream.

All the environmentalists and climate change people had tried to warn us. They said that the ice caps would melt…that the seas would rise…that all the polar bears and penguins and puffins would die…They never freaking said we'd be abducted by alien bride hunters, though!

I bet more people would have sat up and paid attention if someone would have mentioned *that* little tidbit of information. I know *I* would have run my AC less in the summer and carpooled to work to keep from being snatched by aliens. I was betting a lot of other girls would too. But who was telling them? Nobody, that's who. So now they were fair game for this crazy AMI organization.

Thanks for nothing, Al Gore.

"The moment the hole in your ozone layer was wide enough, the Commercians moved in, as they always do with newly harvestable planets," the butler voice which Sarden had called "A.L." informed me.

I was beginning to think the voice coming from the dragonfly sounded like a cross between C-3P0 and Jarvis, the mechanical servant in the Iron Man movies. It sounded damn strange, coming from an insect. But before I could answer, it continued.

"The Commercians injected your atmosphere with trillions of tiny viruses—some for universal translation so that brides from your planet might understand their future mates, some for immunization that our alien pathogens would not infect or kill you, some for surveillance so that every female may be watched in any reflective surface, and some for transportation—which process you have just undergone. Then they opened their base for business."

"Hold on—go back," I said. "Did you say *any* reflective surface?"

The dragonfly fluttered its jewel-like wings.

"Indeed. Surveillance and transport viruses work together. They are silicone based life forms which are able to live in glass, metal…even water."

"So you're watching every woman on Earth every time she

checks her lipstick or does her hair?" I was horrified at the idea. Freaking peeping-Tom-pervert aliens!

"As you see." Bambi made a gesture with one of his many clawed hands (come to think of it, he looked more like a centipede than a worm) and a large screen made of golden light suddenly appeared behind him. My heart caught in my throat when I saw who it was displaying.

Leah was standing there with her phone pressed to her ear, talking rapidly and looking worried. The angle we were looking at her from seemed strange and her image was elongated and distorted but I could still see her long waterfall of silky brown hair and her big, brown eyes as she spoke.

"Fix distortion—switch viewing area," Bambi commanded in his squeaky, innocent-sounding voice.

At once, the angle changed and we appeared to be looking at Leah from the side—as though we were staring in through the small window of the break room at her work, I realized.

"What…how were we looking at her before?" I asked, aloud, my mouth as dry as cotton. "You said, any reflective surface, right?"

"The scanner picks the first reflective surface it can find," Bambi explained. "This was our initial viewpoint." He pointed one clawed hand at the curved, silver side of the toaster which was sitting on the counter in front of Leah.

"Oh my God," I muttered. "And I thought it was weird that you dragged me through the bathroom mirror. Now you're telling me it's not even safe to make *toast?*"

"Any reflective surface can be used for viewing and transport," Bambi assured me. With another wave of his clawed hand, another image came into view.

I bit my lip—this time it was Charlotte but she was upside

down.

"Switch viewing area," Bambi said again.

The view changed to a more normal look and I saw that Charlotte had a half-empty Greek yogurt container in front of her and was toying with a silver spoon as she spoke on the phone. A spoon—so that was why she had appeared upside down! Not only was it not safe to make toast, yogurt was out too!

Breakfast was never going to be the same again.

Charlotte looked as worried as Leah had. As always, her thick, wavy blonde hair was confined in a tight, no-nonsense ponytail and her sharp green eyes were intense as she spoke into her phone—no doubt she and Leah were discussing what had happened to me and what they should do about it.

I felt my gut twist.

"Those are my best friends—please, you have to leave them alone!"

"We will leave them in peace," Bambi promised.

"Oh, thank you," I whispered, but my relief was short lived.

"At least until a customer comes who wishes to buy them," Bambi finished. "After all, both are Pure Ones and either or both might have hidden gifts from the Ancient Ones—it is difficult to tell without further testing."

"You leave them alone!" I snapped at him. "And better yet, send me back to them. They're worried sick about me already—can't you see that?"

"Regrettably, your former life and friendships must now be left behind," Bambi informed me. He made a gesture and the screen made of light that showed Charlotte's face disappeared as if it had never been there in the first place. "Currently you are no less than three hundred miles above the surface of your planet on our base."

"Your base? Is that where I am?" I looked around again at the plain metal walls and floor. There was a row of what looked like holographic lights blinking in one corner. Was that some kind of control panel? It looked about the right size and height for the worm-like Commercians to use, though Bambi hadn't needed it to show me the light screen and my friends.

"Their base is a ship orbiting quite close to your planet," A.L. informed me. "It's quite easy to conceal amidst all the space junk you have floating in your outer orbit. Your people certainly seem bent on being harvested—it appears that you dissolved the lock the Ancient Once put around your planet yourselves."

"Yeah, right, whatever," I muttered, feeling like a scolded child. "I guess we did. But we had no idea there were aliens looking to abduct us as mail order brides!"

"How could you not?" Bambi asked in his piping voice. Now that I'd been watching him for a while, I realized he looked different from the other Commercians—his wormy hide was a slightly lighter shade of blue. "For the past fifty to seventy Earth years or so we have been testing our transfer equipment by abducting one or two Earthlings every year and then returning them," he informed me.

I looked at him in horror. "So all those stories about being taken by aliens are true? Not just crazy people saying crazy things?"

"I am afraid so. We had to test and perfect our equipment, after all." Bambi shrugged—or what I assumed was his version of a shrug. His wormy body rippled with the gesture.

"Oh my God," I whispered. "But in all those stories—or most of them—the abducted people get...get *probed*." I looked at Sarden quickly. "You're not going to...I won't let you! I'll fight every step of the way if you try to stick something up my..."

I trailed off, finally registering the look of amusement on his sharp features.

"No, no—please go on." He made a sweeping gesture at me with one big hand. "Where exactly did you think I wanted to, ah, *probe* you?"

"Never mind," I said grumpily, seeing he was laughing at me. Clearly some of the crazy abduction talk was just that—crazy.

"The captured Earthlings were probably referring to our sensitivity tests," Bambi informed me, making me feel nervous all over again. "We are required to run certain examinations to be certain that our subjects are healthy and that the transportation process did not injure or mutate them in any way."

"*Mutate* them?" I looked down at myself, wondering if I had grown a third nipple or an eleventh toe or something awful like that.

"Don't worry," Sarden rumbled, giving me that annoying, sardonic smile I was beginning to really dislike. "You're fine."

"Technically we cannot say that for sure until she is tested," Bambi pointed out.

"No—no tests!" I insisted, trying to keep my chin up and my voice strong. But the awful reality was, if they wanted to test me—to *probe* me—they could. There were too many of them and I was just one naked, unarmed Earth girl.

God, what I wouldn't give for the little canister of mace I carried around in my purse right now! Or maybe Charlotte's taser—she'd been attacked once in college and now she doesn't play around. She will straight up taze a guy if he comes at her in any kind of threatening way. I wished she was here with me now to taze the big, red son of a bitch alien who was smirking down at me.

Speaking of the red son of a bitch, he seemed to read my mind.

"No need to fear, little Pure One—no one will be probing any part of your lush body. Though I confess it's a tempting idea," he murmured. "You're safe enough while you're with me. Of course after I trade you, I can't say." He shook his head. "You're even more beautiful than your image on the viewer. It's a damn shame to trade you to Tazaxx."

The way he was eyeing me made me realize I was exposed—my arm had slipped and one of my nipples was peeking out at him. I readjusted quickly, but I was damn tired of feeling at a disadvantage just because I was naked.

"Listen, you're going to have to stop talking like that because you can't buy or trade what's not for sale," I said, glaring up at him. "Now give me some clothes and let me go home because you're not trading me to *anyone.* Read my lips—*you don't own me and I am not going with you!*"

It's hard to make a point sitting down while the other guy is looming over you. I started to struggle to my feet—not easy with one arm locked in a death grip over my ta-tas and the other shielding my lady-bits.

"Here." Sarden reached down a hand to help me up. My impassioned little speech didn't seem to have phased him at all. Not surprising since he apparently thought he held all the cards. Well, to be honest, he pretty much did, I had to admit to myself. But still, I'm no quitter! I wasn't going to let him just steal me away and march me off to some Godforsaken planet where—

My thoughts cut off abruptly when his big hand made contact with my skin for the first time. I felt a shock of something like electricity go through me—a jolt that seemed to sizzle through every nerve in my body. It raised chill bumps over every inch of my skin and made my nipples into two painfully tight points.

"Ah!" I gasped, stumbling back from him and nearly falling.

"Gods!" he growled at the same time, jerking his hand away. Whatever the weird jolt was, clearly he had felt it too.

"What...what *was* that?" I gasped, standing shakily, still trying to cover myself.

Sarden didn't answer me. Instead, he looked at the blue wormy Commercians.

"You didn't tell me when I picked her that she was a La-ti-zal! Quick — get an inhibitor on her — *now.*"

"A what?" I demanded but the wormy little aliens were already snapping some kind of bronze metal bracelet around my wrist. I looked down at the band and saw it had a little window on it that had glowing, incomprehensible symbols jiggling across it.

Great, I was wearing the Alien version of a Fitbit.

I could imagine the readout now — *You've already gone three hundred miles today, just a few million more into outer space and you'll reach your abduction goal!* Har-har, very funny.

The strange jolt I'd felt was still making me tingle in the most uncomfortable places. And it appeared to be affecting my captor too. Sarden was pressing his thumb and fingers to his closed eyelids and rubbing like a man trying to drive back a migraine.

"Gods, the colors I saw," he muttered. "Whole spectrums of light..." Looking up at me he said, "Your hair — it's the color of flames. And your eyes...I've never seen anything so blue."

"Um...*okay*," I said carefully. "Are you just now noticing all that? Look — what just happened anyway? What was that word you called me before you jerked away like I was a hot stove?"

"A *La-ti-zal*," the proper butler voice informed me and the golden dragonfly fluttered on Sarden's shoulder. "One especially bred by the Ancient Ones to have extra gifts. They are very rare and valuable. A tingling sensation during first contact between such a gifted one and one of another of the Twelve Sentient Peoples she is sexually compatible with is normally the sign of a *La-ti-zal*. Which is, I believe, how Master Sarden ascertained your abilities."

"Which is good. It means Tazaxx will *have* to make the trade. He won't be able to resist her." Sarden straightened up and I saw for the first time how truly immense he was.

Earlier I'd thought that he just looked big because I was sitting and he was standing—but it hadn't just been a trick of perspective. This alien was *huge.* He had to be seven feet tall at least, I estimated. In fact, the top of my head barely came up past his elbow and his shoulders were easily twice as broad as mine. He was muscular too but not in a gross, over-the-top, ropey-veiny way. He just looked incredibly cut and intimidating, standing there in his tight black trousers and his black sleeveless t-shirt looking thing.

With his incredible abs, neatly clipped mustache and goatee, and those intense golden eyes he looked positively mouthwatering. If you're into Devil worship, that is, which I most certainly am *not*.

But hot or not—and he was, most definitely huge and hot—I didn't like the way he thought he'd bought me and he was already planning to trade me away.

"She'll do," he said to Bambi who was watching, his stalk eyes wide. "I'll take her back to my ship at once since our transaction is completed."

"Negative," Bambi protested in his piping voice. "You paid only enough credits for a standard Pure One—an Earth basic female. The charge for an elite *La-ti-zal* is much higher."

"Then you should find a way to test the females and be sure of what they are before you sell them," Sarden growled. "All sales are final—it says so in your own brochure."

For the first time, I noticed he was wearing a large, chunky silver ring with a black stone on the middle finger of his left hand. He made a motion with it and a holographic display, showing all kinds of Alien symbols I couldn't read, appeared and started scrolling through the air.

"There—see?" he said, pointing to a bit of floating green text that looked like squiggles and lines to me. Apparently the translation viruses the aliens had sent down through the hole in the ozone layer only worked for spoken communication. I was on my own if I wanted to read something.

"This is true," Bambi agreed, sounding very unhappy about it. "But we have been meaning to refine our testing for some time. If you had not come so early, we would have had time."

"So now you're complaining that I'm your first customer?" Sarden raised one arched black eyebrow at him. "You shouldn't have opened for business if you weren't ready."

"You must at least allow us to perform the sensitivity tests," Bambi exclaimed.

"Well…" Sarden appeared to consider the idea. "It would make trading her to Tazaxx easier if I had a certificate of sensitivity on file."

"Very good." Bambi made a motion and two of the wormy Commercians slithered away only to return with a large contraption that floated through the air between them, guided by the lightest touches of their long claws.

I bit the inside of my cheek, trying not to freak out and scream. The weird machine the Commercians were bringing looked like a high-tech version of the Iron Maiden I'd seen in a Medieval museum once. It had a padded upright table with straps on one side to hold the victim in place. The other half, which was clearly meant to close over it and trap the victim inside, was a bristling mass of needles and wires with sparks coming out of them.

Worse even than the awful instruments of torture I saw sticking out of the second side of the upright table, was their placement—they appeared to be clustered into three specific areas. Studying them, I was certain if they strapped me to the table, those needles and wires were going to be aimed straight and my breasts and crotch. Which, I think we can all agree, are the areas you specifically *don't* want needles and sparking wires making contact with.

Great. I was about to be the star of an alien torture porn film.

"Is…" I had to clear my throat before I could get the words out. "Is that going to hurt?"

"Oh, yes—of course. It should be quite excruciating, in fact, as long as all your nerve endings are intact," Bambi said cheerfully, as though he tortured girls just for fun every day. As far as I knew, he did. Who knows what gets an alien centipede off?

A low humming sound filled the air as it got closer and I could feel the short hairs on the backs of my forearms standing up as though I was in a room with an immense generator. My heart was pounding so hard it seemed like it was trying to get out of my chest and run away—which was pretty much what *I* wanted to do. But one look at Sarden's long, muscular legs told me he would catch me before I got three feet from the torture table. My only hope was to change his mind about letting the Commercians test me.

"No," I whispered, my voice almost too dry to speak. "No, *please.*"

But the other four Commercians already had their long, chitinous claws on me and were dragging me over to the table. They pushed me back against the cold, padded part of the table which felt like some kind of slick plastic against my bare skin. They forced my arms down by my sides and I felt my cheeks grow hot with embarrassment as my breasts and the small patch of red curls between my thighs was revealed. Oh God, if this was a nightmare, I needed to wake up *now!*

"Please," I begged, looking at Sarden, feeling so scared I was sick to my stomach. "Please don't let them do this to me. I don't like shots or sparks or being electrocuted. I promise I'm *really* sensitive — you don't have to test me to know that."

He frowned but said nothing.

"Ready the testing subject," Bambi declared in his high, piping voice. "Start with one hundred volts and continue from there until maximum pain threshold is reached."

"No!" I gasped as the other side of the table started moving towards me. I could see the silver needles gleaming and the wires were spitting sparks in my direction with an ominous sizzling sound.

I couldn't believe this was actually happening. How could I be hiding in the restroom bitching about my boss to Leah and Charlotte one minute, and strapped to an alien torture table about to have my ta-tas and coochie pierced and electrocuted the next? I wished like hell I was back in the office brewing yet another pot of coffee for Dayton Lauder the third and listening to him yell-talk while he waved his arms and wafted his awful BO everywhere.

Suddenly having a stapler thrown at my head didn't seem so bad.

*This has to be a dream! It **has** to be a dream!*

But so far I wasn't waking up.

"No, you can't!" I heard myself begging shamelessly. "You can't do this to me!"

Forget suffering in silence, I'm much more of a plead-for-my-life-at-the-top-of-my-lungs type of gal.

"Please!" I cried again, through a throat that had grown so tight I could hardly get the words out. My eyes were stinging with unshed tears and I felt like my heart was going to gallop right out of my chest. Every nerve in my body was on edge, ready to feel the pain. The tip of one bright, shiny needle was just about to poke my right nipple (my right boob is slightly perkier than my left. Don't tell me you don't have one that's just a little perkier—I won't believe you. Everybody does.)

Anyway, as I was saying, I could feel the cold, sharp tip of the needle just about to pierce my nipple…

And then Sarden barked, "Stop!"

Chapter Three

Sarden

I don't know what made me stop the testing. It was certainly true that having a certificate of sensitivity would make the little Earth female easier to trade. And the Gods knew I needed every advantage I could get when dealing with that two-faced bastard, Tazaxx. But still…I couldn't let it continue.

I suppose it was the look on her face…the tears standing in her large, lovely eyes. Throughout the ordeal of being transported and informed that she had been bought and would be leaving her home world and her friends forever, she had remained stubbornly courageous—refusing to cry. I knew many females who would have been weeping and howling long before they were strapped to a testing table but not this little Pure One—only now when she was about to be subjected to intense pain did she allow tears to rise to the surface.

I admired her courage, that was all, I told myself. Also, though I am half Vorn and have the horns and markings to prove it, I'm no sadist to take pleasure in the pain of females. My other half—the *refined* half, as my little sister, Sellah, is always laughingly pointing out—is Eloim. We don't worship our females as the Ma*jo*rans do or feel the need to share them in the manner of the Denarins, but neither do we believe they are inferior.

"Females are equal to males." I could almost hear Sellah's voice

echoing in my head. *"Just because you're stronger doesn't make you any better or smarter!"*

The thought of my little sister raised an aching pain in my chest. She was the reason I ought to let this testing continue—she was the cause of all this in the first place. But I knew what she would say if she could see me—she wouldn't want the little Pure One punished or hurt. After all, the Earth female had simply had the bad luck to catch my eye on the Commercians' light-viewer when they powered up the Alien Mate Index.

The mercenary Commercians had showed me many females— flicking first through images of what was considered attractive by Earth standards. Many tall, thin, boney creatures with long, sleek hair and wide eyes had cycled over the light-viewer. They had put me in mind of the graceful *tallaths* which galloped with impossibly long, fragile legs over the fields of Yanus Six. With their cool, vacant stares and slender, brittle-looking limbs they did nothing to arouse or excite me. I doubted they would interest Tazaxx either.

Then the AMI happened to flicker over this particular female— I realized I didn't even know her name. Anyway, she had been having a heated discussion with an Earth male—a puny creature in rumpled clothing who shouted and threw something at her head. She ducked, her wild curls flying, and went storming out of the room. Char'noth, the lead Commercian had been about to flip to another subject but I stopped him.

"Wait," I had told him, fascinated by the plump little female. "I want to watch her—this could be the one."

And so she had been taken on my request—because I bought and paid for her. But not *just* because she was beautiful, I was quick to tell myself. After all, I wasn't looking for a mate for myself—I was looking for a female that would tempt Tazaxx. I was certain she would do that—watching her with her luscious curves exposed certainly tempted *me*. And the fact that she was a *La-ti-zal* could only help. My head was still ringing with the vivid colors she'd shown me when we touched, although my vision had mostly gone back to its usual shades of sepia.

At the moment, though, I had other things to think of beside her beauty or her unique abilities. Such as the fact that Char'noth and the other Commercians were staring at me in incomprehension, wondering why I had stopped their sensitivity training.

"What is the problem?" Char'noth demanded, his eye stalks wiggling in a way that showed intense displeasure. "The table is all charged—the test will take but a few moments."

"I...er..." I cleared my throat, feeling foolish. "I don't want my property damaged."

"There will be no damage," Char'noth protested. "The test is pain through nerve conduction. There will not be a mark on the female when we are finished."

"Yes, but your little test will still hurt like a bastard and I've never been interested in causing females pain," I snapped. "There *are* other ways to test sensitivity."

In fact, there were several. I even had an old sensitivity tank back at my ship, if I remembered correctly. I had won my ship, *The Celesta*, in a hand of double-blind-Trill from an old bastard who'd used to be a science officer for the Assimilation before it had been defeated. Though I had cleaned it out and outfitted it for smuggling, there was still quite a bit of obscure medical equipment left in the hold that I thought I might sell to a collector some day. It would be worth a pretty credit if I could ever find the right buyer. Now, maybe I could put some of it to use. It certainly couldn't be as painful as what the Commercians had in mind.

"But—" Char'noth started to protest.

"Let her go," I growled. "I'm taking her now—I have no more time to waste on you lot."

"Master, don't forget her documentation!" A.L., still in travel mode, fluttered on my shoulder. He had also come with the ship and his mainframe was located aboard *The Celesta*. I found it useful to take him with me during trade negotiations. His compact travel form could fit into some very tight spaces so he was good at gathering information and watching my back.

"Right—documentation," I said.

"It will be sent directly to your ship," Char'noth said sullenly. "But first—"

"First, nothing. Unstrap her." I made my voice low and commanding, glaring at Char'noth until he acceded.

"Do as he says," he snapped at his underlings.

Muttering angrily in their high voices, the Commercians set about freeing the female. I was fairly certain they'd wanted to do more than just test her sensitivity—they wanted to find a way of identifying other rare and valuable assets like her before transporting them to their base. If they could pinpoint which females were *La-ti-zals* before they transported them, their profits would treble. Well, too bad—the female was coming with me. I'd lingered long enough around this tiny, benighted blue planet. I needed to get to Tazaxx and make the trade before it was too late. Before he—

I pushed the thought aside as the little Pure One was finally freed of her bonds. She collapsed on the floor, her breath coming in tight gasps. I could tell she was trying hard to hold back her tears.

"Come," I said, lifting her by the arm. I felt a tingle and there was a quick flash of color behind my eyes but it was nothing compared to the jolt I'd experienced earlier. The inhibitor was doing its job—barely. I reminded myself to check it later and see if I couldn't find something stronger for her to wear in *The Celesta's* stores of medical equipment. She had an immense untapped talent—good thing she was still latent or she might have fried my entire nervous system when we touched.

"I can't." Her legs wobbled and she nearly fell.

"What do you mean, you can't? Will your legs not work?" I lifted her more firmly. She was tiny but substantial, I noted. I liked that—no male wants to be with a female he fears he might break. Not that I planned on being with her, I reminded myself sternly. She was for trade purposes only.

"I mean, I can't go with you. I can't leave my home and my friends and family. I *won't.*"

She struggled in my grasp, much to my amusement. It may be true that females are equal to males in intelligence but when it comes to physical strength, we have the upper hand. In this case, I used it.

Swinging the struggling female into my arms, I headed for the exit where my short range shuttle was docked. My ship was in orbit around the fourth planet from this system's sun—Mars I believed the Earthlings called it. It was only a short trip in the shuttle to get there and it was far out of reach of any immediate pursuit from Earth. Not that the ignorant Earthlings knew I was here or even that their planet was being harvested. But even if they had, there was nothing they could do about it.

For a moment I felt a stab of pity, remembering all the innocent, unknowing faces I'd seen on the AMI. None of those females knew they might be taken and transported at any moment. Stripped of their identities and sold to the highest bidder—the male with the most credit looking for an expensive, exotic plaything or a bride with the finest pedigree the Universe could offer…

Then I pushed the emotion away. There was no point in feeling bad for the Earthlings—they'd done this to themselves. Dissolved the lock around their planet little by little until finally the Commercians were able to take not just one or two people but as many as they liked and as often as they liked. There were going to be a hell of a lot of disappearances down on that little blue ball— soon the inhabitants would be paying for their carelessness.

But that had nothing to do with me. The little Earth female I had picked, however, did. And she was currently doing her best to wriggle free of my grasp.

"No! No, put me down! I said I'm not going with you!"

She beat against my chest with her little fists and her eyes were bright with unshed tears. Because of our proximity, I could see her in her natural tones—her hair was a deep shade of red like *Proxian* rubies and her pale, lovely skin was dusted with little specks of pigmentation that should have been detrimental to her appearance. Instead, I found them charming—I wondered what they were called. They were especially thick across the bridge of her petite nose which was currently wrinkled in anger.

"I said let me go!" she cried, struggling in my arms. I liked the feel of her soft body close to mine and the way her full, bare breasts heaved as she moved. Her nipples were a soft, innocent pink and the little patch of curls that decorated her mound was the same color as the flaming strands on her head. I felt my shaft harden as I considered if she had other pink areas I might like to explore.

Before my lust could carry me too far though, one of her flailing hands caught me across the face, causing me to jerk back with a growl.

"Careful, little Pure One," I told her, tightening my grip. "My patience isn't limitless."

She stopped struggling abruptly and contented herself with just glaring at me.

"You... you Devil-looking son of a bitch!" she spat.

I tried not to smile. It amused me that she compared me to the fallen deity that tortured her people after death. My own version of damnation was The Pit and I had long ago accepted that I would go there after death. A male can't commit the acts I have and not have a soul so stained even the Goddess of Mercy would turn her face from him. I was probably adding to my burden of sins at the moment but I told myself I didn't care—I was doing what was necessary. What was right, even if it might not look that way to an outsider.

"Call me what you want," I told her, going through the airlock and settling her in the interior of my shuttle. "But the fact is, you're coming with me, little Pure One. And there is nothing you can say or do to stop it."

Chapter Four

Zoe

Sarden got me settled in some kind of a spaceship looking thing—at least that was what I assumed it was. There was a complicated looking control panel with lots of blinking instruments that looked like a high-tech plane cockpit.

I considered grabbing them and pulling as many levers and pushing as many buttons as I could but two things stopped me. The first was that I could see space outside—cold, dead, empty space. (Well, empty except for the moon floating by. It was way bigger than I could ever remember seeing it which made sense—I'd never been this close to it before.)

What if I accidentally pushed the wrong button and opened the window? I would freeze and my eyeballs would bulge out and explode. At least, that was what happened on that awful scifi horror movie my ex-boyfriend had made me watch. He'd said it was a classic—what was it called again? Oh yeah, *Event Horizon.* Don't get me wrong—I actually love science fiction but I'm *not* a big fan of horror movies. Especially horror movies where people's eyeballs explode.

The second thing that kept me from trying a little space-sabotage was the fact that Sarden strapped me into the seat—and I do mean *strapped.* As in, he made sure the weirdly modified seatbelt harness—which seemed way too big for me at first—fit over my arms, fastening them securely to my sides. My bare boobs stuck out between the straps and I thought I had never felt so exposed.

Then he reached between my legs.

"Hey!" I kicked out, trying to get free. "Don't touch me, you big red pervert!"

"What's the problem now?" he growled, looking irritated. Which at least was an improvement over his general air of amusement when I'd struggled to get free of his arms earlier, with absolutely zero results.

"What's the *problem?* I don't know how it is on your planet but on Earth you can't just grope somebody like that!" I snapped, pressing my thighs together as tightly as I could.

"Grope you?" He looked at me as if it was honestly the last thing on his mind. "I'm simply trying to fasten you into the shuttle so you aren't injured during our flight to my ship."

"Yeah, right—by strapping me down naked and reaching between my legs?" I demanded.

He glared at me. "Should I assume you'd rather be strapped to the Commercians' testing table?"

Well, that shut me up—almost, anyway. It *was* true that he'd made them stop the testing. But then, I wouldn't have *been* in a position to be experimented on by a bunch of blue alien worms if he hadn't told them to snatch me in the first place!

"Fine," I muttered. "But just don't make the straps so tight. And don't touch me, uh, *there.*"

"You mean here?" His voice dropped to a soft growl and his long fingers stroked the tops of my thighs, making me squirm.

"Stop," I whispered, wishing my voice didn't sound so breathless.

"Little Pure One…"

"Zoe," I interrupted him. "You abduct a girl, you should at least ask her name. My name is Zoe—not 'little one' or 'Pure One' or anything like that. Just Zoe."

"Zzzoooeee…" He rolled my name thoughtfully on his tongue. "I like it. It fits you, somehow."

"Unlike this damn harness you're putting on me," I snapped.

"It has to be tight to withstand the forces the shuttle will undergo during our trip," he said. "But I'm just strapping you in—I won't harm or molest you, Zoe." His golden eyes grew hard. "I may be an evil, half-breed son of a bitch but I'm no rapist."

"How do I know that's true?" I demanded, and realized I'd said the wrong thing when his face went darker red and his eyes flashed.

"You *don't*," he growled. "You'll just have to trust me. Or not—I don't care. Now spread your legs and let me fit the straps to your body. I don't want to hurt you by forcing them open—your flesh is so delicate I'm sure it bruises easily and—"

"And Tazaxx doesn't take damaged merchandise. Right, I got that," I finished for him.

He looked somewhat surprised. "Exactly. So will you open for me or not?"

The look on his face told me I had little choice in the matter.

"Fine, you big, red pervert," I muttered. "But I swear if you so much as touch me, I'll…I'll…"

"You'll what?" He sounded amused again which pissed me off even more.

"I'll wait until you're not looking and kick you so hard you'll be wearing your balls for a bowtie—if you even *have* balls, that is!" I snapped.

"In fact, I do," he said, conversationally. "Since I, like yourself and many sentient species in the universe, am descended from the Ancient Ones, I have much of the same anatomy an Earth male would have, including balls and a shaft."

Okay, we were getting into uncomfortable territory here—both literally and figuratively. But I couldn't help asking,

"If you've all got the blood of the Ancient Ones, why is Earth so special?"

"Because as we told you earlier, only on Earth has their original DNA been preserved. Not only preserved but sown with seeds of greatness—hidden talents like your own."

"About that..." I shifted uncomfortably as he started to reach for the straps between my legs again. "I think you must be mistaken. I don't have any hidden talents. Like, I don't have visions of the future or hear people's thoughts and I can't move things with my mind—I mean, I'm not a freaking X-man, okay?"

He looked at me as if I was crazy.

"Who said anything about your talent affecting *you*, Zoe? It's the way in which you affect others that makes you so damn special. Now be still and let me finish getting you in the harness before the Commercians think of some legal way to get you back on their testing table."

I shut up then and let him finish strapping me in, though I really didn't like it. Or I told myself, I didn't.

I should have hated his touch on my skin—this was abduction and it might turn into something a hell of a lot more in a minute, despite his claim that he wasn't a rapist. Still, the way he was leaning over me, I could feel his warm breath against my bare breasts. And despite his harsh words, the touch of his big hands was gentle. There was a scent around him too—a warm smell, like a campfire burning. And under it was something else—some musk that was clean and crisp and somehow completely male. I didn't know what it was but it made me feel dizzy to breathe it in.

I told myself I didn't care—that I hated him. That I hated this. I tried to hold absolutely still as he fastened the straps, not moving an inch even when his knuckles brushed against the soft curls on my mound. I *did* gasp at that point though—even though I tried not to.

"Sorry." He shook his head and muttered to himself. The only words I caught were 'extremely sensitive and 'testing,' which made me go rigid in my seat, like I wasn't stiff enough already.

"What?" I demanded in a voice that came out in more of a squeak. "I thought you weren't going to let them test me!"

"I won't let the Commercians test you, no," he said, frowning. "But you *will* have to be tested before I can trade you. Don't worry—I'll manage it myself."

This hardly made me feel any better. I couldn't help wondering if he had a scary, pointy testing table of his own back at his ship. I kept quiet through the rest of the harnessing process, even though the metal buckle was pressed right against my crotch in a very cold and uncomfortable way.

"There," Sarden said at last, looking pleased with his handiwork. "You're secure."

Secure my ass. Trussed up like a Christmas turkey was more like it, but what could I do?

He settled himself in his own seat, getting his own harness fastened much quicker than he'd done mine. Then he did something to the controls and a rush of cold air blasted through the small cockpit, making me shiver uncontrollably.

"Oh m-my G-God," I gasped out, my teeth chattering.

"What's wrong? Why are you trembling?" he demanded, frowning at me.

"B-because it's suddenly f-f-freezing in here, that's why!" I exclaimed. I couldn't even get my hands up to rub some warmth into my arms and legs. Everything seemed to be going numb and cold.

Sarden frowned, a look of concern coming over his sharp features.

"It's simply the ship's drivers warming up. But I see that you're more delicate than I had hoped. Very well—here."

He pulled his shirt over his head, baring an absolutely mouth-watering torso. Forget a six-pack—this guy had an eight-pack of pure, hard muscle. Not that I could enjoy looking at it when I felt like I was getting frostbite in all my extremities—not to mention my nipples which felt like they had turned into little pointy ice cubes.

"What are you—" I started but then he draped the black fabric of his shirt over me, making sure to cover as much of me as possible.

Immediately, I felt a wave of warmth rush over me. It tingled from my neck all the way down to my toes, even though the shirt didn't reach that far.

"Better?" Sarden demanded, frowning at me.

"Yes, but how?" I looked down at the shirt. It was a sleeveless t-shirt looking thing and the fabric was thin. Any of his body heat it had held should have dissipated almost immediately in the chilly cabin. Yet it continued to radiate warmth that seemed to penetrate my entire body.

"It's made of temp-fabric," Sarden explained, seeing my confusion. "It retains and radiates heat during conditions of extreme cold. It also cools the wearer off when it gets too hot."

"Sounds like something we could use in Tampa," I murmured, looking down at myself. "But won't you be cold?"

He shrugged, his broad, muscular shoulders doing that sexy, yummy roll I really needed to ignore. He was my captor and kidnapper, after all, the big, dumb jerk.

"I'll be fine—it's just a short trip to my ship. We're only going to the planet you call Mars."

"What?" I nearly choked. "We're *only* going to Mars? Do you know how long it would take to get there from Earth? Especially if the orbits aren't aligned. Months and months—I mean—"

He looked at me pityingly. "It might take that long for your puny Earth vessels but not for my shuttle." He patted the dashboard fondly. "And my ship is ten times faster. *The Celesta* has a hydrogen scoop hyper-drive."

"Meaning what?" I demanded. "Sorry but quantum mechanics wasn't offered as an elective at my school."

"Meaning that it's capable of faster than light travel. *Much* faster than light." He grinned, showing white teeth almost as sharp as the horns growing out of his temples. "Which further means I'll be trading you to Tazaxx before you know it."

"Um…Master." The golden dragonfly, which had fluttered up and out of the way when he took off his shirt, settled on his shoulder and fanned its wings in agitation.

"What is it, A.L.?" he growled. I wondered what the initials stood for but before I could ask the dragonfly fluttered again.

"About the hyper-drive, Master," its voice said.

"Yes?" Sarden's voice was dangerously quiet.

"Well…it…I hate to be the bearer of bad news…"

"Just spit it out, A.L.," he growled.

"It's malfunctioning. It's only at fifty percent at the moment and levels are dropping as we speak."

"What?" Why didn't you tell me before?" Sarden demanded.

"Well, you may recall that I warned something like this might happen some time ago. The panels in the scooping mechanism are warped and have needed repair or replacement for some time and—"

"Repair. Fine, I'll repair them." Sarden sighed as though repairing his spaceship was a boring chore you put off as long as you could—like taking out the trash or dusting the stuff in the china cabinet.

"I don't know if repairs will work at this point." A.L.'s butler voice sounded apologetic. "Or they may work but only temporarily. Not long enough to get us to Giedi Prime."

"Damn it, A.L.—you know we have to get there before the auction!" Sarden growled, his eyes flashing deeper gold. "If we don't—"

"I am aware, Master." The dragonfly fluttered again. "Forgive me—I am running a full diagnostic now. Hopefully I will have more information for you when we reach the ship."

"Let's go then." As he spoke, Sarden did something to one of the instruments on the control panel. Suddenly we were whizzing forward at an incredible speed.

I gasped, the sound ripped from me as what felt like a huge, invisible hand pressed me back against my seat. From the corner of my eye I caught my last glimpse of Earth—a round blue marble floating in the blackness of space.

Then it was gone and I wondered if I would ever see it again.

* * * * *

Sarden

I gritted my teeth in irritation as I locked the shuttle on course and steered towards the tiny desert planet the Earthlings called Mars.

I'd known that the panels on the hydrogen scoop were warping—there was no way they couldn't at the rate I'd been pushing *The Celesta* lately. But I hadn't had time to deal with it—I'd had a lot on my mind. Like finding the right item to trade to Tazaxx for one. It had to be perfect—something special and unique or he wouldn't even consider it.

Tazaxx is one of the slimiest crime lords in the galaxy—I ought to know, I've smuggled for him often enough. But he has a weakness for beauty and for one-of-a-kind items no one owns but him.

In the little Pure One strapped into the seat beside me, I believed I had found what I needed—something Tazaxx absolutely couldn't resist. Only that something was actually a some*one*, a fact I was trying strenuously to ignore as I piloted the shuttle closer to Mars.

There are plenty of smugglers who make their living in the slave trade, dealing rare and exotic inhabitants from distant planets to the rich, wealthy investors who collected them. I wasn't one of them. My soul might be stained but that was one sin I'd tried to avoid.

Now I couldn't help it. There was no other way—not if I was going to get Sellah back. But that would only happen if I could reach Tazaxx before he held his annual auction. If he decided he didn't want her, if she got auctioned off to the highest bidder, perhaps one who lived on the far flung reaches of the universe where he could never be found, then Sellah might be lost forever.

No. I tightened my grip on the steering yoke, refusing to accept that possibility. I would *not* be too late. Somehow or other I would reach Giedi Prime in time.

And as for the little Pure One... I shot a glance at her from the corner of my eye. She was staring out the viewscreen at the side of the shuttle, her gaze trained on her planet, now just a speck in the blackness. Her chin was still lifted defiantly but her eyes were wide and I thought I saw a glimmer of unshed tears in them as she watched her home world disappear forever.

I would have told anyone who asked I didn't have a heart or a conscience—a smuggler has no need of either one. Then why did I feel a stab of guilt as I watched her try to put on a brave face while I took her away from everything she'd ever known?

I turned to face the viewscreen, concentrating on my instruments as I pushed the emotion ruthlessly away. This was the only way—I had no other choice.

Though I felt like the worst kind of scum for doing it, Zoe would have to be traded.

Chapter Five

Zoe

We got to Mars faster than I could get to the nearest WalMart from my apartment back home. Not that I go there a lot, but sometimes in the middle of the night when there's nothing else open and you have a craving for some Ben and Jerry's, you *have* to go. The nice part is, you don't even have to change out of your PJs if you don't want to.

I have personally been guilty of wearing my favorite sweats and my sleepy bear t-shirt to Wally World and nobody even looks twice. Of course, the sloppy sweats and t-shirt were a hell of a lot more decent than what I had on now, which was just Sarden's temperature regulating wife-beater t-shirt draped over my more sensitive areas. I wondered if he was going to give me anything else to wear once we reached his ship, or if I was just supposed to wander around naked, clutching my boobs and crossing my legs constantly.

I was *really* tired of being naked.

The red curve of Mars was barely looming in the windshield before we zipped around its side and came to a long, needle-shaped ship with a big round bulge at one end of it. Maybe that was the hydrogen scoop thingy Sarden had been talking about?

We were coming in so fast I thought we would crash right into it. A scream was rising in my throat but just at the last moment, the shuttle slowed down dramatically and its nose just barely kissed the side of the huge, needle-shaped ship.

At once, a hole irised open on the silver skin of the ship and our little shuttle was sucked inside. It gave me the creepy sensation of being sucked into a toothless mouth but before I could protest, we were in. The shuttle settled with a soft sigh and Sarden flipped off the ignition—or whatever it was that turned it off and on.

He pressed a button and the doors on either side swooped up—kind of like a DeLorean's. He hopped out and was about to just leave me there when I shouted at him.

"Hey! Are you just going to leave me strapped in here or what?"

"Oh…" He turned back, as though I was the last thing on his mind. "Sorry. A.L.—take care of her."

I was wondering how the golden dragonfly could manage the complicated straps holding me in place. But the dragonfly flew away—upward into the dim recesses of the metal ceiling. A panel opened and it flew inside. Well how was it going to help me up there?

Before I could yell at Sarden's retreating back to ask him, a long, thin, many-jointed silver arm with a six clawed hand came down out of the same panel towards me.

I screamed, of course, because I don't like it when metal claws come at me from out of the ceiling. I'm funny like that.

Though Sarden had been doing his best impression of the disappearing man—or disappearing alien, I guess—he turned and came charging back at once.

"What in the Frozen Hells of Anor is wrong now?" he demanded in a low, irritated growl.

"What do you mean, what's wrong? You leave me strapped down and helpless and then a long metal claw arm starts reaching for me!" I exclaimed. "What do you *think* is wrong? I don't want to die! *That's* what's wrong!"

"Die?" He looked at the silver, many-jointed arm and frowned. "Don't be foolish—that's just A.L."

"My deepest apologies." Suddenly another flexible metal arm came down but this one was topped by a thin rectangular box with a round blinking light in the center. Almost like an eye, I thought. The same proper English butler voice that had been coming from the gold dragonfly was now emanating from the box. "I am so sorry—I did not mean to frighten you, Lady Zoe."

"I thought you were a dragonfly," I told it. "What are you, anyway?"

"I am the computing system which runs this ship," A.L. said. "Do you not have such things on your planet?"

"Only in science fiction movies," I told him. I looked at Sarden who was watching our little exchange impatiently. "You could have warned me, you know."

"How was I to know your people are so primitive you don't even have artificial life-forms? I don't have time for this," he growled, looking really irritated now. "Are you well or do I have to unstrap you myself?"

I thought of the heat of his big, warm body leaning over me, the spicy scent of his skin, and the tingling feeling I got when his long fingers brushed against my more sensitive areas. Then I looked at the six, long metal claws on the end of A.L.'s arm.

"I'll take the claw," I said through gritted teeth.

"Fine. Then I have to go see to the hydrogen scoop." He turned again but I called after him.

"And what am *I* supposed to do?"

"I don't care." He made a dismissive gesture. "Wander the ship if you want. Just keep out of trouble. Oh…" He turned to face me once more briefly and stabbed a finger at me. "But *don't* go into the storage area at the rear. It's dangerous."

"Dangerous for who? Dangerous how?" I demanded but he was already gone, his broad, red back disappearing through the sliding metal doors I swear reminded me of every Star Trek episode I ever watched with my dad when I was a little girl.

"If you'll allow me to unfasten your harness, perhaps I can take you on a brief tour of the ship," A.L.'s proper butler voice said in my ear.

I jumped when I saw that his round light was blinking right by my face — almost as if he was examining me.

"Okay, sure," I muttered. "Just…be careful, okay? Those claws of yours look awfully sharp and some of my most delicate areas are pretty exposed here."

"Of course — I will proceed with utmost caution," he announced. Before I could answer, he had pulled the black shirt aside and was clicking the metal buckles that held the harness in place.

To my great relief, it popped open quickly and I was able to stretch out my cramped arms and legs. There was nothing else to wear, so I pulled Sarden's black t-shirt over my head. It warmed me up immediately and fit like a very snug mini-dress. I didn't love that — normally I wouldn't mind showing off my curves but this wasn't one of those times. Still, it was the best I could do and better than nothing although I wished fiercely I could have a bra and panties to go under it.

It smelled like him too — that warm, spicy, campfire smell that seemed to get in my head and make me dizzy. I tried to ignore it as I hopped out of the shuttle and followed A.L. out of the docking area.

"So you're an artificial life-form?" I asked him as he hummed along, his round, blinking light-eye glowing like a lantern. The metal arm it was connected to slid neatly through the silver ceiling panels which parted with a ripple as he went and closed behind him seamlessly. I wondered what kind of alien technology allowed metal to flow like water. Then again, the fact that they were able to suck me through a mirror was even more impressive.

"I am indeed, Lady Zoe," he answered in his prim and proper voice.

"And is that what A. L. stands for?" I asked. "Artificial life-form?"

"Yes."

"And you don't have any other name?" I asked curiously.

"Do I need one?" His proper butler voice sounded curious. "Master Sarden acquired me along with the rest of the ship in a game of chance. He has never bothered to give me any other name but I did not think I required one."

"Everyone needs a name," I said. "I'd name you Alfred, I think—that's a good butler-type name. Al for short, which also goes with your initials."

"Alfred." He sounded cautiously pleased. "I think I like that, though I am not sure what a butler is."

I explained briefly and Al got excited—in a mechanical kind of way.

"Yes—one who serves. This exactly encompasses my directive." His round eye-light blinked excitedly. "Thank you, Lady Zoe. I shall be pleased to be your butler, Al."

"Just Zoe is fine," I said, smiling a little at his enthusiasm. "Last time I looked I was just a girl from Tampa—not landed gentry or anything."

"Oh, but you must be accorded a title of respect," Al told me seriously. "You have no idea, I think, of how very rare and special you are. You are the first Pure One to be officially taken from your planet. And you are a *La-ti-zal* as well."

"Whatever that means," I muttered. I still thought it was a load of hogwash. "Okay, where are we?"

I had been following Al through a narrow maze of metal corridors that made me feel kind of claustrophobic. But now they had opened out into one long, wide hallway which seemed to run the length of the ship.

"To the left is the navcom and the control area." Al's blinking light indicated the long metal passage with a nod. "To the right are areas for sleeping, eating, and entertainment. I believe these areas will be more to your interest. If you would follow me?"

"What if I don't want to follow you? What if I want to see the control area?" I asked.

"Well, it is not *forbidden,* but I do not think you would know how to use any of the equipment. And even if you could, it would be impossible since all controls are voice locked to Master Sarden," Al explained.

I sighed. No wonder Sarden felt free to let me wander around—I couldn't affect anything since the whole ship responded only to him.

So much for my fantasies of getting in the cockpit, turning the ship around and flying back to Earth. Somehow in science fiction movies, the heroes are always able to figure out the alien tech and use it against the invaders. But I had to admit, though I hated to, that I wasn't a techy kind of girl. Half the time I don't understand everything my smartphone is doing. As complicated as the shuttle had looked, I didn't think I had a chance of learning to fly the huge, needle-shaped spacecraft. Anyway, if it was locked to Sarden's voice, then there was no way I could do anything—even if I'd been the geekiest science-freak around.

No, if I was going to get out of this predicament, it wasn't going to be by learning to fly a spaceship. I would have to appeal to Sarden's good side—if he had one, the big red jerk. I had to make him see me as more than a prisoner or a trading commodity. I had to make him see me as a *person*.

I had read an article about that once—about a girl who got kidnapped by some guys who wanted to hold her for ransom. She turned the situation around and made friends with her captors. They liked her so much they let her go without a scratch on her— she did a kind of reverse Stockholm syndrome thing on them.

That's what I would have to do—reverse Stockholm the shit out of this situation until Big Red *wanted* to take me back to Earth. Which meant I was going to have to be a hell of a lot more charming than I usually was.

Well, crap.

Still, it was the only thing I could think of—Plan A. I had to put it into motion and the first thing to do was to find out more about my captor. I thought I had an idea of where to start.

"Take me to the sleeping quarters," I told Al. "I'm, uh, kind of tired. I'd like to lie down."

"You have, of course, had a very stressful experience, being transported from your home world." Al sounded almost as if he cared. I wondered if he really somehow did or if it was just good programming.

"I have." I manufactured a yawn. "I'm really tired."

"Come this way." His glowing light-eye led me down the corridor, pointing out various other areas along the way. "This is the food prep and dining area, where you may simulate yourself any kind of comestibles for your gustatory enjoyment."

"Nice," I murmured, taking a quick look as we went by. I caught a glimpse of a long bar against one wall with tall stools bolted to the table and a strange gold cylinder that looked like the world's biggest stock pot with lots of brightly colored wires coming from it.

"And here is our entertainment area," Al continued, his light nodding to another area as we passed. "Here you can enjoy written, recorded, or holographic entertainments to pass the time during space travel."

"Holographic?" The thought made me come to a screeching stop. "Like the holo-deck on Star Trek?"

"I am not familiar with the entertainment you mention," Al said.

"I mean, is it a big room where you can imagine any scenario and the computer creates everything to go along with it so you can play out your wildest fantasies?"

The thought made me almost salivate with excitement. I thought of all the fantasies I could play out. I would instruct Al to download a copy of Outlander by Dianna Gabaldon and I would be Claire and he could simulate me a sexy, Scottish Jamie…or I could be Beth from J.R. Ward's Dark Lover novel and he could simulate the hot vampire king, Wrath. (Can you tell I read a lot of romance?)

Or I might just play out a Sherlock Holmes scenario like they did in the Next Generation—remember the one where Moriarty got out and nearly took over The Enterprise? (God, I am *such* a geek.)

But if I did Sherlock Holmes, I decided, I would *definitely* play

Watson and have Al simulate Holmes as Benedict Cumberbatch. Because how hot is he? Yum! It would be the first time that Watson actually jumped Holmes' bones instead of just helping with his cases. Well, the first time outside of fan fiction anyway…

Or, leaving the book fantasies behind, I could just be a rich and famous model, walking the catwalk in fabulous clothes. Okay, I know I said I own my curves and I do. But just once it would be nice to be effortlessly skinny, you know? I'd like to see how it felt to be a size three with paparazzi all around, salivating for a glimpse of my sexy hip bones…

"Ah…I am afraid not. The holograph projector simply shows images of different areas of the known universe. You are not able to interact with them."

Al's proper butler voice brought me crashing down to Earth. Or to the spaceship, anyway.

"Damn." To say I was super disappointed is an understatement. For a minute, I'd almost felt like it was worth being abducted by aliens. I've always wanted my own private holo-deck. But oh well, on with the plan.

"I am sorry if you find the entertainment facilities lacking," Al said apologetically.

"Never mind." I sighed. "Just take me to my room, please."

"With pleasure, Lady Zoe."

He led the way down the corridor until we came to a row of sliding metal doors.

"This will be your room for the duration of our trip." Al motioned at the last door on the left. "Simply wave your hand to break the beam and the door will open."

I didn't see any beam (maybe it was invisible?) but I waved my hand in front of the door he'd indicated anyway and sure enough, it slid open with a nearly silent *whoosh.*

Inside was a metal counter about waist high, a single chair, and a large silver bean bag floating about three feet off the floor. It was really long and looked like it had been built for someone Sarden's size, so it was going to be like sleeping in a king sized bed for me.

"Whoa…" I walked forward and put my hand out to touch the silver material of the bag. It was soft as silk under my fingers. "How cool is this? A hoverbed!"

"It works by simple principles of magnetic deflection," Al said modestly. "It gives excellent support while cushioning your whole body."

"I can't wait to try it," I said and I really wasn't lying. By now, you can probably tell I'm kind of a Scifi geek. If I hadn't been captured with the express intent of being sold off to some alien trader in a galaxy far, far away, being aboard a genuine space ship would have been a dream come true.

"There are bathing facilities as well. Here." Al glided further into the room and then into a smaller doorway set in the wall opposite the bed. I followed him, wondering what alien bathroom fixtures looked like. I really hoped they had a recognizable toilet—it would be super awkward to have to ask Al how to use it if I couldn't figure it out just by looking.

But it wasn't the toilet that caught my eye when I went into the bathroom. There was a rectangular enclosure filled with clear, pale purple liquid standing in the center of the room. It was about five feet wide by five feet across and enclosed by a clear barrier that might have been glass or plastic or some alien material I had never heard of. It was tall, too—reaching almost to the high metal ceiling overhead.

"What's this?" I asked, eyeing it in confusion.

"The pool of personal cleansing. Do you not have such things on Earth?" Al asked, sounding confused. "Do you not bathe?"

"Of course we bathe!" I exclaimed. "But we usually take a shower or a bath."

"A bath—as in you submerse yourself in water or cleansing liquids?"

"Well, yes, but—"

"Then you should feel right at home! The PPC is for exactly that purpose. Simply slide open the entrance hatch…" He indicated a sliding door on one side of the clear enclosure. "And step inside to be thoroughly cleansed."

I frowned. "Are you trying to tell me this thing is a huge vertical bathtub? How can you open the door without all the, uh, water—is that water? Anyway, without it going everywhere?"

"There is a moisture repellant field around it which keeps the cleansing liquid in of course," Al said, as though it should have been obvious. "I really must learn more about your home world. How do your people keep cleansing liquids contained?"

"With good old fashioned gravity, mostly. I mean, we use uh, horizontal bathtubs, not vertical ones," I said.

"But then, how are you able to submerse yourself fully and completely?"

"We don't." I shivered as I looked at the alien "bathtub." As I said, the enclosure was tall—a lot taller than me. If I got into the purple pool, it would be over my head—*way* over.

Just the thought gave me a nauseous, squirmy feeling in the pit of my stomach. I remembered the last time water had closed over my head…looking up through the murky blue light, panicking at the thought that I would never break the surface again as the chlorine burned my throat and my lungs filled with liquid. And then there was Angie…

I pushed the memory away, feeling sick.

"Look, I'm not trying to be difficult but do you have any other way to clean yourself around here?" I asked Al. "I'm, uh, afraid I don't swim and it looks like that stuff would be…would be over my head."

"We do have a misting chamber for refreshment although I do not recommend it for everyday use. It simply will not be able to get you completely clean."

"Misting chamber sounds great," I said, ignoring his warning. After all, it wasn't like I was planning to do any heavy lifting or hard work outs while I was here. A light shower should be able to get me clean and even if it couldn't, there was no way I was getting into that huge vat of purple liquid.

"This way." Al led me to something that looked kind of like a shower stall back home but without a shower head. In fact, I didn't see any knobs or nozzles at all.

"Uh, how do you work it?" I asked, frowning.

"Simply disrobe and step inside. The mister will activate on sensing your presence."

"Okay." That seemed straightforward enough. "And, uh, your restroom facilities?" I asked, feeling embarrassed. I hoped they weren't weird—by this time I *really* needed to pee. Being abducted and dragged through a mirror onto an alien spaceship tends to do that to me.

"This way." Al showed me to another small alcove which had what looked like a silver chair with a solid bottom. Like the silver beanbag bed, it was large—obviously built for someone a lot bigger than a regular human. But there was no hole in the middle of it. No place for anything to *go*, if you know what I mean.

"Uh..." Just what I was afraid of—I was going to have to ask for an explanation.

"Simply remove any encumbrances to elimination and seat yourself upon the waste disposal unit," Al said helpfully. "The center will open for your convenience and remove the products of elimination via air suction." He nodded at a grouping of three silver buttons mounted on the wall beside the unit. "There are three suction strengths to choose from, depending on your need."

Okay," I said again. "That all sounds nice but I don't see any, uh, toilet paper."

"Toilet paper?" Al sounded like he was frowning in confusion. "What is that?"

I could feel my cheeks going red. I'm a private bathroom person so I've never liked talking about this kind of thing—not even to a robot, or whatever Al was. It's embarrassing.

"It's this soft roll of paper—that is, thin sheets of disposable material—that we use to, um, clean up after the elimination process," I told him.

"Oh! Well, rest assured you have no need of such primitive methods here. The waste disposal unit will clean and dry you after each use."

"Wow. Sounds great," I said flatly. I didn't love the idea of the unit "cleaning" me but then, it seemed like I had no choice. Maybe it would just be like an alien bidet. That would be okay, I guessed.

"I am so glad you are pleased," Al said.

"Sure. Very pleased. Okay, well...I think I'd like to, uh, try it out. *Now,*" I hinted as strongly as I could.

I was nearly crossing my legs with the need to pee by now. I shouldn't have had two cups of coffee that morning while my boss was throwing staplers at my head. God, that seemed about a million years ago now.

"By all means. Be my guest," Al said politely. But he didn't leave—his lantern-like eye just kept hovering there right in front of me, as if he expected me to go with him watching me.

"Al," I said at last, my exasperation overcoming my embarrassment. "I don't know how Sarden's people do this kind of thing but for humans it's *private*."

"Oh. Of course—forgive me." His lantern light-eye flickered in acknowledgement. "Shall I withdraw to the next room and wait for you?"

"Actually..." I cleared my throat. "Actually, I'm really tired, like I said. After I, uh, take care of business, I'll probably just go lie down for a nap. So you can help Sarden do...whatever it is he's doing. I'll be fine."

"I see." Was it my imagination or did he sound a little hurt? "You want privacy and solitude."

"Something like that," I said, gritting my teeth and crossing my legs. I didn't want to hurt his feelings but I *really* had to go. *I swear, if he doesn't leave soon...*

Luckily, Al finally got the hint.

"Very well, Lady Zoe. I will check on you later. For now, I wish you a very pleasant waste elimination experience."

"Thanks," I said tightly. "I'm sure it's going to be just *fabulous*." God, I was about to *explode*.

"Goodbye for now." Al finally withdrew, his snaky metal neck sliding through the ceiling and away from the little alcove the strange alien toilet was located in.

The minute he was gone I pulled up the black t-shirt and plopped down on the flat bottom of the silver toilet-chair. At first nothing happened and I was afraid I would have to go pee in the sink or the mister or anyplace else that had a drain. But just as I was about to get up, I remembered the three silver buttons Al had pointed out for "suction needs." One had a small dot on it, the second had a slightly larger one, and the third had a large black dot that filled almost the whole button.

At that point I had to go so bad I thought I was going to die. Without hesitating, I pushed the far button with the biggest dot, thinking that since I really had to go, that would be the right choice.

It was the wrong choice. The wrongest choice possible.

A hole in the seat of the silver toilet irised open and immediately an incredibly strong, cold wind started sucking at me. Remember how I said the toilet was big—like it was built for a species of people way bigger than human? Well, despite my much more than generous ass, the hole was plenty big enough to suck me in. And the suction was so strong, that was exactly what it started to do. I could actually feel myself folding in half like I was doing some kind of crazy bend in yoga class, and being sucked down into the wide hole in the silver toilet.

"Oh…Oh my God! No! Help!" I blurted, grabbing at the walls, since there was nothing else to hold on to. Was this the end? Was this how I died? Sucked down into the depths of an alien toilet and probably ejected into space? "Help!" I cried again.

"Lady Zoe?" Suddenly I heard Al's voice right outside the alcove. "Are you quite well? Master Sarden heard a disturbance and sent me to check."

I was about to scream that *no*, I was not well, I was about to be flushed like a used burrito, when my grasping hand happened to hit another one of the silver buttons—the one with the tiny dot on it.

At once the suction eased and I found I was able to extricate myself from the grip of the monstrous alien toilet. I stood up quickly, almost expecting to hear a *pop* like a cork coming out of a wine bottle. There was no such noise but at least I was free.

"I…I'm fine," I lied shakily to Al, since I didn't want to explain what had almost happened. Not to him and *especially* not to Sarden.

"Oh, good. I just wanted to warn you that you might not want to use the facilities set on the highest suction level just at the moment. When Master Sarden is working on the hydrogen scoop, it tends to send some of the ship's functions into flux."

"Now you tell me," I muttered. And then louder, "Uh, thanks. I'll be sure to only use the, uh, light suction for now."

"Very good." There was a nearly silent hum and I had a mental picture of Al gliding away again, his lantern-eye glowing as he went about his business.

I was left standing there, still having to pee. Because as strong as the suction had been a moment ago, I hadn't let go of a drop. Probably because my body had immediately shut down 'let's pee now' mode and gone into 'let's not get sucked into space through the toilet' mode instead. So I still really had to go—but could I trust this thing a second time?

Mistrustfully, I eyed the toilet, which seemed perfectly normal now. It was sitting there peacefully, barely sucking at all. I wished I was back in the bathroom stall at Lauder, Lauder and Associates—it might be a lousy job but at least I knew I could take a pee break without getting killed. Still, this was what I had to deal with.

My screaming bladder decided me. I would go—I would just have to be really careful.

Gingerly, I sat down again, keeping as far to the front of the silver metal seat as I could. The suction was still slight—barely noticeable. It *seemed* safe enough—I decided to take a chance.

It took me a while to unclench but finally I was able to pee. *Ahhh...* I moaned in silent relief. There's nothing to make a tense situation worse than having to pee. Ever sit in the dentist chair and realize you really have to go in the middle of a root canal? Well multiply that times a hundred and you'll know how I felt being trapped on an alien spaceship going who knows where in the universe with a full bladder.

When I was finally finished, I wasn't sure what to do. Was there another button somewhere to engage the, uh, cleaning mechanism for want of a better word?

As I was looking around, I felt something cold and damp come up from below and swipe at me. It felt like the Creature from the Black Lagoon had made a grab for my coochie.

"Ahh!" Though Al had warned me about the toilet's cleaning function, I still nearly jumped out of my skin. I almost fell off the seat but just then the cold, damp thing retreated and I was buffeted by a blast of hot air instead.

Wow—Al hadn't been kidding. I was clean and dry in no time. Clean and dry but *not* happy. The simple act of using the bathroom felt like an assault. I was pretty sure it was going to take me a while to get used to the whole process but it didn't look like I had much of a choice.

I got up, straightening my t-shirt mini-dress as well as I could, and hobbled out of the bathroom, trying to ignore the giant purple vertical bathtub as I went. I might be stuck using the alien toilet but there was no way in hell I was going to take a bath in that drowning tank-looking thing. Just a glance at it made me shiver.

The huge silver beanbag was still hovering invitingly in mid air, about three feet off the ground. The scifi geek in me wanted to try it in the worst way. But I hadn't maneuvered to have time alone just to lie around in bed. If I wanted to put plan A into action, I needed to find out as much about my captor as possible. After all, how could I make him see me like a person if I didn't see him as one, or understand his motivations?

Cautiously, I moved towards the sliding metal bedroom door. It slid open obligingly when I broke the invisible beam and I found myself out in the long silver corridor again.

Okay, I thought, eyeing the three other doors on the wall beside mine. *One of these has to be Sarden's.* I hoped, anyway. And I also hoped it wasn't locked.

Well, only one way to find out.

Going to the door directly beside mine, I reached forward to break the invisible beam that held it closed.

Sure enough, the door slid open. But disappointingly, I found the room was almost an exact duplicate of my own, right down to the floating silver bed, the chair toilet, and the tank of purple liquid for "personal cleansing."

Okay, strike one. But I had to keep trying.

The next door opened into a storage area filled with all kinds of alien equipment I didn't understand. I was about to leave when it occurred to me I might find something useful. Stepping inside, I scanned the shelves which seemed to be arranged in a haphazard fashion.

Most of the items just looked like tools or spare parts for the ship, which made me nervous. After all, Sarden was making repairs right now. What if he decided he needed something from this room and found me snooping around where I didn't belong? Then again, he *had* told me I could look around the ship, as long as I stayed away from the storage area in the back, that was.

Still, I wasn't seeing anything of interest and was about to leave when something caught my eye. It was a soft, blue glow, almost hidden by a pile of rusty metal pipes in the far corner of the room. Hoping that mysterious blue glow didn't equal radioactive, I pushed some of the pipes aside — they were *heavy* — and found what looked like a pair of thick iron manacles.

They were kind of like handcuffs only the cuff part that went over the wrist was three inches long and *very* large — again like they were made for a species bigger than human. Well, Sarden was certainly that. I wondered if all the sentient species in the universe were. Maybe Earthlings were the runts of the litter. I've always been kind of height challenged so I'm used to being short but I was betting some of the macho guys back home would be in for an unpleasant shock if they found out.

I examined the manacles more closely. The glow was coming from a blue light, embedded in the length of silver chain that linked the thick cuffs together. I didn't quite dare to touch it but I noticed it flickered when I lifted the manacles — which was *not* easy — they had to weigh twenty pounds at least. I wondered why someone had buried them under all these rusty pipes? Were they trying to hide them or was it just a mistake or an oversight?

Looking down at the heavy manacles and the equally heavy pipes, suddenly plan B formed in my brain. It was a hell of a lot more dangerous than plan A and I wasn't sure I could pull it off. But it seemed like a good idea to have a backup plan in case my Reverse Stockholm thing failed completely. Which was entirely possible given that Sarden had been completely upfront about trading me away and didn't seem likely to change his mind.

Holding the manacles against my belly to keep them from clinking, I chose a piece of rusty pipe that was about two feet long. It was thick, and comfortingly solid in my hand. I hefted it experimentally. Yeah, it was heavy enough to do the job, though just thinking of what I might have to do with it made my stomach feel like a flock of nervous butterflies had taken up residence there.

Well, whatever — I was committed now.

Sneaking back to my own room, I looked for a place to store my ill gotten goods. There was no nightstand, unfortunately and I couldn't just leave them lying under the bed. Finally I just stashed them in a fold of the floating silver beanbag. Then I went back out to explore some more.

At first I thought Sarden's room was just another guest room, like mine. It was bare of any personal touches and looked exactly the same except for a desk in one corner.

I walked over to it curiously. The top of the desk was completely clear — so at least my captor was neater than my old boss. Dayton Lauder the third always had messy stacks of half-finished paperwork everywhere. I thought longingly of the coffee-stained piles which I used to curse because it was my job to clean them up and try to organize them. What I wouldn't give to be staring at my boss's messy desk instead of this sterile, blank alien one.

I actually felt tears coming to my eyes before I got hold of myself.

Get a grip, Zoe, I lectured myself. *Whining and moping aren't going to get you home!* Taking a deep breath, I reached out to touch the desk. It was made of some kind of black, shiny material I thought must be glass or plastic at first but it felt warm — almost alive — under my fingertips.

I don't know what I expected but the minute my fingers brushed the desk, it vibrated and came to life. Panels flipped over to reveal several long, feathery instruments about the size of pencils what I could only assume were alien office supplies. There were some thin, transparent sheets piled in stacks too and several other things I had no idea about. But what caught my eye was a clear, crystal cube sitting at the far end of the desk. It was about as big as a softball but square and its many faceted sides caught the dim light in the room and reflected rainbow patterns across the walls.

"Beautiful," I murmured, reaching out to pick it up. Yeah, I know it was probably stupid but I have a weakness for pretty, shiny things.

I held the cube—which was surprisingly heavy—in one hand while I examined it from all sides. There seemed to be a smudge on one jewel-like surface but when I tried to wipe it off, the smudge grew until it was a picture.

A laughing young woman with smooth brown skin, long black hair and big golden cat eyes like Sarden's suddenly filled the cube.

"Sardie!" she exclaimed as the picture came to life, playing like a video on my smartphone back home. "You're incorrigible! Stop it—my hair is a mess!"

I heard the deep rumble of Sarden's laugh, though I couldn't see him. Presumably he'd been the one making the recording.

"You look fine, Sis—stop being so vain."

"I am not vain—you are, *big brother*" she protested.

I frowned. So was this Sarden's little sister? Her eyes were like his, sure enough, but her skin was brown instead of brick red and she didn't have any horns. I frowned, trying to think how it could add up.

"I'm not vain," came Sarden's reply. "Got nothing to be vain about—ugly half-breed bastard that I am. But you're beautiful and you know it."

"Well..." She tossed her shiny hair and I had to agree with Sarden—she was gorgeous.

"Are you ready for your coronation?" he asked, still off camera — or off whatever it was he had used to record this.

"I am." She looked suddenly sad. "I wish it was you up there with me, though. I don't want to rule with Hurxx — come to that, I don't want to rule at *all*."

"I know, little Sellah — always got your head buried in your books and you don't give a damn about the outside world. But the planet has to have a female of the blood as well as a male of the blood to prosper."

"I know, but you'd be better at it than Hurxx — you know you would."

"Hurxx is purebred Eloim and I'm not — you know that," he said flatly. "The people would never — "

"What in the Frozen Hells of Anor do you think you're doing in my room?"

The muted roar from behind me almost made me drop the crystal cube. As it was I fumbled with it comically and barely managed to clutch it to my chest. Then, just when I thought I had it, it squirted out from between my fingers and dropped like a rock to the metal floor below.

Or it would have if Sarden's long fingers hadn't reached out with surprising speed and delicacy and plucked it out of the air.

He pressed something on it that cut off the scene and made it go cold and blank again. Then he spun me around and glared at me.

"I said *what are you doing in my room?*"

"You…I…you said I could go anywhere," I blurted. "I was just exploring. I didn't know this was your room."

Which was true — I hadn't actually known but I *had* hoped.

"I would *think* that a desk full of very personal objects would give you a clue about that," he snarled. "Are all Earthlings this rude and nosey or is it just *you?*"

"I'm s-sorry," I said, trying not to be scared and failing. When he did that glaring thing where his eyes got all glowy he looked positively terrifying. Think—I had to think! *Remember the plan—plan A!* whispered a little voice in my head.

"Um, was that your sister?" I asked, nodding at the cube which he still cradled protectively in one hand. "She's really pretty."

"Yes, Sellah is my sister—not that it's any of your business," he growled. "What of it?"

"Nothing. It's just that…I had a sister once, too. Her…her name was Angie."

My sister's name stuck in my throat. Still, even after all these years, it was hard to talk about her. But I had to try and make a connection with him. *Reverse Stockholm,* I reminded myself fiercely. *It's the only way you're getting out of here!*

Sarden's response was less than enthusiastic.

"Good for you," he growled. "So you have a sibling. It doesn't give you the right to go rifling through my things."

"And what gave you the right to buy me and kidnap me?" I demanded, losing my temper. "What gave you the right to take me away from my entire planet and bring me on this God-forsaken ship where the toilets try to eat you?"

"What?" He stared at me as though I wasn't making any sense. Well, maybe I wasn't but at that point I was so mad I didn't even care. Even though he was huge and muscular and scary, my anger had erased my fear—at least for the moment. Who was he that he thought he could just buy me and steal me away from my ho-hum life and crappy job back on Earth? What the hell was wrong with him?

"What would your sister think of you now?" I demanded, seizing on the only thing I could think of—the only piece of emotional leverage I could find. "What would she say if she knew what you were doing?"

Yet again, I seemed to have said the exact wrong thing. Or maybe it was the right thing, I don't know—but the consequences were the same. Sarden seemed to grow even bigger somehow, his face turning dark as he glared at me. Had I thought he looked scary before? It was nothing to how he looked now. Still, I stood my ground and refused to back down, even though my heart was thumping and my palms were sweating with terror.

For a moment we just stared at each other. And if you've never had a staring contest with a seven foot tall guy who looks like a sexy Devil and could break you in half with his pinky finger, let me tell you—I don't recommend it. Finally, though, Sarden spoke.

"My sister," he said in a low, grating voice. "Is the reason I took you."

"What?" I shook my head. "What are you talking about?"

"Never mind." He made a sharp gesture with one hand. "I'll excuse your intrusion in my room this once on the grounds of ignorance. But never come in here again. *Never.*"

"Fine." I lifted my chin. "I was just leaving, anyway."

"Go back to your room," he ordered. "And don't leave again. I won't be so lenient next time."

As if there would be a next time. It looked to me like plan A wasn't panning out—maybe it was time to consider plan B.

"Fine," I said again. But just as I turned to leave, Al glided into the room, his snaky metal neck sailing smoothly through the metal ceiling as though it was silver water.

"Ah, Master Sarden," he said sounding pleased. "I'm glad to

see you found Lady Zoe. Did you invite her to dine with you, as you had intended?"

I turned around and raised an eyebrow at Sarden.

"Dine? We're *dining* now?"

"I thought you might be hungry," he said, still scowling. "There's time to get something to eat while A.L. runs a diagnostic on the hydrogen scoop."

"The food prep area can simulate almost any human delicacy you desire," Al put in helpfully. "I have been making a study of your Earth cuisine — though I could only devote a small portion of my processing algorithm to it. I hope you will find the results pleasing."

"Thank you, Al. You're by far the most courteous person on this ship," I said, staring at Sarden pointedly.

Sarden frowned, ignoring my jibe. "Why do you call him that? His designation is *A.L.* which stands for artificial life form."

"As to that, Master Sarden, I have been meaning to ask you to call me by my new name," Al told him.

"What?" Sarden looked startled. "You have a name now? Who said you could have a name?"

"Lady Zoe was kind enough to name me," Al said promptly. "I am named Alfred but Al for short. Apparently it is a good butler name — a butler is one who serves on Earth. And the name still goes with my designation of A.L. Is it not fitting?"

For a moment, Sarden looked like he was going to protest. Then he shook his head as though he just couldn't deal with this right now. "Fine. Al is fine, if that's what you want."

"It is. I find I enjoy having a name and not just a designation." Al sounded happy again, in his proper butler way.

"Great. Well…" Sarden looked at me. "Do you want to eat or not?"

"That depends." I crossed my arms over my chest. "I thought I was going to be confined to my room."

"Confined to her room? Oh no—why would you refuse Lady Zoe the freedom of the ship?" Al now sounded properly horrified. I was liking the artificial life-form more and more all the time.

Sarden didn't answer, instead he glared at me.

"I'll give you one more chance to behave," he growled. "Don't pry into my life or my business and I'll let you have the run of the ship. But one more incident and you're going into your room and staying there until we get to Giedi Prime."

"Sounds like somewhere out of a Frank Herbert novel," I said. "But fine. I'll stay out of your room." Which wasn't exactly the same as not prying—I was still determined to do plenty of that. I had hit a nerve with his sister, I was certain. And he'd said she was the reason he'd taken me. I had to find out more about that—I had the feeling it was the key to my freedom. But for now, I would let it drop.

For now.

"Fine," Sarden growled. "Then let's eat."

He turned and left the room and I followed him, with Al whizzing along by my side, his lantern-eye blinking.

Sarden

I tried to control my irritation as I led Zoe down the corridor and into the food prep area. How dare she go snooping around my room, rifling through my private things? I was especially irritated by the fact that she'd gotten me to reveal my relationship with

Sellah. It was none of her business, damn it! And she shouldn't have touched my memory cube!

Seeing the little Pure One handle the precious crystal cube I'd stored so carefully in my desk had nearly turned me feral. It was the best memory I had of my sister, although I hadn't been able to bear to listen to it in a long time. But when I walked in my room, there Zoe was—playing it as though my most private, cherished memories were hers for the taking.

But even worse than the invasion of my privacy was hearing Sellah's voice. Her sweet tones were like a blade piercing my heart. My beloved, innocent little sister now lost, possibly forever…

No! I shoved the thought aside. Sellah wasn't lost forever—she couldn't be. I was going to get her back, Gods damn it! No matter what depths I had to sink to in order to do it.

But I couldn't help feeling a flash of guilt when I remembered Zoe's words. *"What would your sister think of you now?"* she'd asked. *"What would she say if she knew what you were doing?"*

I had the uncomfortable feeling that Sellah wouldn't like it one damn bit.

Trying to shrug off the thought, I turned my attention to the task at hand—teaching Zoe how to use the food-simulator.

The little Pure One would be gone from my life soon enough, I told myself. Though she looked distractingly lovely, dressed as she was in my shirt and nothing else so that all her ample curves were on display, I was determined to ignore her. Ignore her loveliness and the guilt I was tempted to feel when I got too near her.

As soon as the diagnostic was run and the panels of the hydrogen scoop were fit to travel, I would take her straight to Giedi Prime and trade her to Tazaxx.

Before she could worm her way any further under my skin.

Chapter Six

Zoe

So here's the deal with simulated food—if you ever get a chance to try it, don't. Just don't, okay?

It started out all right. Sarden seemed to have simmered down a little which was good. Being around him when he was pissed off was kind of like walking into the middle of a thunderstorm, wondering when the lightning was going to strike. But Sarden calm was not so bad—even if he did still look huge and scary.

First he showed me into the kitchen—excuse me, the *food prep* area—and proceeded to explain how the food-simulator worked. The food-sim, as he called it, was the big gold stock pot looking thing I'd seen earlier when Al took me on my short tour. The one with all the wires coming out of it.

As it turned out, the wires all had sticky pads attached to them and they were supposed to be placed at just the right spot on your temples so the food-sim could read your thoughts and know what to make you.

"Why can't I just *tell* it what to make?" I asked as Sarden pressed one of the sticky pads to his left temple.

"You are telling it—with your mind. You can provide a much more complete idea of whatever it is you're telling the sim to make, including taste, texture, and smell, by sending direct thought messages to its processing unit," he explained.

"So once you think what you want it appears in the pot?" Without waiting for an answer, I took the lid off the big gold pot and recoiled. "Ewww!" It was about two thirds full of green slime that looked an awful lot like snot.

I'm sorry—I know that's gross, but I have to be honest. That's what it looked like.

"You're not supposed to remove the lid until the food-sim is finished," Sarden snapped, snatching the lid back from me. "Are you paying attention? You'd better be because I don't have time to make food for you and even if I did, I doubt you'd like the cuisine from my home world."

"I doubt I'd like *any* cuisine that's snot-based," I said, fighting not to gag. "What's *in* that pot, anyway?"

"Nutrient slime—the raw material from which all foods are simulated, of course," he said impatiently, as though it should be obvious.

"So...the food-sim uses this stuff..." I pointed at the green slime. "To make things to eat? And then you actually *eat* them?"

"I'm beginning to wonder if the transport process from your planet affected your mind after all," he growled. "Of *course* you eat them. What else would you do with food?"

"Throw it away if it was made of green slime," I remarked. Not that I'm a super picky eater—one look at my hips and you'd know that. But a girl has to have some limits.

"The finished food product doesn't retain any of the texture or flavor of the nutrient slime," he said, frowning. "Watch."

Putting the lid back on the pot, he closed his eyes and pressed his fingers to the pad at his temple. He looked like he was thinking really hard about a difficult math problem. I was beginning to wonder how long this whole process took when the food-sim made a small, discrete chime that sounded like someone ringing a fancy door bell.

"There." Opening his eyes, Sarden took the lid off again and a puff of fragrant smelling steam escaped the pot.

I looked in. It was still filled two-thirds full with green slime but a small platform, which was completely slime free, had risen up from the center of the pot. On it sat a clear plate that might have been plastic or glass—I couldn't tell. On the plate was something that looked like a blue spaghetti sandwich. By which I mean that the bread-like stuff it was wrapped in was blue. The spaghetti itself was red and yellow with black specs I took to be some kind of pepper.

"Perfect." Sarden nodded with satisfaction and lifted the plate out of the pot. Picking up the sandwich, he took a large bite. "Delicious," he declared after swallowing.

"It doesn't look *too* bad," I conceded. "I mean the coloring is a little weird and having a bread and pasta combo like that is a *lot* of carbs, but it smells good."

"What is pasta?" he asked before taking another bite.

"That stuff—the long skinny noodles you're eating. On Earth we make it from wheat. What do your people make it from?"

"We don't make it at all—this is *churn.* We catch them in the Great Depths."

"The *what* now?" I frowned, not sure I understood him.

"I said we *catch* them," he repeated. "*Churn.* They're a kind of water snake that comes from my home planet of Eloim. Would you like a bite?"

He pushed the sandwich near my face and I suddenly saw what I hadn't before—the "noodles" all had little black eyes—that was what I had mistaken for pepper. Some even had tiny forked tongues hanging out of their itty-bitty mouths.

I think I made a sound like, "Urrgh," because Sarden withdrew his snake sandwich quickly.

"See? I told you that you wouldn't like the cuisine of my home world—*either one* of my home worlds. If you think the *churn* are disgusting, I can imagine what you'd think of Vornish *yigba* stew."

"I didn't say it was disgusting," I protested weakly. "I'm just not used to, uh, eating snake sandwiches. That's all. But…" I cleared my throat. "You said you have *two* home worlds?"

He looked suddenly guarded. "I should not have mentioned that. But yes, I am half Vorn and half Eloim."

"I, uh, noticed that your sister doesn't have horns like you do," I said, busying myself with securing a sticky thought patch to my left temple and hoping I wasn't overstepping my boundaries. "Is that because she's a girl and only the men, er, males of your people have them, or…?"

I left the question hanging, wondering if he would get mad again.

"The horns are from my Vorn heritage," he growled. "Sellah doesn't have them because she's pureblooded Eloim. Not that it's any of your Gods' damned business."

"Sorry!" I protested. "I didn't know it was such a touchy subject."

"Well it is. You might not know much about the universe—how could you, living on that uninformed ball of rock you call a planet—but the Vorn are hated and feared throughout our galaxy. They are considered violent, dangerous, and most of all, *unpredictable.*" He glared at me, as though daring me to say something.

Okay, I wasn't touching that one with a ten foot pole.

"And what are the Eloim known for?" I asked instead, glossing over the whole violent and dangerous thing.

Sarden took another bite of his sandwich and swallowed before answering.

"Eloim are highly civilized with an elaborate set of social customs for every occasion. They value art, beauty, and learning above all else."

"Wow." I frowned. "So the Vorn and Eloim are kind of polar opposites, huh?"

"Something like that," he agreed guardedly.

"So how did your parents meet and fall in love, if they're from such different cultures?" I asked, genuinely interested.

"They didn't," he said briefly.

"But then how—"

"Why are you so interested in my heritage, anyway?" he interrupted, frowning at me.

"I'm just trying to get to know you," I said. "I've never met an alien before. Hell, I didn't even know there *were* aliens outside of scifi books and movies until you had Bambi and his minions drag me through that bathroom mirror."

"Who is Bambi?" he wanted to know.

"Oh—that's what I was calling the head wormy guy—the main Commercian, I mean. He had a voice like a character from a children's story back on Earth so I sort of started calling him by that character's name."

"That was actually Char'noth and despite his voice and appearance, he's not a male you want to make angry with you," Sarden said dryly. "You really seem to enjoy re-naming things and people."

"Oh, you mean Al?" I asked. The artificial life-form had gone back to the control area, presumably to run the diagnostic test Sarden had talked about so he wasn't there to hear us talking about him. "I just thought he needed a name. He seems to like it, don't you think?"

"Yes, he does." Sarden didn't sound completely happy about it. "I don't understand you—I've owned *The Celesta* for ten solar cycles and A.L.—*Al*—has been nothing but a control system for the ship. Then you're on board for less than a solar hour and suddenly he wants a name."

"Maybe it's because I treated him like a person—not just a thing," I said pointedly.

Sarden looked grumpy again. "Are you going to sim yourself some food or not?" he asked, pointedly changing the subject.

"Yes, I am." I still didn't like the idea of eating something made out of green slime but it seemed like the best offer I was going to get. And besides, it was better to keep the big alien talking—asking for help with the whole food-sim process might take another step towards making him think of me as a person, not just a commodity to be traded. *Reverse Stockholm*, I reminded myself. I had to keep it up.

I closed my eyes just as I had seen Sarden do and pictured a single piece of sushi. Nothing too fancy or complicated—just a California roll with crab and avocado and cucumber like they make at Origami, my favorite sushi restaurant in Tampa. Leah and Charlotte and I always go there for girl's night out and then we head up to Ivarones, a little Italian place, and split a piece of their decadent chocolate cherry cheesecake for dessert.

Just thinking of my two best friends made me want to cry. I wonder if they had gone to the police yet. Probably not—I still hadn't been gone from Earth for a whole day, even though it felt like years. They wouldn't be allowed to file a missing persons report until at least twenty-four hours had elapsed. And even then it wouldn't do them any good. I was gone, on my way to a galaxy far, far away…

Suddenly I realized I was dangerously close to tears.

Get a grip on yourself, Zoe! I took a deep breath and redirected my thoughts back to the piece of sushi. I thought about it as hard as I could until I heard the soft chime from the food-sim.

"All right." Sarden opened the lid for me and peered inside. "Is that what it's supposed to look like?"

I peeped in myself and was surprised to see a perfectly delicious-looking piece of sushi sitting on another one of those clear plates.

"Oh, look! Just like I imagined!" I clapped my hands in surprised pleasure.

"So glad we could meet your expectations," Sarden said dryly, but I thought I saw the ghost of a smile tugging at the corner of his mouth. He lifted the plate out and handed it to me, waiting to see me eat the results.

Picking the piece of sushi up, I sniffed it carefully. Well, it certainly *smelled* like sushi and there was no green slime anywhere on it or near it. Deciding to give it a chance, I popped it into my mouth and began to chew.

After a moment I was looking for a napkin to spit it into. There wasn't anything available though, so I had to swallow.

Sarden must have seen the look on my face.

"What happened? Did the food-sim get it wrong?"

"You could say that." I grimaced. "It looked like sushi but it tasted like something else."

"Like what?"

I frowned. It was hard to place the wrong taste because the sushi the food-sim had made for me had the right shape and color and texture and smell. But the taste…the taste had been completely off. Finally I had it.

"Chocolate cherry cheesecake!" I exclaimed. "That's what it tasted like!" Maybe the food-sim had made it taste like that because I was thinking about how I used to share it with Leah and Charlotte after we had sushi.

"What's that?" Sarden wanted to know.

"It's this kind of cake only not a cake—it's made from soft cheese flavored with chocolate—"

"Cheese?" he interrupted me. "Chocolate?"

At that moment I felt truly sorry for him. He might be a big, tough alien with a super fast spaceship but he was living on snake sandwiches and he'd never had cheese *or* chocolate which are like, two of the holy trinity of foods as far as I'm concerned. (Wine is the third, in case you're interested.)

"Cheese is an Earth food made from milk, which is this white liquid we get from domesticated animals called cows," I explained.

"Ah." He nodded. "We make a similar concoction on Vorn 6 from the bile of the *sprag*."

"Remind me never to go out to eat with you on Vorn 6 then," I said. "Anyway, there are lots of varieties of cheeses—we use a soft, sweet one to make cheese cake."

"And you said it was flavored by *shauckolat?*"

"*Chocolate*," I corrected him. "It's made by taking the beans out of these big pods that grow in the jungle and roasting them and grinding them—then mixing them with sugar and more milk—"

"You certainly eat a lot of this 'milk' you're talking about," Sarden remarked. "If we ate that much *sprag* bile we'd be sick."

In my personal opinion, any amount of bile would be too

much, but I didn't say so. See? I can be tactful.

"There's no such thing as too much cheese or too much chocolate," I told Sarden fervently. "Look, I don't think I'm explaining about the chocolate cherry cheesecake the right way. Let me try to make a piece for you — or let the food-sim try, anyway."

"Very well." He nodded and crossed his muscular arms over his still bare chest which made his pecs dance around in a yummy and distracting way. "I'd like to see this Earth delicacy."

"All right." Closing my eyes to shut out the sight of his muscles, I took a deep breath and concentrated hard on making cheesecake. I thought about the dense, creamy texture…the rich, chocolately taste…the sweet, slightly tart cherries…

The food-sim dinged again. I opened the lid eagerly to see a perfect piece of cherry chocolate cheesecake sitting there on the clear plate. It looked just like it did when we ordered it from Ivarones.

"Perfect!" I exclaimed, picking it up. I was certain that this time I had gotten it right. It looked amazing and smelled so sweet and creamy and delicious. I couldn't wait to taste it — but I wanted Sarden to try some too. He, however, was looking at it with an uncertain expression on his face.

"It looks like a triangular wedge of soil with blood clots on top," he pointed out.

"What? Eww! Don't say that about my cheesecake!" I protested. "Look, just try it and you'll see how delicious it is. Just *try*."

He shrugged his broad shoulders. "I don't see why I should try your cuisine when you refused a bite of my perfectly good *churn* wrap, but all right. I'll try."

"You need something to eat it with — do you have any forks or spoons — any kind of utensils?" I asked when he raised his eyebrows at me in confusion.

"Oh. Of course." He tapped the long bar the food-sim was located on twice with his fingertips. A portion of it flipped over, revealing a tray which held the most bewildering array of cutlery I'd ever seen, all made of some shiny black metal.

There were several knives of varying lengths, some things that looked like really sharp chopsticks only they had curly ends like corkscrews, a ladle-like spoon that would have held almost an entire bowl of soup—if his people ate soup—and some things that looked like weird 3-D forks with tines sticking out in all directions.

"What in the world?" I said, staring down at the bizarre instruments.

"Sorry." Sarden looked slightly embarrassed. "It's inherited from my mother. Eloim have elaborate customs for everything, including dining."

"And they use all this for *every* meal?" Carefully, I chose a spork-looking thing with a very long handle—it looked like the best bet for eating the cheesecake the food-sim had made.

"Mmm-hmm." Sarden nodded. "I don't usually use it myself. Or at least, only when Sellah comes on board. She—" He stopped abruptly and for a moment I thought I saw his features twist into an expression of deep pain and regret. Then his face went blank and he shrugged. "Anyway, do you want to try this cakecheese first or should I?"

"*Cheesecake,*" I corrected him. "And you try it."

"Very well." He took the long handled spork from me. "And this is the correct utensil to use?"

"Uh, sure. It's fine."

"All right." He dug gamely into the chocolate cherry cheesecake despite his earlier opinion that it looked like dirt and blood. He popped the bite in his mouth and I watched anxiously, wondering if this taste of Earth cuisine would make him think differently about me.

"Well?" I asked anxious after he had chewed and swallowed.

Sarden frowned. "It tastes good enough. Only...did you say it was supposed to be sweet?"

"Yes—so sweet it makes your teeth ache. Why—isn't it?" I asked anxiously. "Here, let me try it." I reached for the spork-thing but he held it out of arm's length.

"Don't you want me to wash it first?"

"Why?" I asked impatiently. "Do you have a cold? I mean, are you sick?" I asked, seeing the look of incomprehension on his face.

"Well, no. But...I am Vorn. Half Vorn anyway," he said, as though that was supposed to make a difference.

"So? I'm human. Now let me try the cheesecake." I held out my hand for the spork and he reluctantly surrendered it. (For those of you who are squeamish about eating after someone else, I'm sorry—it just doesn't bother me.) Besides, I *really* wanted to try that cheesecake. I hadn't even been gone from Earth a whole day yet and already I was having chocolate withdrawal.

I took a big bite of the chocolate cherry cheesecake, making sure to get one of the plump, gooey cherries too. I popped it in my mouth and chewed...then nearly spit it out.

"Wrong again? Is it not supposed to taste like that?" Sarden guessed, apparently reading the expression on my face.

"No," I said swallowing with some difficulty. "Not at *all.*"

In fact, it tasted exactly like sushi. Not the mild California roll I'd tried to make earlier, either. The cheesecake tasted like the time I'd tried a piece of really strong salmon skin roll that Charlotte had ordered once. She'd gotten me to take a bite by telling me I wasn't adventurous enough—I wondered what she would think if she could see me now.

Now, I know what you're thinking—so what if they look wrong, you have something that tastes like cheesecake and something that tastes like sushi. Why not just close your eyes and eat them and enjoy?

Well, because it wasn't just the *taste* I was dealing with. It was the texture and the smell. The smooth, creamy mouth-feel of the cheesecake and its rich, dark chocolate smell did *not* go well with the flavor of raw fish.

In fact, it was disgusting. So I was surprised when Sarden plucked the spork from my hand and ate another bite himself.

"Not bad," he remarked thoughtfully. "At any rate, I've had worse. But I take it you want to try again?"

I sighed. "I'll try something different this time—I think the food-sim thingy has sushi and cheesecake completely mixed up."

He shrugged his shoulders. "Go ahead. I have an entire drum of Nutrient Slime in the cargo hold—you can make as much shauckolat cakecheese as you want."

This time I didn't even try to correct him. Instead, I closed my eyes and pictured a cheeseburger. The biggest, juiciest cheeseburger ever, with pickles and onions, a deep red slice of tomato and a crispy piece of lettuce, all served on a big, fluffy sesame seed bun.

The food-sim dinged and out it came—exactly as I had pictured it. It smelled *amazing.*

Sarden eyed my creation with interest. "You Earthlings certainly have strange looking food."

"Says the man who just ate a snake sandwich right in front of me," I said, lifting the plate out of the food-sim's big gold pot.

"Do you need a utensil to eat that?" he wanted to know. "What is it called, anyway?"

"A cheeseburger. And no utensils—this is finger food."

"Finger food?" He frowned. "Is it made from the ground up digits of some animal?"

"Ugh, no!" I exclaimed. "Finger food just means it's meant to be eaten with your fingers—with your hands. Don't your people have any food like that? Aside from snake sandwiches, I mean."

"The Eloim do not," he said. "Even the *churn* wrap I ate was supposed to be carved into pieces with a vunnel knife and then consumed with the trillers." He nodded at the cork-screw chopstick looking things. "The Vorn, however, are very fond of *chabeth* knuckles. We cover them in a type of sweet blood sauce and gnaw the meat from the bones. It's a very messy affair."

"It sounds like it," I muttered. Actually, neither one of his cultures sounded like much fun. The Eloim sounded like overly fancy prigs and the Vorn appeared to be the galaxy's equivalent of thuggish ex-cons with the table manners of a hillbilly. I wondered again how in the world his parents had gotten together. Maybe his mom had a thing for bad boys.

"Well? Are you going to try it?" Sarden asked, nodding at my plate.

"Absolutely." I eyed my creation reverently. This time I was *completely* certain the food-sim had gotten it right. It looked so *perfect*—like a cheeseburger out of a commercial. I mean, it really was a thing of beauty. Closing my eyes, I took a big bite and tasted...

Chocolate éclair.

"Oh, *no,*" I moaned, putting the cheeseburger down.

"Wrong again?" Sarden picked it up, sniffed it, and took a bite.

He frowned, putting it down. "That is *much* too sweet."

"It's not supposed to be sweet at all," I said sadly. "It's supposed to be salty and crunchy and chewy and delicious." Not that chocolate éclairs aren't delicious—but that taste just doesn't go with the smell and texture of a cheeseburger.

"Possibly A.L.—*Al*—did something wrong when adding the new Earth cuisine to the food-sim's program," Sarden remarked. "Maybe you should wait and let him tinker with it some before you try again."

"No." I frowned. "I'm *not* giving up."

He gave me a surprised look. "For such a small female, you certainly have a lot of determination."

"I'm not a quitter," I said grimly. "And I'm not *that* small—it's just that you're so freaking huge. Does that come from the Eloim side or the Vorn side?"

"Vorn," he said. "The Eloim are only a little larger than you Earthlings." He sighed. "I was much feared growing up for my size. Only Sellah—" He frowned and stopped himself abruptly. "Keep trying if you want to. I have to see if A.L. has finished the diagnostic on the Hydrogen scoop's panels yet."

He started to leave but just then Al came gliding into the room.

"Master Sarden, diagnostics complete," he said in that proper voice of his. "But I'm afraid you will not like the results."

"What?" Sarden growled. "All I want to hear is that we can get to Giedi Prime."

"Not immediately, I'm afraid," Al said apologetically. "One of the panels is fatally flawed and must be replaced. The repairs you made will only hold for a little while—long enough to get us to the nearest spaceport—Gallana—which orbits Proxima Centauri."

Sarden groaned. "Not Gallana! It's run by the Gods' damned Majorans."

"I'm sorry I don't have better news, Master." Al sounded genuinely sorry, too. "I know that speed is of the essence. But once the panel is replaced we should be able use the Hyperdrive to make up time and still get to Giedi Prime at the appointed hour."

"We'll be cutting it awfully Gods' damned close though," Sarden growled. "But I guess if that's our only option, you'd better set a course to Gallana."

"At once, Master." Al glided away again.

"What's wrong with going to, uh, Gallana?" I asked, thinking it sounded like a super-expensive and ritzy shopping mall.

"Besides the delay? The fucking Majorans. They have…strange ideas about their females."

"What kinds of ideas?" I asked.

He shook his head. "Never mind. The point is, whenever you visit a Majoran base, you have to follow their rules. Of the twelve overlord races—the Twelve Peoples, we call them—that the Ancient Ones left behind, the Majorans are in ascendancy right now. So their empress rules our galaxy."

"Huh?" I stared at him, my chocolate-éclair cheeseburger completely forgotten now. "Our galaxy has an *empress?*"

"Of course. Who do you think rules us all? Her throne is located on Femme One, on the edge of the super-massive black hole in the center of the galaxy."

"Okay, wow. That's a *lot* to take in," I murmured.

"You'd know all this if you hadn't been locked away by the Ancient Ones," he remarked.

"But we've been searching for extraterrestrial life for years," I protested. "We've been sending out signals and scanning the stars… How is it we never came across anything at all?"

He snorted. "With the primitive instruments you have? You couldn't find a black *kalk* in the white sands of Quendor with Earthling tech."

"Hey, that *tech* got us to our moon and back—more than once," I said stiffly.

He snorted again. "Oh yes—the journey of a single light-second. A *mighty* achievement."

"It was for us," I pointed out. "Everyone has to start somewhere."

"That's the point—you're just starting out. Which means you're far, *far* behind even the more primitive peoples of the universe. Besides," he added more kindly. "Your planet is located in an out-of-the-way arm of the galaxy. It's not like you're close to any of the major space hubs. You're just a forgotten little world the Ancient Ones put off limits." His face grew dark. "And if you're lucky, you'll stay that way. Although I doubt it now that the Commercians have sunk their blue claws into you."

I thought of other girls just like me being sucked through their mirrors or toasters or spoons or any shiny, reflective surface in their house and winding up on Bambi's ship, just as I had. Not just one or two—hundreds, thousands, *millions* maybe, depending on how popular Earth brides turned out to be with alien men. If the Alien Mate Index really took off, we could be looking at the end of the human race.

The thought made me sick and a cold finger of dread skittered down my spine. I wrapped my arms around myself and shivered.

Sarden frowned. "Are you chilly? Char'noth said you came from a very warm region of your planet. I'm…sorry I didn't give you more protective clothing. Although you *do* look tempting in just my shirt."

His golden eyes roamed over me, making me shiver for a different reason. For some reason while we'd been using the food-prep machine, I'd managed to forget how very huge and imposing and *shirtless* he was. Now, as he took a step closer, I was faced with the broad planes of his muscular chest and I could smell his scent again—that warm, spicy, campfire aroma that made my knees turn to jelly for some reason.

"I'm fine," I lied, keeping my chin up and trying not to let him affect me. "Just…just trying to decide what to ask the food-sim to make next."

"So you're determined to try again?" Sarden sounded surprised.

"I told you—I'm not a quitter." There was nothing I could do about the situation with Earth—not now. If I could ever get back there, maybe I could warn my home planet. Although I was pretty sure everyone would think I was just plain crazy if I tried. Still, I would have to get home first to test that theory and right now, plan A was all I had to get there. *Reverse Stockholm,* I reminded myself.

Looking at Sarden, I gave him what I hoped was a flirtatious smile.

"How would you like to try another rare Earth delicacy? We call this one *bacon and eggs."*

Sarden

The little Pure One never ceased to amaze me. She was determined to force the food-sim to get the food of her home world correct and she refused to stop trying.

She made me the Earth food called bacunandeggz—which consisted of long, crispy strips and fluffy, pale yellow chunks. But they tasted sweet, as the cheezburger had. Zoe said they had the flavor of pankakes which are apparently flat, spongy disks soaked in the sweet sap of a tree indigenous to Earth.

Rather than being discouraged by yet another failure, she was happy.

"I'm getting close," she remarked, eating a bite of the crispy bacun. "At least these are all breakfast foods. And this pancake-tasting-bacon isn't half bad."

She tried several other things too but none of them came out the way she wanted. There was a thick piece of grilled meat which was supposed to be salty and tender but which Zoe said tasted like a sweet confection made of red berries and cake. Then she tried two slices of plain white Earth bread, much like the blue crust of my *churn* wrap, with a small amount of yellow Earth cheese melted between them. Again, it was supposed to be salty but Zoe said it tasted like something she called *shauckolat* pudding.

Though none of her Earth recipes came out to her satisfaction, she kept trying anyway. I don't know why, but I stayed with her, tasting the strange Earth concoctions she coaxed from the food-sim and laughing with her as each came out worse than the last. We shared utensils and at one point, she asked me for a drink to wash the various tastes out of her mouth.

I got her a squeeze bulb of purified water but before giving it to her, I took a sip myself. Zoe didn't hesitate to put her lips where mine had been—she took the water and drank it thankfully, apparently not bothered that her mouth had touched that which had also touched the mouth of a Vorn.

Watching her do that roused a powerful sensation in my

chest—more powerful than I liked to admit. The Vorn are hated and feared through most of the universe and especially here in our home galaxy. We are considered an unclean species, especially by the fastidious Eloim. I could still remember the pain in my childhood of the other children refusing to touch me—washing their hands after even the slightest and most incidental contact. Only Sellah stood by me, refusing to act like the others. She never saw me as a half-breed or a Vorn—only as her beloved big brother, and nothing anyone said could shake her love or her loyalty.

I tried to push the thoughts of my lost sister away and thought of the days ahead instead. Stopping by Gallana to get a panel replaced was going to put a serious crimp in my schedule. And that was *if* I could find someone to fix the panel right away—a mechanic willing to deal with a male alone who didn't have a female companion with him.

Just thinking of it made me grind my teeth. The damned Majorans are sexist and it irritates the piss out of me to have to deal with them. Not that I mind them worshiping their females—a male can worship any damn thing he chooses, as far as I'm concerned. But the fact that they make everyone conform to their ways or refuse to do business with them is damned irritating.

The other worry, besides our time constraints, was how I could pay for the new panel and the work to replace it. With the exception of a few hundred credits I had kept back for fuel, buying Zoe from the Commercians had me all tapped out. It looked like I would have to search a little harder for someone who wanted to buy the Assimilation medical equipment in the storage area of *The Celesta*.

But could I do all that and still get back to Giedi Prime and Tazaxx before the auction? I didn't know. I sent a swift prayer to the Goddess of Mercy—hoping she'd hear me, despite what a bastard I am. And I tried to concentrate on Zoe instead.

It wasn't hard – she had a bubbly personality that reminded me of Sellah, though she was more outgoing than my shy, bookish little sister. She kept talking and laughing, drawing me into conversation while she continued to work with the food-sim.

I wondered at her apparent ease around me. I was her captor – her kidnapper – and I had already told her I was trading her to Tazaxx. But she didn't cry with fear or sulk or try to get away. She just kept giving me new things to eat and laughing at her failures.

I couldn't help watching the way she moved – this close to her, the hidden spectrum of colors erupted across my vision, showing me her true beauty despite the inhibitor she wore. Her pale skin with its many dots of light pigment seemed to glow in the dim illumination of the food-prep area. Her hair was a long, silky tangle of auburn curls and her curves – those sweet, generous curves I'd admired so much when she'd first been brought aboard the Commercians' base – were barely covered by the thin black temp-shirt I'd given her to wear.

I knew it was wrong but I couldn't help wishing I could taste the merchandise, just a little, before I sent her on her way. If I kissed her or touched her it would likely be the last such contact she'd ever receive.

That was because Tazaxx was a Gord – a species sexually incompatible with the descendants of the Ancient Ones. He kept his "special collection" in a zoo-like exhibit area – for display purposes only. Zoe would be put into a beautifully built case with all the luxuries her heart could desire and there she would spend her days, behind a force-field, being lovely and innocent for Tazaxx and his friends to admire.

It was where I hoped and prayed Sellah was now. Knowing that Tazaxx didn't physically abuse or sexually violate those in his "special collection" was the only thing that kept me sane. I imagined my little sister in that guilt cage, behind the force-field, and then I pictured Zoe there, in her place.

I didn't like either image.

So though my palms itched to caress Zoe's curves and cup her full breasts…though I wondered more than once what her soft pink lips would taste like, I kept my hands to myself. I am, as I said before, no rapist. No matter how much she tempted me, I was determined to trade her to Tazaxx untouched.

But I couldn't help watching her—she shone so brightly in the dimness of my ship. Like a star I had stolen from the heavens, though I had no right to do it.

Zoe

I don't know how long we spent trying to get the food-sim to make anything decent to eat—it might have been a couple of hours. I *do* know the level of green Nutrient Slime in the gold pot had gone down considerably by the time I finally gave up.

By that time I had made bacon and eggs that tasted like pancakes and syrup, a t-bone steak that tasted like strawberry shortcake, a grilled cheese sandwich that tasted like chocolate pudding, and too many other things to count.

The closest I got to something edible was the pancake flavored bacon, but mostly because you eat those two things together a lot anyway. At last, I had to stop. I was determined to try again after Al worked on the program some more, but I was afraid I would make myself sick if I ate any more mixed up food.

Sarden didn't seem bothered by the strange taste and texture combinations. He gamely tried everything I made, even the awful banana cream pie that tasted like sauerkraut.

I noticed he kept watching me as we worked and he got quiet once or twice but I counted it as a victory anyway. We were getting to be friends—well, sort of. And it's a hell of a lot harder to trade your friends to some oily alien salesman than it is to trade away some girl you don't even know.

Reverse Stockholm—I was sure it was working. Pretty sure, anyway. And I tried not to notice how those glowing gold eyes watching me made me feel. How when his fingers brushed my skin, even by accident, it sent shivers down my spine and made my nipples turn into tight little points.

Friendly or not, he was still the enemy. I might pretend to like him but that was all it was, I told myself sternly—just pretend. All an act to get him to care about me too much to trade me. And hopefully enough to get him to take me back to Earth.

At least we had this layover in the spaceport to look forward to. It would give us more time to spend together—more time for Sarden to get to know me. Maybe I should go even further and try to make him fall in love with me?

Maybe I should try to seduce him.

The thought made me shiver all over. Sarden was *huge* and I hadn't been with anybody since I broke up with my ex almost a year ago. He'd probably split me in half if I tried something like that.

I tried to push the extremely scary thoughts to the back of my mind but the longer I was with him and the more I smelled his warm, spicy scent, the harder it got to do. I was almost relieved when he finally told me I should get some sleep.

"Being transported as you were is a very tiring process. You probably need to rest," he told me as he walked me to the door of my room.

"All right." I stopped beside the door and looked up at him, wondering what was going on behind those golden alien eyes. "I'm looking forward to trying out the floating hoverbed. We don't have anything like that on Earth."

"You want to go to bed, little Pure One?" His voice was a soft, deep growl that seemed to send tingles all though me.

"I...you know what I mean," I stammered, feeling my cheeks get hot.

"Yes, I know," he murmured, brushing a strand of hair out of my eyes. "I just thought maybe you were interested to try the bed's pleasure settings."

I didn't know what he meant by that but I shivered as his warm fingertips brushed my skin and then tried to pretend I hadn't.

"I'm tired," I said and it wasn't a lie. Suddenly I felt as though all my energy was leaking away. It really *had* been a very long day—from getting staplers thrown at my head, to being dragged through the bathroom mirror into an alien space ship, to spending hours with Sarden trying to make food out of green slime. It was the longest and strangest day I'd ever had in my life and I was suddenly completely exhausted.

Being abducted by aliens really takes it out of a girl—out of me, anyway.

"Go to sleep then." Sarden's deep voice was almost a caress and I thought for a moment he was going to cup my cheek or stroke my hair. He raised his hand for a moment...but then he brought it back down to his side and clenched it tight instead.

"What about you?" I asked. "Are you, uh, going to bed too?"

He shook his head. "Not for a while. I have a lot to do before we reach Gallana."

"The spaceport, right." I nodded. "Um, do I get to go with you? I've never seen an alien spaceport before."

"I don't think so." His face darkened. "You'd be a target there if anyone found out you were a Pure One. Especially if it was known you're a *La-ti-zal.*"

"I still don't understand that," I complained. "What does it even mean?"

"That you're special," he murmured and this time he did lift his hand to cup my cheek.

I felt my heart pounding and my face getting warm under his touch. God he smelled good! And he was so close I could feel the heat from his big body radiating against my own. I wondered what it would be like to be cuddled up in his arms...to kiss those cruel but sensual-looking lips...

"*Very* special," Sarden murmured again and he bent lower. Was he actually going to kiss me? Was I actually going to *let* him?

"Too...too special to trade, maybe?" I blurted, my stupid mouth talking without consulting my brain first. (This tends to happen to me a lot.)

At once, Sarden's eyes went cold and he pulled back from me. He'd been leaning over so that we were almost eye-to-eye but now he drew himself up to his full height and glared down at me.

"No," he said coldly. "Not too special for that."

"But...but I thought..." I shook my head, knowing I was making it worse but unable to stop my big fat mouth from saying things I knew it shouldn't. "We had fun today," I said. "I mean, we talked, we got to know each other, we made food out of slime...it was *fun.*"

"Very enjoyable," he agreed but his face was still cold. "I'm sorry, Zoe, but no matter how much I enjoy your company or how beautiful you are, I'm still going to trade you. I have no choice."

With that, he left me standing there, feeling like someone had just dumped a bucket of ice water over my head.

The big red jerk.

Chapter Seven

Zoe

I admit, I spent a couple of hours curled in a corner crying and poor-pitiful-me-ing after I got into my room that night. I had really thought I was making headway with Sarden—I thought he actually liked me. Hell, for a minute there when we were saying good night, I thought he did *more* than like me. I could still feel the heat of his big body radiating against mine, could still trace the line of warmth his hand had left on my cheek...

But it all meant nothing. He was determined to trade me no matter what and I was never going to get back home again. I was never going to have a cheeseburger that didn't taste like chocolate éclair or a steak that didn't taste like strawberry shortcake. There would be no more girl days with Charlotte and Leah, no more three-way bitch sessions on the phone, no more late night movie marathons. No more of a hundred thousand little things that had made up my life on Earth.

No more.

But a person can only cry so much. After a couple of hours when my eyes were all red and weepy and swollen, I finally took a deep breath and got hold of myself.

Back home, when I was miserable, I always took a hot shower and felt better afterwards. Unfortunately, that wasn't an option here. It was either get in the tank of purple liquid (no, no, and *Hell* no) or take a shower in the mister.

I chose the mister. After shedding the black temp-shirt, I turned the alien shower on and stepped into a cloud of cool mist which collected in chilly droplets that ran down over my bare skin.

Honestly, it wasn't very good as showers go. I mean, I *was* able to get my body clean but I knew right away I wouldn't be able to wash my hair in there. My curly mop is too dense to wash under anything but excellent water pressure which was pretty much the exact opposite of the mister.

But since I didn't have any shampoo anyway, I decided not to bother. I twisted my hair into a thick knot at the nape of my neck and just concentrated on getting my skin clean.

After turning off the mister, I looked for something to dry off with. There were no towels that I could see but suddenly a blast of hot air surrounded me, coming from the same fine jets which had previously sprayed the water. It nearly knocked me off my feet but I put out my hands to brace against the wall and managed to stay upright. When the hot air finally subsided, I was dry.

"Whew," I muttered to myself as I stepped out. "What is it with these people and the hot air on your sensitive areas?"

There was no answer forthcoming but I didn't expect one. It was just another aspect of alien life I would have to get used to unless I could get back home. *All right, so let's think about that,* I told myself. *How can I get home?*

I pulled Sarden's t-shirt back on, since I had nothing else to wear, and settled gingerly into the floating silver bed. It dipped and swayed dangerously as I scrambled in but once I was in place, it supported me beautifully. I thought it would probably be like sleeping on a cloud—only I had no intention of sleeping. Not tonight.

It was time to get serious.

Fact 1—I was on a spaceship headed away from Earth and I was getting farther away all the time.

Fact 2—Plan A had failed spectacularly.

Fact 3—I had only one option left, that I could see.

It was time for Plan B.

Reaching into the folds of the silver, floating beanbag bed, I withdrew the heavy length of pipe and the thick manacles. The manacles glowed a soft blue, the light in the center of the chain connecting them winking like a star.

I finally dared to touch it and when I did, the light changed from blue to green and both of the thick cuffs popped open with a soft chime. Hmm… I touched the light again—which was cool but buzzed and vibrated under my fingertip—and they snapped closed and the light turned blue. So *that* was how they worked. Good thing because I didn't see any key to go with them.

I hefted the pipe in my hand and stared at it. Could I really go through with this? I've never been a violent person. I mean, I have a temper on me and I got in a pretty good fight once in fifth grade when Grace McLaughlin stole the charm bracelet my Granny had given me for my birthday and started telling everyone it was hers. But other than that, I've never been much of a fighter.

Well, it was time to change all that. The longer I waited, the further I got from Earth. It was time to turn this ship around and if Sarden wouldn't do it, I would find a way myself.

Tucking the heavy, cold manacles under my shirt-dress to mask their glow, I held the pipe by my side and slipped out into the hall.

I had half expected to see Al somewhere watching me, but the artificial life form's round lantern-eye was nowhere to be seen. The lights aboard the ship had been dimmed and the long metal corridor was filled with black shadows.

It was seriously creepy. My mind kept wanting to show me images and scenes from that *Event Horizon* movie my ex had made me watch—the horror scifi one where the people's eyeballs explode. I really should have insisted on watching something else that night. You can bet I wouldn't be having frightening flashbacks of Richard Gere and Julia Roberts having sex on the piano if I'd gotten my way and we had watched *Pretty Woman* instead.

Taking a deep breath, I pushed the scary images aside and slipped down the hall to stand in front of Sarden's door.

Some time ago I had heard his door whoosh open and closed, so I knew he was in there. The question was—was he asleep? And was he deeply enough asleep for me to carry out my plan?

Well, only one way to find out.

Leaning forward, I broke the invisible beam and the door opened with a soft, almost silent *swish.* Inside it was very dark except for a tiny bit of light coming from the bathroom. As my eyes adjusted, I realized it was the purple liquid in the awful personal cleansing tank—it was glowing ever so faintly like a vast aquarium nightlight thing.

The light wasn't much but it was enough for me to see Sarden's large form sprawled across a vast silver beanbag bed. Like the one in my room, the bed was floating about three feet above the floor. Just the right height. I gripped the pipe tighter and stepped forward.

Sarden didn't stir. He was lying on his back with his head turned to one side which was good. I had read in a self-defense book once that the best way to knock out your attacker with one blow was with a single hit to the temple. I planned to avoid his horns though—I wasn't sure what hitting one of them might do to him and I wanted to knock him out, not kill him.

Sliding closer, I kept my left hand pressed to my belly to keep the manacles from clinking and raised the pipe in my right.

Then I hesitated.

It was really hard to do this—much harder than I'd expected. You spend your whole life from preschool up being told "don't hit, don't kick, don't punch…be careful, don't hurt anyone and if you *do* hurt someone, say you're sorry!"

Well, I could say sorry later, after I had him cuffed and under my control, I decided. Right now, this was my only option.

Taking a deep breath, I swung down, landing the pipe as hard as I could.

Only it landed on the soft, billowy fold of the silver beanbag bed. Because at the last moment, Sarden rolled to one side and popped up on his feet.

I knew I was in trouble from the way his golden eyes glowed in the dark. He looked huge in the dim purple light—a mountain of muscles and it suddenly occurred to me what an extremely stupid idea Plan B was. Here I was, in the dark with a massive, seven foot tall, extremely muscular alien who bore more than a passing resemblance to the Devil and I had just tried to brain him with a metal pipe.

I was so, *so* screwed.

"What in the Frozen Hells of Anor do you think you're doing?" he demanded in a low, angry growl. "And what do you have in your hand?"

"I…um…" Like a scared little girl, I tried to hide the pipe behind my back because I tend to get stupid when I'm terrified.

"Give me that." With one stride he was around the bed and

grabbing my wrist. His long fingers squeezed tight and my hand went numb at once.

"Ow!" I cried and dropped the pipe which landed on the floor with a metallic clatter.

"I see," Sarden said grimly. Still holding my arm, he scooped up the pipe. "So you were planning to kill me in my sleep—is that it?"

"No, honestly," I gasped. "I wasn't going to kill you—just knock you unconscious and chain you up."

"A likely story," he snarled, shaking me. The sudden motion dislodged the manacles from under my shirt and they landed on my bare foot.

"Ouch!" I yelped in sudden agony. "Son of a *bitch* that hurts!"

"Force Locks?" Sarden dropped the pipe and kicked it under the bed, then bent to scoop up the manacles instead. He looked at their glowing blue light and then at me. "Where did you get these?"

"I...I found them," I gasped.

"No doubt when you were snooping around the ship earlier. I knew I was being too soft on you. I should have locked you in your room—that might have kept you from sneaking around in the middle of the night trying to kill me."

"Well, what did you expect me to do, you big red bastard?" I flared at him. "Just wait like a good little prisoner to be sold or traded? Get it through your head—*you do not own me!*"

"No, you get it through *your* head, Zoe..." He leaned down until we were eye-to-eye, his golden, glowing eyes burning into my own. "I *do* own you and I'll do whatever I damn well please with you."

Scooping me up with one arm, he lifted me and threw me on

my back in the middle of the silver beanbag bed.

Then he climbed in beside me.

Chapter Eight

Sarden

I didn't know whether I should be angry with her or admire her courage. I still couldn't believe she'd had the nerve to come to my room in the middle of the night and try to brain me with a pipe.

It's a damn good thing I have a Vornish watchfulness and Eloim reflexes. I'd been awake from the moment she entered my room, but I had wanted to wait and see what she would do. After our almost tender scene at her door, I'd been hoping she might try crawling in bed with me. No such luck though—she just wanted to kill me and take over the ship.

Wouldn't you do the same thing? whispered a voice in my head that sounded uncomfortably like Sellah's. *Wouldn't you try to kill or incapacitate your captor if you were being taken away from your home to be sold as a slave?*

I tried to ignore it as I got into bed beside the little Pure One and held her down.

"Sarden…Sarden, *please!*" Her voice was soft and breathy and her body felt lush and ripe under my restraining hand. I wanted to use both hands to hold her but I was still gripping the Force Locks in my other fist. Seeing their blue glow in the dim room gave me a sudden flash of inspiration—*let her have a taste of her own medicine.*

With two swift moves I had her arms stretched over her head and the Force Locks snapped around her slender wrists. Of course they were much too large for her but the field generated inside the manacles held her in place as securely as the metal outside would have. Then I pushed her hands down until the blue lock-light touched the silver fabric of my hoverbed. At once, they locked into place, as secure as if I'd driven a nail through them to hold them there.

"Hey! Hey, let me go!" Zoe wriggled and squirmed, clearly surprised that she couldn't wiggle her way out of the locks.

I thought it was a good thing she wasn't a Vorn and so was unable to activate the Force-Locks. They were keyed to the ship so if she *had* been able to activate them, she could have released herself by simply applying a firm pressure to the lock-light with her skin. She also could have gotten anywhere in the ship, using the Locks as a key. But of course, not being a Vorn, these things were impossible.

And even if she had been Vornish, she wouldn't have been able to reach the light—not in the position I had her in now. The position I intended to keep her in until she learned her lesson. And how exactly was I going to teach her that lesson?

I didn't know yet but her luscious curves, all laid out like a feast before me in the middle of my bed did give me a few ideas...

Zoe

"Help! Let me go!" I demanded, wiggling futilely. But though the heavy manacles looked like they should be much too big for me, they held me firmly and I couldn't get away. The metal wasn't even touching my skin—it felt like I was being held by a cushion of air—

completely inescapable air.

"You're not going anywhere until you learn your lesson," Sarden growled, leaning over me.

I stopped wiggling and looked up at him, feeling my eyes grow wide and my breath grow short. So much trouble. I was in *so* much trouble now. I could feel the heat of his big body again, hovering just over my own much smaller one.

"What…what are you going to do to me?" I whispered in a voice that trembled a lot more than I liked.

"What do you think I'm going to do?" he snarled softly and then I felt something pinch my nipple.

"Hey!" I nearly jumped out of bed—I would have if the manacles hadn't been holding me in place. "Hey, stop it, you big red pervert!"

"Stop what? I haven't even started yet." Frowning, he pulled away but then I felt something teasing my other nipple.

"Yes, you are!" I exclaimed, twisting to try and get away from him. "You…you're *touching me.* Stop it—stop it *right now!*"

"I tell you, I'm not doing a damn thing," he growled and held up his hands to prove it.

I stared at him in disbelief. Sure enough, I could see both his hands and neither one was anywhere near my body.

So then who or what was playing with my nipples?

The thought made me wiggle some more just as whatever it was tugged on both of my tender buds, sending sparks of scary pleasure through my whole body.

"What the hell?" I gasped, looking down to try and see what was going on. "If you're not touching me then who is?"

"I have no fucking idea. I…wait a minute." Frowning, Sarden

leaned over me and looked at something in a fold of the silver beanbag. "I see what it is," he said, straightening up and looking back down at me. "When you aimed for my head with that pipe, you hit the bed's pleasure settings."

"What?" I vaguely remembered him saying something about that – about the bed's pleasure function when he was saying goodnight to me. But the fact that he'd then acted like a huge jerk had driven it clean out of my head. Now I was being reminded of his words – in the most vivid and visceral way possible.

"You heard me. Your assassination attempt turned on the bed's erotic functions," he repeated and was there a slight smile tugging the corner of his sensual mouth? Yes, there absolutely was, the bastard.

"Well turn it off!" I demanded as the silver material of the bed cradled my breasts and teased lightly at the points of my nipples.

"No." Sarden was openly grinning now, a self satisfied smirk pasted to his handsome, Devil-looking face that made me want to slap him. Only I couldn't get my hands free to do it. "In fact," he continued, "I think this is an excellent punishment for your attempt on my life. I think I'll turn the pleasure settings up a bit."

"I told you," I protested as the perverted beanbag tugged at the hem of my shirt, raising it to bare my sex and breasts for him. "I *wasn't* going to kill you! I was just going to chain you up and have Al turn the ship around to take me back to Earth."

"And what makes you think A.L. would obey any order from you?" he growled softly. Putting a fingertip at the hollow of my throat, he began to trace a line of fire down my body, between my breasts and over my trembling stomach and belly.

"Well, because…because he *likes* me," I said breathlessly. The silver bed had stepped up its "erotic functions," cupping my breasts and circling my nipples relentlessly. Between that and the feel of Sarden's warm finger tracing down my body, I thought I might scream.

"Just because he 'likes' you doesn't mean you can get what you want from him," Sarden murmured in my ear. "We're a lot alike in that way." His breath was hot against the side of my neck and I thought I had never felt so naked and exposed. Suddenly it got worse—something was sliding between my thighs—was it the damned beanbag again or was it Sarden?

"Stop it!" I demanded breathlessly, my chest heaving. "Don't...don't touch me there. You said...you told me you're not a...a rapist."

"I'm not." He gave me a dangerous smile. "You have my word that I won't touch you sexually at all tonight, Zoe. But you're still going to take your punishment and come for me."

"I...there's no way!" I protested.

"There's *every* way," he murmured. "You're going to lie here and be pleasured while I watch. I want to see your face while your sweet pussy is teased."

"*No,*" I protested again but already I could feel the silver bed parting my thighs, baring me to him completely.

Oh God, could he see how wet I was? Because I have to admit it, I was. I didn't get off on BDSM and 50 Shades kind of stuff—at least I didn't *think* I did. So then why was being restrained and touched while Sarden leaned over me and watched me wiggle and moan making me feel hot and cold and crazy all over?

"Oh yes," he murmured, his long finger still stroking up and down my body, from the hollow of my throat all the way down to the top of my mound. "Yes, my little Pure One, you're going to come very, *very* hard. And you're going to do it while I watch."

"Please…" I whispered but by now the silver bed was touching me between my thighs. The soft, silky material seemed to have formed a kind of finger and I felt it tracing around my outer lips, teasing the neatly trimmed curls on my mound, getting closer and closer to my center.

"Tell me something, Zoe, does it feel good?" Sarden murmured, looking down at me. "Does it feel good to be held down and pleasured? To be touched until you come?"

"Of…of course not," I whispered but the words came out with no force at all.

"I don't believe you," he murmured. "And now I'm going to kiss you."

"You…you try to kiss me and I'll bite you. I swear to God I…I *will.*" My last words came out as a kind of moan because the silver finger between my legs had finally gotten to the point. It was stroking me gently, caressing around and around my aching little button until I thought I might scream.

"I'll take my chances." With that, Sarden lowered his head and took my mouth in a kiss like nothing I'd ever felt before.

It wasn't just that it he was an alien, or that he was seven feet tall, incredibly muscular and much, much stronger than me—it was the gentle dominance he used when he took me.

He didn't force himself on me or pry my mouth open. No, he started slowly, kissing my lips and nipping them gently, sucking my lower lip into his mouth to bathe it tenderly with his tongue.

His breath was warm and smelled like some sweet alien spice I couldn't name but it reminded me a lot of cinnamon and chili peppers. In fact, his kisses stung just a little bit but they felt good too—so good I almost forgot my promise to bite him. But then part of me spoke up.

Hey, you can't just lay here and let this happen to you! shouted a little voice in my head. *You can't just give in this easily! Fight him! Bite him!*

The voice was right and I knew it—I couldn't just give up without a fight!

With a little cry, I lifted my head and obeyed my inner badass.

I sank my teeth into his full lower lip and started to bite. But just then the silver finger between my legs started circling my clit in long, slow, gentle strokes and my bite turned into an open-mouthed moan.

Sarden took immediate advantage. I felt one big hand tangle in my hair to hold me in place as the other continued to stroke my trembling abdomen and belly. At the same time, his tongue entered my mouth, sliding between my lips to taste me more fully.

His kisses were scorching...stinging, reminding me of the hot cinnamon candy I used to love as a little girl that burned my mouth and yet tasted so sweet I couldn't stop sucking it. *Hot Lixx* it was called.

Somehow I found I was kissing him back although I told myself I really, *really* didn't want to. Between my wide-spread thighs the silver finger was stroking faster, pushing me closer to the line I didn't want to cross.

"Please!" I gasped at last when he finally broke the kiss. "Please, make it stop or I'm going to...going to..."

"Going to come?" he murmured, his voice rough with lust. "Of course you're going to come. Didn't I tell you it's your punishment?"

"But I don't...don't want to!" I gasped. I didn't either—or part of me didn't. I didn't *like* this bastard—he was going to trade me away to some alien slave merchant and I would never see Earth again! There was no way I wanted to give him the satisfaction of making me come.

But another part of me was starved for sex and was having a damn hard time resisting.

Look, don't judge me. Have I mentioned it was almost a year since my last uh, *encounter?* And that was with my ex, Scott, the world's fastest lover. Seriously, he'd make a jackrabbit jealous when it came to screwing and as for foreplay, well, I don't think the word was even in his vocabulary. Scott's idea of sex was to squeeze my boobs a few times, tell ne I was "looking hot tonight," then jump my bones before I was even really ready. A few pumps, a squirt, and a tickle and we could be done before the commercial break was over so he didn't miss a second of the game.

Needless to say, it wasn't very satisfying. It was also one of the reasons I had broken up with him—although not the only reason. He'd also been a complete slob around the house and ridiculously cheap when it came to money.

But enough about my ex. What I'm trying to tell you is that he never held me down and kissed me like my mouth was the most delicious thing he'd ever tasted. Never spread my legs and teased me so slowly that I thought I would die of pleasure and embarrassment. And he certainly never talked dirty to me, while he looked into my eyes and took sadistic enjoyment from pushing me closer and closer to the point of no return.

"Let me *go,*" I begged Sarden in a moan.

"I'm not the one who's holding you, Zoe," he reminded me in his deep, growling voice. "You did that to yourself when you hit the bed's pleasure function. While you were *aiming* at my *head.* Are you sorry for that?"

"No," I whispered recklessly, unable to lie, even now. "I'd do it again if it would get…get me back to Earth."

His face darkened for a moment and then he kissed me again, harder this time.

I felt the sting of his hot mouth on mine and I couldn't help opening to him, even though I knew I should bite instead. One big hand tightened in my hair as the other slid up and down my body, using a much firmer stroke than his earlier light, erotic caress. I had the feeling that he really, *really* wanted to touch me but he was true to his word. Though the silver bed continued to twist and tease my nipples and stroke my swollen clit, his big, warm hands carefully avoided my sexual hot spots.

"Please," I whispered again when he let me come up for air. "Please, I…I can't…can't come like this."

"Yes, you can," he murmured. "And you're *going* to."

"No…" I closed my eyes, trying to shut out the sight of him leaning over me, his golden gaze glowing in the dark. *"No."*

"Yes," he whispered in my ear. "Now, Zoe — come for me *now.*"

As he spoke, I felt the silver finger between my thighs stroke firmly against the side of my aching clit — moving just the way I moved when I touched myself.

How? I thought deliriously as I tipped over the edge at last. *How does it know how to do that?*

And then all rational thought slipped away and I was coming, coming and crying out in the night because I couldn't help it…because part of me didn't *want* to help it and never wanted it to end.

Sarden didn't say anything else, he just leaned over and took my mouth again, eagerly swallowing my cries and moans as I shook and gasped…as my body took over and I came and came until I couldn't think any more…

I don't know how long it lasted — it seemed like forever. But at last I felt the pleasure ebbing and my body went limp as I panted, trying to catch my breath.

"So beautiful."

I opened my eyes to see him looking down at me, those golden eyes glowing like two candle flames in the dark. "So fucking beautiful when you come, Zoe." His deep voice was hoarse and the expression on his face was beyond intense.

"Let me go," I whispered brokenly, unable to help begging. "Take me back to Earth — *please.*"

"I can't," he murmured and for a moment I thought I saw genuine regret in his eyes. "I told you, I have no choice."

"I don't understand." I blinked back tears, trying not to cry. I hate it when I get emotional after sex. It usually only happens when it's a very intense experience — needless to say I hadn't shed a single tear with Scott, even though we'd been together for over two years.

I hadn't been with Sarden for a whole twenty-four hours yet and I was already getting weepy — and we hadn't even really had sex, I reminded myself.

Right — tell that to my stupid eyes which insisted on producing tears. I sniffed hard, refusing to let them fall.

"I don't understand," I said again.

"You don't have to understand." Sarden's deep voice was surprisingly gentle.

Up until now, he'd been leaning over me, propped on one elbow. Now he shifted so that he was lying beside me in the silver bed which had thankfully stopped its "erotic functions" after I came. Our heads were even but he was so much taller than me, the tips of my toes only came about to his knees. It made me feel like a little girl beside him.

"Sarden…"

"Sleep now," he murmured in my ear.

"What? Like this?" I protested. "I can't…can't sleep like this," I said and yawned despite myself. I still had my arms fastened firmly over my head and the black shirt was rucked up, leaving me exposed.

"You can and you will." Sarden's deep voice was stern. "If I can't trust you to be alone in your room, you'll have to stay in mine. It won't hurt you to stay restrained — the bed will support you in every way."

"But I'm *cold*," I said. "At least pull down my shirt."

"It's *my* shirt. And I won't pull it down — I like looking at you. I *will* warm you up, though." He turned over on his side and put a big, warm hand right in the middle of my belly. It seemed to radiate heat and I felt tingles and tendrils of warmth running through my entire body. His hand was so big that the tops of his fingers were right under my breasts and his palm was down past my belly button.

"You bastard," I said but not as angrily as I wanted to. I really was completely exhausted by this time. I could feel the weariness I'd fought off earlier in order to enact Plan B dragging at me — a slow, relentless tug like the tide pulling me out to sea.

"Yes, I'm a bastard," he agreed amiably enough, his long fingers tracing a lazy pattern across my stomach. "I've been meaning to ask — what are these little patches of pigmentation all over your skin? I've never seen anything like them."

"They're called freckles," I told him. "We don't like them much on Earth. At least, the people who have them don't like them." I yawned again. Even though I was mostly naked in bed with a huge alien, I could hardly keep my eyes open.

"They're beautiful," he murmured. "Unique — just like you."

"I…I'm sure Tazaxx will…will think so too," I said, trying to be sarcastic through my yawns. Even sleepy, I can be snarky — it's one of my special talents.

"I'm sure he will."

Was it my imagination, or did the big alien sound sad? I wanted to ask but my eyelids were so heavy — it felt like someone had dipped them in lead.

The last thing I felt was his large, gentle hand stroking my skin and his warm breath in my hair. Then the sleep tide came in completely and dragged me out into a deep sea filled with unfamiliar stars — each of them further away from Earth than the last.

Part Two: In Over my Head (literally)

Chapter Nine

Zoe

They have a phrase they used to use in old romance books—bodice rippers I think they're called. My mom had a ton of them lying around the house and I used to sneak and read them whenever I got a chance. Anyway, in all those old books whenever the heroine gets caught by the hero and they end up in some kind of sexual situation which she *says* she doesn't want but she *actually* totally does, the books always say, "Her body betrayed her."

I hadn't really understood what that phrase meant until now. Waking up beside Sarden and remembering the events of the night before, I finally, totally got it. Oh boy, did I get it.

Stupid body—how could it have let me down like that? How could I get so hot and bothered for a man I didn't even like? How could I let him make me come—well, technically it hadn't been him, it had been the bed that made me come—but still!

The light in the room had brightened and had the same quality as early-morning sunlight coming through a window. That what had woken me up—but what kept me awake was the way I was pressed against Sarden. I still had my hands fixed over my head but sometime in the night he had pulled the shirt down so at least I wasn't exposed anymore. We were both turned on our sides and he was spooning me, his long, muscular body wrapped around mine protectively, radiating warmth.

It felt really good.

Which of course, made me mad. I didn't *want* to feel good with him. I wanted to hate him, especially now that Plans A and B had both failed and I didn't have a Plan C.

Well, maybe it's time to think of one, I told myself. But I had nothing. I sighed and wiggled in the plush bed restlessly. Sarden stirred and tightened his grip on me, like I was his favorite teddy bear or something. Give me a break.

I was about to wake him up when Al came zipping into the room.

"Master Sarden?" he asked in his proper butler voice. "Oh, and…Lady Zoe." If a robot or A.L. or whatever can be surprised, he certainly was. "Why are you not in your own room?" he asked me. "Was it not to your liking?"

"No, she thought bashing in my head would be more to her liking." Sarden's deep voice rumbled through me, vibrating every inch of my body. He still hadn't let go of me, despite his sarcastic words.

"What? I fear I do not understand." Al sounded perplexed and his lantern-eye blinked uncertainly.

"It's nothing, A.L.—I mean, Al." Sarden yawned. "Did you come to tell me something? Have we reached Gallana?"

"We are in orbit around the main port now, about to land in their docking area," Al reported. "But I have even better news—I have found a collector who is most interested in the medical equipment left behind by Herr Misener."

"Who?" I asked.

"The previous owner of this ship," Sarden replied absently. "That's excellent news, Al. Did you set up a meet?"

"The buyer will meet you in the unattached males district at a café called The Suck Hole in one solar hour."

"Perfect." Sarden sounded extremely pleased. "That's good work Al. Now all we need is a mechanic's shop that will deal with unattached males as well."

"That...might be more difficult. Such commerce is closely regulated," Al said hesitantly. "Perhaps the Lady Zoe—"

"The Lady Zoe is going to stay right here aboard *The Celesta* under lock and key. It's the safest place for her."

"What? But I want to go too," I protested, wiggling around so that we were face to face. "I told you—I've never seen an alien spaceport. Hell, I've never seen *any* spaceport!"

"That's too bad," Sarden growled, sitting up. "Because you're not going to see one now either. I told you, the area I'm going to isn't safe for you. And even if it was, I wouldn't reward your treachery last night by allowing you to come."

"It wasn't treachery, it was self preservation!" I protested. "I just wanted to lock you up and go back to Earth."

"You couldn't have locked me up with those, even if you'd managed to get them on me." He nodded at the manacles encircling my wrists. "They're keyed to Vornish skin signature. One firm press of the lock-light would have set me free and then you'd be in the same position you are now."

"I was just trying to get back home!" I snapped. "Can you honestly tell me you'd have done anything different in my place?"

"I most certainly would have—I wouldn't have missed," he said grimly as he did something to the manacles which were still keeping my arms above my head. "Now get up—I have just time enough to feed you first meal before I have to go meet this collector."

"Feed me?" I protested, sitting up and rolling my shoulders as well as I could with my hands still cuffed in front of me.

Sarden raised an eyebrow at me.

"Would you rather I let you go hungry?"

"No, I'd rather feed myself. Like I did last night," I said pointedly. "I know how to use the food-sim now, remember?"

"I don't think so." He frowned. "You lost your ship privileges when you snuck into my room and aimed a pipe at my head. From now on, I'm going to treat you like I should have from the first— you're going to be shackled in your room from now until we get to Giedi Prime."

"But—"

"Now what do you want for breakfast?" he asked, cutting off my indignant protest. "It will have to be something from one of my home worlds, unfortunately. Perhaps some Eloim *pandan* broth would do you good."

I started to protest again but he was already up and out of the bed, busy getting ready to go and apparently not caring if I watched.

He'd been wearing a pair of long black sleep trousers kind of like pajama pants. Now he shucked them off and threw them into a small chute I hadn't seen earlier.

He sauntered naked into the bathroom—which I could see from the bed—and got into the vertical bathtub tank. The purple cleansing liquid—which would have been well over my head, barely came up to his impossibly broad shoulders.

I shivered as I watched him dunk his head, letting the purple liquid close over him as though it was no big deal. For most people I suppose it wouldn't have been. But for me…it was a whole different story.

I thought again of sinking in the watery depths, of the panicked cries ringing in my ears…and quickly pushed the memory away.

Sarden didn't take long in the personal bathing chamber. In less than two minutes he was out and standing in the mister. He did something to the controls and warm jets of air came out instead of mist. Hmm, so apparently it could be used as *just* a dryer—you didn't always have to get wet. Good to know if I was ever going to go into that freaking drowning-tank bathtub—which I absolutely was not.

Of course, I was watching the big alien's bathing routine from the corner of my eye, trying to pretend I was concentrating on something else. I didn't *want* to watch him at all but somehow I couldn't help it—I'd never seen anyone so huge and muscular outside an action movie. Or maybe a male revue. One time Leah and Charlotte and I had gone to see The Thunder from Down Under—a male strip show from Australia. Those guys were in amazing shape—all muscular and oiled up but somehow none of them was half as hot as Sarden, though I would rather die than admit it.

The other reason I was trying not to look, was that my eyes kept getting drawn to his crotch. He was every bit as big as I'd suspected and I couldn't help staring once or twice, when he came into full frontal view. *God—hung like a Clydesdale and with about as much modesty,* I couldn't help thinking as he took his time pulling on a pair of tight leather trousers and tucking his considerable endowment into them.

When he was done, there was a substantial bulge that ran down the inside of his left thigh—and he wasn't even hard. I didn't want to think about how big he'd be if he was. The mental image that formed in my brain was downright scary.

I couldn't imagine trying to accommodate equipment that large. I wondered if Eloim and Vorn women were better able to take someone like Sarden—presumably so, or their respective species would have died out years ago from terminal too-big-to-handle-dickitis.

"Enjoying the show?" Sarden asked, pulling another sleeveless temp-shirt over his head. This one was white and it stood out nicely in contrast to his deep red skin. His thick black hair was slicked back and his horns were even more prominent. His golden eyes glowed with amusement. It was no lie to say he was devilishly good looking—more of an understatement, really. Which really pissed me off. Why couldn't I be kidnapped by an ugly alien so I could hate him a little more?

"I don't...don't know what you're talking about," I lied, looking away as I felt my cheeks get hot.

"*Sure* you don't." He did a little bump and grind and since he was standing and I was still sitting on the bed, his crotch was almost eye-level with me. The bulge in his trousers was a lot closer than I liked.

"Get that thing away from me," I said irritably. "So you've got a huge wang. So what?"

"So you *were* looking." He grinned, apparently in a good mood this morning. "And actually, I'm about average for my species."

"Which one? An Eloim or a Vorn?" I asked, interested despite myself.

He frowned, some of his good mood evaporating.

"A Vorn. As I told you, Eloim are a much smaller people. But we don't have time to talk." He rubbed his hands together. "I'll make you first meal, as I promised."

"So I'm just supposed to sit here and wait? Can't you at least take off the cuffs so I can take a shower?" I pleaded.

Sarden shook his head. "You should be fine with the Force Locks on—the cleansing liquid won't affect them."

"What?" I looked at the awful vertical bathtub. "No, I didn't mean that thing—there's no *way* I'm getting in there! I just wanted to take a shower in the mister."

He frowned. "The mister won't truly get you clean—it's only for momentary refreshment."

"I don't care," I said stubbornly. "I'm *not* getting into that huge purple drowning-tank thing. *You're* really tall but that purple cleanser stuff would go clear over *my* head."

"Only until you kicked your way to the top," he pointed out. "Or can't you swim?"

A convulsive shudder went through me—I couldn't help it.

"No," I said in a low voice. "No, I...I can't swim."

"And the idea of getting in over your head scares you?" he persisted.

"What do you think?" I snapped. "Look, I'd rather not talk about it, okay?"

Sarden leaned closer, studying me closely.

"It *does* scare you," he murmured. "The idea of water closing over your head scares you nearly to death, doesn't it?"

I refused to answer this and only looked away.

"Poor little Pure One. I'm afraid you'll have to wait. Maybe I can help you bathe when I get back from this deal." He cupped my cheek in an irritatingly condescending way as though I was a frightened child or a puppy that needed to be comforted.

"Asshole." Since my hands were cuffed with the heavy manacles, I couldn't really bat him away. So I snapped at him instead.

He withdrew his long fingers just in time to get them out of reach of my teeth, his eyes widening.

"Feeling feisty this morning, are we?" he remarked mildly.

"All *kinds* of feisty, which you'll find out if you try petting me like a scared puppy again," I told him.

"I don't know what a puppy is but I'll keep it in mind," he said dryly. "Well, I don't have time to bathe you now but I *can* give you a change of shirts—I'm afraid all of my trousers will be too big for you, though."

"All right," I said at once, thinking he would certainly have to uncuff me in order to get the shirt over my head and arms and put a new one on me. And once I had the cuffs off, maybe I could convince him to leave them off.

"Get off the bed," he directed. He had done something to the wall that made a kind of closet appear and he was rummaging through his shirts. Finally he pulled out another sleeves shirt identical to the one he had one.

"Wait," I said. "Don't you have something with a little more, uh, coverage?"

"Why? Are you cold?" He raised an eyebrow at me. "The temp-shirt should keep you warm all over."

"It does," I said. "But it's kind of, um revealing."

"So it is." His golden eyes roved over me again, as though I was some luscious dessert he was dying to take a bite of.

I tried to ignore the lascivious way he was eyeing me.

"Look, do you have something else or not?"

"As a matter of fact, I do." Reaching in the closet again, he pulled out a long-sleeved shirt in black. Were black and white the only colors he owned? Then again, with his deep red skin, I was betting his color choices were probably pretty limited. You don't want to clash with your own clothes. I have kind of the same problem with my red hair—I've never been able to wear pink although I've always wanted to.

"That looks good," I said and held out my hands. "Take these things off so I can put it on. Please," I added, hoping that being polite would help.

But Sarden shook his head.

"Not necessary. Look."

He touched the light between the manacles and it glowed green for a moment, just as it had for me the night before. Then he did something else to it and it glowed purple.

"What does that mean?" I asked, frowning.

"You'll see."

Before I could ask anything else, he knelt in front of me, grasped the bottom hem of the black t-shirt I was wearing and pulled it right off my head and over my arms. Somehow the fabric passed right through the chains of the manacles though he hadn't unlocked them at all, leaving me completely naked.

"Hey!" I tried to cover myself with my arms but with my hands cuffed in front of me, there were limits to what I could hide.

"What's wrong?" Sarden asked.

"What do you mean, what's wrong? I'm *naked*." I could feel

myself blushing furiously as I scrambled to shield myself.

"So you are." He was giving me that look again—that big, bad wolf look that made my pulse race for some reason. "Is nudity really such a problem for your people?" he murmured.

"Yes, it freaking well is," I snapped.

"But it shouldn't be. And besides, I've seen you without clothing several times before," he pointed out.

"Yes, and I was embarrassed every time."

"Embarrassed? Hmm…" He came closer and traced one long finger over my collar bone. "Is that what this red flush means? Your skin is almost as red as mine."

"Yes, that's what it means," I admitted. He was still giving me that intense look and I felt like my heart was trying to pound its way out of my chest. "Stop that," I said, wishing my voice didn't sound so breathless.

"Stop what?"

"Looking at me like that. Like…like you want to eat me up."

"As a matter of fact I would *love* to eat you," he rumbled, his golden eyes half-lidded now. "Vorn and Eloim both are very partial to pleasing their lovers with their tongues. There is no finer flavor than a wet and willing female."

"I didn't mean like *that*." My cheeks were getting hotter and hotter and I couldn't help crossing my legs.

"What's wrong?" He looked surprised. "Don't you enjoy letting a male taste you?"

As a matter of fact, I didn't. It always made me intensely uncomfortable whenever I let a guy try it—not that many had offered. Scott couldn't be bothered and the boyfriend I'd had in college had done nothing but a few perfunctory licks before deciding he'd done his duty and it was time to get down to actual sex, which was always the main event, of course.

But there was no way I was telling Sarden all that.

"Don't talk like that to me," I said, lifting my chin and frowning at him. "If my hands weren't cuffed, I'd slap your face." If I could reach it, that was.

"Really?" He frowned. "Don't you give open and honest sexual compliments on Earth?"

"Not unless you're a freaking construction worker," I snapped. "It's considered rude and invasive."

He shook his head. "On Vorn 6 it's considered extremely polite to tell a female how sexually arousing you find her and how you would enjoy pleasuring her."

Well, that certainly explained why he felt so free to constantly talk about how sexy he thought I was. Which really didn't make any sense, as far as I was concerned. I mean, I've got a pretty face and a lot of guys like my hair, but I'm still rocking a plus-sized booty which has kept more than one man from looking my way.

"I don't understand you," I said, frowning at him. "You could have picked anyone—any female—on Earth, right?"

"Of course." He nodded.

"And you chose *me?* I mean, you could have had a supermodel and instead you picked a paralegal. You should have kept looking on that AMI thingy."

"A supermodel?" His forehead creased in concentration. "Oh yes, I think I know the females you're talking about. The Commercians showed them to me as an example of what Earth males find attractive."

"What?" I couldn't keep the incredulous note out of my voice.

"You actually *saw* the supermodels and you still picked *me?*"

"Yes, I saw them. The Commercians showed me Bianca and Ellsbeth and several others."

I could feel my eyes getting wide. "Those girls are at the *top* of the industry. I can't believe you passed them up and went for me instead!"

"Do you really think so poorly of yourself?" He looked at me curiously.

"Well, no…" I cleared my throat. "I mean, I have a pretty face and pretty good hair when it's not too humid. But I'm not tall enough or thin enough to be a supermodel." Then again, almost no one is, and the fashion industry makes damn sure we never forget it.

Sarden shrugged his broad shoulders. "Those females were all long, skinny limbs with no padding—nothing to hold on to. They most certainly didn't tempt me so I was pretty sure they wouldn't tempt Tazaxx either."

The reminder that he was planning to trade me away kind of put a damper on his compliment but I still couldn't get over the fact that he'd picked plain, ordinary me over the highest paid models on Earth. I guess there's no accounting for alien taste.

"When I saw you," Sarden continued. "I knew you were the one. You were angry with a male who had thrown something at your head. You shouted and stormed away from him. Anger made your eyes bright and brought a flush to your cheeks. It was most fetching. And when I saw how ample your figure was, well…" He gave me his little one-sided grin. "How could I resist?"

"Wow…just wow." I was literally at a loss for words which almost never happens to me. He'd picked me *because* of my figure, not in spite of it. Maybe I should have gone back to Weight

Watchers and tried harder to lose my luscious hips and overlarge ass. If I'd known it might keep me from being abducted by aliens, you bet I would have counted points until Doomsday.

"It's a shame to cover such beauty but I need to get your first meal if I'm going to feed you before I go," Sarden remarked.

Deftly, he slipped the sleeves of the black shirt over my arms and again, they went over the chain between the manacles as though it wasn't there. There were no buttons on the shirt—instead it tied on both sides and made a V-neckline in the middle. Sarden knelt in front of me again to get it right. He was so tall that even kneeling, his face was at the level of my breasts.

When he was done, I felt like I was wearing a wrap dress that was a little too big for me. The sleeves, of course, were more than a little too big—they came down about a foot past my fingertips. Sarden rolled them up for me and then stood back to admire his handiwork.

"Perfect," he murmured, nodding. "You look a hell of a lot better in my dress shirt than I do."

Eyeing his broad, muscular shoulders I had to disagree with that. I was betting he would look freaking spectacular in this shirt. However, it did set off my pale skin and red hair nicely and the V-neckline was really sexy.

The look was kind of ruined by the big heavy manacles clamped around my wrists though.

Sarden left to make me some food and came back with a steaming bowl of some kind of broth with wide, flat noodle things floating in it. Did I mention the noodles were bright green and the broth was pink? I wasn't overly thrilled to try it but the big alien wasn't taking no for an answer.

He got me seated at the desk, which was back to its blank,

empty state, and dragged up another chair to face me.

"Eloim *pandan* broth," he said dipping a long-handled spoon-like utensil into the pinkish broth and offering it to me. "Exactly like I had as a child. Eat it—you'll like it."

"I...don't know." I eyed the pink broth uncertainly. It wasn't pale pink, mind you—it was full on Barbie Dream House hot pink. It's not a color you expect to run across when you're eating soup. Still, I didn't' like to insult what was clearly a comfort food for him.

"Come on..." Sarden brought the spoon, which was black and shiny like all his silverware, closer to my lips. "I tried all of your creations last night," he pointed out. "And besides, if you don't eat, you'll become too thin."

I nearly laughed at that.

"Haven't you ever heard the saying, 'you can never be too rich or too thin?'" I asked him.

He frowned. "I agree with the rich part. But a female can certainly be too thin—it is most unpleasant."

"If you say so." I shrugged. Who was I to argue with his love of curvy women? I sighed and looked down at the soup. "All right, I'll try it. But I reserve the right to puke all over you if my system can't take it."

"Let's hope it doesn't come to that," he remarked dryly. "Come on—open up."

Obediently, I opened my mouth and tried a spoonful of the bright pink soup which I was afraid would taste like a combination of Pepto Bismol and melted plastic.

Surprisingly, it wasn't bad. You know how they say everything tastes like chicken? Well so did this—in a way. It tasted like some kind of chicken noodle soup with some funky (but not in a bad way) herbs thrown in.

"Well?" Sarden pulled back the spoon and looked at me, eyebrows raised.

"It's not bad," I admitted grudgingly. "What are the noodles things?" I nodded at the flat, bright green pieces floating in the pink broth.

"*Fardles,*" he said, scooping one up for me to try. "Have one."

"*Fardles? Seriously?*"

"Try one." He nudged the spoon towards my lips.

"All right," I agreed warily. Again, it wasn't bad. The *fardle* had a dense, almost meaty texture but not much taste of its own—it mostly took on the flavor of the broth, which was nice.

"Well?" Sarden asked.

I swallowed and nodded. "Not bad. So what are *fardles* made of?"

He scooped another one into my mouth before answering.

"They are a type of deep sea algae," he said as I started chewing. "They live off small aquatic creatures that attempt to hide among their fronds for safety from predators."

I nearly spit out the bright green *fardle*. I didn't enjoy the idea of eating algae, especially not a kind that was the Eloim equivalent of an undersea Venus fly trap.

Sarden must have seen the disgusted look on my face because I saw an amused smirk hovering on the corner of his own mouth.

"You're enjoying this," I accused after I swallowed the somewhat slimy mouthful. "Teasing me...feeding me...keeping me chained up and helpless."

"So what if I am?" He raised an eyebrow at me. "You're my prisoner—I can do what I want with you. Believe me, you would have been treated much worse if almost any other male had bought you."

"What makes you so sure?" I demanded. "I thought your species was hated and feared throughout the galaxy. Are you saying there are worse guys out there than the Vorn?"

"Much worse," he said soberly. "We're only hated and feared for the way we treat our enemies. With our females we are extremely protective and possessive. But there are males in the universe who would mistreat and abuse an Earth female if they could get one in their power. And make no mistake Zoe, they *will* come for the females of your planet, as soon as word gets out that the Commercians have Earth open for business."

I thought of Leah and Charlotte and the billions of other women on Earth, all completely unaware that they were being watched, evaluated, considered as possible mates and slaves and concubines. I had to warn them somehow – or at least take steps to protect the friends I loved. But how?

Sarden fed me a few more bites of the *pandan* broth and a couple of *fardles* as I considered, thinking silently of the danger to my home world. When the broth was almost gone, he put down the spoon and looked at the big, chunky silver ring with its black stone on his middle finger.

"It's nearly time – I have to go. You've had enough?"

I nodded grudgingly. "Yes, thank you. It was…surprisingly good."

"Almost as good as the creamy yellow concoction you made last night which had a sour flavor," he remarked. "You'll have to make that for me again soon – if you can behave long enough to regain your food-sim privileges."

"Really? You want more banana cream pie that tastes like sauerkraut?" I looked at him incredulously. "That stuff was *awful*."

He shrugged. "I liked it. Reminded me of a Vornish dish my second mother used to make."

"So you had two mothers?" I asked, as he rose from his chair and prepared to leave.

A guarded expression came over his face.

"In a way. She was the female who raised me when I was sent to live in the court of my father on Vorn 6. That was long after the death of my first mother on Eloim, of course."

"You lost your mom?" I felt a stab of compassion. "I'm so sorry."

"Don't be." His expression hardened. "It was many cycles ago when I was a child—I'm over it."

"I don't believe that," I said softly. "You never completely get over losing your mom. You just don't."

"I disagree." He frowned. "I have to go now and I'm taking Al with me. Come on—I'm putting you in your own room until I get back."

"Why? You don't trust me not to snoop in your room?" I demanded.

"No," he said shortly. "I don't." He wouldn't say anything else, even though I tried to get him to talk.

Before I knew it, I was back in my own room, still cuffed, with nothing to do but stare at the wall and wait for him to return.

Chapter Ten

Sarden

The little Earth female was really getting under my skin. I knew I shouldn't let her but it was extremely difficult to keep my distance for some reason. The night before, for instance, it had taken every ounce of my willpower not to cup her full breasts and suck her ripe pink nipples...not to stroke lower and cup her sweet sex in my hand. I'd been able to smell her heat—a warm, feminine scent that drove me wild. I'd wanted badly to dip my fingers deep into her wet well, to pleasure her and to taste her.

But if I did that, I knew it would only make it that much harder to trade her away to Tazaxx. Already I greatly regretted the fact that I couldn't keep her for myself. If I'd had enough credits and more time, I would certainly have gone back to buy another Pure One to trade to the crime lord so I could save Zoe.

Unfortunately, I didn't have enough of either.

I hoped to at least solve my credit problem during this meeting with the collector of medical artifacts. As for time, there was no helping that. Even once (if) I got the malfunctioning hydrogen scoop panel fixed, I would have to push *The Celesta* to her limit in order to get to Giedi Prime before the auction took place.

If Tazaxx decided Sellah wasn't right for his private collection, if he decided to auction her off instead...well, the males who liked to abuse females I had told Zoe about were very real. And Earth females were not the only ones they were interested in. If Sellah got sold to a T'varri for instance...

But no. I couldn't let myself think such things. I pushed the worried thought to the back of my head as I left the ship and went down the long corridor which led to the spaceport proper. Ducking through to the unaccompanied males doorway, I bypassed the Majoran males and their treasured females. *I* would get my ship fixed in time to save my little sister, I told myself—I *had* to.

My only regret was that I couldn't save Zoe too.

* * * * *

Zoe

You wouldn't think you could get bored on an alien spaceship light years from Earth, surrounded by amazing new technology you'd never seen. But you'd be wrong. I *was* bored—bored to *tears.*

I had nothing to do but sit on the silver bed and stare at my hands, still bound in the thick, heavy manacles. I didn't even have Al to talk to because he had taken his golden dragonfly form and gone with Sarden to meet the prospective buyer for the old medical junk they were trying to sell.

Plan B had seemed like a good idea at the time but look where it had gotten me. Maybe if I hadn't tried to brain Sarden and cuff him I might be out with him at the spaceport right now. I could be seeing things no other human had ever seen. I might even have found a way to escape—maybe a friendly alien freighter who wouldn't mind giving me a lift back to the big blue marble I called home.

Instead I was sitting around staring at my hands waiting to be sold.

The glowing blue light on the chain between the heavy cuffs blinked and glowed, almost seeming to taunt me for my stupidity. I couldn't help remembering what Sarden had said—that I couldn't have held him with the manacles, even if I'd been able to get them on him. Because they were keyed to a Vornish skin signature or something like that. *"One firm touch of the lock-light would have set me free,"* he'd said. Or something to that effect.

So Plan B was doomed to failure right from the start.

Staring at the light, I remembered the way he'd touched it— getting it to glow first green and then purple. When the color changed, the properties of the manacles seemed to change as well.

But the light turned green for you last night too, whispered a little voice in my brain. *Don't you remember? Before you snuck into Sarden's room?*

I sat up a little straighter. It was *true*. They had turned green and popped open when I pressed the light. Sarden had seemed so sure that the manacles wouldn't work for anyone but him or another Vorn. But what about the way I had popped them open when I was examining them? Had that been an accident?

I wasn't Vorn but the question wouldn't leave my mind and I was plenty bored enough to entertain it. What if I *could* somehow unlock myself? Well, it was worth a try—it wasn't like I had anything else on my busy social schedule at the moment.

Experimentally, I tried to reach the glowing blue light with one of my fingers. But the cuffs were too thick—no matter how much I reached and stretched, I was still half an inch shy from making any kind of contact.

Well, do you have to use a finger to press it? whispered that sly little voice again. *Try something else. Don't give up!*

I didn't intend to. Feeling slightly foolish but also very

determined, I lowered my head and pressed the blue light firmly with the tip of my nose.

At first there was nothing but a ticklish buzzing in my nose, the faint, metallic smell of the manacles, and the sound of my own breathing. Then I heard that faint chiming sound I remembered from the night before and the thick cuffs popped open and fell from my wrists.

"Yes!" I jumped up and almost fell off the floating bed which swayed dangerously with my erratic motions. That didn't stop me from doing the happy dance on the silver beanbag, though. I jumped and danced and pumped my fists in the air—they seriously felt so much lighter now. I hadn't realized how much those damn manacles had been weighing me down!

"Suck it, Sarden!" I said aloud, as I finally sat back down on the bed, panting. My victory dance had been the most aerobic exercise I'd had since the big red jerk had captured me. I normally try to hit the gym with Charlotte at least three times a week, just for stress management. Only here on this stupid alien ship I had all the stress and no way to manage it. I felt better just for getting my heart rate up.

Once my elation faded a little though, I realized I was just as stuck as ever. My door was still locked—Sarden had made sure of that before he left. So yes, I was uncuffed, but I was still confined to my room.

"Great going, Zoe—you're still trapped," I muttered to myself. And still no closer to ever seeing Earth again.

In a fit of irritation, I picked up the heavy manacles by their chain. Squeezing the stupid lock-light as hard as I could, I threw them at the locked door.

I expected them to smash and scrape against the door,

hopefully leaving a nice, long scratch in the shiny silver metal.

Instead, the door *whooshed* open and they flew out into the hallway with a musical clatter.

"What the…?" I hopped off the bed again, stumbling in my haste. What had happened to the door? Why had it opened? Did the manacles have something to do with it?

Walking over, I bent over and examined the empty, open manacles carefully. The light on the chain between them was now glowing a deep, steady red. Huh. What did that mean?

I didn't know but I sure as hell intended to find out.

Scooping up the heavy manacles, I went to another door I was pretty sure was locked—Sarden's. Sure enough, when I passed my hand through the invisible beam, nothing happened and the door stayed closed. But when I put the manacles through the beam, it slid open at once. Yay!

I stared down at the heavy cuffs in my hand, thinking hard. Okay, so I had a way to unlock doors and get wherever I wanted on the ship. But I probably had a limited time before Sarden came back and found me out of my restraints and wandering the halls. Or hall, really, since the ship was mostly just a lot of rooms leading off one long hallway. What should I try next?

My first thought was to get out. I went for the door where Sarden had brought me in, through the confusing maze of claustrophobically tight passageways into the place where the little shuttle was docked.

Sure enough, there was a door—a really big hatch, actually, that looked like it was made to open and let the shuttle out. Heart pounding in my chest, I walked up to it and waved the glowing manacles in every direction, trying to break the invisible beam and get it to open.

Only it didn't work. No matter how wildly I waved the heavy metal cuffs, the door stayed obstinately closed. I grew more and more frustrated until I finally saw something blinking in one corner of the large hatch door. Kneeling down, I saw what looked like some kind of combination lock. It had a dial with alien markings in glowing green script all around it. Of course, I couldn't read them. I had another moment of regret that the translation viruses the Commercians had sent through the hole in Earth's ozone layer only affected spoken language and not written.

Still, even if I *had* been able to read Sarden's language, it probably wouldn't have done me any good. I still wouldn't know the combination or code or whatever was needed to get out of the ship.

I tried twisting the dial this way and that anyway, unwilling to just give up. I even put my ear next to it and tried to listen for clicks the way burglars always do in the movies.

I may be a lot of things, but a safe-cracker I'm not. After a few minutes of futilely twisting the dial, I gave up. This thing wasn't going to budge for me and it was time to stop wasting my time.

Strike One but I wasn't done yet. Time to find another way out of this ship.

I threaded my way back through the narrow passages and into the main corridor. It was weird how quiet it was—except for the soft hum of the ship's engines, I couldn't hear anything at all. At least Sarden had left the lights on—it made the long, empty hallway a little less spooky.

A *little*. God, I *really* wanted to get out of here!

The next thing I tried was the control area of the ship. The manacles opened the door for me with no problem but then I was faced with a bewildering array of blinking, glowing, buzzing instruments. What *was* all this? It made the control panel of the shuttle look like a kiddy car. There was no *way* I could get any of this to work—even if it hadn't been voice locked to Sarden's voice. Also, there was no door anywhere—at least not any I could see.

Strike Two. But I still wasn't ready to give up.

I left the control area with its crazy Christmas light display instrument panel and went the other way down the long hall. After the food-prep area, the entertainment room (which had some really intriguing-looking tech that would have made any gamer pee his pants with excitement) and the bedroom and storage room doors, there was nothing for a long way.

Then, just as I was beginning to wonder if the ship went on forever, I came to a small door at the very end of the corridor. Suddenly I had a thought—when Sarden had first brought me aboard, he had specifically told me to stay out of the storage area in the back because it was dangerous. Was that what this was? And what had he meant by dangerous?

Maybe he just wanted to keep me out of a place that had a possible exit, I thought. I wouldn't put it past him, the big red bastard. I didn't care what he had said—I was going to take my chances.

I pushed the manacles through the invisible beam and the door slid open with more of a wheeze than a whoosh. It seemed I might have come to a part of the ship that wasn't used very often. Well fine, that didn't bother me as long as there was an exit door.

The room revealed by the open door was dim—almost dark, in fact. There was, however, a faint yellow rectangle of light at the very end of it. The glow reminded me of sunshine—of daylight.

A-ha! My heart jumped in my chest and I took a step inside and nearly tripped. The big dark room—it was seriously almost as big as a football field—seemed to be packed with all kinds of objects.

I held the manacles up, using the faint glow of their lock-light to try and see what they were. I saw lots of shiny metal and glass—or plastic maybe, I couldn't tell—but none of it made sense to my eyes. There were many large, complex machines and some smaller ones as well. I lifted a small, heavy device from a shelf and held it up to the manacles' light. It looked like a round blue glass paperweight but it had a silver corkscrew-looking arm sticking out from the center of it.

I studied the small instrument carefully, looking closer. There was a reddish-brown stain on the sharp, jutting end of the corkscrew. Was it just rust…or something worse?

Then, a faint noise began. Soft, at first—so soft I could barely hear it. It was a tinkling melody kind of like an old fashioned music box. I frowned—was that coming from the corkscrew paperweight in my hand?

It seemed that it was. I brought it closer to my face, examining it, trying to figure out how it could make music. The blue glass part of it was clear and I didn't see any kind of mechanism for music inside, but the soft, tinkling tune was definitely coming from the strange device.

That was when it came to life in my hand, the corkscrew stabbing out at me with no warning.

"Oh my God!" I gasped, feeling a line of fire slice across my cheek. I dropped the thing as a bolt of terror surged through me, and hopped back a step as though I'd seen a spider. Or something *worse* than a spider.

I expected the blue paperweight part of it to shatter but it didn't—it bounced once and then lay there on the floor, retracting and stabbing the bloody metal corkscrew over and over as the soft, inviting tune played on an on, echoing eerily in the vast, dark room.

I waited for a long, breathless moment to see if the thing was going to grow legs and come skittering after me, but the stabbing motion appeared to be the only movement it was capable of. Well, that and the weird song, which now reminded me of the kind of music you hear in a horror movie when the doomed character opens an ancient, cursed puzzle box they're supposed to leave strictly alone.

Anyway, it answered my question over whether the reddish brown stuff on the corkscrew end was rust or blood. I put my fingers to my cheeks and winced—it had really sliced the hell out of me! What a horrible device—who would invent something like that?

I wondered if it as a Vorn thing but somehow I doubted it. I didn't know Sarden very well, but he struck me as a straight-forward kind of guy. If the rest of his people were anything like him, they wouldn't invent a device so subtle. One that invited you to get closer and closer with its faint, tinkling music until you were within stabbing distance.

What about the Eloim then? I didn't think so. To hear Sarden describe them, they sounded stuck up and priggish. This kind of weapon or whatever it was, would probably be considered crude.

Another thought occurred to me—maybe this was part of the medical equipment Sarden had gone to the spaceport to try and sell. That seemed most likely although I couldn't imagine any medical exam that would require you to be suddenly jabbed in the face with a metal corkscrew. Another inch to the left or right and the damn thing would have burst my eardrum or popped my eye like a grape! Ugh!

Okay, enough messing with the equipment, I told myself. Sarden hadn't been lying—it *was* dangerous. So from now on I was going to keep my hands strictly to myself and just try to get to that rectangle of light I saw at the end of the huge room.

I stepped carefully over the stabby-stabby corkscrew paperweight and picked my way carefully through the room, being extra careful not to touch a thing. Though I tried to blot it with my sleeve, blood was running down my cheek from the long, shallow scratch on my face. I really hoped I wasn't going to need stitches—I was millions of miles away from the nearest E.R.

Shaking my head, I kept going.

Sarden

I didn't know why, but I had a bad feeling as Al and I made our way back to the unattached males district. It's a small area of synth-sex shops and delusion parlors that the Majoran peace keepers usually don't bother to patrol. In contrast to the rest of Gallana, there were almost no females here and I could see why. The whole district was about males getting their most savage needs met without female interference.

Synthi-whores trolled the streets, crying their wares in cracked, mechanical voices. Cloning-mechs called that they could make the female of your dreams…and you could do anything you wanted to her.

Anything at all.

A male cloaked in a shadow-coat whispered to me from a dark alley, asking if I wanted any dream dust. Further down the dirty, rutted road another male offered me fantasy implants.

"See yourself as you want to be…live the life you cannot have in reality," he rasped hoarsely, dangling the long, silvery synthec-worms which would burrow into a host's eyeballs and attach to the optic nerves. While he lived—while they fed on him—they would

send him the sweetest of visions, stimulating every part of the brain in turn even as they devoured his neural function. They would refuse to let go until he was effectively brain dead—a useless husk with nothing left to give. Then they could come slithering out of his skull and return to their master who would sell them to another fool wishing to escape from reality.

I passed them all by and kept on walking, keeping my head low as I looked for my destination—a bar the buyer had named. At last I found it.

Outside the bar—The Suck Hole—was a row of artificial mouths mounted on adjustable metal poles. The red lips gleamed obscenely and made sucking and kissing noises when I got close enough to trip their sensors.

"A credit a minute—best blow job this side of Endora Six, big boy," one of the mouths said. I ignored it—public gratification holds no interest for me. And besides, who knew the last time those things had been cleaned? Like everything else in the unattached males district, they were dirty and disreputable.

Not everyone was as fastidious as me, though. Down the line, a male—a Xlexian by his greenish brown, mottled skin—stepped up to a mouth and slid a cred-card into the slot on the side.

"Mmm, give it to me, baby!" the mouth moaned and the Xlexian obliged by unfastening his trousers and shoving his engorged member between its lips.

Obscenely loud sucking sounds began as the mouth took him in. The Xlexian groaned and pumped his hips enthusiastically, oblivious to anyone watching his pleasure. I looked away, disgusted.

"*He* seems to be enjoying himself," a voice remarked beside me.

I jerked around and found myself facing a tall male with

smooth, even features. His skin was tan and didn't change color—a sure sign that his lineage was closer to the Ancient Ones than mine—but I couldn't immediately tell his people. His hair appeared to be a deep, Majoran blue, though it was hard to tell with my sepia-toned vision. Maybe a half-breed like myself then? He had a long, boney nose and a thin mouth—barely more than a slit, which was currently turned up in a sardonic smile.

"What does it matter?" I said, frowning. "It's a common enough sight."

"Not on Gallana," he said, shifting. He was dressed in a long, black cloak that fell from his narrow shoulders and swirled around him as he moved. "This is the only place on this Gods-forsaken spaceport where a male can get a little peace and quiet away from the meddling of females."

"You are sahjist?" The sahjists were a group of dispossessed males—mostly half or quarter Majorans that didn't like the way their society was run. They refused to believe in the Goddess-hood of the Empress or the sovereignty of females in general. It went further than that for some of them, though. They said they only wanted equal rights for males but some of them, I knew, fucking *hated* females with every bone in their bodies. Those were the types—the radicals—you had to watch out for. Especially in a place like Gallana.

"Not a sahjist, exactly," the male with the blue hair said. "But I don't believe in letting females run your life. Of course, they have their uses…" he nodded at the row of sucking, artificial mouths where the Xlexian was just finishing. "But to claim they are superior or in some way divine, well…that's just foolish. They ought to be kept in their place—preferably chained to a male's bed. Am I right?"

He laughed heartily but I didn't join in. Instead, I took a step away, looking around the district.

"You'd better keep your voice down," I told him. "Expressing sentiments like that is liable to earn you a night in lock-down."

The Peace Keepers don't patrol the unattached males district often but when they do, you'd better look out. That's when all the shady characters you meet on the street melt away and the dirty, rutted walkway is deserted. We were safe for now though—I could still see a cloning-mech trying to sell his services to a male dressed in a trawler pilot's uniform.

"Anyone you want—any female that ever caught your eye but you couldn't have her," he was saying. "You can have her now—and do whatever you want with her. Doesn't matter if she wants it or not—take what you want—what's *rightfully yours*. It's perfectly legal because you'll *own* her. All it costs is a hundred creds and a small sample of her DNA."

The deal turned my stomach. The idea of treating a helpless female so harshly was repugnant to me—even if she was a clone. My thoughts must have shown on my face, though I tried to keep my expression impassive, because the male beside me spoke again.

"Forgive me. I see you don't share my views," he said smoothly.

"I'm Vorn. Half Vorn, anyway. We don't believe in worshiping our females like the Gods-damned Majorans but we don't mistreat them either," I said harshly. As I spoke, I had a guilty flash of Zoe as I had left her, held tight by the Force-Locks and secured in her room. I pushed the image away irritably—locking her up for safe keeping had been necessary. There was nothing else I could do.

"Forgive me," he said again. "Let us speak of more pleasant things, shall we? Such as the fascinating collection of Assimilation medical equipment I understand you have for sale?" Seeing my startled look he added, "I am Count Doloroso, collector of oddities. Your A.L. contacted me about your collection. You *are* Sarden de'Lagorn, are you not?"

"I am," I said. "But I don't intend to conduct business here. Let's go inside and get a drink."

In the dim interior of The Suck Hole we found a seat and Doloroso pressed the chipped call button for service.

A fembot waitress with long, matted blue hair and hugely inflated breasts tottered over.

"How can I service you?" she asked in an artificially seductive tone, batting her eyes—one of which had been blinded by an angry patron and still had the stump of a serving fork sticking out of its empty socket. "Would you care to try my pleasure holes?"

Lifting the tattered skirt she wore, she displayed a flat, fleshy pelvis with three vaginal slits—one in the center, between her legs where it should be, and two set above it, beside her hip bones. They formed a kind of obscene, inverted triangle.

"I am able to service all manner of species, not just the Twelve Peoples," she reported mechanically. "Even three-shafted Yarons are welcome."

"Thank you my dear, but we just want something to drink," Doloroso said smoothly. "A pitcher of your finest Majoran ale, I think." He looked at me. "Have you ever had it dirty?"

"No," I said. "What's that?"

"They bring the pitcher and drop a shot of Black Terbian Fire Brandy into it. It's quite good."

I shrugged. "Works for me."

"Make it dirty," Doloroso told the fembot. She nodded jerkily and tottered off. She returned shortly with a full pitcher of amber ale and a small glass filled with murky black liquid. Setting the tray down with erratic movements, she dropped the entire glass into the pitcher.

A small splash and tendrils of black began to infiltrate the amber. For some reason my stomach lurched uneasily and I thought of Zoe again. Was she all right?

Of course she's all right – she's safe, I told myself sternly. *She can't get out of those Force-Locks no matter what she does and she can't get into any trouble locked in her room. She's fine. Relax.*

I tried to but the worried feeling kept nagging at my mind, even as I made the deal with the Count.

Zoe

Making my way through the crowded, dark room with only the dim light from the manacles to help me wasn't easy. There were some areas where the large pieces of medical equipment were packed too tightly together to squeeze through so I had to find a way around. I went carefully, but as quickly as I could. Who knew when Sarden would be back? I wanted to be long gone by the time he got to my room and found I had done a disappearing act. Always, I kept my eyes trained on the pale golden rectangle of daylight outlining the door at the back.

Keep it up, Zoe – you can do it! You're almost there, I told myself. *Daylight and freedom are on the other side of that door.* I hoped, anyway.

Finally, after what seemed like hours of fumbling through the darkness, I got to the end of the vast room and found myself standing in front of the door outlined in golden light.

Only it wasn't a door.

When I stepped forward and waved the manacles at it, instead of whooshing open, the entire rectangle lit up. Rather than a door, I saw a tall tank, not unlike the vertical bathtubs in the bathrooms. The whole thing glowed with the pale, golden light I'd thought was sunlight and it was filled with some kind of clear yellow liquid.

The top part of the tank was empty, with just a few lazy bubbles rising to the surface. The bottom, however, had a layer of some kind of shiny black sludge.

"Great. Just great," I said aloud, putting my hands on my hips so the manacles clanked. "Not a door at all."

At the sound of my voice—or maybe it was the clinking of the manacles, I don't know—the sludge at the bottom of the tank stirred. It had collected mostly in one corner and it billowed lazily in an invisible current, looking almost like a piece of black cloth. Or maybe…a tentacle?

I frowned, whatever it was, it *wasn't* a door, which meant I had to keep searching. Damn it! My heart sank all the way down to my shoes—or would have if I'd been wearing any. Actually, my bare feet felt like ice from walking on the cold metal floor. Well, I could see the back wall by the deceptive yellowish glow of the tank. Maybe the best thing would be to go to it and start making my way around the perimeter of the room, feeling for an exit as I went.

Something stirred in the tank again—another faint billowing motion—and I felt something wet and warm touch my wounded cheek.

What the hell?

I jerked back involuntarily—it was almost as though someone with a very wet, cold mouth had just given me a sloppy kiss. I put my fingers to my face and they came away wet. But when I examined my fingertips in the faint glow of the manacles, all I saw was blood – the dripping must have been what caused the weird feeling on my cheek.

Well, crap – and here I'd thought it was beginning to clot over.

"Better get going, Zoe," I told myself aloud. Sighing, I began to make my way around the tank, blotting my cheek carefully as I went. Was I *ever* going to stop bleeding? Maybe I really did need stitches although I had no idea where I would get them.

Just as I was right beside the tank, I saw something move from the corner of my eye. A flash of shiny obsidian that seemed to glimmer in the dimness like a black star.

Then something curled around my waist and I was yanked up into the air.

Sarden

"Tell me about your collection," Doloroso said, taking a swig of his black infused ale. "Are the pictures your A.L. showed me accurate? He sent me only a few but what I saw intrigued me greatly."

"Absolutely accurate," I assured him. "I've had the lot for almost ten cycles now, stored in my hold. Never used any of it – it came with my ship when I won it."

"Won it from who?" he wanted to know, taking another sip.

"Male by the name of Heir Misener," I said, taking a drink myself. The ale was smooth but the Fire Brandy burned my mouth and sinuses fiercely. I liked it. "Science officer with the Assimilation before they were defeated."

"And who says they were all defeated?" His eyes gleamed strangely. "Maybe they just went underground, waiting for a more opportune time to ah, emerge."

I frowned at the idea. The Assimilation was an empire which started on the inner ring world of Sha-meth. The Sha-methians had worked hard to build a completely automated society. Predictably, their control systems had been given too much sentience and power and had taken over. These sentient systems downloaded themselves into the brains of the living occupants of Sha-meth and ran them like living corpses which they called "The Assimilated." Their rise to power had happened with dizzying suddenness and in the ensuing conflict — called the War of Assimilation — they had nearly overthrown the current regime some fifty cycles earlier.

Led by the Majorans, the rest of the Twelve Peoples descended from the Ancient Ones had fought and died to keep them from taking the entire galaxy. Their soldiers were notoriously difficult to kill and impossible to subvert — some said due to the obedience chips implanted at the base of their skulls. Heir Misener, the old bastard I'd won my ship and the medical equipment from, had gotten his chip removed, shortly after the war's end. He'd been able to think for himself — not too well, though, or he wouldn't have bet his whole ship on a single hand of double-blind-Trill, but those were the breaks.

We had learned from the War of Assimilation and now all Artificial Life forms had built in controls which kept them from desiring power. But if the Assimilation had won, it would have been a different story — every sentient creature in the known galaxy would have been implanted with an obedience chip and we would have lost our free will forever.

"You better *hope* the Assimilation isn't just waiting underground somewhere," I told my buyer, frowning. "I sure as hell don't want to be wearing an obedience chip — I wouldn't think you would either."

"Obedience is a small price to pay for a galaxy run with perfect order and precision. So the Assimilated used to say," he remarked.

"They had fucking robots living in their skulls. They'd say anything they were told to say," I pointed out. "Why are you so interested in the Assimilation anyway?"

He shrugged eloquently. "As I said, I am a collector of oddities. The War of Assimilation is an area of particular interest to me so I collect relics from it in my spare time to amuse myself."

"Uh-huh," I said, not completely convinced. There was something strange about this male — something I didn't quite trust. His Majoran hair and smooth, light tan skin weren't the only features that didn't match. His scent was confused too — mixed up — almost as though he was two separate people. Of course, being only half Vorn, my sense of smell isn't as strong as it could've been. But it was strong enough to let me know something wasn't right with Count Doloroso.

"There is *one* piece I'm especially interested in." He leaned across the table, his eyes gleaming strangely again. "A chip-drill. Here — let me show you."

He activated his holo-ring — a hell of a lot nicer than my own — and a small image appeared hovering above it. It looked like a round, blue glass ball with a twisted metal blade coming out of it.

I stared at it uneasily and for some reason Zoe rose to my mind again. *No, she's fine,* I told myself and pushed the worry away.

"It's an instrument for making just the right pathway for chip implantation," Doloroso explained. "Once it tasted the subject's blood, it knew exactly how far to drill." The holo projected by his ring jerked as the curving silver blade shot out without warning.

I actually jumped back a little.

"Hell of a nasty thing," I growled. "I think I've seen it. Pretty sure it's with the rest of the stuff in the hold."

"Good—excellent." He gave me a very satisfied look. "And there's just one more thing I hope you have. A sensitivity tank. Looks like this I believe."

He made another motion and the chip-drill disappeared to be replaced by a yellow, glowing tank with murky black tendrils waving inside it.

"Those are sensu-pods," he said, indicating the tendrils which now looked more like tentacles. "The tank sustains them with its liquid but they feed best on the emotions and sensations of sentient beings. They're quite good at measuring sensitivity. How long did you say you'd had this equipment?"

"Around ten cycles," I said absently.

"Hmmm…" He nodded. "I imagine the sensu-pods in your particular tank are quite *hungry* by this time."

I stirred in my chair, remembering my own plans for the tank. I needed it for Zoe's sensitivity test. Although knowing what I did now about her fear of being submerged in liquid gave me pause about using it. Still—what else could I do since I had refused the Commercians' testing? I pictured her floating in the tank and felt another stab of worry. Again I pushed it to the back of my mind.

"I do have that as well, I know," I said. "But it's the only piece that's not for sale. I need it for…personal matters."

"You have a subject you wish to test?" His eyes gleamed. "One who has been recently transported, perhaps? From what world did you buy her? A newly opened one? There have been rumors recently…most intriguing ones."

"Where I got her is my business," I said shortly. I didn't like the idea of Count Doloroso tracking down the Commercians and scanning the Alien Mate Index for an Earth female of his own. I was fairly certain whoever he picked and paid for wouldn't be treated well at all.

He shrugged his narrow shoulders. "Very well, but do be careful if you use it. The liquid that sustains the sensu-pods is toxic to most sentient beings if left on the skin for too long. Whoever you're testing must be thoroughly cleansed of it if you don't wish them to go into cardiac shock."

"Is that right?" I felt more uneasy about using the tank than ever.

"Really," he said seriously. "Honestly, after such a long time without use, the tank is really not fit for anything but a collector's item. So I hope you'll reconsider my offer. I really need it."

"You *need* it?" I frowned. "I thought you just collected this stuff for fun."

"I mean, I need it to complete my *collection*," he answered smoothly. "And I'm willing to pay handsomely to get it."

"How much?" I asked.

He named a price that nearly made me spit out my mouthful of ale and brandy.

"Goddess of Mercy!" My voice rasped a little.

"And twice that for the entire lot," Doloroso assured me. "But only if it's *complete*. Just think—you can clear your hold of a lot of old junk, and I can complete my Assimilation collection—we both win."

"Show me your credit," I said. "I don't know many people that have that much just to spend on a hobby for the hell of it."

"Here you go—test it yourself." He handed me a cred-card— black with gold bands. When I pressed the emerald chip embedded in its center, a small holo-figure popped up and hovered briefly over the card before dissipating like a whiff of smoke.

He was telling the truth.

"You can see that's from the First Bank of Femme 1," he said, taking back the card when I handed it to him. "A guarantee of authenticity and secure funds. So…are you interested?"

"You know I am," I said evenly. I still didn't like to give up the tank but with this much credit, fixing the hydrogen scoop's panel wouldn't break me—that was *if* I could find a mechanic to fix it. As for Zoe's testing—I would have to get it done elsewhere. I didn't like the idea of her in that tank, especially knowing that the liquid could be toxic—didn't like it at all.

Zoe

It happened so fast, I didn't have any idea what was going on. How could I be standing on my own two feet one minute, and then hovering three feet above the weird tank filled with yellow liquid the next? Before I could answer the question, I found myself plunging down as something pulled me into the liquid which closed over my head.

At once I was back in the swimming pool, back when I was so little—almost too young to remember, and yet much too old to ever forget. I heard myself crying my little sister's name, saw her sinking in the water below me, eyes open wide, limbs flailing. I couldn't reach her…couldn't reach her because neither of us could swim…

My head was yanked back above the surface and I took a choking, gasping breath. I wasn't in the swimming pool at the neighbor's house—I was in a tank in an alien spaceship and something had me by the waist. What was it?

Looking down, I saw a thick, slimy tentacle wrapped around my waist like some kind of belt. I grabbed it and tried to push it down—to push it off. It was slimy and horribly warm under my hands—almost hot. What the Hell was it?

My heart was pounding in my chest as I pushed at it, my pulse skittering like a frightened rabbit's. The sleeves of Sarden's black shirt had unrolled themselves and they kept getting in the way as I tried to get a grip on the damn thing.

"Let me go," I muttered under my breath. *"Let...me...go,* you bastard!"

And suddenly, it did.

I dropped to the bottom of the tank like a stone, the weight of the sodden shirt pulled me down.

"No!" I tried to say but I sucked in a mouthful of the yellow liquid which was more viscous than water, and choked it out again. I looked up, clawing to find a way out but the sides of the tank rose around me, slick and high and unclimbable. I thrashed as hard as I could, the glowing yellow tank mixing with the vision of the murky blue pool in my past to make a confused vision of horror in my head. *Angie,* I thought. *Angie, I'm so sorry...*

Suddenly the slimy black tentacle grabbed me and lifted my head above the water again. I took another ragged, gasping breath and coughed it back out again, trying to rid my lungs of the horrible liquid, which tasted like mud and blood mixed together.

Then, as if things couldn't get any worse, more tentacles appeared and started tearing at the black shirt I was wearing.

"Hey...hey, stop that!" I gasped as they managed to get it open. Two more tentacles stripped it off my shoulders, leaving me naked and flailing in the slimy liquid. What the hell was going on? What were they going to do?

I found out sooner than I wanted to.

Two thin, shiny black tentacles suddenly appeared right in

front of me, their tips pointed at my chest. I looked down at them stupidly, unable to move since the thicker tentacle was still wrapped around my waist.

As I watched, the end of each tentacle began to grow and change until, instead of a blunt tip, they had both turned into starfish-looking appendages on the end of the long black arms.

Before I could wonder what the starfish-hands were for, both of them surged forward and plastered themselves to my boobs.

"Hey! Hey, stop it, you perverts!" I began to thrash even harder, trying to get away from the awful things. But they were stuck on me like suction cups. And speaking of suction, it seemed like they were determined to suck my nipples right off my breasts. In fact, it felt like someone had put a vacuum hose against each of my boobs and flipped the switch to high.

It hurt like hell and felt perverted at the same time. And then another tentacle brushed at my inner thigh.

"Oh, no," I said, kicking out at the thing as hard as I could. "Oh, *Hell* no, I don't think so—*get away from me!*"

I was shouting at the top of my lungs—dimly I could hear my own voice echoing in the vast chamber. But there was no one to hear—no one to save me. Was this how my story ended? Could I really die like this, molested to death by some creepy alien creature, like some hapless schoolgirl in Japanese hentai tentacle porn?

"No!" I screamed as the tentacle brushed between my legs again. "No—no, you son of a bitch! *Get off me!*"

And then the main tentacle around my waist yanked me down again. My mouth filled with the awful yellow slime and I couldn't shout any more…

Chapter Eleven

Sarden

I didn't care for Count Doloroso—there was something strange about him. But I told myself he was just an odd male with a weird Assimilation obsession. What could it hurt to let him buy the medical instruments in my hold?

We made the deal, to be finalized when he came to my ship for the Assimilation equipment in a few standard hours. Though Gallana isn't actually on a planet, it orbits around a star and its rotation is paced to mimic the thirty hour day of Femme 1, where the Empress lives. Since the day is long, it was still just mid-morning. I should still have time to find a mechanic to replace my panel after Doloroso made the pick up—I hoped, anyway.

Doloroso and I took one last drink on the deal and I left The Suck Hole, the thought of Zoe still in the back of my mind like a nagging song that won't leave your brain.

"Call the ship," I told Al, who had been keeping silent in his travel form during the negotiations. "Check on Zoe—make sure she's well."

"Don't you wish to hear what I have found out about the local services and mechanics, Master?" he asked. "I have one you might care to visit but—"

"Not now," I snapped, quickening my pace. "Check on Zoe."

He was quiet for a moment, humming softly on my shoulder.

"No answer, Master," he said at last.

"What? What do you mean, no answer?" I frowned. "She's probably sulking because she wanted to go with me." As if I'd bring her to a place like The Suck Hole! "She's probably just refusing to answer."

"No, Master—I don't think so." Now Al sounded worried as well—if an Artificial Life-form can be worried. "I've scanned her room twice now and I don't detect a heartbeat or breathing. Either she is not there. Or…"

He didn't finish and I didn't need him to. I remembered Zoe's big blue eyes, filled with tears she refused to shed last night when she'd begged me to take her home. Frozen Hells of Anor! What if she'd hurt herself in order to avoid being traded? What if she'd decided it was better to die than to live the rest of her life away from her home planet? What if she'd…?

I couldn't let myself finish the thought. I sped up until I was almost running, drawing concerned looks from the Majoran Peace Keepers stationed in the docking area. I didn't give a damn though—the worried feeling that had been tugging at me almost the entire time I'd been making my deal had worsened into a sick dread in the pit of my stomach. I hadn't known the little Pure One even an entire solar week yet but somehow the idea of losing her was unbearable.

I tore into the ship, barely giving the hidden side panel door enough time to open before I was squeezing inside. As I pounded down the main corridor, I feared what I would find when I came to her room.

"Al, unlock her door," I ordered, my boots *thunk-thunk-thunking* on the metal floor.

"No need, Master—it is already open. Look."

Sure enough, as I skidded to a halt before the bedroom I had assigned to Zoe, I saw the door standing wide open. A quick look inside the room revealed no trace of her. My own door was unlocked as well but she wasn't in there either.

"Frozen Hells of Anor!" I swore angrily, coming out into the main corridor again. "Where is she? Al—scan the rest of the ship."

"Yes, Master. Scanning." He hummed softly, still in his travel form on my shoulder. And that was when I heard it—over the quiet humming of Al's processing, a faint splashing noise, like water sloshing in a tank.

And then a single, piercing scream which was cut off abruptly.

"Fuck!" I pounded down the corridor as fast as I could, feeling like my heart might burst. I didn't know how in the Frozen Hells I'd known it or how she had gotten out of the Force-Locks and escaped her room, but my uneasy feelings had been correct—Zoe was in trouble.

The splashing sound came again from the back of the ship. But what was she splashing in? There were no personal cleansing pools located in the hold, where the sounds were coming from. So how in the hell…

Suddenly an image rose to my mind's eye—the holo projection of the sensitivity tank Doloroso had been so eager to buy. The yellow liquid with its nest of black, writhing tentacles, the sensu-pods. *"I imagine they will be quite hungry by now"* he had said…

"Zoe!" I shouted, running for the door to the hold which I could now see was standing wide open, as were all the other doors along the corridor. She must have opened every one, looking for a way out. "Zoe, where are you?"

A faint splashing and the noise of liquid sloshing onto the ground was my only answer. I reached the darkened hold and started shoving my way through the medical equipment stored there, not giving a damn if I broke any of it or not. Up ahead I could see the yellowish glow of the tank and something was writhing inside it…black tentacles were whipping around like some creature from the Great Deep gone berserk.

And then I saw her—her long, red hair floating like a corona around her still face, the filthy tentacles wrapped around and around her smooth, pale skin.

It was Zoe—and she didn't seem to be breathing.

Chapter Twelve

Zoe

I don't remember much about what happened after the last time the shiny black tentacles dragged me under. The putrid yellow liquid filled my mouth and lungs and everything started to go gray.

Vaguely I thought I heard someone — some familiar voice — calling my name. But the voice was too deep to be Charlotte or Leah. Could it be my ex? But no, I hadn't seen Scott in nearly a year and besides, he hadn't had a very deep voice for a guy. My father had, but he'd been dead for the past five years — he had passed in his sleep only a month after my mother had died of cancer. He just couldn't stand to live without her.

Whoever was calling me sounded like that — like he couldn't stand to live without me. But there was no one in my life who felt that way about me. No one I knew of, anyway.

The next thing I knew, someone was unwinding the choking tentacles from around my waist and pulling them off my lady bits. Then he hauled me out of the glass tank and started pounding me on the back.

I began coughing and choking, trying to get the awful blood-mud tasting stuff out of my lungs. It burned like fire coming up and several times I thought I might pass out from the pain.

"Zoe? Zoe!" someone said in my ear. "Can you hear me? Tell me you're well."

"'s aw-right," I said, my stubborn tongue slurring over the words it refused to pronounce. "'m fine." Which was a total lie but it's what you always say, isn't it? Even if you've just been half drowned in alien slime by molesting tentacle monsters, you still say you're fine.

I do, anyway.

The person who'd hauled me out of the tank clearly wasn't buying it.

"Little, liar—you're *not* fine. Not even close to it," he growled and then strong arms were lifting me and taking me out of the dark room while the black tentacles thrashed in their yellow tank, angry to have lost their prey.

"Lay some cloths on the bed. She's soaked in this Gods-damned stuff," the person carrying me commanded.

"At once, Master," a prim and proper voice replied. It sounded familiar and memories began to come back to my oxygen-starved brain.

"Al," I mumbled as I was laid on a cool surface that seemed to rock gently, cradling me in comfort.

"Yes, Lady Zoe?"

"Lady Zoe? Not...'m not..." I choked again, my eyes still closed. I wanted to open them but they felt glued shut by the sticky slime that still covered me.

"Zoe, look at me," the deep voice ordered. I wanted to ignore it—now that I was finally out of the tentacle-tank I just wanted to rest. But there was an authority in his tone I couldn't ignore. "Zoe," he said again.

Reluctantly, I pried my sticky eyes open to see the Devil, complete with red skin, horns, and glowing golden eyes, staring at me anxiously. *No, not the Devil—Sarden,* a little voice in my head reminded me. I was lying on one of the silver, floating hoverbeds and he was standing over me.

"I'm okay," I said and then I started shivering uncontrollably.

"It's all right, little one," he murmured, pulling me close. His warmth and the spicy campfire scent of his skin was comforting, and I felt my heart do a funny little flutter.

"The t-tank," I whispered, my teeth chattering. "The t-tentacles…they p-pulled me in."

He frowned. "I'm sure they didn't reach all the way from the hold to your room. How did you get out of the Force-Locks anyway? And why did you go back there?"

"I p-pressed them with my n-nose," I managed to say. "They turned g-green and unlocked. Then I u-used them as a k-key to explore. I was l-looking for a way out."

"I see. Although why they worked for you I have no idea. They're supposed to be keyed to Vornish DNA and I know you don't have any of that—you're a Pure One."

"I was almost a d-dead one," I told him. "The liquid…the slime…I was d-drowning."

The memory of the yellow, slimy stuff closing over my head made me want to retch. It made me think of Angie again…of how I couldn't save her…of how I nearly died trying.

Her face swam in my memory and a sob burst out of me before I could stop it. I clamped my lips shut against the next one that wanted to follow. I hadn't cried for Angie in a long time. I didn't want to start again now.

"Zoe? What is it?" Sarden still looked concerned.

"N-nothing. I'm f-fine." But my teeth wouldn't stop chattering and my heart was doing that flutter thing again. I put a hand to my chest, trying to calm it down. I didn't like the way it seemed to be jumping around in there like a Mexican jumping bean.

"What is it?" Sarden asked again, more urgently. "Tell me!"

"N-nothing." I glared at him defiantly. "My heart just s-skipped a b-beat—that's all." Actually, it was still skipping beats but I told myself that was only because I was still so upset from the trauma I'd just been through.

"Your heart?" Sarden frowned at me.

"Master," Al, who was in his dragonfly form, spoke up. "Didn't Count Doloroso tell you that the liquid in the sensitivity tank was toxic to most sentient beings?"

"Frozen Hells! He *did*," Sarden growled. "Come on." He lifted me again, as though I weighed no more than a doll.

"Where…where are we g-going?" I whispered. By now my heart was pounding in such an erratic rhythm I felt sick and it was hard to breath.

"To the PPC," he said grimly. "We have to get that slime off you *now*."

"What? You mean the weird purple bathtub thing? No!"

Despite the fact that my heart was going crazy and my teeth wouldn't stop chattering, I somehow managed to twist out of his grip. Probably the slippery slime on my skin helped. Anyway, I fell to the ground with a thud, landing bruisingly on my knees. It hurt like hell but it was better than going in over my head again in yet another vat of alien liquid.

"Look, I know you're frightened of being submerged but you *have* to," Sarden said, bending to try and scoop me up again. "The slime in the sensitivity tank is toxic—we have to get it off you."

"No," I said stubbornly, scooting away from his seeking hands.

"I d-don't care — put me in the mister. I won't go in that drowning-tank. I *w-won't*."

"The mister won't get it all off," he objected. "It's not strong enough."

"Well *I'm* not strong enough to g-go through another n-near drowning," I said, glaring up at him defiantly. "You d-don't understand. My...my little sister..."

I couldn't go on but I didn't have to. Sarden hunkered down on his booted heels beside me, looking me earnestly in the eyes.

"I can see there's a story here — a reason you're afraid," he murmured. "But I'm not just going to throw you in the cleansing pool, Zoe. I'll come in with you."

"You...you wh-what?" My heart was pounding in an irregular rhythm, the sound filling my ears and I wasn't sure I'd heard him right.

"I'll go with you," he repeated patiently. "After all, I've got the slime on me too — we'll get clean together."

"Will...will my head have to go under?" I asked at last, tremulously.

"Only for a moment," he promised. "I'll hold you up and I won't let you fall — I promise. If you go under, I'll go under too."

"Well..." My heart was going crazy now, stopping and starting, making me feel like someone was squeezing it mercilessly in an iron fist.

"Listen to your body," Sarden urged me quietly. "You're going into cardiac shock — you need to get that damn slime off your skin so it can start beating properly again."

I looked at him uncertainly. There was anxiety but also patience in his golden eyes. If he'd wanted to, he could have picked me up by sheer force and thrown me into the vertical bathtub—he was certainly strong enough to do what he wanted with me. But he didn't—he waited for me to make up my own mind to go with him. To trust him.

Chilled to the bone, teeth chattering, and heart pounding I made my choice.

"All r-right," I said at last. "As long as you p-promise not to leave me."

"I promise," he said gently and scooped me into his arms.

Sarden

She felt so light in my arms and I could hear how erratic her heartbeat had become. It scared the hell out of me and I wanted nothing more than to rush her into the cleansing liquid of the pool. But the fear in her eyes told me I had to take things slowly, no matter how worried I was.

I cradled her close to my chest as I pressed the switch on the side of the vertical tank. The door slid to one side—the force field holding the cleansing liquid in place—and I stepped into it, holding Zoe high to be certain it didn't go over her head.

"Sarden," she whispered and I felt her shaking—not from cold but from fear—as we got fully inside. The warm liquid was up to her neck, though it was only up to my shoulders, and her eyes were shut tight, as though she didn't want to look.

"It's all right," I assured her, holding her closer. I felt the slime from the Gods-damned sensitivity tank beginning to melt away at once. Good—I'd been feeling somewhat shaky myself. Doloroso had been right—the tank was no good as anything but as part of a collection. The slime inside it was much too strong and the sensu-pods were far too aggressive to use on a living sentient being.

I wondered again how in the world she'd been able to get out of the Force-Locks and use them to get back in the hold in the first place. She obviously had no Vornish DNA—maybe it was because she was a *La-ti-zal*. But could her gift really be that strong, even with the inhibitor in place?

Zoe was still trembling against me, her arms clutched tight around my neck. I rubbed her back soothingly and murmured to her that everything was going to be fine, that I had her and wouldn't let her go.

But you'll have to let her go, won't you? whispered a nasty little voice in my head. *Once you get to Giedi Prime you'll trade her to Tazaxx and never see her again, unless he extends an invitation to his private zoo.*

I thought of that, of only seeing her from behind a clear force field, of never being able to hold her or touch her again and my heart felt like someone was twisting it.

It's the toxin, I told myself trying to push the feeling away. *I haven't even had her for two solar days yet. Trading her to Tazaxx should be no problem.*

So why couldn't I make myself believe it?

Looking down, I saw that the slime had melted off both of us. I was completely clean since I hadn't gone in under my head. Unfortunately, the same couldn't be said for Zoe. Her long red hair—so vivid when I held her despite the inhibitor she still wore—was matted with the stuff, and it still clung to her face and her long lashes and eyebrows too. She was going to have to go under—there was no other way to get rid of the slime completely.

"Zoe," I said, as gently as I could.

She opened her eyes a crack and peeked at me.

"Yes?" Her voice sounded tiny and uncertain—very different from her usual confident banter—but at least she'd stopped trembling in my arms.

"We have to go under," I told her. "Just for a moment. Just to get your face and hair clean."

"I...I know," she whispered, looking up at me with those big, impossibly blue eyes. Even coated in the thick slime of the tank, I thought I had never seen a lovelier female. Her freckles stood out against the skin of her face—probably because she was pale with fear.

"Can you trust me?" I asked her. "I'll go under with you, I promise. Will that help?"

"Maybe. If...if I can see you."

"We'll be face to face the entire time. Look." I shifted her around so that her legs were wrapped around my waist and we were facing each other directly.

"Okay." She clung to me tightly, her arms wrapped around my neck as she pressed as close to me as she could. Her lush, naked curves were distracting but her fear was too obvious for me to become aroused. I've known males who got off on the fear and pain of females but I have never been one of them.

"All right," I murmured. "On the count of three take a deep breath and we'll go under. We'll stay under for a count of three and then come back up. Understand?"

She nodded, her eyes big with fear. It hurt me to see how terrified she still was but I couldn't help it—this had to be done.

"One," I told her. "Two...three." Taking a deep breath, I ducked us both beneath the purple liquid of the cleansing pool.

Zoe's long hair floated free, the liquid in the pool going to work at once on the slime left by the tank. I hoped it would do its job quickly. She was trembling against me so violently now that it vibrated my entire body. I had the sense that this was bringing back some old trauma for her and that she was barely holding on to her self control.

I made a count of three and then lifted us both, breaking the surface.

Zoe gasped in a breath, her eyes huge in her pale face. Then she squeezed them shut and a deep, hitching sob came from her throat. She clamped her lips shut as though to keep another from following it. Clearly this experience was absolutely terrifying to her—and just as clearly she was determined not to give in to the fear and cry.

"Zoe?" I looked at her with concern.

"Is it done?" she whispered in a small, choked voice. "Please tell me it's done, Sarden."

I felt her thick hair with my free hand. Unfortunately, there was still slime caught in its curly locks.

"I'm afraid not," I said regretfully. "Your face is clear but your hair…"

"It…it always takes forever to rinse the shampoo and conditioner out," she said and tried to laugh. "So I guess I shouldn't be surprised. Do…do we have to go under again?"

I was about to say yes but I had a sudden thought.

"Not if you don't want to," I told her. "Not if you trust me enough to support you."

"You're supporting me now," she pointed out.

"Yes, but I mean support you while you float on your back," I said. "I'll hold you up and you can lean back and let your hair drift in the water. That way at least your face doesn't have to go under. What do you think?"

"I think…I *guess* that would be okay." She nodded. "Only I don't know how to float."

"You don't really have to—I'll hold you up," I promised. "Just relax and trust me. Can you do that?" I very much wanted her to say yes, to know that she trusted me, though I didn't know why. When she nodded her head, I felt as though something clenched tight inside me had loosened a little. "Good," I told her. "On the count of three, then?"

"Yes, okay." She took a deep breath. "Just…just put me where I need to be."

"I will," I promised her, stroking her cheek. Gods, she was lovely.

"Thank you," she whispered.

"Thank me later—when we've gotten all this off of you," I told her. "One…two…three."

Zoe

It was both awkward and terrifying, floating on my back in the purple liquid. I'd had boyfriends before who promised to teach me how to swim and I knew this was how you were supposed to start—just floating with someone you trusted holding you up.

I hadn't trusted a single guy enough to let him do that for me. Not until Sarden. And I didn't know why I was trusting him now. I barely knew him, so why was I okay with believing he would hold me up and not let me go?

I couldn't answer that question, even to myself. I tried to think up some snarky explanation but my mind was too tangled in knots with the past and the future merging together to make one big nasty mess of my emotions.

When the snarky part of me goes into hiding, I know I'm in

trouble.

I tried closing my eyes but I kept seeing Angela's face — Angie, little Angie that I was supposed to be responsible for. That I was supposed to watch. Guilt and sorrow flowed through me until I couldn't bear it and had to open my eyes to look up at Sarden who was holding me firmly and patiently, just waiting for the cleansing liquid to do its job.

I tried to help it along some by lifting my arms very, very carefully over my head to scrub at my hair. But then I suddenly became aware of the fact that I was naked and my boobs were floating very obviously, my nipples like two little pink boats bobbing on the surface of the purple liquid. More like two *red* boats actually — those damn starfish suckers on the end of the tentacles had really done a number on me!

"Oops." I lowered my arms hastily to cover myself, feeling both shy and more vulnerable than I could ever remember feeling before. Yes, even more vulnerable than the night before when the damn hoverbed had been touching me while he watched.

Sarden frowned but never let go of me — his large, warm hands were spread carefully under my back and the top of my butt, holding me up.

"Are you still so shy with me?" he murmured. "You have nothing to be ashamed of — your curves are lovely."

"Thank you but that doesn't mean I want to go parading around naked as a jay bird," I said tartly.

"What?" He frowned. "Is that some kind of Earth creature?"

"Yes, a bird — you know, they fly through the air?"

"We have such creatures on Vorn 6 and also Eloim," he said, nodding. "The Ancient Ones sowed the seeds of life everywhere. But the birds on my home worlds usually have feathers. On Vorn 6, some have scales as well."

I tried to picture a scaly bird and shuttered. *Ugh.*

"They have feathers on Earth, too," I said.

"Then how can a bird be 'naked'?" Sarden asked reasonably. "I don't understand."

"Honestly, I don't either," I told him. "It's just a saying. Look—do you think we're almost done here?"

He felt my hair carefully, making sure to keep me well supported with one large hand under my back.

"I think so." He nodded. "I take it you're ready to get out?"

"More than ready," I said fervently. "Seriously, so, so, *so* ready."

"All right." He gathered me close to his broad chest and prepared to exit the vertical bathtub. The fabric of his sleeveless shirt was soaked and clinging to him transparently in an extremely yummy way but it was hard to appreciate when I wanted so badly to get out of the water.

But then he just stopped. Instead of taking me out of the PPC, he just looked at me.

"What? What is it? Why are we stopping?" I asked nervously. "Please, Sarden, I *really* want to get out of here!"

"I can tell you do. But I'd like to understand *why.*"

"Why what?" I asked, feeling exasperated.

"Why you're afraid of going in over your head." He was still looking at me intently. "What happened to you, Zoe, that made you so fearful of water or swimming?"

"Angela...my little sister," I said stiffly. "She...there was an accident. She was only five. I..." I shook my head. "I don't....I can't talk about it."

"You did tell me you had a sister — I remember." Sarden looked at me thoughtfully.

"*Had* being the operative word," I said, my throat tight.

He raised an eyebrow. "She died?"

I looked away, unable to meet his gaze.

"Look, can we please just get out? I am so past ready to leave this damn purple bathtub thing it's not even funny."

"Right." He nodded and, to my infinite relief, let the subject drop. I'd had enough trips down Memory Lane today, first in the awful tentacle tank and then in the weird vertical bathtub. I just wanted to let the memory of my sister and what had happened to her fade away — at least for now.

We stepped out and I started shivering again — the liquid in the Personal Pool of Cleansing, as Al had called it, was as warm as bathwater. The outside air felt incredibly chilly in contrast.

"Here." Sarden carried me over to the mister and stood me on my feet in front of him. I wobbled a minute but then I was fine — my heart was beating normally again. Well, as normally as it could when I was naked and so close to the huge, muscular alien.

Sarden changed the controls so that blasts of hot air started coming out to dry us. It felt wonderful against my chilled skin but not so good against my tender nipples, which still felt like they'd been half sucked off by the awful tentacles in the tank. You know how it is when you burn your hand and then you try to cook something over a hot stove? The heat hitting your burn is almost more than you can stand. That's how it was with my nipples…and between my thighs too. Those tentacles had been *awful*.

"Ouch!" I winced involuntarily and took a step back from the hot air.

"What is it? What's wrong?" Sarden sounded concerned. I

turned to him.

"Nothing, it's—hey, you're naked!"

"Of course I am." He kicked the heap of sodden clothes he'd shed to one side. "I have to dry off too." Rivulets of the purple cleansing liquid ran down the hard planes of his abdomen and beaded on his broad, bare shoulders. Between his long, muscular legs his shaft was every bit as big and impressive as I remembered. It was also more than half hard.

"All right, well…fine." I started edging away from him.

"Where are you going?" he demanded. "Don't be foolish, Zoe. Just because I'm naked doesn't mean I'll suddenly try to molest you."

"Right" I said, still moving away. "You're not just naked. You're also, uh, *excited*." I nodded at his half-hard shaft.

"I can't help being aroused when I see your naked body," he said, as if it was a totally reasonable thing. "Especially when I was just holding you against me. But that doesn't mean I'm going to act on it. Come back and dry off—I don't want you getting sick."

"It's not just that I'm embarrassed to be naked with you," I said, although I totally was. At least, partly. "It also hurts. The hot air, I mean."

"It hurts? What are you talking about?"

"It's too hot—it's burning me." I wasn't about to say where but Sarden's eyes flicked to my nipples, which I was trying unsuccessfully to hide with one arm, and narrowed at once.

"The sensu-pods—what did they do to you?" he demanded.

"The *what?*" I asked.

"The tentacles in the tank. They're meant to test nerve conduction and sensitivity—the same way the Commercian's table does," he explained. "But those had been dormant for over ten cycles — they're starving and extremely aggressive."

"Tell me about it," I said, my teeth chattering. "Not to mention extremely *rapey.*"

His face darkened and he took a step toward me. "What did they do to you? Did they hurt you? Did they —"

"There was no, uh, penetration," I said quickly, seeing where he was going with this. "Just a lot of really, really aggressive suction. It hurt. A *lot.*"

"I need to see if you're injured — I need to examine you," he announced.

"What? No!" I took another step back.

"I'm not going to hurt you, Zoe." His deep voice was soft and coaxing. "I just need to make sure you're all right. You could have a life threatening injury and not even know it."

"I'm not injured, just sore," I protested. "It's not like being dunked in that damn tentacle tank is going to kill me."

"It almost *did* kill you," he pointed out. "Look, at the very least we need to be sure you got the slime that housed the sensu-pods off you completely. We need to be certain there isn't some left somewhere."

He looked pointedly between my legs and I could feel my cheeks getting hot.

"I'm fine. I'm sure I got it all off," I protested.

"Then it won't hurt to let me check," he countered.

"*I'll* check," I said quickly.

He raised an eyebrow at me. "Are humans so flexible, then? You're able to see that area with no problems?"

"Um...yes..." I didn't sound very certain, even to myself.

"It will only take a minute. Come." Sarden started for the bedroom but I hung back. "What is it?" he demanded, looking over his shoulder and seeing that I was still in the bathroom. "Is it that I'm still nude? Look."

He made the closet appear in his wall again — (how did he do that?) — and quickly got dressed, pulling on another pair of the tight, black trousers and a black sleeveless shirt. Then he turned to face me and held out his arms.

"See?"

"Great. So you're dressed," I said flatly. "That doesn't exactly qualify you as a gynecologist."

"A what?" He shook his head. "Never mind. Look, Zoe, what if I swear to you that I have only your wellbeing in mind? I promise not to hurt you or touch you in a sexual way — I just want to make sure you're all right." He made his voice softer. "You trusted me to take you in the cleansing pool. Please trust me again."

I don't know why I went to him but somehow I did. I was mostly dry by now, just from standing around in the air arguing. Well, except for my hair which still hung wet and dripping down my back. Sarden handed me another one of his long sleeved shirts to wear — between the two of us, we were really going through his wardrobe at a quick rate, I wondered who did the laundry around here — and gave me a clean, dry cloth to blot my hair.

While I did that, he cleared the blankets that had covered the bed and still had slime on them, throwing them down the laundry chute in the wall. At least, I assumed it was a laundry chute.

"Does that lead to the laundry room or something?" I asked, nodding at it. "Or wherever you keep the washer and dryer?"

"The what and the what?" He threw a frowning glance over his shoulder.

"That chute—where you threw the slimy blankets and where you put your dirty clothes earlier today? Are there machines for cleaning clothes at the bottom of it?"

"No, the chute itself cleans them. It's a clothing cycler," he explained. "It connects to my storage unit." He pointed at the closet. "The dirty items are washed and dried and hung or folded back where they belong within the space of about one standard solar hour."

"What?" I stared at the chute, suddenly green with envy. "You have a system that washes, dries, folds, *and* puts clothes away? Forget your hydrogen scoop engine, we'd *kill* for something like that on Earth!" Especially those of us who had to deal with slobby boyfriends or husbands. Scott had been *awful* about leaving his dirty clothes all over the place and I was constantly picking up after him. It was either that or live in a pigsty.

"Really?" Sarden was fiddling with the controls on the bed. "It's actually very simple tech. Here—I'm ready."

He stepped back and I saw that he had converted the floating silver beanbag bed into a kind of semi-reclined chair.

"Umm..." I wasn't sure what to do.

"Come sit here so I can look at you." He patted the silver material. "Come on, Zoe—it won't take long. I just want to be sure you're all right."

"Well..." Reluctantly, I went and sat in the chair. Sarden had lowered it somehow but once I was settled into it, he raised it again so that it was hovering in mid-air once more.

"Now, let's see." He pulled the sides of the shirt apart first (it was another black one which really did look good with my pale skin) and examined my nipples. "Hmm..." He frowned as he looked but didn't touch. "These *do* look painful. And extremely red."

"They, uh, they are." I wished my voice wouldn't come out sounding so breathless but he was so close I could feel his warm breath against my tender flesh. It made a rash of goosebumps break out all over my body.

If Sarden noticed my discomfort, he didn't say anything—he just kept staring at me. Then he ducked lower, kneeling in front of me so that his face was level with my thighs—which were tightly shut.

"Open." He put one big hand on my knee, making me shiver. "Please, Zoe—I need to see."

Biting my lip, I spread my legs for him.

"Hmm..." Sarden leaned closer and now I could feel his hot breath against my sex, stirring the neatly trimmed reddish curls on my mound. Oh God, this was so embarrassing! I swore to myself if I could just get through this, I'd never complain about going to the gyno again.

"The outside looks all right, if somewhat red," Sarden remarked at last. "But I can't see your inner depths. I'm sorry, Zoe, but you'll have to spread yourself for me. Unless you'd rather I do it?" He looked up at me and I bit my lip and shook my head.

"No. I...I'll do it."

Had I said I was embarrassed before? Well up that by a factor of about a thousand. I was *mortified* as I made myself reach down between my legs and spread my outer pussy lips for him.

Sarden leaned closer until he was close enough to kiss me. To— *no!* I pushed that thought away as quick as I could. Only it wouldn't go. I kept thinking about how he'd said that Vorn males loved tasting their females. It made me feel hot and cold and trembly all over. Especially since I could feel his hot breath right against my open pussy.

"Hmm," Sarden murmured again but this time he didn't sound quite so clinical and detached.

"Well?" I asked at last because it seemed to be taking him an *awfully* long time. "All clear?"

"I believe so. Although your skin is as red as mine here – is that normal?"

I looked down – really looked – and saw that my inner pussy was cherry red, just like my nipples.

"No," I said, sounding worried, even to myself. "No, it's not at all."

"I didn't think so." He frowned and looked up at me. "Do I need to look further in? You said that the tentacles didn't...penetrate you, correct?"

"Right." By now I was sure my face was probably cherry red too. "There's no need to look any further – honest."

"I hope you're right. You know..." He looked up at me. "You shouldn't have been back in the hold in the first place but I'm sorry you were hurt by the sensu-pods."

"You and me both." I thought of the shiny black tentacles again and shivered. "They were awful!"

"I know." He stroked my thigh soothingly. "I can heal this for you, if you'll let me."

"Heal it?" I looked at him suspiciously. "Heal it *how?*"

He shrugged. "The usual way of course."

"And what's the usual way? You have a first aid kit? Some kind of antiseptic cream or numbing ointment?"

He frowned. "I don't know what any of that is. I meant I can heal you with my mouth."

"What?" I nearly jumped out of the chair but he held me back firmly with one large hand and frowned at me.

"Why are you upset? Because I'm not your mate? I know unmated people don't often heal each other—at least they don't on my home worlds—but—"

"It's not *that*," I burst out. "You can't heal me with your mouth! That's just an excuse to be perverted."

Sarden looked startled. "You can't heal each other orally on Earth? What do you do when you have a minor injury like a cut or burn?"

"We get a freaking Band-Aid," I snapped. "We don't offer to *lick* each other on the…" I trailed off, blushing.

"Hmm…" He frowned. "Maybe there are some disadvantages to being so purely bred and sheltered on your little planet. Most of the rest of the Twelve Peoples descended from the Ancient Ones have the ability to heal."

"Well maybe you evolved it or whatever," I said. "But we don't have it on Earth. And I don't know that I believe you have it either."

He raised an eyebrow at me.

"So you think I'm lying just to get a chance to taste your pussy?"

"Well…yes," I said, feeling my cheeks get hot as I pressed my thighs together and crossed my arms protectively over my breasts. "Ouch!" I jerked my arms away quickly—my nipples were more tender than ever. In fact they were absolutely *throbbing*. Between my legs didn't feel too great either.

"Zoe, please—you're clearly in pain. And I'm afraid that the sensu-pods might have injected you with some kind of nerve stimulator to heighten your sensations. Which means it's only going to get worse unless you let me heal you."

He sounded very reasonable and concerned but I was still reluctant to let him "heal" me orally, as he put it.

"I don't know…" I said stubbornly. "I mean, I just don't know if I believe it."

"Let me prove it to you then." He rose from the metal floor smoothly and leaned over me again so that we were eye-to-eye. "Let me lick just one of your nipples once. If you don't begin to feel better again right away, you'll know I'm lying and I won't touch you again."

"Well…" I bit my lip, considering it. Then I thought of something else. "Your mouth—last night when you, uh, kissed me—it's hot. I mean, it stings like hot cinnamon. I don't need that when I'm already in pain."

"What you tasted was my healing factor," he said reasonably. "It's what makes me able to heal you orally in the first place. It may sting your mouth but I promise, it will soothe your injuries."

The sincerity in his eyes finally decided me. I didn't know why he cared if I was in pain but he did seem to really want to help me.

"All right," I said at last. "But just one lick."

He nodded. "Absolutely. Do you care which one I heal?" He nodded down at my breasts with their bright red nipples. Ugh—I looked like something out of a weird porno for people who fetishize maraschino cherries or something!

I shook my head, my cheeks burning.

"No. Uh—take your pick."

"Very well." He leaned closer and reached for me, one big, warm hand sliding from my thigh, up my side to cup my right breast.

"Hey," I said breathlessly as he lifted my breast to his lips.

"You don't have to uh—"

"Watch me," he cut me off, his deep voice a soft growl. "Watch me heal you, Zoe."

I twisted my hands into the silver material at my sides and tried not to make a sound as he brought my nipple to his mouth. Then, looking me in the eyes the whole time, he put out his tongue and dragged it slowly…so *slowly*…over my tender peak.

"Oh!" I gasped as the burning sensitivity in my nipple was replaced by a tingling coolness. As I watched the cherry-red flesh went back to my normal pink color. It was like some kind of magic trick—only I don't know many magic tricks that make you hot and bothered and I was definitely both.

"See?" Apparently finished with his long, leisurely lick, Sarden leaned back and looked at me. "Was I lying?"

"No," I whispered, all the wind taken out of my sales. "No, I…I guess not."

"So will you let me heal the other one?"

I looked up at him. His golden eyes were blazing into mine, making my heart pound.

"Y-yes," I said in a shaky voice.

"Good." Sarden repeated his performance, his eyes locked with mine the whole time. It was incredibly intimate holding his gaze while he licked me but somehow, though my pulse raced and my palms grew damp, I couldn't look away.

He spent a little more time on my left nipple, swirling his tongue around it slowly until I thought I might scream from the gentle torture. I knew he was just supposed to be healing me but God, it felt so *good.*

At last he drew back and gave me a serious look.

"Zoe," he said softly. "You know what comes next."

"I don't know about...about that part." I still had my thighs crossed though I had to confess that my pussy was really in pain at this point.

He raised an eyebrow at me.

"Why not? Don't you want to be healed?"

"I'm not sure." I was blushing and biting my lip, feeling uncertain and scared and embarrassed all over again. "I mean it's just...very intimate. You're sure you don't...don't mind?

He frowned. "Why would I mind?"

"Because, well...some guys don't want...I mean...what if you don't like it?" I blurted out at last. My boyfriend in college never had much and Scott had never even asked if he could go there.

"How could I *not* like tasting you?" he murmured, reaching out to cup my flushed cheek. "Even if it's just for the purpose of healing you, it's a privilege. Your scent is intoxicating and your pussy is so beautiful and delicate — it reminds me of a *yonah* flower."

"A what kind of flower? No — never mind." I took a deep breath and made a decision. "You can do it," I told him. "But only...only on the outside. Okay?"

Sarden frowned. "But your inner pussy is in pain as well. I saw how red you were, Zoe."

"I don't care about that," I said stubbornly. "I'll manage. Just...just lick the outside — that's all."

He shrugged, his broad shoulders rolling.

"If that's how you want it but I'm afraid you're going to have a lot of pain and discomfort later."

"Let me worry about that," I said. "Do you want to do it or not?"

His gold eyes flashed. "More than anything. All right—spread your thighs and let me heal at least the outside of your sex"

Heart hammering, I did as he said, forcing myself to spread my thighs as he knelt in front of me again. Sarden leaned forward slowly, taking his time, making me even more nervous, the big red bastard!

"So beautiful," I heard him murmur and then his long, hot tongue was lapping slowly over my swollen folds, making me moan and gasp and squirm in the silver beanbag chair even though I tried really, *really* hard not to.

"Sarden…" I gasped breathlessly.

"Hold still." He frowned up at me. "You moved too much—I have to do it again to be sure I got everything."

He spread my thighs even wider, putting his big hands on my legs and opening me so wide I could feel my pussy lips parting with the gesture. Again my hands clenched into fists in the silver material. Oh God, I couldn't stand this…

But I had to. Once more he dragged his hot tongue over my swollen pussy. But this time there was a difference. The first time, he'd used the flat of his tongue and I'd felt it stroke over me smoothly. This time I felt it enter me. Not a lot, but enough. I felt just the tip of his tongue slide lightly over my throbbing clit and I had to bite the inside of my cheek to keep from moaning. God, it felt so *good*…

At last he finished and looked up at me.

"You're delicious, Zoe." His deep voice was thick and his eyes were heavy-lidded with lust. "I'd love to heal inside you now—would love to lick your sweet pussy until you're all better."

"I…I don't' know what you mean by 'all better,'" I whispered in a breathless voice.

"Oh, I think you do." His eyes gleamed. "I mean I want to taste you until you come. Until you come all over my face."

"I...you...we shouldn't," I protested weakly.

"Why not? If it makes you feel good. Besides..." His voice took on a lecturing tone. "Having an orgasm would help facilitate the healing process."

"It...it would?"

Slowly, he nodded.

I knew it was an excuse to let him continue but hell, at this point I *wanted* an excuse.

"Okay, well I guess so," I whispered. "If you think it will help...help to heal me."

"I know it will," he growled. "So just lie back and let me work on you. Let me *heal* you."

"I...I'll try," I said in a shaky voice, but he was already at work. Leaning forward again, he parted me with his thumbs and began circling the swollen bud of my clit with his tongue. I moaned and bucked up against him, unable to help my reaction. Damn, he was good at this! So good I could hear myself panting, unable to catch my breath as he licked and licked, tracing and stroking my hot little bud as though he'd been born to do it.

This was nothing like my boyfriend in college, nothing like anything I'd ever experienced before. The hot cinnamon of his mouth felt tingly against my inner folds and seemed to intensify every sensation until I was almost begging for release.

"Sarden!" I gasped, arching my back as he lapped me eagerly, like an ice cream he didn't want to melt. "Oh, *Sarden!*"

He paused for a moment, his thumb taking the place of his tongue as he looked up. His mouth was shiny with my juices and his eyes were filled with a flickering, golden lust. "That's right, sweetheart, give it up," he growled. "Gonna make you come. Gonna make you come so *hard* now."

"Sarden—" I wailed as he started to duck back down between my legs. I could feel my orgasm beginning—my insides tensed in a knot that was destined to explode as the broad pad of this thumb slid over my tender bud again and again and again.

He was right, I was going to come. Going to come harder than I ever had in my life while he tasted me with his long, talented tongue...

Just then, Al buzzed into the room, still in his firefly form.

"Master!" he said in his proper voice. "Forgive me for interrupting you and Lady Zoe while you are..." He paused delicately. "Well, I am not certain *what* you are doing. But—"

"Go away, Al," Sarden growled, glaring at him. "*Go away.*"

But it was too late—the mood was lost and so was my orgasm.

Feeling ashamed of myself, I clamped my thighs shut and sat up straight.

"We weren't doing anything Al," I said, trying to make my voice sound normal.

"Yes, we were," Sarden growled. He looked at me, his eyes still hungry. "Come on, Zoe—I was about to make you come."

"Come where? Where were you going?" Al wanted to know.

"Nowhere, now," I said and sighed. I looked at Sarden and shook my head. "Sorry. I just...can't. But, um, thank you for, uh, healing me."

"Fine." He sighed and sat back, looking at Al. "What do you want? Spit it out."

"Forgive me, Master, it's just that Count Doloroso is here to pick up the collection of Assimilation medical artifacts. I have asked him to wait outside the ship but I cannot keep him waiting forever."

"Frozen Hells—I completely forgot he was coming." Sarden jumped up, leaving me feeling exposed. Immediately I started refastening the shirt I was wearing.

"Bring him around to the back entrance to the hold. I'll meet him there," he said.

So there *was* an exit from the ship in the hold! I bet myself I would have found it if I hadn't been grabbed by the damn rapey tentacles. I wanted to go see exactly where this Doloroso guy came in at so I could get out if I wanted to. But I was steering well clear of that awful tank.

I hopped up but Sarden pointed a finger at me.

"You stay here."

"What? Why?" I demanded.

"Because every damn time you leave this room you get into some kind of trouble or other," he growled. "I mean it, Zoe—*stay here.*"

"Fine," I said. "I'll go finish drying my hair in the mister if I can figure out the controls."

"An excellent idea." He gave me one last stern look and left with Al buzzing behind him.

Chapter Thirteen

Sarden

I left Zoe in her room and went to make certain the Assimilation artifacts hadn't been damaged by my hurried rush through the hold to get her out of the tank. I knew she was upset that I'd confined her to her room but it was for her own safety. She needed to stay far away from this area—especially now that the damn sensu-pods had gotten a taste of her. Who knew if they might want more?

They aren't the only ones that got a taste of her, whispered a little voice in my head. *What were you thinking, offering to heal her orally? What are you trying to do—form some kind of bond with her?*

Right. As if I could bond her to me, even if I wanted to. It wasn't possible and I knew it.

She was in pain, I argued with the little voice. *What was I supposed to do—just let her suffer?*

She'll suffer even more if you let her form an emotional attachment to you, even if it isn't a bond, and then you trade her to Tazaxx and never see her again, the voice pointed out implacably. *And she won't be the only one suffering.*

Shut up! I pushed the voice away as well as I could. It was true that only bonded mates usually healed each other orally and I never should have offered it to Zoe. But I was just trying to keep her healthy enough to trade, I told myself. After all, Tazaxx didn't take damaged goods. So there was nothing else I could have done.

Soon enough I was in the hold and calling for lights. A few of the medical artifacts had been pushed aside to make a path to the tank but none of them looked that much worse for the wear. Even the tank itself wasn't damaged although much of the yellowish slime inside it had slopped over the edge when I'd dragged Zoe out. The many-tentacled sensu-pods were sulking in one corner. I tapped the glass but they barely stirred. No doubt they were angry at being deprived of their meal.

"Master, Count Doloroso is asking for admittance to the ship," Al told me.

"Let him in," I said. "Then send a household droid to clean up this slime—it's damn slippery."

"At once," Al said and buzzed off. No doubt responding to his order, a rectangular door opened in the far wall and one of the small, silver household droids which are usually kept dormant within the interior of the ship came whirring out. A pink mop attachment which looked a lot like a tongue shot out and began lapping up the slime from the floor. Good, at least now no one would slip in the mess.

The door at the far end of the hold slid open, revealing Doloroso's angular form, framed in the bluish light from the spaceport.

"Sarden," he said, waving at me. "So good to see you again. I've come to transfer the credit to your account and take possession of my new collection. I hope you don't mind—I brought some moving droids to do the heavy lifting."

"That's fine." I picked my way over to him through the medical equipment. "But don't you want to examine everything first?"

"I'll take a look, of course. But the chip-drill and sensitivity tank are the two items I'm most interested in." He stepped inside, followed by several lumbering moving droids, each with a shell on their backs capable of lifting and holding items weighing up to three metric tons. He would need them—the hold really was crammed full of the Assimilation equipment.

"So…the tank?" He raised his eyebrows inquiringly. "Or would you like to show me the chip-drill first?"

"The chip drill is this way." I wanted to give the household droid a little more time to clean up the slime. We made our way around the perimeter of the room with Doloroso commenting delightedly from time to time over the "priceless collection" and "wonderfully preserved artifacts."

I was glad he liked what he saw—I wanted him to pay and get the hell out as soon as possible. My feeling from The Suck Hole had only grown stronger—though he was paying an exorbitant amount for the medical equipment and had been nothing but courteous, I didn't like him. Not one damn bit.

"All right, now where did I put it?" I looked on the shelf where I'd last seen the chip-drill but it wasn't there.

"Is there a problem?" Doloroso looked concerned.

"No. It's here somewhere, I know it is. I must have misplaced the damn thing."

Exasperated, I looked around—where in the Frozen Hells could the chip-drill be?

"Ah-ha!" Doloroso said from behind me. "Here we are—it must have fallen and rolled—the bottom part is round, you know."

I turned to see the round blue bottom and twisting curved metal end of the drill at his feet. He was just bending over to pick it up when a familiar voice cried,

"Stop!"

"Well, well and who have we here?" Doloroso murmured, picking up the chip-drill by its round, bulbous blue end anyway.

I turned to see Zoe standing in the doorway to the hold. She was wearing another one of my formal shirts with the sleeves rolled up and the black material made her pale, lovely face glow like a distant star. Her long curly hair was a wild mass of ruby red around her shoulders and her bare legs were both shapely and tempting.

All in all she looked fucking gorgeous. I felt a surge of possessiveness fill my chest—I didn't want Doloroso seeing her like this. Or at all, for that matter. Zoe, however, seemed oblivious to the way he was looking at her.

"Really, get rid of that thing—you don't want to touch it," she said, gesturing to the chip-drill in Doloroso's hand as she came forward. "It's extremely dangerous. Look—see what it did to me?" She pointed to a long scratch across her cheekbone which I hadn't noticed earlier. I would have to heal it for her later—if I didn't kill her for disobeying orders first, that was.

"I see. So this is your blood, my dear?" Doloroso asked, examining the end of the drill.

"I'm lucky it wasn't my eye," she said. "Another inch to the side and it would have been. Just don't get it too close to your face—it stabs out with no warning."

"Zoe," I growled, feeling another surge of possessiveness fill me. "What are you doing here? I thought I told you to stay in your room."

"Well, I got *hungry*," she said, crossing her arms over her chest which caused her creamy cleavage to become more prominent in the v-neck of the shirt. "So I was going to make something in the food-sim but just as I was passing by the hold—"

"The food prep area isn't anywhere near the hold," I pointed out.

"*As* I was passing by," she went on, ignoring me pointedly. "I saw your, uh, friend here about to pick up that extremely dangerous stabby-stabby corkscrew thing. I was just trying to warn him—you don't want him to lose an eye, do you?"

"I assure you, my dear, I am quite safe. I collect antiquities and oddities like this for a living." Doloroso gave her a greasy smile I didn't like a bit and set the chip-drill down on the shelf to hold out his hand. "Might I know your name and planet of origin? It isn't every day I meet such an enchanting creature."

"Oh, well..." Zoe gave him her hand—the one with the inhibitor on it—and I saw Doloroso look at it sharply though he made no remark about it. Instead, he bent over the back of her hand and kissed it wetly, as though he was a Gods-damned courier from the Court of the Divine Empress on Femme 1.

"Charmed, I'm sure," he murmured, looking up to smile at her as he licked his lips, almost as though he was tasting her skin.

"Uh, thank you." Zoe smiled uncertainly and took her hand back as soon as she could. I saw her surreptitiously wiping it on the side of my shirt when she was certain he wasn't looking.

"And you are from *which* world in our fair galaxy?" Doloroso asked.

"From—"

"Salex Prime," I said quickly, before she could finish. "Not many people know it—it's on a far arm on the other side of Femme 1."

"Ah—close to the court of the Empress. That would explain why you look so radiantly divine," Count Doloroso said smoothly. "And tell me, how do you like life on Salex Prime?"

"It's, uh, nice," Zoe said, frowning at me.

"Very nice," I said. "And now, if you'd like to see the tank, Count Doloroso..."

"What?" Zoe interjected. "You're going to let him get *close* to that thing? I nearly drowned in there!"

"You were in the sensitivity tank today?" Doloroso gave her a sharp look. "Were you being tested?"

"An incomplete test only," I assured him. "And an accidental one at that. Zoe wandered out here to the hold—where she *doesn't belong*..." I glared at her and she glared back. "And the sensu-pods apparently grabbed her and dragged her into the tank."

"Where they nearly drowned me," she repeated stubbornly, crossing her arms over her chest again. "So be really careful around it. In fact, if I were you, I wouldn't even go near it."

"Oh, don't worry my dear—it won't hurt *me*." Doloroso gave an irritating, tittering laugh. "But I would be most eager to hear what happened during your little, ah, attack."

I felt a jolt of possessive rage surge through me and had to fight to keep my features calm.

"You know damn well what happens during sensitivity testing," I growled. "There's no need to ask her to rehash it for you."

"Ah—forgive me. I misspoke." The Count made an elaborate bow of apology in Zoe's direction. "What I meant to say was, I'd like to know the events that *preceded* the attack. The sensu-pods, you see, don't normally reach out of the tank and take a subject of their own volition."

"Well, this time they did," Zoe said, frowning. "One of them kissed me on the cheek—well, that was what it felt like anyway—my cut cheek, here..." She pointed to her wounded cheek again. "And then the next thing I knew, they were dragging me into their tank. Ugh!" She shivered.

"So first the chip-drill stabbed out at you and cut your cheek and then the sensu-pods tasted you and liked you so much they pulled you in?"

Doloroso's eyes were bright for some reason and I *really* didn't like the way he was looking at Zoe. There was a hungry, avid light in his shiny eyes that made my protective instincts kick into high gear.

Mine, an angry voice whispered inside my head. *He can't look at her like that – she's fucking* **mine.**

"Yes, I guess so. That's pretty much what happened." Zoe nodded.

"But my dear, do you have any idea how extraordinary that is? What a unique specimen you must be for both the drill and the sensu-pods to react as they did to you?"

He took a step towards her but I put myself between them. I was damned if I'd let him touch her again.

"Hey, Sarden! We were *talking,*" she protested, trying to get around me. I blocked her with one arm.

"Zoe, go to the food-prep area and make me that cakecheese concoction you made last night," I ordered her. "I'm hungry and I'll want to eat as soon as Count Doloroso and I conclude our business here."

"What?" She poked her head around my arm and glared up at me. "Did you just do the alien equivalent of telling me to get to the kitchen and make you a sandwich?"

"Whatever you call it, go make it," I growled. "*Please.*"

"Fine." Zoe stormed off—I could hear her little bare feet slapping against the metal floor as she went and knew she as angry.

But I couldn't stand to have Doloroso lusting over her. I didn't like the way he looked at her—not one fucking bit.

"But Master, I thought once this deal was concluded we were going to try and find a mechanic?"

It was Al again, this time in his shipboard form. I had to have a talk with him about interrupting. Lately he was showing up at the most inopportune time possible, damn it.

"Al—" I began but Doloroso interrupted.

"If you're looking for a mechanic who deals with unattached males, I'm afraid I have bad news for you—you won't find one on Gallana. Such services are strictly monitored by the Majorans and they refuse to deal with any male without a female. Luckily…" He smiled at Zoe's retreating back. "You have a *lovely* female to accompany you and make the deal for whatever repairs you need. *And* I happen to know of a fine and reputable shop who will give you an excellent discount if you mention my name."

I ground my teeth at the idea of taking Zoe into Gallana. In the spaceport proper and wearing traditional Majoran garb, she would stand out with her pale skin and vivid hair. Her beauty would shine like a star and I was afraid it would attract all the wrong kinds of attention.

Then again, I didn't know if I had a choice.

I sighed. She'd probably be thrilled to see the port and as long as I kept a good eye on her, no harm would come to her.

I'd see to that myself.

Zoe

Of course there was no way in hell I was staying put in my room. Especially after I heard strange voices down the long hallway. I'd meant to just creep quietly over and peep into the doorway to see who it was. But when I saw the tall man with blue hair bending over to pick up the stabby-stabby corkscrew, I had to say *something*. Strangely though, it didn't try anything with him. Maybe it was all stabbed out and I had been its last victim.

I hadn't loved the weird way the new guy—who I guessed was there to buy all the strange medical equipment, which looked more like torture devices—had looked at me. The way he kissed my hand and then licked his lips was kind of creepy too. But at least he was polite, damn it! Which was a hell of a lot more than I could say for Sarden, the big red jerk!

And here for a little while I'd actually begun to think he had some kind of feelings for me. I mean, after the way he was so patient and kind—the way he held me in the purple bathtub tank and soothed me when I started to panic because of my bad memories.

And don't forget the way he healed you, whispered a little voice in the back of my head. My brain tried to show me an image of the big alien kneeling before me, licking my nipples and then moving lower…what if Al hadn't come in at just that minute? I would have come for sure. Come all over his face, just like he wanted me to…

Stop it! I ordered myself sternly, pushing the naughty images out of my head. *He was probably just healing me because Tazaxx doesn't take damaged goods.*

Sarden wasn't a nice guy at all, I told myself. He was a big, sexist alien jerk who'd ordered me to go to the kitchen and make him a damn sandwich!

"Asshole," I muttered to myself as I stomped back to the food-prep area and slapped one of the sticky pads from the food-sim against my temple. "He wants a sandwich, let's make him one."

I tried to think of the worst combinations I could and since the food-sim was still messed up, it didn't take much work on my part. I had managed to make a crème brulee with the flavor of pepperoni pizza, a plate of spaghetti and meatballs that tasted like pistachio ice cream, and a ham sandwich which tasted like a nasty-ass batch of oatmeal raisin cookies — (I *hate* raisins) — when Sarden finally came sauntering in.

"Zoe?" he said cautiously, approaching me as though I might bite. Well I *felt* like biting, damn it! But I plastered a smile on my face and turned to face him instead.

"Hello dear, you're just in time for supper. Here's that sandwich you ordered," I said sweetly, handing him the plate with the ham sandwich on it.

"Hmmm." He took it, sniffed it, and took a wary bite.

To my disappointment, he didn't immediately spit it on the floor and wash his mouth out. Instead, he chewed meditatively before taking another bite.

"It's good," he said, nodding. "Thank you. I was afraid you'd try to make something disgusting because you were mad at me."

"It *is* disgusting," I said, completely exasperated. Honestly, couldn't the man tell when he'd been fed a sandwich that was all kinds of nasty? "And I *am* mad at you! There was no need for you to be so rude to me in front of your friend."

"Count Doloroso is *not* my friend," he growled, putting the sandwich down. "He was a business deal and that's all."

"Well why did you send me to the kitchen then?" I flared. "Were you afraid I was going to mess up your deal by warning him that the stuff he was buying could put his eye out or drown him or both? I mean, *caveat emptor* and all that but you have to at least *warn* someone when you're selling them something that could kill or maim them."

"Doloroso knows exactly how dangerous the Assimilation equipment is — he collects it," he said, frowning. "So your oh-so-generous warning was of no consequence to him."

"Then why did you kick me out if you weren't afraid I'd mess up the deal?" I demanded.

Sarden's face grew dark. "Because I didn't like the way he was looking at you, all right? You look too damn tempting running around like that." He made a gesture which took in my appearance.

"What? But I'm just wearing your shirt," I protested. "What's so special about that?"

"It's not the shirt that's special," he said, sounding exasperated. "It's *you* Zoe. You're fucking gorgeous — didn't you see the way he was looking at you?"

It's hard to stay mad at someone who thinks you're so fabulously beautiful they picked you over a Victoria's Secret model to kidnap. But then I reminded myself *why* Sarden had picked me — to trade me to some scummy alien on the other side of the galaxy — and I managed to stay mad anyway.

"The way he was *looking* at me? Are you hearing yourself?" I asked. "You sound just like my friend Leah's jealous, controlling fiancée. He doesn't even want her going to the grocery store to buy milk alone because he's afraid other men will look at her."

"Well if she's as beautiful as you, I don't blame him for being wary of other males," Sarden said, frowning.

"You're missing the point," I glared at him.

"And the point is?" He raised an eyebrow.

"The point is, I'm a person, not a possession," I said, thoroughly exasperated now. "You don't *own* me, you know."

"As a matter of fact, I do," he pointed out, taking another bite of the nasty oatmeal raisin-tasting ham sandwich. "I bought you, remember?"

"Alien asshole," I muttered. "Fine. You own me. But that doesn't mean I'll do everything you say like a good little puppet. I'm still a person with feelings and thoughts of my own."

I turned back to the food-sim, preparing to make something even worse for him to eat. I wondered if I could get it to make me a chocolate pudding that tasted like dog crap or something horrible like that. Maybe a cupcake that tasted like earthworms? Or apple strudel that tasted like mashed up spiders. Then again, he'd probably eat it all and ask for more. He *had* liked the pie that tasted like sauerkraut…

"Since you have all these feelings, how would you *feel* about going out to see the spaceport this afternoon?" Sarden asked quietly.

His words caught me completely by surprise. I turned back to him slowly, peeling the sticky thought pad from my temple.

"Are you serious?"

"Completely." He took another bite of sandwich, finishing it off. "You get to come with me and see the spaceport. He frowned and pointed a finger at me. "But *only* if you promise to stay at my side at *all times.*"

"What? You afraid I'm going to try and escape so I can hitch a ride home?" I said carelessly. It was, of course, exactly what I planned to do.

"Zoe, listen to me." He took me by the shoulders and looked into my eyes. "I'm telling you to stay by me because it isn't safe for you to wander off alone. And because anyone you asked to take you back to Earth would probably be happy to agree and take you aboard their ship."

"Then why shouldn't I ask?" I demanded.

"Because." His voice dropped and his eyes narrowed. "Once they had you aboard, they could do anything to you — anything at all. And I wouldn't be there to stop them." He shook his head, his eyes serious. "I...I couldn't stand that."

"Right," I said. "I'm supposed to believe you care about me? When you've told me over and over you're determined to trade me away?"

"That's different," he growled. "I *do* care about you, Gods damn it, although I don't know why, exactly. And the male I'm trading you to won't molest or harm you. He won't chop you up into bite sized pieces for cloning, either."

"What?" My stomach did a weird little flip and I was glad I hadn't eaten too much of the mixed up food. "What are you talking about?"

"You're beautiful and unique and Gallana has a black market for clones second only to Tiberium 3," he said. "When I told you they could do anything they wanted, did you think I only meant whoever took you could rape you? Believe me, it can be much, *much* worse."

His words made my stomach do that weird flip again and I took a step back.

"If it's that dangerous, why are you letting me go at all?"

"Because, well..." He ground his teeth, looking irritated. "Because I need you to get the hydrogen scoop's panel fixed," he admitted at last.

"What? Why would you need *me* to get your ship fixed?"

He took a deep breath. "Remember I told you that the Majorans are in ascendancy and their Empress rules the galaxy?"

"Yeah. So?" The idea of the galaxy having an Empress was still weird to me but so many strange things had happened in my life in the past forty-eight hours, it didn't seem quite so shocking anymore.

"So…" He ran a hand through his hair. "So the Majorans are a matrilineal society and Gallana is a strictly Majoran port."

"Oh…" I was beginning to get it. "So it's all about girl power, huh? Females rule the roost and the men are at their beck and call?"

"Not *exactly*. It isn't as if the females own the males as slaves – nothing that extreme. It's that Majoran males worship their females as goddesses."

"Wow!" I was beginning to like the idea of Majoran society – *a lot*. "That sounds pretty extreme to me," I told Sarden. "They really worship their wives?"

He nodded. "They believe in each female resides a small bit of divinity from the Goddess of Mercy and so they treat them like goddesses and refuse to do business without them. Also, they refuse to do business with a male who does not have his own personal goddess with him."

"Your own personal goddess," I mused. It sounded like a song from the 80s. I put a hand on my hip and looked up at him. "And why should I agree to act as your goddess? What's in it for me? I mean, you get that panel fixed and then it's off to Giedi Prime to trade me to that Tazaxx guy. Why should I help you?"

"Because it's not just for me I'm doing this." He ran both hands through his hair this time. "I'm doing it for my little sister. She's been sold to Tazaxx and I have a limited time to get her back. That's why I bought you – to trade for her."

"What?" Sold by who? How?" I was intensely interested and couldn't quite hide it. I had been able to tell by his reaction to me touching his crystal picture cube how important his sister was to him. But to hear that all this was about her, that he hadn't just kidnapped me to sell or trade for profit, put a whole new perspective on things.

"I don't like to talk about it," Sarden growled.

I raised an eyebrow at him. "Well that's too bad. You'd *better* talk if you need my help. And begin at the beginning."

"All right—I'll tell you. *Briefly.*" He sighed. "You know that I am a half-breed—both Vorn and Eloim. My mother was the daughter of the Rae and Ria of Eloim—the rulers of the planet. She was kidnapped by a high ranking Vorn and taken back to Vorn 6. There she became pregnant with me. Then her parents—my grandparents, the Rae and Ria—paid her ransom and she was returned to Vorn."

"Wow." I nodded. "Okay. Go on."

He started pacing the kitchen. "In due time, I was born. My mother hid her pregnancy until it was too late to abort me although that was what my grandfather, the Rae, wanted when he finally found out. But she wouldn't allow it, even though I was a half-breed and a product of rape she..." He shook his head. "She was always protective of me."

"Oh, Sarden..." I whispered but he shook his head and continued, his face stony.

"My grandparents married my mother to a respectable Eloim male for a considerable sum of credit so that he would overlook the fact that she was 'used goods.' About seven cycles later, my sister, Sellah was born and my mother died shortly after from complications of childbirth."

"I'm sorry," I said softly. "I lost my mom too. I know how awful it is."

He shook his head, his face dark. "It was a long time ago. I *do* remember the last time I saw her though—she was holding Sellah in her arms. She introduced me to my little sister and made me promise to always take care of her and protect her."

"Oh…" His words caused a stabbing pain in my heart. I had to sink down into a chair because my knees suddenly felt wobbly.

"You're the oldest one—the one in charge," I heard my mother's voice whisper in my memory. *"You have to look out for Angie. Sisters look after each other. The oldest looks after the youngest, remember that Zoe. Take care of your sister!"*

"It's a promise I was unable to keep." Sarden had his back to me so he couldn't see my reaction—I was glad.

"How…what happened?" I asked, my voice coming out hoarse and whispery.

He sighed. "Normally the oldest male child of the Rae and Ria will grow up to become the Rae in his own right. His mate will be the Ria so that the planet is balanced. However, if he has no mate, he can choose a female relative to help him rule. Because I was a half-breed, I was…*discouraged* from claiming my birthright. And so the honor of being the next Rae fell to my cousin, Hurxx. He had no mate so he chose my little sister, Sellah as his Ria."

I remembered all the talk about her coronation on the crystal cube. So that was what it had been about. Sarden wasn't just some common smuggler—he was the rightful heir to a whole freaking planet. Or would have been if he hadn't been half Vorn. Also, his sister was a queen. Wow.

"So what happened? Was there some kind of political coup?"

"You could say that," he remarked grimly. "Not three solar

days after her coronation, Sellah was walking in the palace gardens when a band of pirates somehow got past security and took her." He ran his hands through his hair again in a distracted, anxious way. "I traced them for months—so afraid of what might be happening to her. Then finally I found out she was with a male I already know."

"Tazaxx?" I asked.

He nodded. "Tazaxx. He is a collector of rare and beautiful females which is why I bought you—there is no rarer female than one from a closed planet. Especially a *La-ti-zal* like yourself." He looked at me and there was desperation on his strong features. "You're so fucking gorgeous and unique, Zoe. I knew if I could get you to him in time, he wouldn't be able to resist a trade—you for Sellah." He lifted his hands, palm up. "And now you know why I need your help."

"Wow..." I didn't know what else to say.

"Of course," Sarden went on. "I realize that my troubles are my own. Why should you care about helping to save my sister? Especially when her freedom means your own imprisonment? But there *is* something else I can promise you, Zoe—"

"I'll do it," I said quietly.

"I can go back to Earth when this is over and buy the contracts on your two best friends," he went on. "That way no male searching for a mate can pick them from the AMI and take them away as I took you. It will guarantee their safety forever. It—"

"I said, I'll do it," I said, louder this time.

"It will—what?" Sarden looked at me uncertainly. "*What* did you say?"

"I said I'll do it. I'll help you." I looked up at him, letting him see the sincerity in my eyes.

"You will? But…why?" He shook his head, puzzled.

"Because family is important. And I know…" I cleared my throat. "I know about feeling responsible for them."

He bowed his head and looked down for a moment. When he looked back up, his golden eyes were suspiciously bright.

"Thank you," he said in a low, hoarse voice. "I…thank you."

"You *did* say that this Tazaxx guy just wants me to put me in some kind of display case?" I asked uneasily. "I assume I'll still be alive, right? Not stuffed like some taxidermied gator hung up on a poacher's wall?"

"You'll be alive and well, living in a place as close to your home as possible," he promised me. "He'll consult you about your home planet and build you a beautiful habitat which resembles it in every way."

"Huh. Like an exhibit at the zoo," I said, thinking of how zoo designers always tried to make the animals feel at home by crafting them a place as close to native environment as possible.

Sarden nodded. "Exactly."

I decided right then and there that I was going to have Tazaxx build me a private movie theater and see if he could catch the signal from Earth to get some chick flick and scifi movies imported. And also, a Godiva chocolate shop and maybe a Krispy Kreme as well. After all, if I was going to be an exhibit at a zoo with no dating scene to worry about, I might dump the 80-20 rule of eating and go something more like 60-40 or maybe even 70-30. What the hell, right?

"You'll be perfectly safe and secure and comfortable," Sarden promised again. "And I will keep my promise about your friends too — I'll buy their contracts so no other male can choose them from the Alien Mate Index."

"That's good—that's important to me," I said, nodding. "But how much danger to you think they're really in? Will the Commercians start importing five hundred thousand women a day or something? Because honestly, something like that is going to cause people to notice and wonder what in the hell is going on."

"No—they won't want to attract undue attention. Not at first, anyway," he said grimly. "But I'm afraid your friends will be at more risk than most because of their proximity to and relationship with you."

"What? But we're not related or anything. Even if I am this *Lata* thingy whatever it is you keep calling me, it's not like Leah or Charlotte could have inherited it or anything."

"I don't think you understand at all how the gifts of a *La-ti-zal* work at all," he remarked. "Or how they are formed. The Ancient Ones sowed seeds of greatness all over your planet, but only in certain females do they sprout and take root."

"Well, what causes them to do that?" I demanded.

"Sometimes a traumatic event in their past causes it," he said. "Sometimes it has to do with the proximity of another *La-ti-zal*. How much time did you spend with your friends?"

"All the time," I whispered. "Every weekend, practically. Plus we got together at least two or three times during the week. We...we were inseparable."

Thinking of Leah and Charlotte put a lump in my throat but I swallowed hard and tried not to think about never seeing them again. Could I really do this? Could I really give up any chance of going back to Earth? *"Take care of your sister,"* I heard my mother whisper and I knew that I would do it.

"And when you spent time with your friends, did you eat from the same utensils and drink from the same vessels?" he wanted to know.

"Well, I mean sure," I said thinking of all the times we'd split dessert to avoid scarfing down too many calories. "So…you're saying they could have caught this, uh, specialness from me?"

"They may or they may not have. But the Commercians have them in their sights now," he said seriously. "And they're probably already refining their process so they can pick out latent *La-ti-zals* and sell them at a higher price."

"All right," I said, lifting my chin. "I'll do it. If it will help you get your sister back and keep my friends safe from what I'm going through right now, it's worth it."

"I'm sorry," Sarden said in a low, rough voice and looked away.

I couldn't exactly say "it's all right." Because it wasn't—no matter how good and noble the reasons were, I was going to be sold into a kind of slavery. A nice, cushy slavery if what Sarden was saying was true, but slavery nonetheless. And I would never see Earth again. Would never see Leah or Charlotte or…

Okay, if I let myself keep thinking this way, I was seriously going to bawl. I squared my shoulders and took a deep breath. If I was going to spend the rest of my life behind glass being a zoo exhibit, I'd better have as much fun as I could before we got to Giedi Prime. And that meant exploring the spaceport—well, as much as Sarden would allow me to.

"Hadn't we better get going?" I asked him. "I mean, if we're going to find a mechanic before it gets too late?"

"Yes." He straightened up and nodded. "But first you have to get dressed. What you're wearing now won't do for Gallana, unfortunately."

I opened my eyes wide, as though shocked.

"Really? Walking around in a man's shirt ten times too big for me with no panties or bra underneath isn't considered Goddess couture? *Imagine* that."

He made a face. "Your humor knows no bounds, Zoe. Just go to your room and I'll have Al synthesize you something that's more in keeping with Majoran fashion."

"Wait—you said he can *synthesize* clothes? The same way you make food in the food-sim?" I asked, frowning.

Sarden nodded. "Of course."

"Well in *that* case, how come you didn't give me something else to wear before now?" I demanded. "Why in the world do you have me running around the damn ship in your shirts with no underwear?"

His eyes suddenly went half-lidded. "Maybe because I like you that way. You look good in my clothes…and nothing else."

His voice was a soft growl I swore I could feel right through my entire body, even though we weren't touching.

My heart did a little jump and started to pound. I could feel my cheeks getting hot at the way he was looking at me.

"Big red pervert," I muttered.

"Perhaps." He gave me a lazy grin. "Don't worry, Zoe—you'll have some new clothes soon. Just wait in your room and I'll bring them shortly."

"Fine," I said, turning to leave and hoping my blush wasn't too evident. "But before you go, try the pizza-flavored crème brulee—you'll probably like it."

Then I left, trying not to feel his eyes on my backside as I walked away.

Aliens can be *so* annoying.

Chapter Fourteen

Zoe

"Okay, I am *so* not going out in public like this." I surveyed myself in the 3-D mirror-like thing Sarden had called out of the wall somehow, the same way he'd accessed the closet. How did he do that anyway? It seemed to be a series of taps but when I had tried it, nothing happened. Maybe it was just keyed to his fingerprints?

I didn't know and at the moment, I didn't care. I was more concerned with the weird M*ajor*an outfit Sarden had gotten Al to make for me.

It was see-through.

I'm not kidding, either or saying that it was really sheer fabric—I'm talking *totally transparent.* As in, I might as well have been wrapped in Saran Wrap—which actually was kind of what it felt like. The dress—(if it could be called a dress)—really was just one long strip of fabric which was wrapped around me and somehow adhered to itself like it was Velcro. But there was no Velcro scratchiness—the fabric was as soft as silk. In fact, I rather enjoyed the sensation of it against my skin—although I would have enjoyed it a Hell of a lot more if it actually covered anything.

"What's wrong with it?" Sarden asked, frowning. "You look gorgeous."

"I look *naked,*" I pointed out.

"Not true. The modesty patches cover your most private areas."

"Barely," I said.

In fact, the three black dots he'd given me to paste over my nipples and crotch reminded me of the stick-on stringless bikini I'd seen once while looking for a new bathing suit on the Internet. *Almost no coverage! Our most daring suit! Turn heads everywhere you go!* screamed the site that was selling it. At the time, I had assumed that only porn stars would want to buy and wear such a thing. I had certainly never imagined putting my own size sixteen ass into one.

And yet here I was—looking like a plus sized porn star wrapped in cling film. The shoes that went with it didn't help either—they were platforms with three inch heels, more like stilts than shoes. I totally looked like I should be pole dancing to dirty, sexy music somewhere.

I sighed and looked at myself again. What is it they say about when life hands you lemons? No wait—a lemon would cover more than this freaking outfit. I *wished* someone would hand me a good sized lemon right about now. I'd put it to good use, damn it!

"You can't seriously expect me to believe that the women of Gallana go around dressed like this," I said, looking at myself again. The only good thing I could say for the Saran Wrap dress was that it had good support. My boobs had never looked perkier—or more exposed.

"Actually, you'll be dressed more conservatively than most. Only virgins wear modesty patches," he said, pointing to the three black dots again.

"Well I'm not a virgin," I said tartly. "But I'm not a freaking exhibitionist either!"

"I promise you, you're dressed like every other female on Gallana," he said patiently. "They believe in showing off their divine beauty."

"Because they're all like some kind of manifestation of the Goddess of Mercy, right?" I said.

"Well, one of her aspects, anyway. Most of the galaxy worships the one Goddess. She created the Ancient Ones and commanded them to sow the seeds of life throughout the galaxy," Sarden said, reaching out to adjust the part of the dress that went around my shoulders. "But to the Majorans the Goddess wears many faces. The Virgin, the Whore, the Lover, the Healer, the Comforter…and too many more to name." He sighed. "It's a complicated religion but then, Majorans are fucking complicated by nature."

I raised an eyebrow at him. "The whole idea of worshiping a woman pisses you off, doesn't it? Careful, Sarden—your misogyny is showing."

"I'm no Sahjist," he said, with surprising vehemence. "So don't insult me. But I believe that males and females are equals—neither one needs to worship the other."

"You'd better put a pin in that attitude if you want to get this deal done," I pointed out. "What am I supposed to do, anyway?"

"So you'll go?" he asked, sounding surprised. "You're done complaining?"

"Oh, I'm not done complaining—not by a long shot," I said dryly. "By making me wear this dress, you just gave me a free pass to complain as much as I want. But yes, I guess we'd better go. Just tell me what to do."

"Simple—when we get to the mechanic, just treat me the same way you see every other female treating their male. That should do the trick." Sarden said, though he didn't sound very happy about it.

He held out an arm to me and I looked at it, surprised at the courtly gesture. Apparently the male escorting a female on his arm wasn't just an Earth custom.

"Well?" he asked. "Are you ready to go?"

I took a deep breath and smoothed down my transparent dress. My women's study professor back at USF would either be extremely proud or totally horrified by this outfit. I decided to go with proud—I wasn't objectifying myself or letting anyone else objectify me, I told myself. I was owning my curves and revealing my inner beauty—projecting positive body image all over the damn place.

I hoped.

I took Sarden's arm and looked up at him.

"Let's go get 'em tiger," I told him. "Go big or go home."

Or in this case, go naked but I was trying really hard not to think about that.

Sarden

I couldn't help feeling both proud and possessive as I squired Zoe into the spaceport proper through the entrance designated only for males accompanied by their females. Or goddesses, if you believed the way the Majorans did. I didn't but I had to admit, my little Earth female was looking particularly divine in the Majoran garb. Her beautiful curves and lovely freckled skin were fully exposed in the thin, silky dress and her wild, curly auburn hair floated around her shoulders like a burning corona.

Gods, she was fucking gorgeous. The whole world was more vivid now that she was mine. And she *was* still mine—at least for a little while longer. I wouldn't have to give her up to Tazaxx until we reached Giedi Prime. I pushed away the emotions that tried to rise at that thought and concentrated on the business at hand.

I had left Al back with the ship to get the Scoop ready for

repairs. I missed having him at my back but I wanted everything in readiness as soon as I lined up a mechanic. I just hoped the one Doloroso had recommended was good.

The entrance to the spaceport was a big place—a high dome with duty-free shops and merchants of all kinds lining its wall. It was packed with people from every known species in the galaxy going here and there. Yet even in that busy crowd, Zoe stood out as I had known she would.

All around us, I saw the other Majoran females catching glimpses of the little Pure One and talking among themselves, buzzing like a hive of Rigelian bees. Some of them even changed their skin color to match hers on the spot, though none of them managed to copy her charming pattern of her freckles with any kind of accuracy.

Zoe caught sight of what they were doing and gasped. She looked up at me and jerked her head at a Majoran female with the traditional long, blue hair who had just turned from deep lavender to Zoe's own creamy pale shade.

"How did she do that?" she asked, under her breath. "How are *any* of them doing that?"

"Majorans are chromatacromes," I explained. "Able to change their skin color at will. Some can also change hair and eye color but that's much more challenging."

"So they just go all day changing all the time? Like chameleons blending in with their environment?" she wanted to know.

I barked a short laugh.

"Hardly. If anything, the Majoran females want to stand out. That's why they're copying you—see?" I nodded at a female who must have been especially skilled in the ways of her people. She had managed to copy not only Zoe's skin color, but also the warm, changeable ruby-auburn of her hair and the blue of her eyes.

"Hey! That's creepy," Zoe protested, moving closer to me uneasily.

"No, it's a compliment," I corrected her. "They recognize your beauty. I knew they would."

"Well…thanks, Sarden." Her skin grew pink and I realized she was blushing, as she did so often when she was embarrassed. It struck me again that she didn't understand how lovely she was, though it was hard to comprehend how she couldn't. She was the most stunning female I had ever seen. It amazed me that she couldn't see her own beauty.

"*Ambergeis* for sale here. Buy your goddess that which compliments her beauty," a voice shouted, almost in my ear.

"Ooo, what's that?" Zoe slowed to stare at what the merchant—a swarthy Fenigan with a mustache above his first mouth and a beard below his second—was selling.

"*Ambergeis*, lovely goddess," the Fenigan merchant said, holding out a small silver pot with a yellowish paste inside. "Made from the purified nectar of the *ish'tha* flower."

"What does it do?" Zoe wanted to know.

"Ah, it is truly *wondrous*," the merchant said, both mouths speaking as one. "You put just a tiny dab behind each ear and a dab on your wrists and soon your scent is irresistible."

"Is it some kind of perfume, then?" she asked.

"It enhances your own natural scent," a new voice answered her.

It was one of the Majoran females who had copied Zoe's skin color, though at least her hair was still blue. Behind her was a Majoran male. His skin was a warm, neutral brownish-tan at the moment, though I knew that could change according to mood or whim…not his, of course. Though the female's skin color would be dictated by what she thought fashionable, the male's color would be dependant on the mood of his female. At the moment the soft, neutral color was an indication that she must be feeling well.

"How does the, uh, *Ambergeis* enhance your scent?" Zoe asked, turning to her.

"By bringing out your natural musk, my goddess," the merchant assured her.

"Your musk?" Zoe wrinkled her pert nose. "Um, sorry but I don't want to smell *musky*."

"He doesn't mean it will make your skin smell unpleasant, only that it will intensify the natural scent of your skin," the Majoran female explained.

"Yes, for it takes on the scent of your skin and *magnifies* it." The merchant nodded. "It can also be put on articles of clothing if you wish. In this way if you have to leave your mate for a time, he is able to keep a little of your scent to comfort him during the loss of his goddess."

"Leave my mate? Goddess of Love prevent it!" The Majoran female sounded shocked and her male, who had been silently watching, came forward to comfort her. His skin was as blue as his hair now—the color of sadness, which she was obviously feeling at the idea of the two of them being parted.

"Come, *Leelah*," he murmured softly. "Don't fret. You know I'll not leave you."

He put an arm around her shoulders and she leaned against him, obviously drawing strength from his embrace. For a moment I wondered what it would be like to have Zoe trust me enough to lean on me that way, to seek me out when she needed to be held and touched — then I pushed the idea away.

"I did not mean that you would leave him *forever*," the Fenigan merchant said smoothly. "Perish the thought! But any absence, no matter how brief, may be traumatic. Think how he must feel when you go to spend time with your friends and he is left without you. The scent of your skin on a scarf or other such object would comfort him greatly."

"Sheesh," Zoe muttered to me. "He's acting like her guy is some kind of sick puppy who can't stand to be without her for an hour or two while she has a girl's night out. That's ridiculous."

"Not at all," the Ma*jor*an female, who had unfortunately overheard, gave Zoe a very cool look. Her skin remained pale and creamy, like Zoe's, but her mate's skin suddenly went a deep maroon indicating anger and offense.

"Oh, uh…" Zoe seemed taken aback. "I…I didn't mean…"

"Prether is *very* attached to me, aren't you my darling?" she asked, looking up at the tall male beside her.

"I would rather die than live without you, my goddess," he rumbled and there was a sincerity in his eyes that told me he truly felt that way.

"Oh, Prether…" The female entwined her arms around his neck and began to run her hands through his hair. "You're so sweet."

"And you are the star which sheds light into my otherwise dark life," he murmured, drawing her closer. His skin had turned from maroon to a deep violet now, indicating passion, I guessed.

They were eye-to-eye, running their hands all over each other and I thought they might start mating right there. However, the Fenigan merchant wasn't about to let love-making get in the way of his spiel.

"As you are so attached to your goddess, good Sir," he said, addressing the male. "I would think you would want her scent with you at all times."

The couple ignored him, however. They were far too wrapped up in each other with the male murmuring, "Oh *Leelah,* my goddess, how I long to worship you," into his female's hair as she writhed against his caressing hands.

"Sheesh, get a room" Zoe muttered, but in a softer voice this time. She turned to the merchant. "So this *Ambergeis* stuff...it just smells like whoever wears it only more so?"

"Exactly." Seeing that he had lost the Majorans completely, he leaned forward eagerly, offering the little silver pot to Zoe. "Try some, my goddess."

Shrugging, Zoe leaned forward and reached for the pot with one finger.

"Oh, no-no-no!" Both the Fenigen's mouths turned down at once giving him a double frown. "Forgive me but I must give you the trial with a neutral object. The moment you touch the pot with your fingers, it will smell only like you and it will be useless as a sample thereafter. Now, here..." He dug in the folds of his voluminous purple robe and came out with a long green *yillo* reed. Delicately, he dipped just the tip into the pot of *Ambergeis* and put a tiny amount on Zoe's outstretched forefinger.

"Thanks, I guess." She pulled her finger back, looking at the little dab of yellow paste as though she didn't know quite what to do with it.

"Dab at your pulse points—go on." The merchant nodded eagerly.

Zoe looked at me and I nodded.

"It should be safe," I told her.

"Okay." Shrugging, she dabbed the *Ambergeis* on one wrist and then rubbed it against the other, rubbing the tiny amount of yellow paste into her skin. Then she looked at the merchant. "Now what?"

"Now let your male scent you, my goddess." His purple eyes gleamed. "Let him decide for himself if he likes the change."

"All right." Zoe looked up at me, her blue eyes filled with mischief. "Would you like to scent your *goddess,* my darling?" she asked in a breathy imitation of the Majoran female, who by now was lost in the crowd with her male.

I wasn't about to play along with her act—not until I had to at the mechanic Count Doloroso had recommended, anyway. But I took her arm and brought her wrist to my nose, inhaling deeply.

Immediately her rich, feminine smell filled my senses, making me almost dizzy with desire. Her personal aroma had a sweet note deepening into a luscious feminine musk that made me think of the delicious scent of her sex. I'd only been between her legs for a few moments but already I longed to go back, to taste more of her nectar, to hear her moan my name as she pulled my hair and caressed my horns while I tasted her sweet sex…

"Gods," I muttered hoarsely and Zoe looked at me, clearly concerned.

"Does it not smell good? Should I wash it off?"

"Possibly," I growled. "But not because it doesn't smell good." I couldn't help remembering the Majoran male telling his female that he longed to worship her. I felt the same way about Zoe—I wanted to drop to my knees and worship her pussy with my tongue.

No—get hold of yourself. You've got business to conduct.

With an effort of will, I released Zoe's arm and took a half step back. There. Better.

All this time the Fenigen merchant had been watching me

sharply.

"It is intoxicating, is it not?" he asked, smiling with both mouths. "There is nothing more bewitching as the scent of the female you love. And remember, once she touches the *Ambergeis* in the pot, it will take on her scent. Then you can keep it with you for always."

I thought of the long days ahead after I made the trade with Tazaxx and Zoe was gone from my life forever. I thought of never seeing her again and a fierce ache started in my heart.

"How much?" I heard myself asking.

"A thousand credits," the merchant said promptly.

"That…seems like a lot," Zoe objected. "Unless credits are like pesos or something. But if they're on par with dollars or pounds or Euros then that's *way* too much for a little pot of perfume." She sniffed her wrist. "It really doesn't smell like much of anything at all."

"I'll take it," I told the merchant. After the price I'd gotten for the Assimilation equipment, I could afford it. And I wanted it. Wanted a way to keep her scent…the memory of her, even after she was gone.

"But, Sarden," she protested. I ignored her and waved the temp chip card I'd be using for all transactions on Gallana. It was untraceable and theft proof.

"Very nice doing business with you, good Sir." The merchant nodded agreeably and handed me a little silver pot filled with the yellow paste. "Have your lovely goddess put another dab behind her ears for extra added effect."

I nodded back and took the pot, then pulled Zoe along by the hand before she could protest any further.

Zoe

"Hey!" I protested, digging in my heels to try and stop our forward progress. "Hey, why did you do that?"

"What?" Sarden looked down, stopping at last along one wall of the huge area. The spaceport reminded me a little of a cross between a crowded stadium and an airport. The center was filled with people and creatures—because they weren't all humanoid—hurrying this way and that, probably to catch a flight or get to meetings in the spaceport. But the outer edges were filled with shops and had a colorful outdoor bazaar kind of feel to it—a little like a high end flea market, if there is such a thing.

Merchants everywhere were selling things from exotic looking fruit that looked like pink bananas, to elaborate orange pastries that made my mouth water, to square brown cubes (I assumed they were candy or some kind of supplement because the merchant kept chanting "sweet—delicious—gooey—nutritious," over and over), to tiny, chittering creatures that looked like green and purple monkeys only as big as my finger. There were also long, furry scarves in every color of the rainbow, tiny silver disks that flew on their own and rained colored mist over their owner, and so many other things, my head was spinning. Not to mention perfumes like the kind Sarden had just bought.

Speaking of which, *why* had he bought it? Was it a welcome home present for his little sister when he got her back? But it didn't seem like something you'd give a sister or relative—more like a gift for a lover.

"What's wrong?" he asked me again. "We need to get to the mechanic."

"But...but why did you buy that stuff? It's so expensive!" I protested.

He frowned. "How I spend my credit is my own business. But to answer your question, I bought it to…to…" He cleared his throat. "To help our act. It's definitely a present a male who worships his female as the Majorans do would buy."

"That's a pretty expensive prop, Sarden," I pointed out. "You could have just bought me one of the little green and purple monkeys. Those guys are *adorable.*"

We were standing next to the monkey vendor as we spoke and I leaned forward to point at an especially cute pair of monkeys. They had their tails entwined and were sitting up in their cage and chattering in high, squeaky voices.

"Buy you a *nib-nib?* I don't think so," he said shortly.

"I'm just saying if you can afford the alien equivalent of Channel number 5 you can certainly buy your 'goddess' a monkey," I grumbled. "At least it would be more entertaining than a boring pot of perfume that doesn't smell like much at all."

"It doesn't yet…but it will. Here—put a dab of it behind your ears, like the merchant said."

He held out the tiny pot of *Ambergeis* to me—it really was only about the size of a large coin—but I drew back.

"What? But…if I touch it, the whole pot will be contaminated with my scent. Wouldn't you rather find something, uh, neutral for me to put it on with?"

"No," he said simply. "Go on, Zoe—touch it."

"Well, if you're sure…" I wasn't sure where we were going with this but I dabbed my finger in the thousand dollar—excuse me, thousand *credit*—paste and put just a little dab behind both ears. Then I sniffed my fingers. Honestly, I didn't smell a thing. I looked up at Sarden. "Um, I really think we should go back and ask for a refund. I'm telling you, this stuff doesn't smell like anything at all."

"Not true." He put the little pot to his nose and sniffed deeply. His golden eyes went suddenly half-lidded and he started giving me that look again—the hungry look that made my insides feel like Jell-O. "It smells like *you*, Zoe," he rumbled. Then he closed the tiny silver pot and tucked it carefully into a pocket of the black vest he was wearing before taking my hand again. "Come on—there are only two hours left in the light cycle. We need to get moving—don't want to be caught in Gallana when it goes dark."

I still had no idea why he'd really bought the alien perfume but it didn't look like he was going to tell me. I followed him out of the crowded area until we reached three vast exit arches with alien markings floating above them in light up holographic lettering.

Sarden took us through the middle arch and then we were out of the airport terminal/flea market part of the port which he told me was the docking area, and onto a paved road. The road was lined by tall, skinny houses built right up against each other. They reminded me a little of pictures I'd seen of Amsterdam, with one big difference—the colors. The narrow, squished-together buildings were painted in jewel tones—deep blues and greens and purples with the occasional splash of ruby red and burnt umber thrown it for good measure.

It was really pretty in an Instagram over-filtered kind of way.

There were moving sidewalks on either side of the road and Majoran women and their husbands, or mates to use Sarden's word, were riding them and speaking in low, intimate voices. The women were dressed like I was, just as he had promised, so at least I didn't feel out of place. But even though I blended in with the crowd—at least fashion-wise—I still felt pretty naked, though I tried not to think about it.

I think what surprised me the most was the sky overhead—it was pink. But also, it was a *sky* with puffy white clouds and everything.

"Hey," I said to Sarden, pointing up. "I thought we were in some kind of enclosed building or area like the International Space Station. So how is there a sky? Come to think of it—how is there even gravity?"

"The spin and rotation of the spaceport provides artificial gravity, of course," he said as though it was obvious. "They have no need for gravity generators like I have aboard my ship."

"Yeah, but what about the sky? The clouds and everything?"

"A projection," he told me. "The actual ceiling is bare metal and only fifteen *flarns* above our heads. But the sky is more aesthetically pleasing and since Ma*jor*ans are all about aesthetics, they went to the trouble of making the illusion."

I had no idea what a *flarn* was but the idea that the very real-looking sky above us was completely fake kind of caught me off guard.

"Wow," I said. "Okay. So what now?"

"Let's see..." Sarden consulted his ring, which made a green, holographic map appear in front of us. "Looks like we have a ways to go. We'd better ride," he remarked. Putting his hand to the small of my back, he guided me to the entryway of one of the moving sidewalks.

There was a Ma*jor*an couple ahead of us and I watched them carefully to see how they acted. Just like the couple at the perfume seller, these two were obviously deeply in love. The male held his mate's hand and helped her carefully onto the sidewalk, then jumped on behind her, making certain to stand so that his chest was directly against her back. She leaned trustingly against him and he stroked her hair gently as they glided off on the moving walkway.

The little scene of silent gallantry and love was sweet, if a bit mushy—and it wasn't unique, either. All around us I saw Majoran males treating their females with gentleness and deference, as though they were precious treasures to be guarded and cared for. Clearly they really did worship them as goddesses.

It was nice and certainly not what I was used to. I thought back on my time with my ex, Scott. He'd never held open doors or pulled out chairs for me, which I didn't really mind, because it was kind of old fashioned. But he'd also never gone out of his way to hold my hand if we were walking together. Mostly he was too busy looking at his phone to bother. I didn't see any constant use of hand-held devices here in Gallana—just lovers looking at each other longingly and whispering intimately as though they couldn't wait to get home and get busy.

The Majorans were tall people—with most of the males being almost as tall as Sarden—and good looking too. Except for the way they changed colors all the time, it was kind of like being in the middle of a romance novel come to life. I glanced at Sarden to see if he was going to treat me the same way, or just wait until we got to the mechanic to put on a show.

He gave me a slight, sardonic smile, almost as though he knew what I was thinking. As we got to the walkway, he held out his hand.

"Allow me to help you aboard, my goddess," he murmured.

"Why, thank you." I took his hand and he helped me onto the walkway. Then he stepped up beside me and pulled me back against him. "Hey!" I protested a bit breathlessly.

"It's all right," he murmured into my ear. "Just making sure you feel safe and protected, my goddess."

He braced his feet on either side of the walkway to keep us steady—which was good because it was moving way faster than would have been considered safe on Earth—and we watched together as the tall, skinny, jewel-toned houses and buildings rushed past.

We went through a business district, a colorful marketplace, and an expensive looking residential area before Sarden consulted his ring again and decided it was time to exit.

"Time to go—come on," he said, pointing to a curving exit ramp.

"All right." I got ready to jump although the stilt-like stripper shoes I was wearing were going to make it a risky proposition at best. Still, never let it be said that Zoe McKinley isn't up for a challenge.

Sarden, however, didn't seem to think I was. He took a look at my shoes and the awkward way I was standing in them and then scooped me up in his arms with no warning.

"Hey!" I exclaimed.

"Can't let you exit the walkway like that—you'll break your neck," he said gruffly.

"I'll be fine," I protested. "I'm short so I'm used to wearing high heels. I mean, not *stripper* heels like these, but the concept is the same."

But Sarden was already hopping off the speeding walkway as casually as though he was simply stepping off a street corner. Even holding me, he managed it with grace and ease and we found ourselves in an area that looked kind of like a warehouse district. The buildings here were wide and squat and painted a dull, brownish-gray that contrasted sharply with the colorful houses and shops we'd passed in the other districts.

"Okay," I said once we were clear of the walkway. "You can, uh, put me down now."

He looked around, frowned, and shook his head.

"I don't think so. I don't like the look of this area."

"Well this is where Count Doloroso sent us. I thought it was supposed to be safe."

"I did too. He said they were reputable." He sighed. "We're not far from the mechanic he recommended so we'll at least have a look. But I want you close to me. Very close."

"But…but I can be close and still *walk*," I protested. "You don't have to carry me around like a baby or a damsel in distress." Which made me remember how he'd carried me into the purple bathtub and held me so tenderly while he got the slime of the awful tentacle tank out of my hair. But I pushed the thought away hurriedly — there was no need to bring it up now, especially when we were so embarrassingly close and I was next to naked in the Majoran dress.

"Look at the road." He nodded to the pitted, rutted pavement beneath his feet. It *was* a lot rougher here and there were plenty of potholes that looked like a twisted ankle waiting to happen. "A Majoran male would carry his female in this area, I'm sure of it."

"It's not as nice as the road by the docking area," I acknowledged. "But I could still manage."

"Why should you when I prefer to carry you?" He raised an eyebrow at me.

"You'll throw your back out," I warned him, trying again. "I'm not exactly a hundred pound Hollywood starlet you can tote around all day like it's no big deal."

"Are you saying I'm not strong enough to carry you? I did before, you know." He frowned and began walking as we talked, which kind of made the conversation moot, but I'm no quitter.

"No, you're obviously plenty strong. And I know you carried me, uh, before." I blushed, remembering the slime tank incident again. "But that was just the length of your ship. I'm just saying I'm not exactly skinny enough to—"

"Oh, this is about your planet's strange ideas about stick-thin females being more attractive, isn't it?" He raised an eyebrow at me.

"Well, I guess sort of…in a way," I admitted.

"Such a strange concept." He shook his head. "I picked you from the Alien Mate Index *because* of your curves—not despite them. Remember that, sweetheart."

"All right," I said, feeling like the conversation had somehow gotten off topic but unsure how to get it back.

Sarden must have seen my uncertainty because he gave me one of his rare smiles.

"Just relax, Zoe—I've got you."

"Fine," I said a bit stiffly. I wished I could do as he said and completely relax—wished I could pillow my head on his broad chest and just watch the scenery go by. Maybe I would have been able to—if I hadn't known that my ultimate fate was to be traded away. But as it was, I was afraid to relax against him, afraid to let myself enjoy being carried so gently because I was frightened of what I might start to feel for the big Alien.

Just deal with it and don't get too close, I lectured myself as Sarden carried me past several deserted looking buildings. *It's going to be over soon and besides, he's only carrying you because that's what a Majoran male would do for his female. But in the end, Sarden's not going to treat you like a goddess—he's going to trade you in like a used car he doesn't want anymore. So there's no point getting all warm and fuzzy just because he insists on carrying you.*

The thoughts made me sad and a little bit angry. True, I'd

agreed to be traded and I stood by my decision. It was, after all, for a good cause. But giving up your freedom and any chance you have of ever going home—even for a good cause—is hard. You go through a grieving process for your old way of life—the life you're never going to have again. And isn't one of the steps in the grieving process getting extremely pissed off?

It's a step in *my* grieving process, anyway.

By the time we turned down a long, dark alleyway and finally found the entrance to the "extremely reputable" mechanic Count Doloroso had recommended, I was in something of a stew. I was feeling sad and homesick and also irritated with myself for being upset about something I couldn't change. I was upset with Sarden too, for kidnapping me in the first place. After all, if he hadn't picked me from that damn Alien Mate Index, I'd still be back at home bitching about my job and having girls' nights out with Charlotte and Leah.

God, I missed them!

"Here we are—finally," Sarden remarked, setting me down on my feet at last in front of a stained and pitted iron door with no sign of any kind that I could tell.

"What? How can you be sure?" I demanded, looking at the door and then at the area around us uneasily. The pinkish daylight didn't penetrate very far into the mouth of the alley we found ourselves in and there were shadows everywhere which made me distinctly nervous. It looked like a really good place to get mugged—if I hadn't been with a seven-foot tall alien, I might really have freaked out.

"The map says so," Sarden said, showing the map that projected out of his ring again briefly.

"I don't like it." I crossed my arms over my chest and shivered, still looking around.

"It's only for a moment," he assured me. "As soon as I can secure their services for tomorrow early, we'll leave and go back to the ship."

"Will you buy me a *nib-nib* monkey on the way back?" I asked hopefully. I was thinking that the little green and purple monkeys could keep me company once I was in my new habitat in Tazaxx's zoo. Having a pet around can make you feel a lot less lonely.

He sighed. "I *really* don't think you'd like them, Zoe."

"What are you talking about? I *love* animals," I protested. "I'd have like *seven* cats if my apartment complex would allow it. In fact, I fully intend to be a crazy cat lady when I get old."

He stared at me for a long moment, then shook his head.

"As usual, I don't understand your cultural references. Please just play your part well here and I promise I'll buy you *something* you want in the docking area."

"Like a *nib-nib,* right?" I persisted.

"You've got a one track mind, don't you? No, I won't promise a *nib-nib,*" he growled. "Now will you please come with me and act your part? We need to make this deal before the light cycle ends and it gets dark."

"Fine." I was pissed off but determined not to show it. "Lead the way."

"Thank you. I will go first but only to check for danger."

Sarden pushed open the metal door which gave with a rusty creaking sound and we entered a dimly lit room with a single counter against the far end and nothing else.

"Hello?" Sarden called. "Is anyone there?"

"Hello, good Sire and lovely lady-goddess." A man popped up

from behind the counter so quickly he looked like a jack-in-the-box suddenly released by its spring.

I gave a startled little scream and took a hop backwards, almost overbalancing in my stripper heels. Sarden grabbed me by the arm before I could hit the ground, however, and hauled me back upright.

"Be careful," he growled. "I don't need you breaking your neck on top of everything else."

Well, so much for gallantry.

"So sorry," I said icily. "I wouldn't want to *inconvenience* you by injuring myself in the ridiculous shoes *you* gave me to wear."

"Well, you—"

"Is there a problem, lady-goddess?" the man behind the counter asked, interrupting our argument before it could really gather steam. "Is this male mistreating you?"

I keep calling him a man but that was a really relative term here. I *assumed* he was a man but he wasn't like any man I'd ever seen before. He wasn't Majoran, that much was clear. His hair wasn't blue—it was green. Also his skin was orange and he wasn't very tall—not much taller than me. In fact, what he most reminded me of was an Oompa-Loompa from the old Willie Wonka movie.

"Lady-goddess?" he asked, still looking at me anxiously.

I looked at Sarden, who was glaring at me.

"He's not mistreating me, *exactly*," I said, after pretending to take a moment to consider it. "He's just not being as, ah, *loving* as he could be." I threw Sarden a sidelong glance. "In fact he's being rather *rude.*"

"Ah—too bad, too bad!" the little counter attended exclaimed. "We cannot serve those males who do not reverence and worship their females. So says the boss-of-All."

"And who might this 'boss-of-all' be?" Sarden growled.

"The boss of all who?" I asked. "Are there a lot more workers in the back?"

"No, no—of course not! The boss-of-All is the boss of *me*." He poked his chest with his thumb. "I am All," he clarified beaming.

"Wait—you mean your *name* is 'All'?" I asked.

"Naturally." He sounded really proud about it. "I am all the workers he has and so he calls me All, the boss-of-All does."

"Right. Now that we cleared that up, All, I need to speak to your boss," Sarden said, frowning. "Is he in the back? Can you call him?"

The little guy got a mulish expression on his green face.

"No, no—I'm afraid not! Not unless you show your lady-goddess proper respect."

"But Count Doloroso sent us," Sarden exclaimed, clearly exasperated.

"It does not matter who sent you—no it doesn't!" All, the Oompa-Loompa, shook his head adamantly. "I will not call the boss-of-All until I see proper respect."

Sarden looked at me and I looked at him and shrugged. *Your move, buddy.*

"I'm sorry, Zoe," he said shortly and then turned back to the counter. "Now get your damn boss out here!"

"No, no!" The Oompa-Loompa shook his finger reprovingly at Sarden. "This is not proper respect. This is not *worship.*"

"Worship, huh?" Sarden looked like he wanted to punch the little guy right in his orange gums. Instead he faced me again, gritted his teeth, and got down on his knees, for all the world as though he was going to propose.

"Zoe," he said, taking my hands in both of his and looking up at me—though he didn't have to look very far—he was tall, even on his knees. "I'm sorry for the way I spoke to you. It was disrespectful and rude."

"Yes, it was," I said, smiling just a little.

"Can you ever forgive me?" Sarden asked. Turning my hands over, he kissed them gently, laying a tender kiss in each of my open palms in turn.

I have to confess, my heart took a little leap, even though I knew it was an act. Not that I was going to show it—I could act too, damn it!

"*Maybe* I'll forgive you," I said slowly. "*If* you promise to buy me a *nib-nib.*"

"What is it with you and the damn *nib-nibs?*" he growled in a low voice. "Really Zoe, I don't think you'd like them—they scratch the inside of your mouth. And besides, you can make something that tastes just like them in the food-sim back at the ship. I'll show you."

"What? Scratch the inside of your mouth? What are you *talking* about?" I stared at him, totally not getting it. "Why would you put a pet in your mouth?"

"A pet?" he said, raising his eyebrows. "Is *that* what you think they are?"

"What else could they *be?*" I demanded. "I—"

"Well now, All, why didn't you tell me we had a customer?" a new voice boomed. Looking up, I saw it was a Majoran male with a dark blue beard and hair to match. His skin was the same tannish-brown of the male we'd met with his wife at the perfume seller's place but he looked less refined and snobby—more of a man's man, if you know what I mean.

"I'm sorry, Boss," the Oompa-Loompa squeaked. "It's true this male came in asking for service but he wasn't showing his lady-goddess proper respect."

"Well, he appears to be respecting her now," the boss boomed. Except for the color of his hair and beard, he reminded me of a retired biker who had decided to open an auto body shop. He even had on a grease-stained coverall-type garment that looked like it had seen better days. He raised his voice — (like it wasn't already loud enough — seriously, he could teach my old boss a thing or two about yell-talking) and roared, "Goddess, is your male treating you with adequate care and attention?"

I looked down at Sarden and lifted an eyebrow at him.

"Goddess," he said in a low voice, really laying it on thick now. "I *worship* you — you know that."

He pulled me closer, pressing his face right between my breasts as though he didn't want even a millimeter of distance between us.

My stomach did a little flip at the feeling of his long, muscular arms wrapped around me so securely. I couldn't help myself — even though it was an act, I still liked it. Taking pity on him, I decided to play along.

"Sarden," I murmured, running my hands through his thick, black hair, just as the female Majoran had been doing with her mate back at the perfume seller. "Sarden, my darling, you know I *adore you.*"

Since they were right there, I started playing with his horns too. I'd always kind of wanted to touch them, almost from the moment I found out he *wasn't* really the Devil dragging me down to Hell. They were fascinating, growing out from the sides of his temples in thick, short, sharp curves. They weren't nearly as long as a bull's horns, though that was what they mostly reminded me of. I ran my hands up and down them, swirling my fingers around their bases and sliding up to the sharp tips curiously.

Sarden trembled against me as I touched him and his grip around my waist tightened as he pressed his face fiercely between my breasts. "Goddess…Zoe, you shouldn't," he groaned in a deep, hoarse voice. Wow, he really *was* laying it on thick.

"Shouldn't what, my darling? Shouldn't forgive you?" I asked sweetly, laying it on a bit myself. Hey, I took drama in high school—I know how it's done.

"Uh, goddess? Goddess?"

It took me a minute to realize that the big biker-looking Majoran was talking to me. He and his Oompa-Loompa were watching Sarden and me with wide eyes.

"Yes?" I asked, still caressing Sarden's horns as I spoke to them.

"Normally I encourage all kinds of worship between a male and his goddess," the boss said. "But…your male is a Vorn, isn't he?"

"He's part Vorn, why? Is that a problem?" I demanded, all ready to do battle if this guy started bringing racial bias into it. From what little he'd told me, Sarden had had enough of that to last him a lifetime.

The Majoran mechanic frowned.

"It *wouldn't* be if you weren't, *ahem*, playing with his horns," he said, frowning.

"What are you talking about?" I asked. "He's just, uh, worshipping me like he's supposed to—that's all."

"Yes, but some kinds of worship are best left in the bedroom," he growled. "I can't have the two of you pleasuring each other right here in my shop—how would it look if another customer comes in?"

"Pleasuring each other? What are you talking about?" I demanded. "I'm just, you know, stroking his horns."

"And look how they've grown!" All, the Oompa-Loompa, squeaked.

"Grown?" I looked down and frowned. Sure enough, Sarden's horns *did* seem longer now. But how was that possible?

"A Vorn's horns are erogenous zones," the boss said bluntly. "Some say they're best used to guide him when he's...*ahem*...worshipping his goddess with his tongue."

"What?" I took a quick step back.

Sarden released me—reluctantly, I thought—and looked up.

"Goddess," he growled softly and I could see that lazy, half-lidded look of lust in his glowing golden eyes again.

"You could have told me," I whispered fiercely.

"Why would I do that when you were playing your part so well?" he murmured back.

"You...I..." I couldn't believe I'd been giving him the equivalent of a hand-job right out in public. And he'd been getting off on it!

This gave a whole new meaning to the word "horny."

"Well, erotic interludes aside, it appears that you worship your female with proper respect," the mechanic said, this time addressing Sarden. "So what can I do for you this fine evening?"

Sarden got to his feet smoothly—really, he was surprisingly quick and graceful for such a big guy.

"I was sent by Count Doloroso," he said, abruptly all business.

"Count who?" The mechanic frowned. "Sorry, I don't know

that name."

"Well he apparently knows *you*," Sarden said, sounding exasperated. "He said you were a reputable mechanic and would give me a fair price on getting one of the panels for my Hydrogen Scoop replaced."

The Majoran puffed out his chest with pride.

"Well, now, we *are* the finest mech shop it all of Gallana, that much is true," he said. "What kind of ship do you have? And what kind of panel do you want as a replacement? I've got corrugated *sythosium*, lacquered *geodesium* or just plain *sonium*."

"*Geodesium?*" Sarden frowned. "I've never heard of panels made of *geodesium*."

"Oh, sure! It's new tech — the best! In fact, if you have the credit, you can get them all replaced."

"I don't know about that — I'm in a hurry at the moment," Sarden said.

"Well, if it's just a matter of replacement — you can do all six panels in just a little longer than it takes to do one. And if it's speed you're after, well, lacquered *geodesium* panels'll make your Scoop up to fifty percent more efficient and your ship fifty percent faster."

"Is that right?" Sarden looked interested. "Do you have the stats to back that up?"

"Sure do — in the back. All," he said to his assistant. "Go in the back and pull up the geo stats in full holo. Then pull out a pair of the geo panels for our customer to admire."

"At once, boss-of-All!" the Oompa-Loompa squeaked and scurried to obey.

"He's a good lad as Goolies go." The mechanic smiled at Sarden. "Now about these panels — you've got to see them to believe them. Come on." He made a motion, inviting Sarden around the counter to the back of the shop, which was located behind a large swinging door.

"All right." Sarden started to go…then turned back to me. "But what about my…my goddess?"

"Well, she's welcome to come too, of course," the mechanic said, nodding. "Although it's a mite dirty back there."

"That's okay," I said. "I'll be fine here. I'll just have a seat and wait."

There was a lone stool, shaped kind of like a dirty gray mushroom, located (or possibly growing, I couldn't be sure) in the corner of the shop. I walked over and plopped down on it, glad to take a load off. Those damn stripper heels really *hurt* after a while.

"Well, if you're absolutely *sure…*" He was still hesitating, a little frown on his face.

"I'll be fine, honestly." As much as I was interested in alien culture and technology, I had no interest in going in the back of a dirty alien mechanic's shop to look at engine equipment any more than I would have back on Earth. I made a 'go on' gesture at Sarden and he finally nodded.

"I'll be back in a moment."

"Take your time," I remarked. "I'll just be sitting here twiddling my thumbs."

"I don't know what that means," he said. "But I'll try to be fast—we don't have much time left in the light cycle."

"Sure. Fine." I shrugged. I didn't particularly like the idea of being out in the bad part of Gallana at night—or during their dark cycle or whatever they called it when they turned off the lights—but I was pretty sure I'd be safe if I was with Sarden.

"All right." He turned and went through the swinging door with the mechanic, leaving me to sit on the gray mushroom and wait.

I hadn't been sitting for five minutes, thinking how bored I was—seriously, couldn't they at least have a magazine to look at? I mean, not that I'd understand what it said but at least I could look at the pictures—when the front door of the shop opened and the last person I'd expected to see walked in.

"Why hello, Zoe," Count Doloroso said, smiling charmingly. "How surprising to see *you* here."

Chapter Fifteen

Zoe

"Why should it be surprising?" I asked, frowning at Doloroso. "*You're* the one who sent us here."

"Ah, yes. I did, didn't I?" he mused, giving me that oily smile of his.

"Yes, you did," I said pointedly. The way he was looking at me gave me the creeps. Especially since I was wearing the damn see-through dress. He looked like he was undressing me with his eyes only he didn't have to—everything was already on display. "So…why are you here?" I asked, trying unobtrusively to cover as much of my goodies as I could with my arms.

"Just a little matter I needed to discuss with the mech tech," he murmured. "But I suppose he's busy with your master?"

"Sarden is *not* my master," I said stiffly. "He's just a guy who…" I was about to say 'a guy who owns me' or 'a guy who bought me' but that made it sound like he *was* my master, after all. "He's just a guy I'm traveling with," I ended at last, lamely.

"Is that right? Well, perhaps I should come back later. The dark cycle is coming soon, after all." Count Doloroso opened the door and stepped halfway out. But before he got all the way back out to the alley, he reached into his long, black cloak—which was twitching oddly—and pulled out a yellow bag with a drawstring. Carefully, he opened the drawstring and extracted something from the bag.

I gasped when I saw what it was—a little purple and green *nib-nib!* Doloroso had it by the tail, pinched delicately between thumb and forefinger, and it chattered desperately in its high-pitched, squeaky voice.

"Oh my God," I said, fascinated. "A *nib-nib* – you've got one!"

"More than one, actually. Would you care for one? They're a bit crunchy but quite delicious."

"What? *What* did you say?" I asked faintly. Please let him not be saying what I thought he was saying. Suddenly Sarden's earlier words began to make an awful kind of sense.

"Some find their flavor bitter," Doloroso went on, dangling the tiny monkey, no longer than my pinky finger—above his mouth. "But I quite like it."

"Their...*flavor?*" I still couldn't believe it.

"Yes, their flavor. They're a kind of snack food, you know. A specialty of Gallana."

"Oh no—you can't be serious. You *can't* be." I was filled with a sick kind of horror.

"Of *course* I am. What did you think they were? A kind of pet?" He laughed and popped the screaming, chattering *nib-nib* into his mouth.

"Stop!" Modesty forgotten, I hopped to my feet and ran as fast as I could in my stripper heels, trying to reach him before he could bite down. "Spit him out! *Spit him out!*" I demanded, pounding on his chest. He was almost as tall as Sarden but the heels made him easier to reach. I slapped and punched and pushed as hard as I could. *"Don't you dare hurt him – spit him out!"* I yelled.

More from surprise than from the effects of my punching, I

think, Doloroso opened his mouth and spat the little *nib-nib* into the palm of his hand. The poor little guy was shivering and all nasty and damp from the awful man's mouth but he didn't seem to be harmed.

"What in the name of The Assimilation is *wrong* with you?" the Count asked, looking at me as though I'd grown a third eye. "I offer you a snack and you *attack* me."

"He's not just a snack. Give him to me! In fact, I want *all* of them—how many do you have in the bag?"

"Only two more. They're quite expensive you know. And you're acting unbecomingly greedy, young lady, if I may take the liberty of saying so."

As he spoke, he moved backward and I found myself following. To my surprise, I found that my momentum when I had pushed and pummeled him to make him spit out the *nib-nib,* had carried us out the door and into the dark alley beyond. The ground under my ridiculous shoes was uneven and rutted and I nearly stumbled as I went after him.

Go back, Zoe—this isn't safe! a stern voice spoke up in my head. But I couldn't leave the *nib-nibs* to be eaten! Count Doloroso had the one he'd spit out clutched in his large fist with only its little head poking out. It was chattering and looking at me with such fear in its large, liquid eyes it twisted my heart. I couldn't bear to think of it going back in his mouth to be ground up to mush. What a horrible fate—to be eaten alive by this creepy man!

Well, it wasn't going to happen on my watch.

"Please," I said, taking another step towards him. "Please, just give them to me. I...I'll have Sarden pay you for them. He promised he'd get me some. He won't mind. He'll pay you double...triple even!"

"Aha, but what if I'd rather be paid in information than credit?" he asked, taking another step backward.

"What information?" I took another step forward—we were far down the alley at this point and I could barely see the pinkish light at the mouth of it anymore. I wondered where it ended.

Count Doloroso's eyes gleamed.

"Information about your home world, of course. I checked, you know. Salex Prime is a rocky wasteland much too close to its sun to bear any life at all."

"Where?" I asked, my eyes still on the tiny *nib-nib* in his hand which was crying pitifully.

"Your *home planet*—according to Sarden, anyway." He smiled triumphantly. "I *knew* you weren't from there. What I want to know is *where* are you from? You are, as I said before, a very unique specimen, my dear."

"That's because…because I come from another galaxy," I said, thinking fast. I wanted to save the *nib-nibs* but I most certainly did *not* want to send a creepy bastard like Doloroso back to Earth to pick out his own "specimen" from the Alien Mate Index.

"Ah, I see." He nodded, still walking backwards. "And what galaxy would that be? And what planet exactly?"

"I'll tell you everything," I lied recklessly. "Just give me the *nib-nibs. All* of them."

"Very well. You may have them." He stopped and I saw that we were at the far end of the alley now, the opposite end from where Sarden and I had entered.

"Here." I held out my hands eagerly and he dropped the first one—still kind of damp, poor little guy—into my cupped hands. "Hey, little guy." I leaned down and whispered to him, trying to use my softest and most gentle voice. "It's okay—I won't hurt you."

The *nib-nib* looked at me doubtfully and chattered softly.

Gently, *very* gently, I used one finger to stroke the soft greenish-purple fur on his little back. Immediately, his large eyes closed and his tail began to twitch in time with my stroking. A soft, musical humming sound came from his tiny throat—so high it almost sounded like the buzzing of a bee.

"Well, well—it seems he's quite taken with you," Doloroso said right in my ear.

"Huh?" I jumped and suddenly realized that he was close—a lot closer than I wanted him to be.

"I'm sure the other two will be as well," he remarked and dumped them out of the sack and into my hands.

Immediately, all three of the tiny monkey-creatures started chattering and scampering all over me, as though I was a giant jungle gym set up just for them.

"Oh—oh my God!" I gasped as they ran up my arms and into my hair, down my neck, and across my shoulders. Their tiny claws had no trouble holding on and they went all over the place, playing a game of tag all over me that tickled horribly. "Stop—stop you little boogers!" I gasped, not sure whether to laugh or panic.

"Here—I was afraid this might happen. Let me try to get them off you."

Suddenly Count Doloroso had me by the arm and dragging me off into another alleyway.

"Hey. Hey, stop!" I yanked my concentration from my three new pets to the creepy man beside me. "Let me go—I need to get back to Sarden!"

"I don't think so." He smiled at me in a way that made my blood run cold. "I think we have a lot to talk about, my dear Zoe. But it's a discussion best held in *private.*"

I can be loud when I need to and I felt the need right now.

"Sarden!" I shouted as loudly as I could. *"Sarden! HELP!"*

"Shut up, you foolish girl!" Doloroso clamped a big, clammy palm over my mouth but I wasn't having any of that. I bit him as hard as I could and one of the little *nib-nibs* – I'd like to think it was the one I rescued from being eaten – scampered forward and bit him too.

Doloroso howled in pain and jerked back as my mouth filled with his blood. It didn't taste like blood though – it had an acrid, oily, bland flavor that made me gag and spit.

I didn't have long to clear my mouth because Doloroso was already coming after me again. I dodged away from him as he made a grab for me, the *nib-nibs* chattering in my ears. They were all in my hair now, maybe thinking it was the safest place to be. I wasn't so sure about that but I couldn't take time to secure them at the moment because Count creepy was determined to get me.

"Get back!" I shouted as loudly as I could, dodging another one of his boney, grabbing hands. "Get away from me! I don't want you anywhere near me!"

They say that shouting definite negative statements like that will often scare off an attacker or possibly bring help. But so far, neither one of those things was happening. Where in the Frozen Hells, to borrow one of his own phrases, was Sarden?

"Come here," Doloroso snarled, his long fingers catching in my hair. "Come *here* you little bitch!" He gave a tug and I screamed and stumbled towards him, grabbing at my aching scalp.

My hair is long and I was bent over, trying to pull away so I had a clear view of it. If I could have, I would have cut off the hank he had in his fist but obviously, I didn't have any scissors. As it turned out, though, I wasn't completely unarmed. I heard one of the *nib-nibs* chattering , almost as if he was talking to the others. They chattered back and then all three *nib-nibs* ran forward and bit the hand tangled in my hair.

"Ow! Filthy vermin!" Doloroso howled, at last releasing his grip on my hair.

With one more yank, I got free, leaving several long curly auburn strands in his grip. My scalp ached fiercely—it felt like he'd tried to snatch me bald, as my Granny would have said.

Unfortunately during our struggle, our places had gotten reversed and now Doloroso was between me and the mouth of the alley where the mechanic's shop was. I cast one last glance in that direction. *Where was Sarden?* Well, wherever he was, I couldn't trust him to save me. I was going to have to get away on my own.

If I can just get back to the moving walkway, I told myself. *If I can just get back, I'll be safe. There are plenty of people there and if Doloroso tries anything I can shout that he's hurting me.*

Mind made up, I turned in the direction I thought was most likely to lead back to the walkway. Then I kicked off the ridiculous stripper heels and ran.

Sarden

"Stop. Did you hear that?" I pulled off the protective ear-shields the mechanic—whose name was Gil, I had found out—had given me to wear as he turned off his equipment.

He'd wanted to show me the new panels and then his assistant had helpfully offered to demonstrate by using a lithium cold laser blowtorch on them. And after that, he'd insisted on showing me that even a blast grinder wouldn't scratch them. And *then* of course, we had to have a simulated meteor shower in their private wind tunnel. All these tests were extremely loud. In fact, even with the ear-shields on, I was beginning to wonder if I would ever hear properly again.

But I did hear *something* — it sounded like someone calling my name.

Zoe? My heart started pounding and I dropped the ear-shields carelessly on the floor as I jogged back to the swinging metal door connecting to the front of the shop.

She'll be fine, I told myself uneasily. *It was just my imagination – I'm sure of it.*

I wasn't so sure when I pushed out into the front of the shop and found it empty. Zoe, who had been sitting on the organically grown stool in the corner of the room, wasn't there anymore.

Well, maybe she just went outside for a breath of fresh air.

I went out of the shop but she was nowhere to be seen in the alleyway either.

"Zoe?" I called and then raised my voice. *"Zoe?"*

No answer. I felt my heart stutter in my chest.

It was just as I had feared — she was gone.

Zoe

I hadn't been running for more than a couple of minutes before I got a horrible stitch in my side. Also, I could hear Doloroso gaining on me. He was panting and letting out a string of curses that didn't make sense but sounded extremely nasty nonetheless.

He'd been acting like such a gentleman back when he was making his deal with Sarden but, he'd turned into a real potty-mouth now. I was pretty glad I didn't understand half of what he was saying—no doubt it would have really hurt my feelings.

Ha—better my feelings than my body though, right? I had no intention of letting him catch me to find out.

I wanted to keep running in the direction of the moving walkway, but the creepy Count was making my plan unfeasible. I had to get away from him any way I could.

I saw a side street coming up but I didn't know if I could make it—or even if I should try. What if I ended up someplace even worse? What if I got trapped?

Then again, maybe I should take a chance.

My feet were getting cut and tattered on the jagged pavement but I couldn't worry about that now. I could practically feel him breathing down my neck and the chattering of my *nib-nibs* was getting more and more frantic when something that was either the best luck or the worst luck ever, happened.

A huge voice that came out of the sky like God talking to Moses suddenly boomed, "Light cycle is over. Night cycle now commencing."

And suddenly, the pinkish glow from the "sky" overhead faded to nothing but a dull, barely-there gray which left everything in almost complete darkness.

The sudden change made me feel as if I had gone blind all at once. I tripped over a rock and stumbled, almost going down. It was a good thing though—as I rocked forward, I felt the wind of Doloroso's arm and hand making a missed grab over my head. Clearly he was trying to get his hands on hair again.

If he gets me now, I'm dead! I thought wildly. I felt like a character in a slasher movie where the bad guy is right behind them with a long, sharp knife and they keep making stupid decisions—like going with the killer, letting him distract them with tiny cute monkeys, then lure them away from safety — until he ultimately catches them and kills them.

Okay, time for a *good* decision.

My eyes were adjusting a bit now and I could still see the side street I'd been eyeing coming up.

Go for it — now or never, Zoe! I told myself in a silent pep talk. Quick and quiet as a rabbit running for its life, I dodged down the narrow side street and came to...

A dead end.

Sarden

The night cycle of Gallana had commenced by the time I ran to the end of the alley we'd entered to get to the mechanic's shop. The street outside was plunged into gloom but that didn't bother me — the Vorn part of my heritage gives me excellent night vision. I could easily see that Zoe wasn't there.

I almost charged out of the alley and went back the way we had come. I was thinking that she must have changed her mind about being traded for my sister to Tazaxx. I guessed I couldn't blame her for that but I was still worried as hell. What I had told her about being taken aboard a strange vessel and cut up for cloning seeds was the absolute truth. She might not want to go live in Tazaxx's private zoo, but at least she'd be safe and well cared for there.

A safe, well cared for prisoner, whispered a voice in my head. *Can you blame her for running? Of course she tried to get away.*

But was *this* the way she had gone? Something — some instinct, maybe the same one that had tried to warn me when she was drowning in the sensitivity tank—told me no.

I jogged back the other way, going to the distant end of the alley instead. She wasn't there either but something else was. First I found an empty yellow drawstring bag—the kind used to hold merchandise bought at the docking area. I sniffed it and drew back, my nose wrinkling—*nib-nibs!* Exactly what Zoe had been asking for so insistently back at the mechanic's shop.

I frowned. What the hell was going on here? Had someone offered Zoe what she wanted and gotten her to follow them out of the shop? But who? And where would they have taken her?

Heart beating fast I walked a few more steps and found some other things. The first was something anyone without my night vision would have missed—a few strands of long, curly hair. And then the ridiculously high shoes I'd given her to go with the Majoran dress she was wearing. She'd taken them off. Why?

It wasn't another visual clue that gave me the answer—it was an olfactory one. Because of the *Ambergeis* amplifying her natural scent, I could smell that Zoe had been here recently. And there was a sharp tang of fear mixed in with her sweet natural aroma. She'd been frightened then—possibly she'd called out for me but I hadn't heard her due to the damn ear-shields.

I gritted my teeth. Gods, what must be happening to her now? Had whoever had lured her out here taken her away?

I thought of how much attention her unique beauty had attracted at the docking area. Every male within the entire area had probably been watching us. They'd seen what she showed an interest in—those damned *nib-nibs.* Then they probably followed us to the mechanic's shop, waiting for the right moment to make their play. And, like a fool, I had given them the perfect opportunity. I had dragged her out to this Gods'forsaken area of a spaceport known to have a brisk black market in cloning and then *left her alone.* What in the Frozen Hells was *wrong* with me?

Should have known better than to leave her alone. Should have known better than to bring her here in the first place. I should have found another way to get the ship fixed. Now she's gone, possibly being cut into little while I stand her like a fool and it's all my damn fault. My heart twisted in my chest and I felt sick, imagining her cries of pain. I don't usually pray but I sent up a prayer now.

Please, Goddess of Mercy – let me find her! Let her be all right!

I took another step, following her scent, so full of fear and desperation, and then I saw it—a spot of blood on the rough and broken pavement. It was just beginning to dry but when I scented it I knew it was hers. There was another further on and then another. The drops were spaced widely apart as though Zoe had been taking long strides when she made them.

Of course—her feet were bare so she was probably cutting herself all to hell. Well why had she taken off her shoes in the first place? I flashed on them again—the ridiculous things were so high I hadn't even wanted her walking in them on this broken pavement. I'd been afraid she would twist an ankle. She couldn't walk in the damn things—let alone run, which was what the length of her strides indicated.

Sudden understanding broke over me and I felt a surge of relief. She must be running away! Running from whoever had lured her out here! So maybe she was still on the move and they hadn't caught her!

I gave a groan. My little Pure One was on the run in the middle of the bad part of Gallana during the night cycle which lasted a full ten solar hours.

Gods, I had to find her—and hope I got to her before her

attacker did!

Zoe

A dead end. Good going, Zoe — you really know how to pick escape routes, a little voice whispered snarkily in my head.

Shut up! I told it. *I don't have time for this — I have to find a way out.*

My eyes had adjusted as much as they were going to, to the deep gray gloom that had fallen over the entire spaceport. Which meant I could see Count Doloroso coming at me just fine. Apparently my sudden dodge into the side alley hadn't fooled him a bit. All I had done was manage to get myself cornered.

I looked wildly from side to side. There was blank, stone wall much too high to climb to my left and a shut door to my right. Was it locked? Probably but you don't know until you try. I went to reach for it but Doloroso made a lunge at me and I had to jump back.

"Come here, you foolish girl." His voice was ugly and sneering, as though he was laughing at me — as though he knew I had no place to go. Well, he was right but I wasn't about to admit it.

"Stay back," I said, trying to keep my voice from shaking. "Just stay away."

"Why? Do you think you can run from me?" He stepped over to the door I'd wanted to try and put his hand flat on a wide rectangular pad to one side of it. It lit up and his large, boney-knuckled hand was outlined in red. "See? Locked. There's no way out."

"There's always a way out," I said, to sound brave even though I was pretty much scared shitless. Sorry for the language, but I *was*.

You would have been too, in my place.

"Not this time, young lady—you're coming back to my ship with me," Doloroso informed me. "And the first thing we're going to do is put you back in the sensitivity tank to finish the scan the sensu-pods started." He licked his thin lips. "They are...*eager* for another taste of you and I can't say that I blame them. You *are* a luscious little creature, even if you are a bit temperamental."

"What? Put me back in that awful tank?" I stared at his shadowy form in horror. "Why the hell do you want to do that? Are you some kind of sadist or something?"

"I assure you, I am not," he said in a way I somehow found completely unconvincing. "I just want to know a little more about you and your home world. The blood sample from the chip-driller and the half-finished sensitivity test from the tank I purchased from your Master were most *instructive*. They let me know that I have much to learn from you and your people. In fact, I believe that you might be exactly what I have been searching for ever since the *Last Day*."

He said "last day" in a way that made me think it was some kind of holiday or a historic date with special significance. Not that I cared. I had been feeling around with my cut and bleeding feet as we talked, searching for anything I could use as a weapon and I had finally found something.

It was a long length of metal—some kind of a pole or pipe maybe?—and I could feel it under my bare toes.

"You're going to come with me now without any more trouble," Doloroso informed me. "The Assimilated have much to learn from you, my dear."

As quickly as I could, I reached down and grabbed the long metal pole. Holding it like a baseball bat and picturing his head as a big, nasty ball, I swung it as hard as I could.

"Learn about *this* you monkey-eating asshole!" I yelled as the pole connected.

Unfortunately, I only hit his shoulder. I can be brave when I want to but I have to be honest, I suck at sports, baseball included. This was my only time at bat and I had struck out.

My blow *did* make Doloroso stagger backwards a few steps, though. For just a moment he wasn't blocking my way to the mouth of the alley. I had a window of opportunity to get past him and run.

Instead, I ran to the door—the one he'd demonstrated was locked. I don't know why I did it—instinct? Stupidity? I don't know—pick one. Anyway, once I got there I pressed my own hand to the same pad he'd used to prove the door was locked.

I felt a tingle in my palm and fingers and then suddenly the pad lit up—green this time.

I shoved hard with my shoulder and the door creaked inward.

"Stop, you little bitch!" I heard Doloroso scream. Yup, when he thought he had me I was "young lady" but the minute I started getting away, I was suddenly a "bitch." Of course, as far as I was concerned, he was an asshole *all* the time.

"Sorry to be such an inconsiderate *bitch* by not letting you kidnap me," I shouted as I shoved the door closed in his face. "But I don't feel like it—I've been kidnapped enough for one week."

He started to snarl something else but just then the door clicked closed and I heard a buzzing sound that I hoped was the lock falling back into place. Sure enough, I heard Doloroso slapping at the keypad and cursing. The door rattled on its metal hinges but he apparently couldn't open it.

I breathed a shaky sigh of relief and the *nib-nibs*, which I hadn't even been thinking about, chattered from their place on top of my head. They were probably making a terrible mess of my hair up there but I didn't care—I was just glad I wasn't all alone.

"It's all right, guys," I told them in a low voice. "It's all right now—everything is going to be all right."

And then I heard a grinding-sizzling sound start just outside the door. To my horror, I saw sparks along the edge of the door nearest the hinges. Did Doloroso have some kind of laser or grinder he was using to cut his way in?

The answer appeared to be yes. Quickly, I backed away.

If the outside had been dark, the inside of the building was pitch-black. I had no idea what this building was or what it contained but I didn't want to stay by the door with Count Creepy cutting his way in. I still had the length of pipe I'd used to wallop Doloroso, but I wasn't interested in going for round two. I had to get out of here—get further into the building and away from the door. It seemed pretty thick but who knew how long it would take my assailant to get in?

My assailant. I gave a shaky little laugh. It made me sound so important—like someone out of a crime drama. Who would have ever guessed plain, plus-sized Zoe McKinley would have an *assailant*? Then again, who would have guessed that I would have an artificial life form as a friend, a hot, Devil-looking captor, or my hair full of alien monkeys?

My life was getting weirder all the time. Not for the first time, I wished I was back at Lauder, Lauder and Associates having staplers thrown at my head.

But we can't have everything we want.

"Okay, guys," I said softly to the *nib-nibs*. "Let's see if we can find a way out before Count Creeps-a-lot get in."

They chattered quietly and I hoped that they were housebroken since they had apparently decided my hair was the best place for a monkey condo. Then, feeling my way forward with my bruised and battered toes, I began moving through the dark.

I managed to find a wall and put my fingers against it, trailing lightly over its cold, metallic surface as I went. I read somewhere once that if you're lost in a maze or an unknown building you should pick one direction and keep going that way. Like stay right and keep turning right every chance you get. And that was somehow supposed to lead you out of the maze.

I had never had a chance to try this bit of trivia before but I can share with you now that it is complete *bullshit*.

I put my fingertips to the right hand wall and I kept taking rights every time I felt a corner but my strategy didn't get me to any kind of an exit. Instead, the wall I was following abruptly stopped. What I mean was, I came to the end of it and there was no corner. It just kind of curved away in a way that made me think maybe the room I was entering was either round or oval.

It was also absolutely *huge*.

I could tell because the soft, shuffling of my bare, wounded feet was suddenly magnified by a factor of about a thousand. I held still in the silence, trying not to breathe for a moment.

It wasn't *completely* quiet in the big, empty space, though—I could hear a kind of rhythmic lapping sound—a soft liquid gurgle that made me shiver. What *was* that? It sounded a little like the indoor swimming pool my therapist had made me go to in order to try and overcome my past. That had been a big, fat failure by the way, but the sound of the water lapping and gurgling, echoing in the huge tiled room reminded me of what I was hearing now.

Cling! I'd been listening so hard that the end of the metal pole, which I was still carrying even though it was damn heavy, dropped a little and scraped the metal floor.

The small sound rang and echoed, flying around the vast room like a flock of bats. God, this place must be bigger than a football stadium! The *nib-nibs* in my hair chattered uneasily and even that small sound was magnified.

"*Shhh*, guys," I whispered to them. "Let's keep it down, okay?"

But it was too late. Somewhere in the darkness in front of me I saw two fiery red spots appear. After a moment, I realized they were eyes. Freaking *eyes* staring at me from out of the pitch-blackness.

And then something growled.

Chapter Sixteen

Sarden

"Zoe? *Zoe?*" I shouted as I jogged down the pitted road as quickly as I could. I kept my eyes down, following her scent and the drops of blood I saw every few feet. She was going to need some serious medical attention by the time I found her.

If I found her.

But I wouldn't let myself entertain that thought. She was out here somewhere—I just had to get to her before whoever was chasing her did.

The droplets led into a narrow alleyway. Down at the end, I saw a dark figure swathed in a cloak doing something to a door. Something that made a lot of sparks, glowing golden in the darkness.

I crept quietly down the alley but it wouldn't have mattered if I had been playing a Grobian *fizzween* and doing the Yakitan stomp dance. The dark figure was completely engrossed in his work. As I got closer, I saw that he was using some kind of hand-held blast laser to try and cut through the hinges of the door. Such tools are highly illegal but also quite useful for getting into places you're not supposed to go. I'd been guilty of using one a time or two myself during a few of my dicier smuggling runs.

Over the smell of the melting, scorching metal, I could still catch Zoe's scent, now with a tang of desperation. Had she held him off down here and somehow gone through the door he was trying to get into? Was she inside the dark building it led into?

"Who in the Frozen Hells are you and what have you done to Zoe?" I demanded, grabbing him by the shoulder and spinning him around.

I grabbed for his wrist, meaning to disarm him at the same time but before I could grab it, the laser flew from his hand, narrowly missing my crotch but burning me just the same.

I got lucky—he didn't have it collimated, so only the outer edge of the beam hit me. It left a long, burning trail down the inside of my left thigh, parting my tough Byrinian leather flight trousers and sending a line of blazing pain through my flesh. It could have been worse though—if I'd been hit by the full force of the beam, I could have lost a leg. Another *flit* to the left and I would have lost my balls as well.

Of course, just because it missed my more delicate areas didn't mean the laser didn't hurt. It did—it burned like fucking hell.

"Ah!" I snarled and lost my grip on the unknown assailant's arm. He whirled away from me, cape swirling so I couldn't see his face, and pounded back down the alleyway.

He turned once for an instant to look at me but all I could see were his eyes shining with a strangely metallic glitter in the dim light.

"You may have stopped me this time but I'll get her," he shouted in a thin, angry voice. "Her or another like her and then the Last Day will be the First!"

Then he sprinted away.

I wanted to go after him but I doubted I could catch him with an injured leg. The good thing about being burned with a laser is you don't have to worry about bleeding out because the laser cauterizes the wound. The bad thing, as I said before, is that it hurts like hell.

But I had more pressing business to attend to than my own pain. The unknown male had almost finished cutting through the door's hinges. I picked up the hand-held blast laser—very, *very* carefully—turned it back on and finished the job. Then I kicked open the door (with my uninjured leg) and shouted her name.

"Zoe?" I yelled into the echoing blackness. "Zoe, where are you? Please, sweetheart—answer me!"

Zoe

I heard someone shouting my name and I was pretty sure it wasn't Count Doloroso—mainly because they were calling my name instead of "young lady" or "bitch." I hoped against hope it was Sarden but I didn't dare answer back. That was because any loud noise on my part seemed to make the red-eyed growling thing in the darkness angry. At least, it growled louder, which I assumed wasn't a friendly greeting filled with joy.

"Easy now…easy," I whispered to it, trying to make my voice low and soothing as I took a step backwards. "I didn't know this was your territory so I'm just going to back up really, *really* slowly. Okay?"

"*Grrrrrrrr,*" was my only answer. Apparently Mr. Red-eyed growlypants didn't like me moving backwards any more than he'd liked me moving forward.

The eyes got closer and I took another step back and gripped my metal pole with both sweating palms. If it came at me, I was going to go down swinging. But we know how well that went last time, when I swung at Doloroso and I had actually been able to *see* him. In this case, all I could see were the red, animal eyes coming towards me and I had no idea how large the animal attached to them might be. From the sound of the rumbling growl coming from its throat, though, I'd say it had to be pretty big. Maybe the size of a grizzly bear?

Immediately I wished I hadn't thought that. Now all I could imagine was a huge alien grizzly bear coming at me in the dark.

I had seen a documentary about how a grizzly savaged and ate an entire group of campers when I was little and watching supposedly "kid-friendly" shows on Animal Planet. The images of human bones with all the flesh gnawed off had given me nightmares for months.

The *nib-nibs* in my hair had gone completely quiet. I got the feeling they were frozen with fear—the same way I would be if I let myself get hypnotized by those glowing red eyes.

Suddenly I heard echoing footsteps running down the hallway.

"Zoe? *Zoe?*" someone yelled. I felt a surge of relief when I recognized the voice—it really *was* Sarden. I dared to look over my shoulder—though what I expected to see in the pitch-blackness I didn't know. Surprisingly, I *did* see something.

Sarden's golden eyes glowed in the dark too. And clearly he could see a lot better in the blackness than I could because he said,

"Zoe! Thank the Goddess!"

"Don't thank her yet," I told him in a low, trembling voice. "We've got company."

As if on cue, the growling started up again and the red eyes started moving closer and closer in a slow and deliberate way. Then I knew for sure—the damn thing was stalking me.

And it was about to pounce.

Sarden must have seen it too because he shouted at me, the tension in his deep voice near the breaking point.

"Zoe!"

I whipped my head over my shoulder again and saw an incredibly bright beam of golden light suddenly appear in his hand. *What the Hell? How did he get his hands on a lightsaber?* my frozen brain demanded.

"Zoe," he shouted again, breaking my train of thought. "Zoe when I say, you have to jump to the left! Do you understand me? Jump to the *left!*"

"*Why?*" I gasped. The eyes were getting closer and now I thought I could feel a hot, damp wind blowing against my exposed skin. It had a horrible smell, too. You know how your cat's breath reeks after you feed it a can of the really stinky fish-flavored cat food? *That* was what it smelled like—a rank, fishy odor mixed with the stench of rotten meat. It was enough to make you gag.

I felt my insides turn to ice water as I realized what was going on. The thing was *breathing* on me. It had its mouth open, ready to take a bite!

"Just *do* it!" Sarden bellowed. "*NOW!*"

At that point, several things happened at once.

The red-eyed growling thing jumped at me and I threw myself to the left. A beam of light flashed over my head and the growl rose to an unearthly pitch—it was like the scream of a wildcat mixed with the roar of a tiger and the screech of some other creature I couldn't even name. Something alien and hungry and angry, anyway.

But I soon had other things to worry about.

I had jumped as far as I could and had expected to hit the ground pretty hard. Instead, I found myself falling—falling and flailing wildly through the air as the *nib-nibs* screamed and chattered in my ears.

And then I plunged into an ice-cold pool of deep, deep water.

Sarden

I knew how Zoe hated the water—hated getting in over her head. But there was nowhere else for her to go. The *chudd'x* was about to spring and she was its target—its intended prey. I just hoped I could finish it off with the blast laser and dive in the reservoir myself before she drowned.

I sliced one of its forepaws—a *chudd'x* has six in all, three on each side—with the first swipe, but I was too far away to do much damage.

It growled and seemed to debate whether it should go after me or jump into the reservoir and pursue its intended prey. Though I was the one who had hurt it, *chudd'xs* generally have a one track mind when it comes to hunting.

"Here! Over here, you big bastard!" I shouted, running forward and swiping at it again with the laser beam. It shook its black, shaggy mane and screamed at me—a shattering sound that echoed unbearably from the rounded metal ceiling. Despite the horrible noise, I could still hear Zoe floundering around in the water. Well, at least she was still alive—if I could just finish off this damn *chudd'x* I could hopefully keep her that way.

"Here!" I shouted again, running recklessly right at it, my boots thudding on the metal deck around the reservoir.

I saw it crouch for a spring and dropped to the ground just in time, sliding on the slick metal floor. As the *chudd'x's* momentum carried it over my head, I flipped over on my back and sliced with the laser set on maximum collimation, as precisely as a surgeon making the first cut.

There are some wounds too big to cauterize and this was one of them.

The deadly beam of light sliced it open from neck to groin and suddenly a rain of hot *chudd'x* guts was falling on my head. Including a glob of something wet and slimy that somehow made its way directly into my mouth, nearly choking me.

The huge creature screamed again but when it fell, with a final sounding *thud* that seemed to shake the entire room, it didn't stir again. Apparently being eviscerated didn't agree with it.

Something *was* stirring though—or *someone*. I could hear Zoe still splashing in the water below me, could hear her ever-weakening cries for help.

Grimly, I spat out the gob of *chudd'x* offal and dove headfirst into the freezing water.

Zoe

"It's okay. It's okay—I've got you," I heard Sarden saying in my ear. And then a strong arm was coming around my waist to help me keep my head above the water. Which was good, because the *nib-nibs* were still up there chattering with fear and indignation at the impromptu bath they'd been forced to take.

I was feeling pretty indignant myself—well, in between being scared to death and having awful flashbacks of my past. God, *why* did I keep ending up in the water when it was the very *last* place I ever wanted to be? Was the universe trying to tell me I needed to learn to swim?

If so, the universe could go screw itself.

It was exactly what my old therapist, Dr. Wainwright, was always trying to get me to do. "If you can just get over your fear of the water, Zoe," she'd say. "You can start moving away from your past." She wanted me to take swimming lessons, which was why I'd gone and stood, shivering , at the side of the indoor swimming pool every day for two months straight before giving up.

Now I kind of wished I'd sucked up the courage to get in and at least learn how to dog paddle.

"Sarden," I gasped, though chattering teeth. "Help!"

"I'm here." His deep voice was warm and steady, making me feel better even though I was up to my neck in icy death-liquid. "We're going to get out of here."

"How?" I tried to keep my chin up as the chilly water lapped against my cheeks. God, it felt like all of me was going numb—I could barely feel my arms and legs anymore.

"This way," he said. "Towards the lip of the reservoir."

"What way? I can't see in the dark!" I reminded him tartly.

"Here—hold on to me and I'll get us there."

He had me hold on to his neck and though I tried not to choke him, I was pretty panicked so I probably squeezed tighter than I should have. Sarden didn't complain though. He just kept swimming with long, slow, even strokes until I felt him come to a stop, as though he'd bumped into something.

"Here's the wall," he said, his low voice echoing softly in the darkness. "Reach up your arms—can you grab the edge?"

I didn't want to let go of him but I knew we had to get out of here somehow. Keeping one hand tightly gripped on his broad shoulder, I reached my left arm up as far as I could. But all I could feel was the slick, ice-cold metal wall with no edge anywhere.

Sarden must have been watching my efforts because he made a disgusted-sounding grunt.

"All right, I see the problem—your arms are too short. Why are you Earthlings such puny creatures?"

"Just because we're n-not all as t-tall as professional basketball p-players—" I began with chattering teeth, but he cut me off.

"Look, *I* can reach the lip just fine. So I'll hang on and you'll have to crawl up on my shoulders and get to the edge that way."

It was extremely awkward and embarrassing—especially since I knew he could see in the dark and I was pretty sure I had lost all of my modesty patches in the icy water. But I was so ready to get out at that point, I didn't even complain. I just climbed up, using his big body as a ladder and finally found the edge of that awful, dark pool.

I dragged myself out and then collapsed in a heap, all my energy spent. To my side, I heard a deep, effortful grunt. Though I couldn't see it, I imagined Sarden pulling himself up with those impressive, muscular arms, his broad shoulders and tight abs working with the effort. Then he was beside me, breathing deeply in the darkness.

I lay on my side, shivering and gasping with the angry *nib-nibs* still chattering in my hair. I felt woozy and ill. Half-drowned and almost completely frozen. I couldn't feel my arms or my legs anymore at all.

All I could think was that back home in Tampa, I had always wished I had enough money to go visit other countries. I wanted to backpack through Europe and hike the Himalayas and explore the Far East and have all kinds of exotic adventures—at least I *thought* I did. Now that I had been abducted by aliens and was actually living the dream I realized something.

Adventures suck. They really do.

"You okay?" I heard Sarden ask.

"Yes," I wanted to say but somehow nothing came out. The cold started leaving my body and I felt toasty warm instead.

"Zoe?" he said again and I thought he sounded concerned. "Sweetheart? Talk to me!"

I wanted to but somehow I just couldn't. My mouth didn't want to work—*nothing* wanted to work. Not even my heart. I swear I felt it stop, although that ought to be impossible. But I did. The steady *thud-thud* that had been my own internal clock since birth went silent in my ears.

The room was dark all around me but I felt Sarden take me in his arms. He shook me and said something else, then pulled me to his chest. I couldn't see him but I heard the panic in his voice. I felt bad about it but I couldn't answer—couldn't do anything now.

And then, I don't want to say everything went dark because it was *already* dark. But I saw a pinpoint of white light in the blackness which slowly grew into a tunnel. A tunnel of light that seemed to be beckoning, just to me.

After that, I don't remember any more.

Sarden

I held her in my arms—her frail, soft body, as cold as ice. I pressed my ear to her chest but I didn't hear a heartbeat. Gods, what had I done? How had I let this happen?

Your fault, a little voice whispered in my head. *Your fault, Sarden, you bastard! She's beautiful and unique—a sheltered flower. And you took her. You plucked her from her home world and brought her out into the big, dirty universe to be hurt and abused and nearly drowned. And now she's gone – gone beyond your reach forever.*

"No!" I don't think I realized I'd said the word out loud until I heard it echo back to me, bouncing off the metal walls of the reservoir. It sounded loud and anguished and hopeless. But I couldn't lose hope—not now.

I held Zoe's limp form close to me, trying to massage life back into her limbs. I needed to warm her up, but how? My own body was almost as chilled as hers. In fact, I was shivering as I held her to me. But before I thought about bringing up her body heat, I had to restore her heartbeat.

"Come on, sweetheart," I told her, willing her to hear, willing her to come back to me. "Come on, my little Pure One, just breathe. Just live. *Please.*"

I squeezed her tight and placed the heel of one palm on her chest, pressing hard and rhythmically, trying to massage life back into her. *Come on…come on…*

I don't know how long I did that—held her and massaged her. I think I prayed at one point—begged the Goddess of Mercy for help. I'm not a religious male but I knew that I couldn't bear this—I couldn't lose her.

"*Please,*" I prayed. "*I'll make things right – just don't let her die. Don't let her be gone forever. Please!*"

But my prayers seemed to fall on deaf ears. Zoe stayed limp in my arms. Limp and cold and silent.

Gone. She was gone. I felt pain such as I hadn't known existed and something seemed to tear inside me. How could she mean so much to me? I had known her such a short time and I never intended to keep her for myself. And yet somehow, knowing she was gone beyond my reach devastated me to the core.

I gripped her to me, too numb to cry out.

"Zoe," I whispered, my voice a choked whisper. "I'm so damn sorry…"

And then I felt it—a single heartbeat. Just one faint flutter under my palm. And then another and another.

Warm her, a voice seemed to whisper in my ear. *Warm her and she will be well.*

Who was it? The Goddess in one of her many aspects? One of the Ancient Ones, looking down from on high? Or maybe just my own common sense telling me what had to be done?

Whatever or whoever it was, I knew I had to listen. I looked around again for a way to get my little Pure One warm and my eyes fell on the steaming hulk of the dead *chudd'x.*

I knew what I had to do.

Part Three: Uninhibited (you figure it out)

Chapter Seventeen

Zoe

"Are you all right, Lady Zoe?" a familiar voice asked. It sounded like a butler only I don't *have* a butler. I have a run-down, one-bedroom apartment in Ybor city, the historic and somewhat seedy part of Tampa, and half the time I worry about being able to make rent on *that*. So there's no way I can afford a butler. Yet, one was talking in my ear right now, as though he knew me.

I pried open my eyelids which seemed to be glued shut somehow, and saw a lantern with a light like an eye hovering over me. It was attached to a long, snaky silver neck which was, in turn, attached to the ceiling.

For a minute I completely freaked out…and then I remembered everything.

"Al," I said weakly, trying to sit up and failing. My chest was really sore for some reason. "What's going on? How did I get back on board the ship?"

"I carried you here. But not before you almost died on me."

The new voice came from the doorway. I looked over and saw

Sarden leaning against the doorframe, frowning at me. His arms and chest were smeared with some kind of black goo and streaks of the same stuff stained his shirt and trousers.

"*Died* on you? What are you talking about?" I demanded, my voice coming out weaker than I wanted it to. "Died from what?"

"Hypothermia. The water in the reservoir was extremely cold — I don't think you would have survived in it for much longer."

"Well, *you're* the one who told me to jump in," I pointed out, tartly.

"It was either that or wind up in the belly of the *chudd'x*, guarding the water supply. Which, as it turns out, you did anyway."

"What?" I wanted to sit up but when I tried, my body disagreed. So I just laid there and glared at him. "What do you mean by that?"

He shrugged, his broad shoulders rolling with the motion.

"Your heart had already stopped once and it was the only way to warm you up. I had already sliced it open so I put you inside its body cavity to bring your body temperature back up to normal."

"*What?*" This time I *did* manage to sit up even though my body protested. Looking down at myself, I realized I was covered in black goo. Not just my arms and hands, either — I was completely coated in the stuff. When I reached up to touch my cheek, I found it was even on my face — no wonder my eyelids had felt glued shut!

Also, I smelled *horrendous.*

"You heard me — I had to get you warmed up. This was the only way. You can say what you want about *chudd'xs* but at least they're hot-blooded. That's what's all over you — its blood. All over me too." He motioned at himself.

"Oh God, Sarden," I moaned, looking down at the gooey black stuff that coated every inch of my skin. "Is there *any* scifi trope you're *not* going to hit? First you pull out a lightsaber —"

"A what?" He frowned. "I used a *blast laser* to slice open the *chudd'x*. And a damn good thing I did too, or it would have eaten us both."

"And then you put me in its awful guts to warm me up," I continued, ignoring him. "I mean, what's next? Are you going to tell me you're my father and cut off my hand?"

"*What?*" He shook his head. "Zoe, are you sure you're feeling all right? Maybe I should have left you inside the *chudd'x* a little longer to let your brain thaw — you're not making any sense."

"I'm making perfect sense," I said grimly. "My point is, this sucks and I want a shower. A hot one. *Now.*"

He sighed. "You know the mister isn't going to get this off. It's the Cleansing Pool or nothing."

I almost said, "nothing then" but I was coated — literally *coated* — from head to foot in alien monster guts. The blankets Al had laid over the silver beanbag bed would probably have to be burned, along with my clothes. "Fine," I mumbled at last. "But…can you at least lower the uh, water level this time so it's not over my head?"

"I am afraid the liquid level of the PPC is pre-set and we are quite unable to change it, even to suit your less than average stature, lady Zoe," Al answered for him, sounding politely regretful.

"Great." I looked down at my nasty, gooey hands. "But I still can't swim."

"I'll go with you, of course." Sarden's voice got softer. "You know I won't let you get hurt."

I felt my stomach do a little flip but I wasn't going to melt that easily.

"Yeah, right," I muttered. "Where were you when Count Doloroso was trying to drag me away?"

"Count Doloroso?" He took a few steps towards me—he was limping a little for some reason. "Is *he* the one who lured you out of the shop with those damn *nib-nibs?*"

"How did you know that?" I asked. "And where are they, anyway?"

"They are quite well and safe, lady Zoe, I assure you," Al said. "I bathed them in warming liquid and gave them a proper home."

"A proper home? Where, in someone's stomach?" I looked at Sarden. "I can't believe that you guys eat them! Poor little monkeys!"

"*I* don't eat them," he protested. "And what are monkeys?"

"Cute little furry Earth animals," I said. "And if you never ate one, why did you tell me they scratched the inside of your mouth?"

"I may have tried one once," he muttered. "But I spit it out and let it run away—they're disgusting."

"Says the man who eats snake sandwiches," I said, but I felt relieved. I didn't want to think that Sarden was the kind of guy who would eat a living creature. Not a cute one, anyway.

"What did Doloroso say to you?" he asked.

"Mostly that I was special and a 'unique specimen'. Of course, this was in between nearly pulling my hair out by the roots and calling me a 'bitch.'" I shivered when I remembered what a close call I'd had.

"He tried to pull your hair out?" Sarden growled, looking angry.

I shrugged. "Basically he was just trying to grab hold of me anyway he could so he could drag me back to his ship. You know, you'd better be nice to my *nib-nibs* – they saved my life. If they hadn't bitten his hand, he never would have let me go. I'd be...be on his ship right now." My throat was suddenly tight with the thought.

"Did he say anything else?" Sarden asked in a low, dangerous voice.

"It's all kind of a blur." I shook my head. "He shouted something about The Last Day, whatever that means. And he said...said that..." I had to swallow hard before I could continue. "He said he wanted to put me back into the sensitivity tank and...and finish the test."

I shuttered again – I couldn't help it. The memory of being dragged into the yellow slime by the long, shiny black tentacles was still fresh in my mind. I would be there right now if I hadn't somehow unlocked the locked door and gotten inside the water storage building. How had I done that?

"Sarden's face was dark. "I should have known he would want you – the way he was looking at you, it was pretty fucking obvious. Zoe..." He took my hand. "I'm so damn sorry – I should never have left you alone in the first place."

"I...I called for you." My throat was still tight and I couldn't seem to summon up even an ounce of snark or sarcasm to lighten up the situation. "I called and called but you...you didn't come."

"I'm so sorry – I was wearing ear shields to protect my hearing while the mechanic and his fucking assistant showed me the properties of the new panels." His golden eyes glowed with fury. "In fact, it turns out the assistant was in on your kidnapping – or almost kidnapping."

"The little Oompa-Loompa looking guy?" I couldn't believe it.

"He seemed so nice and so concerned that I wasn't being treated right."

"Which was exactly how Doloroso convinced him that you rightfully belonged to him and that he needed to steal you away from me," Sarden said grimly. "I'm sure the fight we were having as we walked in the shop just made up his mind for him. So he suggested a lot of very loud tests and gave me the ear shields to wear—by the time I heard you calling, it was almost too late."

"So he confessed?" I asked. "The mechanic's assistant, I mean?"

Sarden nodded. "The mechanic was mortified—he's replacing all the panels for free."

"Wow," I said. "Well, I guess *some* good came of all this then."

"You nearly died, Zoe. I...I almost lost you." His voice went rough and he looked down at our joined hands—both still covered in the black *chudd'x* blood. "There's nothing good about that. The Goddess of Mercy knows I deserve to be skinned alive for leaving you alone in danger like that."

"You didn't know that Count Creepy would come after me," I said, for once not feeling the need to be snarky to defend myself.

"I should've," he said fiercely. "And I swear to you, it won't happen again. I'm going to protect you and stay by your side every minute from now until I can see you safely home."

"You mean safely to Giedi Prime," I said. "Right?"

"No." He shook his head. "No, I'm not going to trade you. I can't. I realized that when I thought I'd lost you for good."

"But...but what about your sister? You have to get her back and trading me is the only way."

This seemed wrong. Was I actually *arguing* that he should trade me? But it didn't matter because Sarden was shaking his head.

"I'll find another way," he said grimly. "You'll still have to come with me to Giedi Prime. I have to get there before the auction Tazaxx holds every cycle to get rid of the exhibits he doesn't want so he can make room for new ones. But after that, I'll take you...take you back to Earth." He cleared his throat. "And then you'll never have to see me again."

"What?" I could hardly believe him. Was he actually being serious? Also, why did the idea of never seeing the big alien again make me feel so sad?

"You heard me." Sarden did something to the bronze metal band he'd had the Commercians put on my wrist when he first got me. All this time it had remained in place, blinking quietly—my Alien Fitbit which he had called an "inhibitor." Now it popped off and lay in my lap. Where it had been was the only clean place on my body—a thin white band in the middle of the black *chudd'x* blood.

I looked up at Sarden and shook my head.

"I don't understand."

"You're free," he said quietly. "You're no longer my prisoner, Zoe. I hope you can forgive me for taking you in the first place."

"Why are you doing this?" I asked.

"Because I nearly lost you. You nearly died—Hell, you *did* die." He turned to me, his eyes flashing. "I can't have that on my soul—as stained as it is, I can't add murder of an innocent to the list."

"I didn't die," I said, and then I remembered the sensation of my heart stilling in my chest and the pinpoint of light that had grown to a tunnel. Okay, so maybe I *had* died, a little. "I'm okay *now*," I said lamely, trying to get out of the silver beanbag bed.

"Like hell you are," he growled. "Here, don't—you'll fall."

He reached me just as I toppled over and caught me in his

arms.

I gasped as an electrical jolt went through me—a tingling sensation that seemed to start at the top of my head and travel all the way down to my toes.

"What in the—"

Sarden took a deep breath, as though he was trying to steady himself.

"The inhibitor's gone," he said in a low voice, cradling me in his arms. "Give it a moment. We should get used to each other soon."

"Get used to each other? I don't understand." I felt like I was saying that a lot lately but really, I didn't. "Does this have to do with me being a, uh, La-ti, um, La-ti-da?"

"A La-ti-*zal*." He frowned. "At some point you really should learn the name for what you are."

"But I still don't know what a La-ti-zal *is*," I protested, finally getting it right. "Or how it's supposed to make me special."

"I'd say you're special in a lot of ways," he remarked. "For instance, how did you open the lock on the Force-Locks which were cued only for those of Vorn descent? Or the door to the water reservoir on Gallana which shouldn't have opened to anyone without Majoran DNA?"

I shook my head. "I don't know. They just…opened for me."

He gave me a look. "And that was *with* the inhibitor on. Gods, I don't know what you'll be capable of now. When I touch your skin, I see such colors…" He shook his head. "Spectrums and rainbows like I've never seen."

"Are you saying skin contact with me is like taking some kind of drug?" I demanded. "Some kind of magic mushrooms or LSD or something?"

"No." He held me close to his chest and headed for the bathroom area. "Nothing like that. It's just that males with Vorn DNA don't normally see in color."

"You don't? You're all color-blind?" I was surprised but then I thought back on the first time he'd touched me. When he talked about how red my hair was and how blue my eyes were.

"Not color-blind exactly," he said. "It's more like…things are washed out. We see in shades of gray and tan and black and white with just a few pastel tints here and there. We don't see true color until…"

"Until what?" I asked, prompting him. Maybe I was just trying to keep him talking, trying to avoid the inevitable dunking in the Cleansing Pool. Although God knew I ought to be used to going into tanks full of liquid by now — I had certainly been doing enough of it lately.

"Never mind." Sarden's face took on a guarded expression. "Sufficient to say, I have never seen anything remotely like what I see when I have skin-to skin contact with you. But it's probably just a manifestation of your La-ti-zal powers — nothing more."

"So glad I could brighten your day," I muttered. "*Literally*, I guess." We were standing right in front of the vertical bathtub with its pale purple liquid and I was feeling nervous and squirmy.

"It's more than that," Sarden murmured. "There's something about you, Zoe. Something I can't put a name to." He shook his head. "Never mind — it's time to get in. Will you be all right?"

"As long…as long as you don't let me go," I whispered, the words squeezed out of my too-tight throat.

"Never," he rumbled and opening the door, he took me with him into the pool.

Sarden

She did well in the Cleansing Pool—much better than the first time. I was almost tempted to think she was getting used to it but her white lips and wide eyes told a different story. So she wasn't getting used to being submerged after all—she was just determined not to show her fear this time.

Her bravery impressed me but more than ever, I wanted to know the reason for her fear. What had happened to make taking a simple dip in the Cleansing Pool such a traumatic experience for her?

And what was happening to me as I held her? Without the inhibitor to block her power, the world around me was brilliant— vivid in a way I'd never seen before. It was amazing and I wondered what she might be capable of in the future if her abilities came to full fruition.

Of course, I was taking her back to Earth so it was possible nothing would happen at all. On her home planet she would just be a latent La-ti-zal with no one the wiser. No one to know how incredibly special she was.

I knew but I couldn't say. Couldn't risk letting her know the truth about my people. Zoe's other latent abilities were impressive—her ability to somehow open locks which were keyed to others and the electrical tingle I felt when we first touched was amazing but it was the colors I saw when I touched her that troubled me the most.

Males with Vorn DNA never saw in color until they met a female they could mate. A female they could bond with.

You can't mate her—you promised to bring her home. And you can't bond with any female — you're a half-breed, remember? It's impossible.

It should be—but what about the colors I saw? Colors I had never expected to see with any female. Could they really be attributed to her powers as a *La-ti-zal?* Or was there some other reason…something more?

Doesn't matter if there is, the little voice in my head whispered. *She probably wants nothing to do with you. And who could blame her after you left her alone and let her get nearly kidnapped by fucking Doloroso, eaten by the damn chudd'x, and drowned in the reservoir?*

About one thing Doloroso was right—Zoe was incredibly unique and special.

And I didn't deserve her one damn bit.

Zoe

We stayed in the pool long enough to rinse all the black, stinking *chudd'x* blood away and then Sarden finally took us out. I was so glad to get out of the drowning tank—as I still thought of it to myself—that I didn't even mind that the filmy Majoran dress he'd had AI synthesize for me had melted completely away while we were inside it.

Yup, I was naked again. It seemed to be my lot in life ever since I was abducted. I would say I was getting used to it—only I wasn't. I still kept my arms firmly in place over my cash and prizes while Sarden stood in front of the mister, which was set to dry us off.

At last I was all dry and toasty warm—which was nice—and Sarden was about to set me on my feet when he appeared to remember something.

"Hey—what's going on?" I protested as he swung me back up in his arms when my soles were a scant inch from the floor. "I thought you were going to put me down."

"I was—but I forgot about your feet."

"What? What about them?" I asked uneasily as he sat me carefully on the edge of the silver hoverbed.

Al had been busy while we bathed and all the black slime smeared blankets were gone—they had been replaced by a single shiny gold coverlet. I wrapped it around myself, glad to have a way to hide my never-ending nakedness.

"You know what about them." Sarden frowned at me as he changed from his own still-damp clothes into a pair of his black silky sleep trousers. Now that I knew he was colorblind, I wasn't surprised that he limited his wardrobe colors to black and white. At least he could be sure those two shades wouldn't clash with his skin.

"No, I don't know," I told him. "My feet are fine." Well, maybe not exactly *fine*—I had actually cut them up pretty badly in my run from Count Creepy McGrabbyHands—but I wasn't about to admit that to Sarden.

"They're *not* fine—I followed the trail of blood you left. It's how I found you, Zoe." His deep voice was surprisingly quiet and the look in his golden eyes was pained. I realized he still blamed himself for what had happened to me and felt sorry for him.

"It's not that bad," I said, trying to make him feel better. "I'll be walking around in no time. In fact, I'd be walking *now* if you'd just give me some Neosporin and some Band-aids."

He shook his head. "I don't know what those are. But I *am* going to heal you."

"Oh no—please don't," I said quickly, thinking of how he'd "healed" the other parts of my anatomy. "I mean, *please* don't tell me you want to lick my foot because sorry, that's just gross. And please don't say it's not gross because you have a foot fetish because that's even grosser," I babbled.

"A *foot* fetish?" he asked, frowning.

"You know—someone who gets off to feet? Sexually, I mean?" I thought of some of the weird stuff I'd run across on the Internet. "I mean, there are some guys on Earth who love that kind of stuff. Toe porn and foot bondage, and sniffing dirty pantyhose and…uh…" I trailed off, realizing he was just staring at me.

Finally, he shook his head. "Your little planet is stranger than I gave you credit for."

"What?" I asked, feeling defensive. "You can't tell me in a whole wide galaxy full of planets that Earth is the kinkiest one."

"Not by a long shot." Sarden was busying himself with a shallow metal basin he'd pulled out of one of his closets. "But we tend to fetishize other races and peoples—not individual parts of their bodies. "For instance, you might say I have a fetish for Earth females." He shot me a grin that made my insides flip.

"But not Earth girls' feet, right?" I clarified. "I mean…how *exactly* are you going to heal me?"

"Don't worry—oral healing is only for…the most intimate areas." His eyes grew half-lidded and I knew he was remembering the way he'd licked me, right here on this very bed. I could feel my cheeks getting hot but I tried not to show it.

"Uh-huh," I said, noncommittally. "So then, how—"

"With this." He held out the metal basin and then pressed a button on the side of it. Suddenly it started to fill up with bright blue fizzing liquid. "Here." Sarden stepped forward, motioning for me to put my feet in. "This will help."

"It also looks like it's going to sting," I said, keeping my tootsies well clear of the fizzing liquid.

"It will—but only a little." Sarden gave me a stern look. "Come on, Zoe—put your feet in.

"I don't want to," I said stubbornly. "Plus, I don't need to—I'm a fast healer."

He frowned. "Wounds like yours will take days to mend without the help of the healing agent. How do you expect to get around? You think I'm going to drop everything and carry you everywhere you want to go?"

"I thought you *liked* carrying me," I pointed out, offended.

"I *do*," he growled. "The Gods know I like it more than I should. But we're going to be leaving for the port on Giedi Prime soon. Once we get there I'll need to go down and scout around—gather some information. I don't like leaving you alone on the ship helpless."

"Then don't," I said, promptly. "Take me with you."

"What?" Sarden stared at me as though I'd lost my mind. "After what just happened on Gallana you want me to take you to *another* port? I don't think so."

"Why not?" I asked. "Can't you give me some kind of disguise? Something to cover my hair—maybe some baggy clothes?"

"But...*why* would you want to go? After what you just went through?"

"I want to help," I said simply. "You're letting me go even though I'm your best chance of getting your sister back. The least I can do is try to help you gather information."

"And what makes you think you'd be good at that? You don't strike me as the stealthy type," he remarked sarcastically.

"Thanks a lot! I *can* be when I *want* to be." I lifted my chin. "Also, I'm *small* which is more than you or most of the other aliens

I've met so far can say. Dress me in dark clothes, maybe give me a pair of dark glasses or something to hide my eyes and I can be *very* unobtrusive. Just a quiet little mouse sneaking around the corners of the room listening to what everyone is saying. No one will even notice me."

"Well..." He frowned thoughtfully and I could tell he was considering my idea. Good — I really did want to help. As strange as it sounds, I felt really bad about him giving me back my freedom with no idea of how he'd get his little sister back. Also, I'd be bored stiff on the ship all by myself.

"Please?" I pleaded. "I really want to help. Look, I'll stick my feet in the bath and I won't complain no matter how much it stings if you just let me go with you."

"All right," he said, nodding at last. "I agree — on one condition."

"Which is?" I was already getting ready to put my feet in the blue, fizzing basin which he had been holding patiently all this time, but his next words stopped me.

"I'll let you come with me and help find information about my sister if you'll tell me what happened to yours."

"What?" I froze, unable to move. "What...what do you mean?"

"You know what I mean, Zoe," he said quietly. "You've mentioned her several times now and I know she has something to do with why you're so deathly afraid of being submerged in water. But I want to know why — the whole story."

"Why should I tell *you?*" I demanded, crossing my arms over my chest defensively.

"Zoe..." He gave me a long look. "I told you about Sellah, about how she was taken."

"That's different though," I whispered. "Your sister — she's still alive."

"Yes." Sarden put down the basin and leaned forward, cupping my cheek in one hand. "Please," he said, staring intently into my eyes. "I *need* to know."

"Fine." I pulled back from him and he withdrew his hand. "I'll tell you," I said. "But I might as well do the foot thing while I do."

He picked the basin back up, held it out, and simply looked at me.

"Fine," I said again and took a deep, shaking breath. After all these years, it still hurt to talk about it.

There was silence from Sarden and I knew he was waiting. Well, might as well get it over with. Gritting my teeth, I put my feet into the blue liquid—which did indeed sting like hell—and began talking.

"I wasn't very old when it happened—not that that's any excuse. I was seven and my sister, Angela, was five. We had just moved to Tampa from Minnesota." I looked at him briefly. "You have to understand—Minnesota is really cold, so almost nobody has a swimming pool. But Florida is really hot so a lot of people have them down there."

"A swimming pool is an artificially made body of water big enough to swim in?" Sarden guessed.

"Exactly." I sighed. "Anyway, our next door neighbor had one. They had a fence around their yard but we could still see it through the chain link. All blue and inviting…" I swallowed hard, remembering how fascinated Angie had been with the pool. How she always begged to be allowed to go over and just *look* at it.

"Zoe?" Sarden prompted, and I realized I'd been sitting there silent for a while, just thinking.

"Neither of us knew how to swim," I told Sarden. "We were

supposed to take lessons later that summer but, well, we hadn't had them yet."

Okay, I was stalling and I knew it. Might as well get the hard part of the story over and done with.

"One day my mom had to go out—I think she got a call from her new job. She was only going to be gone about an hour and she hadn't had time to find a good babysitter in Tampa yet. I guess she thought we would be all right alone, just for that short length of time. So she told me...she told me..." I cleared my throat, forcing myself to go on despite the hard knot of pain and shame that had formed in my stomach. "She told me to watch over my sister," I said, forcing the words out at last. "To take care of her—not to let anything happen to her."

"You were too young for a responsibility like that," Sarden said in a low voice.

"Yeah, well..." I shrugged and looked down at my hands again, seeing it all over again. "Angie and I played for a little while but then she got bored so we sat down to watch cartoons on TV. Um—that's a kind of entertainment for kids," I added for Sarden's benefit. "Then, the next thing I knew, I looked up and she was gone. Just...gone."

The knot in my stomach had grown so big now it was crushing my lungs, making it hard to breathe. But somehow I was still talking.

"The minute I saw she was gone, I got up and went looking for her," I said. "I looked all over the house but it wasn't until I opened the back door to check the yard that I heard splashing coming from the neighbor's place."

"She climbed the divider separating your property from your neighbor's?" Sarden guessed.

I nodded, feeling sick.

"I ran and climbed after her but by the time I got over the fence she was already..." Oh God, this was hard to say. "Already at the bottom of the...the pool."

"What did you do?" Sarden asked softly.

"I think I screamed for help. I must have because the neighbor said they heard someone shouting and screaming as they drove up into their driveway." I shook my head. "But no one came—not right away. And Angie was at the...at the bottom..."

"You jumped in after her, didn't you?" he asked softly. "Even though you didn't know how to swim."

"What else could I do?" I looked up at him and noticed he seemed blurry for some reason. Also, my eyes were stinging. Must be the fumes from that damn blue fizzy liquid or something. "What else could I do?" I repeated. "She was my sister...my *little sister.* I was su-supposed to be t-taking *c-care* of her. But I didn't. I *didn't.*"

My last word ended on a sob and I realized, to my horror, that I was crying. I *hate* crying—especially in front of someone else. It makes me feel so weak and girly and stupid.

Without a word, Sarden put down the fizzing basin and took me in his arms, heedless of the fact that I was dripping blue liquid all over him.

For a long time he just held me and let me cry. I found I was holding him back, my arms wrapped around his narrow waist as I pressed my face into his muscular chest and let the sobs take me.

I don't know why telling him the story affected me so strongly. It wasn't like I hadn't told anyone before. Charlotte and Leah knew. Hell, the therapist I'd seen in high school could recite the details forward and backwards. But this was the first time I'd shared this old, hurtful piece of my past with a guy. Not even my ex, Scott, who

I had lived with for over a year, had known the details. He'd just known that I had a sister who died when she was younger — not that I had anything to do with it.

"I should have been watching her," I told Sarden, between sobs. "I should have kept it from happening."

"Gods," he murmured and stroked my hair gently. "No wonder you agreed to let me trade you for Sellah. You're still trying to assuage the guilt for something that happened back when you were a child."

I swiped at my eyes and looked up at him.

"Maybe," I admitted in a small voice. "I know there's no getting Angie back — she's gone. But I guess I thought, if I could help you find your sister…help you get back Sellah…"

"That's not your responsibility," he said fiercely. "And you shouldn't have been tasked with watching over your sister at such a young age, either. Seven cycles isn't old enough for such adult behavior."

"Weren't you?" I asked. "I mean, I thought you said you weren't much older than that when your mom told you to look after Sellah."

He sighed and nodded.

"You're right. I guess…we always feel responsible for our siblings. But Zoe…" He cupped my cheek and looked down at me. "You tried — you did everything you could. You jumped in after your sister even though you *couldn't swim.*"

"My mom said the same thing," I said, wiping at my eyes again. "She…she never forgave herself for leaving us alone."

"Guilt is a heavy burden," Sarden murmured. He tilted my chin and looked into my eyes. "Thank you for telling me. I know it couldn't have been easy."

"It's not something I like to talk about," I admitted. "It's easier to just keep things light."

He gave me a crooked smile.

"I knew there was more to you than a sense of humor with a thin veneer of sarcasm."

"It's called snarkiness," I said. "And it works just fine for me."

"I like it," he rumbled. "But I want you to know, you can let down the outer barrier of, uh, 'sharkliness' and just be yourself with me if you want."

"It's snark — *snarkiness*," I said. "But thank you, I appreciate the offer."

"You're more than welcome." He cupped my face in both hands and for a moment I thought he was going to kiss me. He did come in close and I held my breath, my heart pounding against my ribs. I didn't know if I wanted him to kiss me or not. Now that I wasn't his prisoner anymore, I didn't know where we stood.

Sarden didn't seem to know either. At the last minute, his lips moved up and he planted a soft, gentle kiss...on my forehead. Great. I didn't know whether to be relieved or disappointed...but I was definitely leaning towards disappointed.

"Well," I said, trying to lighten the mood. "My feet should be all healed now and I told you what you wanted to know so I get to go with you to the spaceport outside of Giedi Prime, right?"

He sighed. "On two conditions — you go in disguise and you stay close to me. I want to keep an eye on you at all times."

"All right," I agreed, just glad I was going to get off the ship again. Gallana had been extremely interesting and exciting. I mean, the part where Count Doloroso had chased me and I was nearly eaten by a huge alien monster and almost drowned in freezing water and then died for just a minute from hypothermia, sucked.

But other than that, it was an experience I would never forget. I had always wanted to travel—I wasn't going to waste my chance to see the galaxy just sitting around the ship twiddling my thumbs.

And on a more serious note, if I could help Sarden get his sister back and avoid the kind of guilt and pain I had in my past, I wanted to do it. Nobody should have to live with that hanging over them—it's a pain you never completely recover from.

No matter how many years pass, it still hurts.

As I watched Sarden examine my newly healed feet—and felt glad I'd had a recent pedicure before he'd abducted me—I thought that I'd like to spare him that pain.

The big alien, who had seemed like such a jerk at first, actually had a heart. The very fact that he'd comforted me and let me cry myself out against his chest without pulling away or making excuses said a lot about him in my opinion. I couldn't remember the last time a guy had done that for me—Scott certainly hadn't. Any display of emotion had made him intensely uncomfortable.

"C'mon, babe," he'd say if I even got a little teary. *"Enough with the waterworks—okay?"* And then I would have to try not to feel what I was feeling and just pretend everything was okay—which was probably one reason I was so good at keeping things light.

Sarden didn't expect that of me. Even when we sniped at each other from time to time, he never demanded that I keep my feelings to myself. In fact, he even seemed to welcome them…

Speaking of keeping things light, that's exactly what you'd better do with Sarden, whispered a little voice in my head. *Stop getting all mushy and come back to reality. He still has to rescue his sister and you're only along for the ride. Plus, the minute he gets her back, you're headed straight back to Earth and you'll never see him again.*

I wondered why that thought made me feel so sad. But it didn't matter—it wasn't as though he'd want some Earth girl tagging along after him on his adventures through the galaxy.

Just keep it light, I told myself again. *Try to do your part to get his sister back and don't do anything crazy.*

Right. Like fall in love. Because that would be the craziest, stupidest thing I could do. It was absolutely, positively out of the question.

So why did I have a feeling I was already falling?

Chapter Eighteen

Zoe

"Not bad. Not bad at all." Sarden surveyed me with apparent satisfaction—satisfaction I didn't exactly share. The 'disguise' he had put me in was pretty much the exact opposite of the Majoran dress I had worn on Gallana. Instead of exposing my goodies, it covered everything and I do mean *everything*.

Don't get me wrong—I wasn't complaining about not being naked. Or mostly naked, anyway. But the bulky black clothes he'd had Al synthesize for me were heavy and hot. They consisted of a shapeless, long-sleeved shirt, thick trousers, and as if all that wasn't enough—a cape.

I mean, really? A *cape*?

"I'm not wearing the cape," I said, frowning at myself in the 3-D viewer thingy. "I'm not freaking Batman."

"The cape probably isn't necessary," Sarden agreed.

I was pleasantly surprised that he was giving in so easily.

"Great! Then just give me a pair of dark glasses to hide my eyes and I'm ready to go."

He frowned. "We need to hide your hair as well. It's so red it really stands out."

"Says the man who has red *skin*," I pointed out.

"Which is normal for a Vorn, even if it's not for an Eloim," he said. "But your combination of pale, silky skin with such a profusion of red hair is unusual—*and* desirable."

"Is that what this is about? Look at me in this get-up." I spread my arms, indicating my bulky, be-caped figure. "Do I look desirable to you?"

Sarden's golden eyes suddenly went half-lidded.

"Always, sweetheart," he murmured. "I find you *extremely* desirable, which I think I've made clear in the past."

"I didn't mean…I mean, I wasn't fishing for compliments," I said, feeling my cheeks go hot at the way he was looking at me. "I just meant, I don't think anyone is going to be lusting after me while I'm wearing a baggy sweatshirt and a freaking Batman cape. That's all."

"I know what you mean, but I disagree." He frowned. "You really have no idea of your own beauty, do you?"

"I, um…" I didn't know what to say about that. When you've been called "chubby" and "chunky" and been freckled and short and pretty much the exact opposite of what society says is beautiful, like I had all your life, it's hard to get a sense of your own "beauty."

"Luckily, *I* do," Sarden continued evenly. "Which is why I had Al synthesize *this*." He pulled something from behind his back and I stared at it in disbelief.

"No," I said at last, when I could talk. "No *way* am I wearing that thing."

Sarden arched an eyebrow at me.

"Then I guess you're not coming with me."

"What? But I did everything you asked. Look, just give me a scarf to wear over my hair or something. But not *this*—how will I even breathe in it?"

I gestured at what he was holding out to me—a mask. But not just any mask—this thing would cover my entire *head*. It looked a little like those caricature rubber masks that bank robbers use to protect their identity when they're committing the crime of the century.

And wearing this thing would certainly be a crime. It wasn't just ugly—it was *hideous.*

Green, pebbled skin that reminded me of an alligator's hide, black, compound eyes like a fly, and pointy, Shrek-like ears stared back at me. The mouth was a small, blue wrinkled hole and the nose wasn't even a nose—just two flat nostril slits.

"What is this even supposed to *be?*" I asked Sarden. "It's awful."

"It's a Grubbian," he said patiently. "They're one of the few sentient species as small as you Earthlings. Also, they're traders, known to frequent the outer ports. You'll fit right in with this on."

"I'll *smother* with this on," I protested."

"It's very comfortable— made out of a special smart-fabric. I ran a shipment of it for a rich merchant in the Acanthion system last cycle and kept a bolt back for myself. Thought it might come in handy." He grinned at me. "It's illegal in most systems, you know."

"Great," I grumbled. "So now you're trying to make an intergalactic criminal out of me."

"Oh, you'll see plenty of criminals in the Giedi Prime port—but only if you wear this."

He nodded at the mask and frowned at me. With a sinking feeling, I understood he wasn't going to let up until I put the damn thing on. And he said *I* had a one track mind!

"All right—*fine.*" Gathering my hair into a loose, messy bun at the nape of my neck, I pulled the weird Grubbian mask over my head.

I had expected the closed in, claustrophobic sensation and the weird, plasticky smell of a Halloween mask. I was pleasantly surprised though—the mask was completely breathable so I didn't get the feeling I was suffocating. I could tell something was over my face, but it was more like a thin piece of fabric or gauze—the same sensation I imagined I would feel if I was just wearing a veil draped over my head.

"Well?" Sarden asked.

"All right." I sighed. "It's not *awful.* But won't it look weird, me not having any facial expressions. I mean, unless, uh, Grubbians just walk around stone-faced all day."

"Oh, you have expressions, all right," he remarked. "Every time your face moves, so does the mask. Even the tiniest twitch is relayed to the smart-fabric."

"Smart-fabric, huh?" I murmured.

"See for yourself," he gestured at the 3-D viewer again.

I looked at it, taking in my weird new appearance and wrinkled my nose.

The ugly green mask wrinkled its nose too—well, the nostril slits did, anyway.

"Hey!" I didn't know whether to be horrified or delighted. I settled for a mixture—hor-lighted?—and made another face which the mask copied perfectly.

I winked my eyes—the big, black bug eyes of the mask winked back. I waggled my eyebrows and the brow-ridges of the mask did the same. I stuck out my tongue—the mask did too. Only the mask's tongue was long and thin and *blue.* Amazing.

Sarden let loose a deep, rumbling laugh and I realized I was acting like a fool. But honestly, it was so cool—I couldn't help myself.

"Okay," I said, looking up at him. "This is pretty awesome. I mean, it's ugly as sin but I like it anyway."

He raised an eyebrow at me.

"So you'll wear it with no more complaining?"

"No more complaining," I promised. "This is going to be *fun*."

"Zoe..." He put a hand on my shoulder and looked at me intently, suddenly completely serious. "All joking aside, the station on Giedi Prime is damn dangerous. There are going to be males there who would cut you to pieces and use you for bait for a *xanthun* hunt without a second thought. So be careful when we're down there and never get too far from me. All right?"

His words made me feel like someone had dumped a bucket of ice cubes into the pit of my stomach.

"Okay," I said, in a much more subdued voice. "I got it. I'm just there to gather information and I won't get too far from you."

"Good." He nodded. "Now here's what to listen for..."

Chapter Nineteen

Zoe

I scanned the dim, smoky area of the VIP lounge carefully, trying to stay to the shadows and look unobtrusive. Not that I stood out at all. Even with my ugly-ass mask on, I was by far one of the least noticeable people in the big, weird room.

There was a kind of round, circular bar at the center of the lounge that was made of what looked like bones. What kind of bones, I didn't know and didn't want to find out. The ivory of alien femurs and tibias and scapulas and whatever the other bones were gleamed in the dim, hazy light. Whoever or whatever it was that had donated the raw material for the grizzly bar must have been big though—freaking huge. Most of the aliens sitting around the bone bar were Sarden's size or even bigger and not all of them were humanoid, but none of them looked like they had bones big enough to make such massive furniture out of.

Well, *almost* none of them. Far at the end of the bar was a creature the size of an elephant, taking up three of the bone bar stools at once with his wrinkled, purple behind. He spoke in a voice so low I felt it as a trembling vibration in the air and seemed to be having a conversation with the bartender—who had three faces and was speaking with several other customers at the same time.

Beside the purple elephant man sat a thin woman—I *thought* it was a woman, anyway—wearing an elegant fur bikini which barely covered her three gigantic breasts. She had light green skin and was smoking the longest, thinnest cigarette I had ever seen. It must have been three feet long and the smoke coming out of it changed colors occasionally, from pink to purple to dark, cerulean blue.

Sarden was working the other end of the lounge, casting an occasional glance in my direction. I was keeping to the fringes of the crowd, listening as best I could while I pretended to drink a weird, fizzing concoction that didn't look too different from the liquid in the healing foot bath he had used on me. I couldn't really taste it through the mask but I pretended to suck it up through the long, tube-like, blue tongue, which was how Sarden had told me Grubbians drank.

A band played in the corner — making loud, unpleasant squawking sounds on bagpipe-looking instruments that appeared to be growing out of the musicians' bodies. I wondered if we were being serenaded by their burps and coughs and other bodily noises — that was certainly what it *sounded* like, anyway. *Ugh.*

Honestly, if this was the VIP lounge, I would hate to see the regular one. It really wasn't a very pleasant place at all. But then, I wasn't there for pleasantries. I needed to collect information and I was hot on the trail of someone I thought might have some.

He was a big son-of-a-bitch — even bigger than Sarden, I estimated, though not quite in the same league as the purple elephant man. I had only seen him from behind because he was hunched over the bar with his head down, saying something into a communications device gripped in one big hand. His skin was a dusky blue, the color of the sky at twilight when the sun is just starting to sink, and he was wearing black leather trousers and a leather vest to match, which left his massive, muscular arms bare.

Between the bass rumblings of the elephant man and the

strange, unmusical sounds coming from the "band" in the corner of the large room, it was hard to hear anything. But I was absolutely positive I'd heard the big blue guy say, "Tazaxx" into his phone-thingy. Trying to be quiet and unobtrusive, I crept closer.

"No, don't know if she's here or not," he was growling to whoever he was talking to. "I'll have to do recognizance and it won't be easy – Tazaxx doesn't let anyone into his compound without a damn good reason. Fuckin' asshole."

There it was again! I was *certain* I'd heard the name this time! I snuck even closer…and that was the moment when a drunk alien with two heads bumped into me.

"Oh, 'scuse me. Pardon me!" one head said, nodding a drunken apology.

"Watch where you're going! Clumsy Grubbians!" the other one barked. Apparently he was an angry drunk, even if the other head wasn't.

"Sorry," I muttered, because I just wanted him to move along and let me listen some more. But that wasn't good enough for the two headed guy.

"Do you even know who you're speaking to?" the second head demanded, looking down his long nose at me.

"Uh, Zaphod Beeblebrox?" I said, hazarding a guess.

"*What* did you call me?" the second head demanded. "Is that some kind of insult?"

"How *dare* you insult my brother?" the first head asked, getting into the act now.

Oh, so they were *brothers?* That must be awkward on dates. Not that having two heads was ever going to be simple.

"Look, I wasn't trying to be insulting. It was a joke and not a very good one." I made what I hoped was a placating "calm down" gesture with one hand. "Why don't we just forget about it and go our separate ways?"

"Such an insult can never be forgotten or forgiven!" The second head proclaimed. He shoved me with one of his three arms (did I mention the three arms?) and my drink flew out of my glass and landed on the back of the big, blue alien's head, dousing his black, skull-cut hair with fizzing blue.

"What the *fuck?*"

The big blue guy spun around, moving much faster than anyone that huge ought to be able to. He took one look at me and the empty drink in my hand and grabbed me by the front of my shirt.

"The *Hell* do you think you're doin'?" he growled in a deep, menacing voice. Up close I was surprised to see that he had horns like Sarden's — only his were thicker and curled like a ram's horns — also they were jet black. There was a curving black tattoo that grew up from one muscular pec to encircle his thick neck in a pattern that reminded me of thorns.

But the weirdest thing about him was his eyes — it was It was as if they had been reversed. The whites were jet black and the pupil and iris were outlined in white.

"Oh, I…I'm so sorry," I gasped, tugging at the bottom hem of my shirt. Al had yet to manage to synthesize me a working bra and I was afraid that if the blue alien pulled my shirt up much further, my bare breasts would be exposed. *That* would certainly blow my cover. Nothing like flashing your titties at an alien bar to let them know you're human.

"The fuck did you throw your drink at me?" he demanded, his white-on-black eyes narrowing and his lips peeling back in a snarl.

Great, he had two short, sharp fangs to go with the weird eyes and black horns.

Some people are just blessed, I guess.

"I...I didn't! I mean, not on purpose!" I exclaimed breathlessly. "He shoved me! He..." I looked around for the two headed alien but he had conveniently disappeared.

"He, *who?*" the big alien demanded, shaking me.

"The two-headed guy. He was just here—he was really drunk and he shoved into me and tried to pick a fight."

"Right. Tried to pick a fight while you were busy listenin' in on my conversation," he growled. "What are you, anyway?" His nostrils wrinkled. "I can tell you're not really Grubbian." He pulled me closer and took a deeper sniff. "And you're not male either. So who in the Scalding Hells..."

"She's with me," Sarden said, suddenly appearing behind the blue alien's massive shoulder. His eyes were glowing molten gold with rage and his voice was a deep, angry growl. "So put her the *fuck* down or suffer the consequences."

The blue guy whipped around to face Sarden with me still clutched in his fist. I was sure at any minute my shirt would rip open or pull all the way up to my neck and then the whole bar would see my fun-puppies. But when he caught sight of Sarden, his expression suddenly changed from one of irritation and anger to pleased disbelief.

"Sarden?" he asked. "Sarden de'Lagorn?"

"Gravex? Grav N'gol? I don't believe it!" Sarden put out an arm and the big blue guy grasped it, his hand closing over Sarden's forearm as Sarden's hand closed over his. "How long has it been?"

"Too long," Sarden said, positively grinning now. "I haven't seen you since our time on Vorn 6 when you, well..." He trailed off, looking extremely uncomfortable.

"You can say it," the blue guy whose name was apparently Grav rumbled. "Since I was tried and found guilty in the High Court."

"Listen, for what it's worth, I never believed you did it," Sarden said earnestly.

"But I *did* do it." Grav grinned, flashing his short, sharp fangs. "Which is why they sent me away to triple max detention. But I'm out now, as you can see."

"All I can see is that I'm about to be exposed here," I said, breaking into their conversation. "I hate to interrupt your reunion but if you guys are friends, could you *please* put me down?"

"Oh — sorry." Grav set me on my feet and I smoothed down the front of my shirt, relieved not to be exposed. He pointed a thumb at me and looked at Sarden. "Who is she anyway and why is she sneakin' around listening in on other people's conversations?"

"She's with me." Sarden pulled me close, draping one arm around my shoulders protectively.

"Yeah, you said that but who *is* she?" Grav's nose wrinkled. "*What* is she? I've never smelled anything like her — so fuckin' *sweet*."

"She's *not* available." Sarden's voice went from friendly to a menacing growl so fast it made my head spin. Apparently his trust in his old friend only went so far.

"I didn't think she was," Grav rumbled, frowning. "Hell, I can smell your scent all over her, Sarden. I was just curious — that's all." He frowned at me. "Curious the same way your little female was about me. Why do you have her skulking around this fuckin' place anyway if you're so protective? It's not very damn safe, you know."

Sarden sighed and seemed to relax a little.

"I know. But she insisted." He gave me a look which I returned with interest. "The truth is, she's here helping me gather any information we can get about Sellah."

"Sellah? Your Eloim blood-sister?" Grav frowned as he grabbed a napkin looking thing from the bar to swab at the back of his head which was still dripping with my drink. "What about her?"

Sarden took a look around the bar. Nobody seemed to be listening but he still frowned.

"Let's take this reunion someplace a little more private," he muttered. "Come on."

"Sure." Grav shrugged amiably and the three of us went to find a dark corner — of which there were plenty in the dim, smoky lounge. Walking between them, I felt like a little kid between two adults — they were both so freaking *huge*.

I wondered if Grav was part Vorn like Sarden. His horns were a little different and his eyes and skin color were completely unlike Sarden's but they both had the same big, muscular build and confident way of walking.

We finally got settled in a booth with extremely high sides and a gauzy curtain at the entrance to keep prying eyes out. Apparently the regular patrons of the VIP lounge valued their privacy. I sat beside Sarden, who kept his arm around me, and across from Grav. The table of the booth was so high, it was almost up to my chin, though both guys rested their brawny forearms on it easily.

"So what happened to your sister?" Grav asked, frowning. "Is she all right?"

"I don't know — I hope so," Sarden said grimly. "She was kidnapped and sold to a wealthy Gord merchant — Tazaxx. He has a compound on Giedi Prime where he keeps his private exhibit — beautiful and unique females from all over the galaxy. Some he keeps but some—"

"He auctions off. Right." Grav nodded.

"So you know about him?" Sarden leaned forward eagerly. "What can you tell me about the situation?"

"Probably nothin' you don't already know. That he keeps his 'treasures' as he calls them, hidden away and it's fuckin' impossible to get in to see them unless you're a wealthy investor who might buy one at an exorbitant price."

Sarden nodded. "I know all that. I've smuggled several shipments for the bastard but he's never once offered to let me see his private collection, even though I've been in his compound twice."

"Excuse me," I said. "Not to interrupt but if he sells his, uh, exhibits sometimes, why not just *buy* Sellah back? I mean..." I lowered my voice and spoke in Sarden's ear. "Don't you have enough money, er, *credit* from selling all that medical-torture stuff to Count Creepy? Especially since you didn't have to pay to have the ship's panels replaced?"

"I thought about that but Tazaxx won't sell to me." Sarden sounded frustrated.

"What? Why not?" I asked.

"Because..." He sighed. "We had a...dispute over the last shipment I smuggled for him. Terrinian quarthogs. He wanted to pay less than he'd offered in the first place so I offloaded the whole lot to another merchant. Once you piss Tazaxx off, he'll never deal with you again."

"But what about...I thought that was why you got *me* in the first place?" I said to Sarden. "So he would deal with you. Make a trade with you."

"That would have been different—a trade doesn't involve

credit changing hands," he said. "It's not the same thing to a Gord." He shrugged. "But even so, I don't know if he would have gone for it. He hates me—he'd be glad to cause me pain by withholding Sellah just because I want her back so badly."

"My employer is in the same situation," Grav rumbled. "He offended Tazaxx and now he's paying the price. Gords never forgive an offense—they hold on to a grudge like it's fuckin' credit."

"Wait—your *employer?*" Sarden raised an eyebrow at him. "You don't strike me as the kind who goes to work for a regular paycheck, Grav."

"Oh, I don't—contract work only. I'm too much of a son-of-a-bitch to work with on a regular basis." Grav grinned. "I'm a Protector now."

Sarden's eyebrows went even higher.

"You? A *Protector?*"

"I'm fuckin' hurt." Grav put a hand to his broad chest. "You don't think I'm Protector material?"

"It's just…surprising, that's all." Sarden shrugged. "But of course a male has to do what he wants with his life."

"Excuse me," I said, butting in again. "But what's a Protector and why shouldn't your old friend be one?"

Sarden looked uncomfortable but Grav answered me without hesitation.

"A Protector is a sentinel for hire—I shield my wards from harm or in some cases, like my current job, I retrieve them when they're in danger. I put my life on the line to keep them safe—but the position requires them to trust me completely."

"Oh," I said. "So, kind of like a bodyguard slash rescuer?"

He inclined his massive head. "In a way."

"But…" I shook my head. "I still don't understand why you think Sarden thinks it's odd for you to be a bodyguard…er, *Protector*."

"Probably because I'm also a murderer." Grav spoke matter-of-factly, as though it was no big deal. I threw Sarden a glance from the corner of my eye and saw that his facial expression hadn't changed. But his hand on my shoulder tightened and he drew me a little bit closer to his big body.

"Ooookay," I said at last, when the silence that had fallen between us was getting really uncomfortable. "Well, *that's* not awkward."

"Just answerin' your question." Grav shrugged.

"So who are you protecting now?" I asked. "You said it's some guy who crossed Tazaxx like Sarden did?"

"No, my employer isn't my ward—he just pays the bills. In fact, I don't ward males at all."

"You don't?" I asked.

Grav shook his head, the polished tips of his horns gleaming in the dim light.

"Fuck no. Any male who can't protect himself doesn't deserve my help. I work strictly for females—I ward and protect those in danger—especially if they're being threatened by a male."

He cracked his knuckles menacingly, making me suddenly glad I had girly parts. I wouldn't want to be the guy he was after for mistreating a female, that was for damn sure.

"That's…very chivalrous of you," I said, my throat dry. "But if you're not protecting your employer, then who—?"

"It's my client's granddaughter—only twelve cycles old. I warded her for over a year and then her grandmother decided to take her on a trip without me—something about the mysteries of femalehood…becoming a woman—I don't know." He shook his head in disgust. "Anyway, pirates attacked their ship. The grandmother was killed and my ward was snatched up and sold to Tazaxx for his damn zoo."

His face had gone cold as he told the story, the easy good humor disappearing from his white-on-black eyes and leaving them hard as stones.

"Only twelve years old?" I whispered, feeling a surge of pity for the girl. "That's awful! Is she…is she all right? Did they…?"

"I don't know exactly *what* they did to her." Grav's voice was a low growl. "I have to get her back first to find out. *Then* I'll punish the ones who took her. And believe me, if they laid so much as a finger on her before delivering her to Tazaxx…"

He seemed to grow bigger somehow, if that was even possible, and if I had thought he was scary before, well, he was freaking *terrifying* now. I wouldn't have been the pirates who had captured and sold his ward for all the world. They were going to be in a universe of pain if Grav caught them and something told me he wouldn't stop until he did.

"And you think Tazaxx has her—your ward—in his exhibit?" Sarden asked.

Grav nodded. "I *know* it. But getting in to find her is a problem."

"But…if there's going to be an auction, couldn't your, uh, employer just buy her there?" I asked. "And the same for Sellah—couldn't you just buy her at the auction?"

"Of course—*if* we were sure that Tazaxx had them marked to go to the auction," Sarden said. "We don't know that. We don't know what he plans to do and he's sure as hell not going to share his plans with *me*. He told me last time we spoke that he never wanted to see my face again."

His words sparked something inside me—an idea. It might be a really stupid idea, I wasn't sure—but that didn't keep me from speaking up.

"Why does he have to see your face?" I asked.

"What do you mean?" He frowned at me.

"I mean, you said that he sells to wealthy investors sometimes, right? So why not pretend to be one and get in his compound that way?"

"That's a damn good idea," Grav rumbled. "*If* you've got technology that will defeat his facial scanning software. If he recognizes you, you'll be out on your ass before you even step foot in the door."

"Will this do it?" I asked, pointing at the Grubbian mask I was wearing. "I mean, can you use the smart-fabric to make something that will fool his tech and get you into his compound?"

Sarden frowned. "Well, technically yes, the smart-fabric should be able to do it. That's the reason it's illegal almost everywhere."

"Well, then—that's it!" I was starting to get excited about my plan. "Just have Al synthesize you a mask and go in pretending to be some wealthy entrepreneur with a taste for exotic females. You could buy Sellah and the other girl—what's her name?" I looked at Grav.

"Teeny," he said promptly. "Teeny Kiv'orop."

"Right. Buy Sellah and Teeny right there and get them out before the auction," I said.

"It's not that easy," Sarden growled. "He won't let just *anyone* in. Gords are very *selective*."

"That's true," Grav said thoughtfully. "You can't just flash your credit and get in the front door. Tazaxx has this idea he's a classy son of a bitch and he doesn't want anyone around him that doesn't meet his 'standards.'"

"Exactly." Sarden nodded. "Tazaxx wouldn't let anyone who wasn't *someone* into his compound. An *important* someone."

"What about Baron Van'Dleek of Armitage 3?" Grav asked.

"Who?" Sarden and I said at the same time.

"Van'Dleek's an emissary from another galaxy—Tazaxx has never seen him. He's supposed to be among the trillion-credit elite and he's named as one of the invited guests on the auction list—paid a hell of a lot of credit to get my hands on that damn list." Grav shrugged. "Why couldn't 'Van'Dleek' come early to get a look at what he's going to be bidding on?"

"Hmm…it *could* work." Sarden looked like he was thinking hard. "You have a holo render of him?"

"Of course." The stone in Grav's ring was dark red instead of black but it projected holographic images the same way Sarden's did. I really had to get myself something like that before I went back to Earth, I thought. It put the Apple watch to shame.

The dim booth was the perfect place to project and the image that popped up was clear. Van'Dleek was about Sarden's size and build—which was good—but he had pale blue skin and was bald as an egg. He was wearing flowing white trousers cinched at his narrow waist, no shirt, apparently so he could show off his chiseled chest, and a big, boxy black jacket that matched the trousers. Also loafer-like shoes with no socks on. I thought he looked like something out of an episode of that old TV show, Miami Vice.

Sitting at Van'Dleek's feet were two females, both skimpily dressed and looking up at him adoringly. One had orange skin and several long, fleshy tentacles growing out of her head where a human's hair would be. The other looked like she could have come from Earth—she seemed to be a regular girl with tan skin and long brown hair—until I looked closer and saw that she had three purple eyes, all in a row under one long black eyebrow. Eww.

"He never goes anywhere without a fuckin' entourage," Grav explained, gesturing to the adoring girls and the muscular bodyguard who stood at Van'Dleek's back with his massive arms crossed and an alert expression on his face.

"So much the better," Sarden remarked. "I'll play Van'Dleek and you can be my Protector. That gets us both in."

"I guess that makes me one of the bikini-babes," I said, gesturing at the holographic projection of the skimpily clad girls.

"Oh, no it doesn't." Sarden frowned down at me. "You're not going anywhere *near* Tazaxx's compound—it's not safe."

"I'll be *fine*," I said bristling. "You need me there to make it look real. Look at this guy..." I gestured to the holo again. "He doesn't go *anywhere* without arm candy. He's probably the biggest douche-nozzle in the universe and he needs a girl with him constantly to tell him how *amazing* and *wonderful* he is."

"*Douche-nozzle?*" Sarden stared at me.

"Actually, from what I can tell about Van'Dleek, she's probably right," Grav said, nodding at the holo apologetically. "About him always having a female or two with him, anyway. I don't know what a douche-nozzle is."

Sarden's face looked like a thundercloud about to break.

"I don't want to risk you, Zoe. I nearly lost you once—I'm not going to let you walk into danger again," he growled.

"Look," I said in a low voice. "I won't be in danger—I'll be between you and Grav here, who looks like he could bench press a city bus. Besides, this is the least I can do since you aren't, you know, trading me away."

"I don't know…" he began.

"Come on," I said. "This is *my* plan—you can't just cut me out of it. Besides, I might be able to see more than you can. You'll be playing the big, important man and I'll be down on my knees adoring you and being unobtrusively nosey."

"Well, if it means getting you on your knees…" His gold eyes flashed for a moment and my stomach did a little flip. For a moment I thought he was going to kiss me but he didn't—maybe because Grav was sitting right across the table, watching us with interest.

"I'm glad you're seeing it my way," I said, trying to ignore the rush of heat his words sent through me. "So let's get started—the sooner we do this, the sooner we can all go home."

I regretted my choice of words almost immediately but it was too late to call them back.

"Home. Yes, I did promise to take you home," Sarden mused, the heat leaving his eyes abruptly. "And I *will* keep that promise, Zoe—I swear it."

"I know you will," I said, feeling suddenly miserable for no reason I could really name. "But we have to take care of this first. We have to get your sister."

"And Teeny," Grav put in. "I've sworn to retrieve her or die trying."

"Wow." I looked at him appraisingly. "You really take this bodyguard stuff *seriously*."

"A Protector is more than just a guard," he said, frowning. "I told you—I lay my life on the line for my wards. That's why I'm very fuckin' careful who I take as a client."

"Duly noted," Sarden said, nodding at his friend. "Hopefully we can get both our females back."

"There is just *one* thing…" Grav cleared his throat. "I picked Van'Dleek from the auction list because he's coming from a different galaxy and it's a pretty sure bet Tazaxx has never met him before. But he's Frellian."

"So?" Sarden shrugged. "What does that mean to me?"

"Nothing, except, well, take a closer look at his clothes—his trousers." Grav fired up the hologram again and made it bigger, zeroing in on the loose, white trousers. Now that he had zoomed it up, I could see what he was talking about.

"Hey—there's no fly in those things," I protested. "His, uh, junk could just fall out at any time. Why is that?"

"Frellians…" Grav coughed. "Uh, they *expose* themselves as a type of greeting to their equals. It's considered an insult not to."

"What?" I exclaimed. "They literally have a dick measuring contest every time they meet someone? That's insane."

"No—that's Frellian," Grav said. "Fuckin' weird but what are you gonna do? Different cultures, right?"

I had a sudden mental image of Sarden opening a pair of loose, white, Miami Vice-type trousers and flopping out his dick while saying hello to the infamous Tazaxx. I couldn't tell if the idea was horrifying or funny. Maybe just scary, considering how freaking huge he was down there. To my surprise, though, Sarden didn't look the least perturbed.

"So, he's Frellian. So what?" he said, shrugging. "Tazaxx isn't—he's Gord. Why should he care about the social conventions of a business partner?"

"Good point." Grav looked relieved. "You probably won't have to do it. I just wanted to, uh, lay it out there before we got started with this."

"No pun intended?" I asked, raising an eyebrow at him.

Grav grinned, his white fangs gleaming.

"Right."

"Is there anything else I should know?" Sarden asked.

Grav shook his head. "That's it for weird Frellian customs as far as I know."

"All right." Sarden slapped the table with his palm. "Now that we're all on the same page, let's go back to *The Celesta* and prepare."

Sarden

I still couldn't believe I was letting Zoe come with me. Bearding Tazaxx in his den was damn dangerous and I didn't want to risk her again. I wouldn't have done it if it was just the two of us alone. But I would have Grav with me and no male could ask for better backup than that.

I watched him from the corner of my eye. He was in the corner of my room, putting on the disguise AI had synthesized for him. It wasn't much—just two black leather straps with spikes that crisscrossed his bare chest and torso. We'd decided to leave his face unmasked because he looked fucking terrifying enough as himself. Also, if Tazaxx's facial recognition tech picked up on him, it would show his checkered past. And the male I was impersonating, Baron Van'Dleek of the Tig'o'bah system, seemed like the type who would hire a Protector precisely *because* of his violent reputation.

I looked away from Grav. To say I'd been surprised to see my old friend was an understatement—especially since I'd been under the impression he was serving three consecutive life sentences for his crimes. I wondered how he'd gotten early release—I would bet my left nut it wasn't for good behavior.

The crime he'd committed was the worst thing you could do on Vorn 6. In fact, if he hadn't been underage at the time he'd committed it, he would have faced immediate execution. I had never believed my friend could do such a thing but he admitted it freely—as he had during the trial, I remembered now.

Grav had never denied his guilt or the savagery of his actions. He had stood before the High Court and laid his crime out for the three judges like a bad hand of cards, never even trying to pretend he was innocent of the gory violence he was accused of. There was blood on his hands and no mistaking it.

Which made it all the more surprising that he'd decided to become a Protector.

He'd been right when he told Zoe a Protector was more than just a guard. They trained for years to earn the title and swore an oath when they took on a new client. Something like… *"Your blood is more precious to me than my own—I spill mine willingly before a drop of yours is shed. Your flesh is my flesh—may I be pierced a thousand times before the blade shall even scratch your skin…"* I frowned, trying to remember the rest of it.

"Well? What do you think?" a soft, feminine voice said, interrupting my ruminations.

I looked up and felt my eyes widen. Zoe had insisted on having a say in what kind of disguise she wore and she and Al had been holed up in the synth closet for almost an hour when we first got back to the ship.

I had wondered what was taking so damn long—Al had made the clothing for my own disguise in next to no time, although the mask had taken a little longer since it had to be an exact duplicate of Van'Dleek's face. My skin I was going to tint with *saphor* solution, which allows the user to change his or her epidermis to any color they choose, but only for a certain amount of time. We would have to get in and out of Tazaxx's compound pretty quickly.

Now, looking at Zoe, I saw why she had been taking such pains with her own clothing—it was eye-catching to say the least.

The top was two intricately curved bronze cups which held her full breasts in place while showing a generous amount of her pale, creamy cleavage. Her midsection was bare, showing the soft curves of her sides. A metal belt was cinched low on her lush hips and from it hung two long, shimmering strips of fabric which barely covered her sex and her luscious ass and left her legs bare. A pair of small sandals which showed off her tiny feet completed the outfit but I confess my eyes didn't linger there for long—I was too busy looking at the rest of her.

"So do you like it or what?" Zoe asked again, twirling so that her long, red curls glittered in the overhead glows. "I figured if you could dress like Crocket and Tubbs I could be 'Slave Leia.' It's perfect, right?"

"It's…you're…" I found I couldn't finish my thought. Though I had seen her naked on several occasions—and almost naked in the Majoran clothing—this particular outfit seemed made to emphasize her curvy beauty. She was absolutely breathtaking and I couldn't take my eyes off her. It made me glad I had closed the slit in the ridiculous white trousers which were part of my own disguise—if I hadn't, my feelings about her outfit would have suddenly become a lot more obvious.

"Fuckin' gorgeous," Grav said. "Hell of a lot better than that damn Grubbian disguise you were wearing at the port lounge."

I tore my eyes away from Zoe long enough to see that my friend was looking at her admiringly. I felt a possessive growl rise in my throat—Vorns don't share their females like Denarins do—but he held up his hands in a gesture of peace.

"I'm just stating the obvious, old friend. You're a lucky son of a bitch to have found such a beautiful, smart female to call your own."

It was on the tip of my tongue to say that Zoe wasn't mine—that she was a free female—but somehow I couldn't make myself say it. That was because part of me rose up inside and growled that she *was* fucking mine and I would kill any male who tried to take her away from me. That I would kill or die for her as surely as Grav would kill or die for his female ward to whom he had sworn his oath.

"Thank you." Zoe was blushing prettily, her pale, freckled cheeks flushed with pleasure at the compliment. I noticed she hadn't denied being mine any more than I had, and wondered about it. She'd been quick to point out I didn't own her before I had given her her freedom, but now she wasn't so quick to mention it. Did it mean anything?

"Any more like you back home?" Grav asked. "I don't think I've ever seen a female quite like you before—where are you from, anyway?"

"A closed planet called Earth," I said, speaking up at last. "It was locked by the Ancient Ones after they seeded it so the inhabitants have never mingled with races outside their own planet."

Grav's white-on-black eyes grew wide. "A Pure One? She's a *Pure One?*"

"And a La-ti-da," Zoe added. "A Lat-ti-*zal*, I mean. Whatever that means—I'm still not completely sure."

"Really?" Grav's eyes grew even wider and he looked at me. "I can see why you wanted to protect her, Sarden. She's fuckin' priceless."

"She is," I murmured, looking down at my little Pure One. "In fact, this is beginning to seem like a really bad idea, flaunting her in front of Tazaxx."

"No, if anything it'll add verisimilitude to our story," Grav protested. "Van'Dleek would *definitely* have a female like Zoe on his arm. And Tazaxx won't be able to resist taking a closer look at her."

I tore my eyes away from Zoe to look at him.

"Excuse me? *Verisimilitude?*"

He shrugged and gave me a sardonic grin.

"Hey, I read a lot in Triple Max. Helped pass the time."

"I bet," I said dryly. "But the very fact that Tazaxx won't be able to resist Zoe is what makes me so reluctant to take her."

"He wouldn't dare steal another male's property—especially not a rich and influential one like Van'Dleek's," Grav pointed out. "But you having Zoe—it'll impress the hell out of him and make him more willing to deal."

I knew he was right but I couldn't suppress the feeling of worry that rose in me when I thought of taking Zoe into danger—even a controlled kind of danger. She was mine, Godsdamnit and I needed to protect her. I wanted nothing more than to lock her away and keep her safe forever.

But I couldn't do that—because no matter how loudly my possessive instincts growled, she wasn't mine. Not really.

"All right," I said at last and pointed a finger at Zoe. "But *stay close.* I'm serious, Zoe, don't leave my side. I don't want a repeat of Gallana."

"Speaking of Gallana, look who's all recovered." Zoe parted the hair at the side of her neck carefully and I saw a tiny, purple-green face peering out at me.

"What in the Frozen Hells, Zoe?" I growled, frowning. "You can't take those damn things with you."

"Why not? They're really tame—look." She put up a hand and the three little creatures came crawling out to sit obediently on her hand.

"*Nib-nibs!*" In two strides, Grav was across the room and reaching for one of the tiny creatures.

"No!" Zoe snatched her hand away and held the chittering *nib-nibs* protectively to her chest. "They're pets," she explained to the startled Grav. "They're *not* for snacking."

"Hey—okay." He held up his hands. "I wasn't going to eat 'em. I've read about them—just never seen any up close."

"Sorry—it's just that *some* people think they're only good for a between-meal snack." She shot me a look.

"What?" I said, defensively. "I told you—I tried one *once* and spit it out before I even bit down."

"You say you've got them tamed?" Grav asked, apparently still interested.

"Look, I've been working with them while Al synthesized my costume. It's amazing how quickly they learn. Okay guys," she said, addressing the *nib-nibs,* "Roll over." Immediately all three of them lay on their backs and rolled over in her hand. "Speak," Zoe told them and they all sat up and chattered. "Play dead," she said and they immediately flopped down and lay motionless across her palm.

"Nice," Grav said, nodding.

"It's more than nice—it's *amazing*." Zoe's big blue eyes shone, making her even more gorgeous, if that was possible. "I taught them all that in less than an hour. It's almost like they *know* what I want them to do even before I tell them."

"That's because they're mildly telepathic," Grav said. "It's how they keep track of each other — if you take one away from its colony, it can still get back, no matter how far away it is, just by zeroing in on the mental energy of the others."

"Wow." Zoe looked at her tiny pets with newfound respect and I knew I'd never be able to convince her to leave them behind now. Well, maybe having a Pure One that had tame *nib-nibs* as pets would also add to the *verisimilitude* of our disguise. It certainly seemed like the eccentric kind of thing a rich *douche-nozzle,* to use Zoe's term, would do.

"What did you name them?" I asked, resignedly. "You *did* name them, right?"

"Of course. This one is Rhaegar, this one is Viserys, and this one — the one I rescued from Count Creepy — is Drogon. He's my main guy, aren't you, fella?" she asked, stroking the little creature gently with one finger. He hummed contentedly and rubbed against her hand in apparent ecstasy.

I felt a tightening in my gut and realized I was actually getting jealous of the damn *nib-nib*! At least it got to feel the touch of her soft little hands. I wanted those hands all over me — and I wanted mine all over Zoe. Seeing her in that damn disguise which showed off all her creamy curves didn't help my desire to possess her either.

"Rhaegar ...Viserys...Drogon. Are those Earth names?" Grav asked, still watching as she played with her pets.

Zoe flushed, her freckled cheeks going pink.

"Well, *sort* of — they're from a TV show I like — a kind of entertainment you watch on a screen. Just call me 'the mother of dragons' — or, I guess 'the mother of nib-nibs.'"

She laughed and Grav rumbled laughter too, not because he got her Earth-centric joke, I was sure. But just because Zoe had such an infectious laugh. Soft, and feminine, and lilting — Gods, was there *anything* about her that didn't arouse me? I didn't fucking think so.

"It's time to go," I said, my voice rougher than I meant it to be. As if on cue, Al came whizzing into the room, already in his travel form.

"Master, I have received an answer from the compound — Tazaxx will be most pleased to meet with Baron Van'Dleek today."

"Good," I said, pulling on my mask and drinking a few drops of the *saphor* juice compound. "Tell him the baron and his entourage are on the way."

Chapter Twenty

Zoe

I don't know what I expected when we got to the surface of Giedi Prime, but it was nothing like Gallana. On the Majoran spaceport, there had been, for the most part, a sense of beauty and grace—an interest in aesthetics which was sadly lacking here.

Giedi Prime was a big, dirty, ugly, industrialized planet where the city seemed to stretch on and on forever with tall towers and huge stacks belching smoke into the air.

The sky was completely black.

"Oh—I didn't know we were getting here in the middle of the night," I remarked to Sarden as he piloted his small shuttle over the planet's surface. The two guys were up front, due to their size and I was squeezed into the back, looking out through the windshield-type-screen at the front.

"We're not—this is the middle of the Giedi Prime day," he said.

"Pollution here is fuckin' awful," Grav growled from my other side. "Just stay in the shuttle and keep the air circulator turned on full blast and we'll be okay."

"It'll be better at Tazaxx's compound," Sarden told me. "He's got his own private atmosphere bubble over the entire property. Probably cost thirty million credits at least."

"Wow." I was suitably impressed and kept my eyes peeled, still curiously drinking in all the alien sights around me as we flew. Not that there was much to see—just lots and lots of dark buildings and belching smokestacks. The whole planet looked like the end the *Lorax* book after the greedy Onceler gets hold of it and ruins it so the humming fish and swammy-swans and barbaloots have to move out.

My *nib-nibs,* Rae, Vis, and little Drogon, my favorite, chattered quietly to each other in my hair but otherwise were perfectly well behaved. They really were the cutest little guys and the perfect pets. I was gladder than ever that I'd rescued them after hearing that they were mildly telepathic. Imagine the poor things having to hear their buddy screaming inside their heads while he got chewed up and swallowed! Ugh! If I ever saw Count Doloroso again— which I never hoped to do, but if I did—I'd give him a piece of my mind and a kick in the balls. What a jerk, trying to eat such adorable little creatures!

At last, after about thirty minutes of flying, we came to a kind of countryside—if you could call it that. Mostly it just looked like a big, open, barren plain with no buildings on it. There weren't any trees or lakes or animals either, but there was a dark, scraggly kind of grass which was apparently what passed for nature on Giedi Prime.

Once again I was reminded of the Lorax, which had been my favorite book as a kid. *"At the far end of town, where the grickle-grass grows and the wind smells slow and sour when it blows…"*

We hadn't opened any of the windows in the shuttle so much as a crack but I was willing to bet the wind on this planet *did* smell sour. It was pretty much the nastiest, most polluted place I'd ever seen and I had visited a friend who lived in the industrial part of Houston once, so that was saying something.

"Heads up. Compound ahead," Sarden said.

"What?" I asked, frowning. "I don't see any…"

And then I saw it. Sitting in the middle of the dark field of sickly grickle-grass, was an enormous dome. It was black too— pure, shiny, bible-black—which was why I hadn't immediately seen it. It rose out of the blighted ground like a bubble of diseased blood that might burst and spew ichor everywhere at any moment. *Yech.*

Sarden brought the shuttle down right in front of the curving, shiny black side and then spoke into some kind of communicator in a technical-sounding jargon I couldn't make heads or tails of.

Whoever was on the other end seemed to get it though, because after a moment, the black bubble started to swell outward and then it just sort of *enveloped* our shuttle. Kind of like an amoeba envelopes its prey, when it eats some other hapless, microscopic creature living in its pond of dirty rainwater. Which is how I felt when the giant black bubble grew to encapsulate us—tiny…microscopic.

Also kind of claustrophobic.

"Um, are we going to be able to get out of here all right?" I asked, trying not to sound nervous and failing miserably.

"They'll let us out the same way we came in," Sarden assured me as the black border of the bubble passed over us. Ir swallowed the shuttle whole, leaving us in a big parking area that looked like a warehouse. "Hopefully with Sellah and Teeny in tow."

"From your lips to the Goddess's ears," Grav muttered, adjusting the knives he had clipped to the spiked leather straps criss-crossing his muscular chest.

"Everybody be quiet now—here comes Tazaxx's emissary," Sarden muttered. "Remember, we need to get in and out of here as quickly as possible. The *saphor* solution I took to change my skin color has a time limit on it."

"How long are we talking?" Grav wanted to know.

"One solar hour—two max. But hopefully it won't be a problem—we should be in and out of here fast—Tazaxx isn't known for prolonging business deals."

"Can't you just take more if it starts to wear off?" I asked.

He shook his head. "Doesn't work that way. The solution has a two solar-hour recovery time on it—it won't work again after it wears off until that time is up."

"Oh, okay. Then I guess we'd better be quick," I said.

"We will be," Sarden said grimly.

"All right—let's go. I'm ready." Grav cracked his knuckles again, making me shudder. He might be Sarden's friend but the fact that he was such a big, scary guy *and* a confessed murderer meant I was still kind of nervous around him.

"All right—I'm popping the hatch," Sarden said.

The door to the shuttle opened and I leaned forward eagerly, trying to see the emissary.

What I saw was a giant piece of crap wearing a rainbow-colored cape.

At least, that was what it *appeared* to be. A giant, man-sized poo that had somehow managed to stand up on end and learned to move.

Okay, sorry for the gross mental image but seriously—that's just *exactly* what it looked like. It slid forward smoothly and I looked behind it, wondering if it was leaving a trail of slime. There was no slime, though, and after a minute I saw why—its bottom half had about a million tiny little legs and feet all over it and they were moving kind of like a caterpillar's legs to carry it along.

It had a vaguely human looking face in the middle of its lumpy head—by which I mean it had two eyes, a sort of nose, and a round, lipless mouth. Out of the mouth came a nasal, croaking voice like a bullfrog with a cold.

"You are Baron Van'Dleek?" it demanded, waving a lumpy arm at Sarden.

"I am." Sarden, who was dressed in his Miami Vice best with the baggy white trousers and black, boxy jacket stepped out of the shuttle and looked down his nose at the moving piece of crap who was apparently our guide.

Sarden was looking good, despite his new light blue skin and the Van'Dleek mask. It was amazing how well the smart-fabric conformed to his face—it even hid his horns. And the fact that the jacket hung open, revealing his mouthwateringly muscular torso didn't hurt either.

I noticed, though, that he was careful to keep his trousers closed when he moved, so as not to expose himself by accident. Which was a good thing—a wardrobe malfunction is one thing but letting his entire wang dangle outside the white pants would definitely ruin the cool, 80s look he had going.

"You and your entourage will have to be scanned before being admitted to the main compound," the moving crap informed him as he stepped down.

Sarden gave our guide a condescending sneer. "Of course. But make it quick—I don't like to be kept waiting."

I stared at him in surprise as I scrambled out of the shuttle with a helping hand from Grav. Wow, he was nailing the rich douche-nozzle part right off the bat!

"Of course." The piece of crap—at some point we would probably learn his name but he was always going to be POC to me—nodded stiffly.

He produced a large instrument that looked like a bullhorn

from under his colorful, rainbow cape. Pointing it at Sarden's face, he pressed a button. A blue light illuminated Sarden's features for a moment, then went dark again.

POC consulted a screen that was on the back of the bullhorn and frowned. "Hmm...these readings are most...peculiar," he said in his nasally bullfrog-with-a-cold voice.

"What are you talking about? Hurry up! I don't have all day," Sarden snapped.

"But...these readings..." POC looked worried and he wasn't the only one. My stomach did a little flip. Was it possible that the smart-fabric wasn't smart enough to do the job? Could the scanner POC was using see through Sarden's disguise? If so we were *so* screwed...

"I can't help it if your equipment isn't up to par," Sarden barked, scowling at POC.

"But—"

"You have exactly two solar seconds to finish this scan and let me pass," Sarden snapped. "If you're not done by then, I'm getting back in my shuttle and leaving and I'm taking my credit *with* me."

"But—" POC said again, helplessly.

"Nor will I be at the auction later, though your Master *specifically* invited me," Sarden continued, giving POC a withering look. "I didn't come all this way to be insulted."

I had to give Sarden credit for his performance—he sounded like every rich, South Tampa customer with a snotty attitude I'd ever dealt with back when I was working retail in college. Poor POC was obviously bowled over by it too. Seeing the look of abject terror on what passed for his face, I almost felt sorry for him.

"Forgive me," he burbled in his bullfrog voice. "Master Tazaxx very much wants to meet with you, Baron Van'Dleek. Please come right this way and bring your entourage with you."

"That's more like it." Sarden straightened his jacket with a few huffy jerks and flicked at an imaginary speck of dust off one immaculate sleeve. "Lead on. And I hope you brought transportation. I don't walk."

"Of course—of course." The POC made an obsequious bow which almost tipped him over—he was kind of top-heavy—and led us from the large landing area, which appeared to be in some kind of vast warehouse, to a large door.

The door slid open at our approach and I caught my breath. The scene here was in direct contrast to the outside of the black bubble.

The sky overhead was a pale, lovely purple, filled with sunlight and big puffy white clouds floating by. We had stepped out onto a kind of rolling meadow, covered in thick, neatly clipped dark blue grass. There were wildflowers and trees with purple bark and blue leaves. Here and there I saw little furry creatures that looked kind of like a cross between a cat and a raccoon nibbling the lush vegetation. Really, except for the color palate, it looked like something out of a Disney film.

"Wow," I breathed, looking around as POC lead us to a device that looked kind of like a large bright green golf cart with caterpillar treads instead of wheels.

"Fuckin' nice," Grav agreed under his breath. Sarden said nothing, just looked around with a faintly bored expression on his face as though he'd seen it all before and this was no different. I wondered how he had learned to play a rich, entitled jerk so well.

"If you'd care to take a seat, Baron Van'Dleek," POC burbled, indicating the cart. "I'll be happy to drive you and your entourage to the main house."

"That's acceptable," Sarden murmured coolly. He settled himself in the back of the cart, leaving POC to take the wheel at the front.

Grav sat beside POC and glared at him, presumably for extra intimidation and I sat beside Sarden, at his feet.

"Hey—you don't have to be down there," Sarden muttered to me, his voice pitched low so POC couldn't hear him.

"Yes, I do," I whispered back. "You're playing your role and I'm playing mine." I batted my lashes at him and leaned against his leg, looking up at him with a flirty little smile.

He rumbled laughter and reached down to stroke my hair, an action my *nib-nibs* objected to by chattering angrily and running to the other side of my neck. Their little claws gave me a ticklish feeling but I was more interested in the sensation of Sarden's long fingers caressing my curls.

I had only meant to get into character—the adoring slave girl staring up at her master. But his hand felt so warm against my head—so right. I nuzzled my cheek against his palm and looked into his eyes. His face looked different because of the mask but the expression he was wearing was unmistakable—desire and tenderness that made me catch my breath with yearning of my own.

Stop it, I told myself. *He's playing a part—that's all!* But somehow I couldn't tear my eyes away from his until the garish green golf came to a jerky halt.

"And here is the main house of Master Tazaxx who is expecting you," POC said.

I tore my gaze from Sarden's at last and looked up to see a large, rounded dome-shaped building that looked a lot like the black bubble dome we were in. But this one was pink. Not pastel pink or even rose pink—it was full on, *blazing* pink—a shade so bright it hurt your eyes to look at it.

There were doorways and windows on the curving side of the hot pink dome and all of them were outlined entirely in what appeared to be solid gold. Apparently Tazaxx liked to flaunt his wealth.

"Wow—classy décor," I muttered to Sarden.

He just gave me a look.

"This way," POC said and led the way up a curving pathway made of smooth, electric blue stones which might have been some kind of sapphires to the front door. I stared in disbelief. The doorknob was an enormous *diamond*. Ostentatious much?

I wished I could twist it off and stick it in my pocket for a souvenir because Leah and Charlotte were never going to believe all this without some proof. But that would be stealing—plus, the Slave Leia outfit I had on didn't have pockets. It was really sexy though— I'd thought Sarden would swallow his tongue when he first saw me in it—which, if I'm honest, was the exact reaction I was going for. I liked the way it swirled around my legs as I walked, even if I *did* feel a little exposed in it.

But enough about my sexy disguise. POC was leading us into the garishly expensive pink dome-mansion and we all had to be on our toes.

Speaking of toes, POC opened the gold encrusted, diamond-handled door and ushered us into the hot pink dome...and right into a half-inch puddle of water.

"Oh!" I jumped back but my toes—and the rest of my feet— were already wet. Then I looked at the vast, pink marble floor (yes, the neon pink theme continued inside too) and saw that it wasn't just a puddle—the entire floor was flooded with a half inch of water. Was Tazaxx having a plumbing problem? "What the Hell?" I muttered to Sarden.

"Apologies but Master Tazaxx is going through his molting cycle at the moment and requires moisture," POC told us. "Be so kind as to leave your footwear outside the door if you do not wish it to get wet."

Molting, huh? *That* sounded interesting. I took off the little strappy sandals I'd had Al synthesize for me and left them on the hot pink doorstep. Sarden and Grav did the same and then rolled up their trousers. Then we all filed into the house barefoot.

Inside, POC led us through several large empty rooms with high, rounded ceilings that had strange artwork on them. I couldn't tell exactly what it was because it kept moving and changing — shifting colors and forms that didn't seem to have any kind of pattern. After awhile, my neck started getting a crick in it so I looked down and stopped trying to figure it out.

Finally we came to an area about as big as a ballroom with only two things in it. The first was a raised dais about two feet tall.

"This is where your interview with Master Tazaxx will be conducted," POC informed us. "If you will please ascend to the platform?"

Well, at least it looked dry up there, which would be a vast improvement over the wet marble floor — my toes were getting pruney. It also faced the only other thing in the room, which appeared to be a giant mud puddle.

"Um, what are we supposed to do?" I asked Sarden in a low voice as we all climbed up onto the platform. It was a high step for me so he simply lifted me by the waist and set me down beside him.

"I don't know. I've never seen Tazaxx during his molting phase," he murmured. "This is all new to me."

"If you will please be patient, Master Tazaxx will be ready to speak with you in a moment," POC said. He hadn't climbed onto the platform with us, (maybe because his tiny little caterpillar legs couldn't reach that high?) and was still standing in the inch-deep water on the floor below us.

We stood silently on the platform—which was carpeted in the same dark blue grass we had seen outside—and faced the mud puddle. It looked brown and thick—more like a mud slick than an actual mud puddle, I guessed. In fact, the more I looked at it, the more I thought it seemed to have patterns in it.

There were two swirls at the top of it that looked almost like eyes, and then another swirl below and between them which could almost be a nose, and a wide curve below *that* which looked like a frowning mouth.

That was when the curve opened and a thunderous voice asked, "Who dares to disturb my molting?"

I nearly jumped right into Sarden's arms.

"Oh my God," I gasped. "It spoke—the mud puddle *spoke!*"

"That's no mud puddle," Grav growled softly from his post behind Sarden. "That's fuckin' Tazaxx."

"Master, this is Baron Van'Dleek of Frellex," POC said quickly. "I informed you earlier that he had come to Giedi Prime early because he wished to see your private collection before the auction. You told me to allow him entrance to the compound. Do you remember?"

"Remember?" roared the mud puddle. "Of *course* I remember. I'm molting—not mentally incompetent, Floosh."

So that was POC's name. Hmm, not much of an improvement as far as I was concerned.

Then the mud puddle—or Tazaxx I guess—began to shift and change. A man-sized column of mud suddenly rose out of the puddle and began to mold itself into something else.

I watched, fascinated, as arms and legs formed and then a clearly defined torso, head, face, and even hair. It was like watching an artist sculpting clay in fast-motion—only there was no artist and the clay was sculpting itself.

Soon a mud-man about six feet tall, stood before us. It was brown all over and completely naked. Its rather large, uh, *equipment,* lay against one thigh.

"There," the man said in the same thundering voice the mud puddle had used. "Now I am better equipped to speak to you."

"That was amazing," I blurted, before I thought about it.

"I was merely being polite," Tazaxx assured me. "Of course, the main part of my being is still on the molting room floor." The mud man nodded at the vast mud puddle, which didn't seem to have shrunk at all. "But I am able to animate a part of myself for a considerable range away from my central mass." He stepped forward and held out a hand to me. "And you are?"

"Oh, uh…I'm Zoe. Nice to meet you." Uncertainly I let him take my hand for a moment in a kind of shake. His mud-fingers were cool and damp like wet clay. I had the immediate urge to pull my hand away and wipe it off but forced myself not to, knowing it would be considered rude.

My nib-nibs, however, weren't quite as disgusted as I was. Or maybe they were just curious. Two of them ran down my arm to take a closer look at Tazaxx.

"Well, well," he remarked. "And what do we have here?"

"Zoe is my bonded concubine," Sarden growled, pulling me firmly away from the handshake, for which I was grateful. "And those are simply her pets."

"Mmm, a most enchanting creature." The mud man took a step

back from the dais and actually *licked* his fingers, as though he wanted to taste where we had been touching somehow. *Ugh.* I tried not to make a face as the *nib-nibs* ran back up my arm to take their place in my hair. "I don't believe I have encountered one of your kind before," he remarked to me, still licking his mud-lips with a brown mud-tongue.

"You do us honor, taking our shape to speak with us," Sarden said, clearly changing the subject. He gave an abbreviated bow which Tazaxx returned.

"Then why do you not do me honor in turn?" he demanded, his mud-brown eyes narrowing.

"I am…not certain what you mean." Sarden frowned. "We are standing on this platform as your, uh, as Floosh instructed us. What more do you want?"

"Floosh said you were Frellian, did he not?" the mud man demanded.

"Well, yes, but…ah." Suddenly Sarden seemed to understand what Tazaxx was talking about.

I remembered at the same time—the mud man was naked, exposing his equipment—apparently he expected Sarden to do the same.

Well, so much for not caring about Frellian customs.

"Forgive me. I was…transfixed by your transformation," Sarden said in a flat voice. He reached into the flap in his loose white trousers to pull out his shaft and that was when I saw it.

His equipment wasn't blue, like the rest of his skin anymore. Or at least, not *all* blue. The broad, flaring head of it was the dark, maroon red—his natural skin color.

Oh no! Oh my God! my mind babbled. What the hell was going on? Then I remembered Sarden's words before we left the shuttle—

he'd said that the saphor stuff he'd taken to change his skin color wouldn't last very long. But surely it was supposed to last longer than *this?* How long had we been here, anyway? Maybe he had gotten a bad batch?

Whatever the case, he couldn't go exposing the fact that he wasn't all the same light blue color Van'Dleek was supposed to be anymore. But if he didn't, Tazaxx would take offense and probably refuse to sell us Sellah and Teeny. Something had to be done, and quick.

I did the only thing I could think of—I dropped to my knees in front of him and took his long, hard shaft in my hands, hiding his multicolored member with my face and hair

"Zoe?" Sarden was plainly startled. I was pretty shocked myself—it wasn't like I was used to doing this kind of thing on the spur of the moment—or in public for that matter. But since I was playing the adoring, sex-starved slave girl, I decided to really go for it.

"Master," I murmured, rubbing my cheek against his long, hard length. "Master, forgive me but you know whenever I see your *hugeness* I cannot restrain myself."

As I spoke, I looked up at him and pointed meaningfully at the broad crown of his shaft.

"Uh..." Sarden's eyes widened as he saw that his skin was turning back from blue to red.

"What is going on here? Why are you perverting the Frellian form of greeting?" Tazaxx demanded.

"You'll have to, uh, forgive my concubine," Sarden said in a slightly strangled voice. "She's *Niciniean*—they're notorious for their sexual appetites."

"Ah, I see," I heard Tazaxx say. "A *Niciniean*, eh? I don't think

I've ever encountered such a female before. Do you find it difficult to keep her satisfied?"

"Not as long as I allow her to, ah, gratify me several times a day." Sarden cleared his throat. "And I gratify her as well. It's one of the reasons I wanted to come alone to meet with you before the auction. I find it…difficult to take her out in public as she's prone to this…this kind of behavior whenever I try to greet someone in the traditional Frellian way."

All this time, I was still rubbing Sarden's shaft — which had grown considerably — and trying to hide him with my face and hair. (Luckily my *nib-nibs* were staying well back, not that I was thinking of them at the moment.)

I know it sounds weird that I was doing this in front of everyone, but actually, I was kind of enjoying it. Sarden's rich, spicy, masculine scent was stronger here and I liked the way the hot, silky skin of his shaft felt against my cheek. In fact, I was feeling extremely sexy, kneeling at his feet in my slave girl outfit and pretending to worship his cock. From the look in Sarden's eyes when he stroked my curls and how hard he had gotten, he was feeling pretty turned on himself.

"And the only way to slake her thirst is to allow her to take you in her mouth?" Tazaxx asked, still sounding extremely interested.

"Yes. Unfortunately." Sarden's deep voice still sounded somewhat choked and a tremble ran through his big body.

"Oh, Master," I moaned, playing it up and rubbing harder. I couldn't help the thrill that ran through me, making my nipples tight under my metal bra and my sex feel wet and slippery between my thighs. This might be just pretend but I liked that I was having such a strong effect on him. I was the one on my knees but just by touching him, I was making him shake. It made me feel naughty and hot and incredibly *powerful*.

"Ah, how interesting. Of course, we Gords divide and reproduce asexually, but I've always been fascinated by the mating rituals of other species," Tazaxx remarked.

And then he actually came around to the side of the dais, as though he wanted to get a better look!

Just like that, pretending went out the window. I had no choice—I put Sarden in my mouth.

The broad head of Sarden's cock was the only thing I could fit—he was that big—but luckily, that was the only part that had changed back to his normal color so I was able to hide what needed to be hidden.

Sarden made a strangled sound and his hand, which had been gently stroking my head, suddenly tightened reflexively in my hair.

"Gods, Zoe," he groaned and I could feel him holding back, trying not to thrust into the wet heat of my mouth.

I felt another surge of lust rush through me. He tasted good— *really* good—and not at all human.

During my relationship with Scott, he'd always wanted me to do this for him but I hadn't liked it much. My ex had a musky, sour kind of flavor to his skin that I found off-putting. And as I said before, it wasn't exactly like he was eager to return the favor.

With Sarden it was different. Salty and hot and sweet…that was what I tasted when I took him between my lips. The broad head of his cock rubbed against my tongue and the flavor of hot cinnamon candy filled my mouth—the same thing I had tasted when he kissed me, only it didn't sting as much as his kisses had.

"Mmm," I purred, sucking harder, trying to get more of him into my mouth. It wasn't just the fact that I was down on my knees, giving him a public blow-job that was turning me on—there was something about his flavor too. In fact, the more I tasted it, the more I wanted. It seemed to do something to me—making my nipples tender and my sex feel wet and so swollen with need, I had to spread my legs to ease the ache.

"Zoe, you should…should stop now," I heard Sarden say, tugging gently at my hair. "We're…being rude to our host."

"Not at all," Tazaxx murmured. He seemed to have stepped back, apparently satisfied at what he had seen. "I wouldn't like to interfere in such an enchanting creature's sexual needs—by all means, allow her to finish you off."

Since the mud man that was Tazaxx had stepped away some, I dared to lean back some and let the broad head slip from my mouth.

"Yes, Master," I murmured breathily. "Let me finish you, please."

Where in the world I got the nerve to talk like that, I don't know. Believe me, I knew I was acting as shameless as an actress in a porno. But Sarden's flavor was still doing something to me—it made me want more and more of him. In fact, I didn't just want to suck him—I wanted him to take me right there on the floor of the raised platform and I didn't care who was watching.

But Sarden shook his head firmly, a worried look in his eyes.

"No, I don't think so. I believe you've had enough for now—maybe too much," he said, making me wonder what he was talking about.

"Master," I moaned as he tucked himself away, making sure to keep the head of his rigid shaft hidden as he did so. "Master, *please.*"

"No. That's enough," he said firmly. "Come now, Zoe, I need to discuss business with our host before it gets *too late.*"

He stared at me meaningfully and I realized what he was saying. If the *saphor* stuff was wearing off this quickly, we really didn't have time for his, uh, *oral gratification*. I sat back on my heels and felt my head clearing a little now that I couldn't smell him or taste him anymore. What was going on with me? Why had I acted like that?

"Well, if you're sure you'd rather have business than pleasure…" Tazaxx remarked.

"I'm positive." Sarden's deep voice still sounded strained and the bulge in his white trousers was evident but he nodded firmly at the mud man, indicating he was ready to deal. "I've come here to talk about acquiring some new females for my entourage and I understand you have the best of the best in your collection."

"That I do." Tazaxx nodded. "Would you like to see some of them?"

"Please," Sarden inclined his head.

"Very well," the mud man said. "Then allow me to lead the way."

Sarden

I didn't know what in the Frozen Hells had gotten into Zoe. Or actually, I was afraid I *did* know, but I could hardly believe it.

Between the different species of bipedal, sentient Terran-type beings the Ancient Ones had brought into existence through their seeding of our universe, there existed certain natural laws that governed absolutely. Most peoples who had grown from the Ancient seeds were sexually compatible in some way but very few were fit to be bonded as mates for life.

What's the difference in being able to have sex with another life form and being able to bond with them? The ability to bear viable children for one thing, but also the possibility of a permanent emotional connection that grows stronger with every year. Bonded partners can feel each other's emotions and sometimes even hear each other's thoughts — it's a very rare and special occurrence.

And it never happens for half-breeds like me.

Because my DNA was mixed, I was physically unable to form such a strong and lasting connection to any female. I simply wasn't enough either Eloim or Vorn for a bond to form. And yet, since I had healed Zoe orally and tasted her sweet pussy and she had tasted me as well, I could feel something forming between us. A longing to get closer…a longing that just for a moment, I could swear I felt coming from her as an emotion that touched my soul.

It's your imagination, I told myself impatiently as we filed off the raised platform and followed the mud creature Tazaxx had become out of the molting room. *You can't bond with anyone — let alone a Pure One.*

But if that was true, then why was her scent so sweet when she tasted me? And why had she been so eager to taste even more? Why had I felt her longing? Her *desire?*

She was putting on an act — hiding you from Tazaxx, I told myself.

But when I glanced down at her, I saw she was still watching me with need in those lovely blue eyes of hers and I swore I could feel it still, as a tingle at my very core. I could hardly look away from her. Gods, the idea that I might ever form that kind of lasting connection with a female…it was an impossible dream. One I had never dared to hope for.

And you shouldn't hope for it now, the implacable little voice lectured. *Especially not with a female you've promised to return to her home planet.*

Of course, I knew it was right. There was no point in getting attached to Zoe or letting her get attached to me.

Which was exactly what I was afraid was happening.

Zoe

Sarden was quiet as Tazaxx led us out of the molting room and through a wide doorway to a dark hallway beyond. I wondered if he was mad at me—I couldn't be sure how he was feeling by the blank look on his face. Well, if he was mad, he would just have to get over it—it wasn't like I'd acted like a porn star just because I *liked* it.

Oh, you liked it all right, whispered an accusing little voice in my brain. *You **more** than liked it—you didn't want to stop!*

I squirmed uncomfortably, but I had to admit it was true. I *hadn't* wanted to stop. There was something about the whole experience—not just the way he tasted or felt in my mouth, it was almost like we were forming some kind of *connection.*

*Okay, **now** you're talking crazy,* the little voice informed me. *There's no connection here. You're just along for the ride until Sarden gets his sister back and then it's back to Earth for you. So stop being all mushy and stupid and get the job done.*

Right—that was exactly what I intended to do. I made myself look away from Sarden and pay attention to the darkened hallway we now found ourselves in. It was a long, vast corridor and every hundred feet or so, there was a large, lighted window. Honestly, what it most reminded me of was the reptile area at the zoo—where they kept the room dark so you could see the animals on display better.

We came to the first window and Tazaxx stopped, his bare, mud feet slapping against the cold stone floor.

"Now here we have a Zulian," he said, pointing to the lighted window. "As you can see, I've done my best to preserve her in her native habitat. She's quite lovely, is she not?"

I looked in through the window and saw a kind of lighted aquarium. Inside long, colorful kelp-like plants swayed in pale pink liquid. Swimming through them was an honest-to-God mermaid. She moved with graceful flips of her long green tail, which shone like jewels in the pinkish water and her hair flowed, long and blonde, over her slim shoulders.

My heart went out to this poor creature in captivity—if Sarden hadn't had a change of heart, that could have been *me*. I thought I had never seen anyone more beautiful and harmless looking.

At least, she *looked* harmless at first.

When we got closer, she swam up to the glass and hissed at Tazaxx, baring a mouthful of sharp, pointed teeth that reminded me of a barracuda. Her eyes went blood red and the tips of her fingers grew three inch long claws—all in the space of a second or two. It was like one of those scary gifs on the Internet where one minute someone looks normal and the next they have a demon face.

"Holy crap!" I jumped back from the window and put a hand to my pounding heart.

"Yes, she is *quite* a spectacle, isn't she?" Tazaxx was the only one of us who hadn't started, at least a little, when the mermaid went all feral on us. "Not for sale, I am afraid. Her planet has since been destroyed so she is the only one of her kind left. Really, I did the poor creature a service rescuing her before her home world was blown to smithereens by an errant asteroid."

I wondered if the feral mermaid felt like he'd done her a "favor." From the way she continued to snarl and gnash her needle-sharp teeth, it didn't look like it to me.

We went on to the next window which contained a kind of desert scene. Bright green sand and dry, spiky plants were the first things I saw. A mercilessly hot light — like the sun at noon — beat down from the roof of the room. I could feel its savage heat right through the glass of the display case.

Then one of the "plants" — a large, purple cactus-looking one — moved. First one slender limb, then another and then another, each of them covered with long, sharp needles, shifted in our direction. It looked like the cactus was creeping up on us in slow motion. Only when it got right up to the glass did I see that it had a face with wide, staring eyes, slits for nostrils, and a tiny, lipless mouth.

"A Dendrite," Tazaxx informed us. "Taken from the barren world of Towen Omega. Also not for sale unless you have the means to care for her properly. She needs a six hundred terra-watt heat ray set to maximum constantly to survive and thrive."

I looked into the wide, alien eyes of the Dendrite girl and she stared back at me. I couldn't help thinking again of how this could have been me. What kind of habitat would Tazaxx have built me? A Starbucks?

Here we see the white girl in her natural habitat — notice the counter where she is able to order unlimited variations of a beverage Earthlings call "caw-fee." There are limitless possible combinations of ingredients for this Earth delicacy but they all taste basically the same…

"If you don't mind, Tazaxx, my time is somewhat limited," Sarden remarked, derailing my train of thought. "So I'd like to see only those females you feel you can part with."

"Very well—can you tell me if you're looking for anything in particular?" Tazaxx's mud-brown eyes flashed in the dark hallway.

"Hmm…" Sarden pretended to consider. "Well, I do prefer young females—one can raise them correctly to service if one gets them young enough."

"Ah, well I *do* have a rather recent acquisition," Tazaxx remarked. "Sold to me by Byrillian pirates—barely twelve cycles old, as I recall."

Behind us, I could feel Grav shifting impatiently but he said nothing, though I knew he was itching to see the girl he was warding and make sure she was safe.

"Well…" Sarden pretended to think again, then nodded. "All right. I'll see her."

"This way, then."

Tazaxx in his mud-man shape, led us further down the long, curving, darkened hallway. We were getting pretty far from the molting room and I wondered how far this form would take him, considering he had left most of himself back in the mud puddle. I remembered he had said that he was able to go quite a distance away from the main part of himself—but how far exactly?

We passed many strange looking females of all different exotic species, some humanoid and some not even recognizable as living beings—at least to me. It really was a zoo and I felt sorry for all the exhibits, even the ones that looked like rocks or plants or—in one case—a cross between a dolphin and a Doberman.

At last we came to a case made to look like a sitting room. There was a fireplace with blue flames dancing in the grate, a large, comfortable looking red chair with a high back and scrolled arms, and a flowered carpet on the floor. Interesting and expensive art work hung on the walls and a low table with five curved legs was set to one side of the chair.

A plate on the table was heaped with what looked like tasty little cakes in every color of the rainbow and there was a triangular cup with steam rising from it. Was it some kind of tea? I didn't know—my eyes were drawn away from the surroundings when I saw a movement in the center of the chair.

Someone was sitting in it—a slender girl was huddled in one corner with her back to us. Her dress was almost the same deep, velvety red of the chair which was why I hadn't seen her right away. I couldn't see her face because she had it buried in her hands. As I watched, her slight shoulders shook and I realized she must be crying.

Poor little thing! My heart went out to her—how homesick and scared she must be in this big, awful, weird place! Tazaxx was a monster for keeping her locked up like this.

Behind me I heard Grav breathe, "Teeny," in a low voice not much more than a growl. I glanced back at him and saw that he was holding himself back with an iron will. Every muscle in his big body was bunched with tension and his huge hands were curled into fists. A vein throbbed in his temple, just to the side of one of his curving, black horns and a muscle jumped in his jaw. I thought he looked like he might rush forward and break the glass of the little prisoner's display case at any minute. But somehow, he managed not to.

"She looks all right," Sarden remarked. "But it's difficult to see her."

"Here…you. Come forward." Tazaxx tapped sharply on the glass.

The girl in the chair jumped, her thin shoulders twitching with the motion. Slowly she stood and turned to face us. She had pale, almost translucent skin in the most delicate shade of sage green imaginable and a cable of thick, black hair.

I could see by her tear-streaked cheeks that I was right—she had indeed been crying. Her eyes were a gorgeous shade of violet, red rimmed now, from weeping. With her delicate coloring and jewel-like eyes, I thought she looked like a little elf or fairy.

"Come here!" Tazaxx ordered her, tapping the glass again.

Slowly, uncertainly, the girl walked forward. It wasn't until she was right up against the glass that she really saw us—or should I say, that she saw Grav.

Her violet eyes went wide as she looked at him and I saw hope fill her thin face and flush her pale cheeks. Her mouth started to form his name but I saw him give her a short, sharp shake of his head.

Biting her lip, the girl looked down, her thin fingers twisting in the skirts of the red dress she wore.

"Hmm…" Sarden nodded. "Yes, I like her," he said, turning to Tazaxx. "She's young enough to train and she'll be quite lovely when she's grown in a few years. What's your asking price?"

"One hundred thousand credits," Tazaxx said, without blinking an eye.

"What?" Sarden frowned. "I thought I might get a better deal here than at the auction. It's ridiculous to ask so much for an ungrown girl with no particular rarity or skill set."

"But she *is* rare—not her species, per say—she's only a common Thonilan. But there are other forms of rarity, my dear Baron Van'Dleek," Tazaxx assured him. "This little female is the last living heir to the House of Yanux—one of the ruling families of her people. As a result, she is very rare indeed."

"Hmm…I *do* like having girls with good pedigrees in my

entourage," Sarden said, sounding for all the world as though he was talking about some kind of purebred animal like a racehorse instead of a sentient being. "Do you have any more like that? Any more *royalty?* Perhaps we can make a deal if so."

"Alas…" Tazaxx made a face. "I *did* have a very fine Eloim female in my collection until very recently."

"You *did* have?" I heard the slightly strangled sound in Sarden's voice but to his credit, he managed to keep his features blank and only mildly interested. "What happened to her? Did you sell her?"

"Unfortunately, no. She had the Crimson Death. I didn't know it when she first came to me — it's lucky I keep my treasures isolated or it might have spread to all of them."

"The…Crimson Death?" Sarden's voice sounded harsh and his cool, indifferent manner was slipping somewhat. "So she's too ill to see — is that what you're saying?"

"Oh, no — you may see her if you like. Come."

Tazaxx led the way down the darkened hallway. Sarden's broad shoulders were tense and his gait was wooden but somehow he kept going. I wanted to slip my hand into his and comfort him the same way he had comforted me when I told him about Angie, but I didn't know how he would take it.

We walked past a few more lighted windows and then we came to one that was dark.

"Lights!" Tazaxx called, raising his voice and tapping on the glass.

At once, the lights came up in the case, revealing a bare room with a single raised platform in the center. On the platform lay a girl — or what used to be a girl.

Her body was bent in a position of agony — the back arched as though she had died trying to get a last breath. Her long, silky black hair was matted and dull and her golden cat's eyes, so much like Sarden's, were open but empty. Glazed and lifeless, they stared at us and I noticed rivulets of dried blood had leaked from their corners. Her full lips were painted red too, and gore ran down her chin.

Clearly she had died in agony.

"Gods," Sarden whispered hoarsely. "Oh *Gods.*"

"Yes, it *is* rather disturbing, isn't it?" Tazaxx didn't sound disturbed by the gruesome sight at all. If anything, I thought he sounded bored. "I've had to leave her here, unfortunately. It would be quite dangerous to unseal the room at this point. We need to give it a full sixty solar days before we break the seal and spray in the anti-viral agents."

"She...she..." Sarden clearly couldn't finish.

I slipped my hand into his, not caring if he wanted me to or not—I had to comfort him, to help ease the numbing pain I saw on his face. A pain I swore I could almost feel in my own heart.

"She's been gone for about a week, I believe," Tazaxx said. "We did the best we could for her but after a certain point, nothing but intervention by the Goddess of Mercy herself would have been enough to save her."

"What...what are you going to do with the...with her body?" I could feel Sarden's big frame trembling, yet still he was trying to keep from showing his pain. I understood why—we had to keep the pretense up at least a little while longer if we were going to rescue Teeny.

Tazaxx shrugged his mud shoulders stiffly, as though he wasn't used to making the gesture and was only copying what he had seen others do.

"Burn it, most likely. It's the only safe method of disposal when dealing with the Crimson Death."

"Her ashes…" Sarden made a choking noise. "I need them."

"What?" Tazaxx frowned. "Whatever for?"

"A gift to the Eloim government," I said quickly, improvising. "My, uh, Master is entering into trade agreements with them. If he could give them…give them her ashes, it might be taken as a sign of, uh, goodwill."

"So it could. Yes, I see." Tazaxx nodded. "Very well. I'll be pleased to send you the ashes — for a nominal fee of course."

"Of course." Sarden's deep voice was wooden.

"And do you wish to see any other females?" Tazaxx inquired, raising one mud-eyebrow.

"No, I…no." Sarden coughed. "Just the one. The little Thonilan."

"Yes, indeed. I tell you what — since I couldn't satisfy your other offer, I'll give her to you for a mere ninety-nine thousand." Tazaxx nodded genially, as if he was being generous.

"Yes, all right. Ninety-nine is all right," Sarden said in a low voice. "I…I really must be going now. If you could just have her delivered to my shuttle."

"I'd be happy to. Come right this way." Tazaxx tapped the wall beside the lighted room with Sellah's body in it. To my surprise, it slid open smoothly, revealing another long, dark corridor. "It's a shortcut," Tazaxx explained when I looked at it in surprise. "An underground passageway from my display area back to the docking accommodations where your shuttle is parked. We can arrange for payment there since you're in such a rush."

"Of course. Thank you," Sarden said mechanically. I was

getting really worried about him—he seemed like he was barely holding it together. I squeezed his hand and looked up at him but he didn't respond. Even with the smart-fabric mask on, I could tell his face was set like a stone.

He's still numb, I thought as we followed Tazaxx through the short-cut corridor. *It hasn't really hit him yet, but it will.* I intended to be there for him when it did. I felt so bad for him, seeing his sister like that! What a terrible, gruesome death. And she had died alone, isolated in that horrible cage with no one to help her bear the pain or hold her hand. *Poor Sellah…*

I squeezed Sarden's hand harder and felt my eyes burning. My throat was tight and somehow I couldn't seem to swallow the lump that had formed there.

"Here we are. I'll just go get Floosh to see to the financial transaction and fetch your purchase," Tazaxx remarked as we came out into the warehouse where Sarden's small shuttle was parked. "I'll return shortly."

He left us alone, disappearing back through the door we had come from, and for a moment we just stood there.

"Sarden…" I said at last but he didn't look at me. *"Sarden."*

At last he turned his head.

"Yes?" he asked in a low, toneless voice. "What is it?"

"Sarden, *please.*" I stood on my tiptoes and put my arms around his neck, trying to bring him down to me, trying to ease his pain.

At first he didn't seem to know what I was doing but then he bent down, letting me hug him even if he didn't exactly hug me back.

"Sarden," I said again, pressing my face to his neck. "Honey, I'm so sorry."

He fell to his knees then, his arms wrapping around my midsection, his face pressed between my breasts. I put my arms around him tight—wishing I could take the pain for him. For a long moment, we stayed like that, with Sarden holding me silently. He didn't cry but I could feel the ache of grief inside him—I swear I could.

"I failed her," he said at last, his deep voice hoarse with agony. "She's been gone a whole week. I should have come sooner. I should have found her before she got sick. I—"

"There was nothing you could have done," I whispered. "You tried—you did everything you could."

"No, I didn't," he said fiercely, pulling away. "I never should have left her in the first place—I should have fought for my place on the throne. But I told myself it wasn't worth it—that the Eloim people wouldn't want a half-breed ruling them. I left the responsibility and burden to Sellah and that idiot, Hurxx, who didn't protect her. Who let her get taken…"

"I'm so sorry." I felt tears running down my cheeks and couldn't seem to stop them.

"Don't be." Sarden's eyes glittered as he looked at me. He cupped my cheek in his palm. "I thank you for your tears, Zoe, because I cannot shed them myself."

"Why not?" I asked, swiping at my eyes. "I don't understand."

"I can't let myself grieve until I get vengeance." He stood and looked down at me, his voice a low, menacing growl. "Vengeance on the pirates who took her in the first place…and on my fool of a cousin, Hurxx, who should have protected her and didn't."

"And Tazaxx?" I asked, knowing he was probably somewhere on that list.

Sarden nodded. "But not now—later when he's least expecting

it. After Grav has had time to take his ward to safety."

"Thank you, my friend," Grav rumbled. He hadn't said a word this whole time but I could see the terrible compassion on his face. "There are no words for the pain you must feel," he told Sarden. "I will help you take vengeance for Sellah's death if you wish."

"Thank you." Sarden nodded formally. "I will take you up on that offer."

"Here we are. I believe this is the female you purchased?" It was Floosh – or POC as I had been calling him in my head. He waddled in from the back door with Teeny in tow. Her eyes got wide when she saw Grav but she didn't say a thing.

Sarden and Grav shot each other one last meaningful look but Sarden didn't utter another word else except to thank POC for bringing the girl.

"If you would like to follow me to my Master's back office, we can arrange for the payment," POC said to him.

"Fine. I'll come." Sarden squared his shoulders. "My new acquisition will be safe with my Protector."

"As you wish." POC waddled towards the door on his tiny little feet and Sarden followed him.

"I'm coming too," I said, hurrying to stay with him. As we left the vast, echoing room, I turned my head and saw Teeny rush into Grav's arms.

"Grav! You came! You came for me!" she whispered breathlessly. He laughed and swung her around, looking happier and less scary than any time I could remember since I'd met him in the VIP lounge.

"Teeny! Didn't I promise I would always come for you? Didn't I swear it on my life?" He squeezed her very gently to his broad chest and she covered his rough face in kisses. She looked like a little girl greeting an adoring uncle—I couldn't believe the big, tough Vorn (or Vorn half-breed? I still didn't know what he was) had such a soft heart.

The sweet little reunion almost made me feel a little better. Then I looked at Sarden's broad back and felt worse again. Poor guy! And he wasn't even going to let himself grieve until he killed everyone responsible for Sellah's death.

He could say that but I knew the truth—there's no way to put off that kind of deep grief. When it comes knocking, you have to open the door because you can't keep it out.

"Just a little further down," POC was saying as he led us around another bend in the dark tunnel. "This is my master's accounting area…"

We were heading for an open door at the end of the corridor and passing several others along the way which all appeared to be locked. They were dark and quiet and I wondered if they were back entrances to some of the "exhibits" we had seen. Then we passed one that was different—it had a window.

Sarden had his head down, looking at his feet as he walked. I could only imagine the effort it cost him to keep up this awful charade. I, however, was looking around and so the window caught my eye—and in it, the flash of a woman's face. A golden eye…a flick of silky, black hair… Had I really seen that?

I couldn't be sure. It was there and gone so quickly I thought I must have imagined it. I stopped for a moment and looked again but I didn't see anything—just a lighted square in the metal door. Just my mind playing tricks on me.

"And here I am afraid you must come in alone," POC said, breaking my concentration. He was gesturing to the open door and talking to Sarden. "Master Tazaxx does not allow anyone but his business partners into his inner accounting sanctum."

Sarden frowned. "I won't leave Zoe."

"You must, I am afraid," POC said. "I assure you she will be quite well. Or she can go back to your Protector to wait if you like – the way back is just down the corridor."

"Yes, do that." Sarden nodded at me. "Go back to Grav. Stay there until this is finished."

"All right." I nodded and watched as he and POC went into the lighted room and shut the door, leaving me in gloom.

I should have gone back down the hallway at once – I know I should have. But something made me go look in that window we had passed one more time and that was when I saw her.

Sellah was alive.

Part Four: Captured, Cloned, and Collared

Chapter Twenty-one

Zoe

I couldn't believe it but there she was—the exact same girl I'd seen in Sarden's crystal memory cube. Her smooth brown skin and large golden eyes, so like Sarden's, were unmistakable. Those golden eyes widened when she saw me watching her and she made motions at me and said something I couldn't hear.

"Hang on," I told her in a low voice, which she probably couldn't hear either. "I'm going to get you out of there."

But how? I pulled on the door handle and it didn't budge an inch—it was unmistakably locked.

I looked at the palm-pad just to the right of the door and wondered. Doubtless it was set to only open for Tazaxx. But then, the door on Gallana had been keyed only for someone with Majoran DNA and the Force-Locks I had opened before that were supposedly only useable by a Vorn.

Might as well give it a try.

Taking a deep breath, I pressed my hand to the pad and waited anxiously to see what would happen. At first my fingers were outlined in red and I was afraid it wasn't going to work. Then, to my excitement, the red changed to green and I heard a soft but definite *click* from the locking mechanism inside the door.

Grabbing the handle before it could change its mind, I yanked it open and ran in to Sellah.

"Sellah!" I exclaimed, rushing to greet her. She was wearing manacles on her wrists and a cruel looking metal collar around her slender throat which was attached by a chain to the wall.

"Who are you?" she whispered, looking at me with wide eyes. "And what are you doing here? I thought...I thought I saw my big brother."

"You did." I couldn't help myself, I put my arms around her and hugged her tight. I was just so glad to see she was alive!

Sellah hesitated for a moment, then hugged me back.

"Where is he?" she whispered in my ear. "You have to tell him to get out of here and you have to go too—you're both in terrible danger."

"We're not going anywhere without you," I told her, pulling back to look into her eyes. "You're the reason we came in the first place. I'm Zoe, by the way."

"Zo-ee?" She made my name sound exotic. "Are you my brother's lover? Or his intended mate?"

"Oh, er..." Well *this* conversation was turning awkward fast. "Neither," I said. "He abducted me to trade for you but then...well, it's a long story. Let's talk about you—we thought you were dead. Tazaxx showed us..." I shivered. "I don't even want to say what he showed us."

"He can take many shapes—different forms," Sellah said in a low voice. "Please..." She looked at me urgently. "You *have* to go while you still can."

"I told you — I'm not going without you," I said firmly. "Now let's have a look at this awful collar you're wearing."

I found the unlocking mechanism around the back of it.

"It's no good," Sellah said, sounding hopeless. "It's keyed only to Tazaxx or the captain of his Gord guard. I don't know what planet you hail from, but it's clear you aren't Gord."

"I come from Earth," I told her. "We're a, uh, closed planet. Or we were, until recently."

"You're a Pure One?" Her eyes widened.

"That's what everyone keeps telling me, though Sister Mary Louise back at The Sisters of the Sacred Heart high school would probably disagree," I said. "Okay…here."

I had been trying to find a way to open the thick, metal collar around her neck. There seemed to be several buttons but none of them responded when I pressed them. Then, by accident, my fingertip slipped into the small, smooth place between the buttons and *that* was when the lock snapped open. I pulled the collar off Selah's neck and helped her stand.

"How did you *do* that?" She looked at me wide-eyed.

"I don't know," I said honestly. "Sarden, er, your brother says I'm a *La-ti-zal,* whatever that means."

"It means that you're very, very valuable indeed. Even more than I had at first imagined."

The familiar voice came from behind me, startling me. I jerked and turned to see Tazaxx in his mud-man form standing just inside the doorway. Before I could move, the door clicked shut and I knew it was locked again.

"What are you talking about?" I asked, my stomach doing a nervous twitch. "And why did you lie to us about Sellah being dead?"

"I might ask why *you* lied to me as well," he drawled, raising an eyebrow. "The smart-fabric mask was a masterful touch — I will give you that. But it wasn't enough to fool me, especially as I knew you'd be coming."

"Someone warned you Sarden was coming?" I asked.

"Of course — Hurxx, who arranged for Sarden's sister to be captured and sold in the first place." He gave Sellah a cold smile. "He told me when he sent her to me that her older brother would never stop hunting for her until he knew she was dead." He shrugged his muddy shoulders. "So I made certain that he knew it."

"You bastard," I snarled. "You have no idea the pain you're putting him through."

"Oh yes, I do — I simply do not care." He grinned at me, showing muddy brown teeth — even in his mud face, the sight was weirdly disgusting.

"Let us go," I said, trying to keep my voice steady. "You've had your fun — your revenge on Sarden. Now let him know his sister isn't dead."

"I don't think so." His smile widened. "In fact, not only will I deny him his sister, he's also going to lose his favorite concubine."

"You can't," I said, wishing my voice wouldn't tremble so much. "He'll hunt for me, too. You can't just…"

But the words died on my lips as Tazaxx began to change.

The muddy outline of his man-shaped body changed, smoothing out, becoming smaller and more feminine. Then I was staring right at myself — or a sculpture of me made out of mud, anyway.

"That's creepy but it won't work," I said, lifting my chin. "So what if you look like me? You still look like me *made out of mud."*

"Because I'm not finished yet. This form is crude yet comfortable—but I can refine it if I wish to."

As I watched, the mud-me became smoother and paler. The hair became red and the eyes, blue. Even the same clothing I was wearing appeared on the mud-me's body. The Slave Leia outfit down to the last detail.

Until Tazaxx looked exactly like me.

"What…" I had to swallow before I could try again. "What do you think you're going to do? Get on the shuttle and leave with Sarden? You'll just be trapped with him and once he finds out you aren't really me—" I shook my head. "You're gonna be in for a world of hurt, buddy."

Tazaxx shrugged. "I don't mind what he does to my scion. I can make many, *many* of them, you see—can mold myself into whatever form I choose. And if I lose one here or there, it is no matter to me. It doesn't hurt me anymore than clipping your fingernails would hurt you."

"So…you can make infinite mud-men? Or women?" I could feel my heart sinking but I tried not to show it.

"More or less. Every time I molt, my mass grows and I can afford to lose more of it. Which is why I didn't mind sacrificing some of it to assure your paramour, Sarden, that his beloved sibling was dead." He nodded at Sellah, who was white-lipped and wide-eyed with terror. "As I won't mind sacrificing a bit more to make Sarden think he has you with him, my dear," he told me.

"He'll know," I said desperately. "You can't fool him that easily."

"Oh, really? Are you *positive* of that?"

Tazaxx smiled at me and suddenly I saw Sarden pass by the

door that kept Sellah and me prisoner. Another me—this one also perfect in every detail—walked by his side.

"Sarden!" I screamed as loud as I could. "Sarden, help! Help— we're in here!"

He didn't even look up. But the other-me did. She looked up and gave me a nasty, knowing smile.

If you've never been smiled at by your evil mud-doppelganger as she walks off with your boyfriend (or at least the guy you really, really like) well, I don't recommend it. It sucks.

"Sarden!" I shouted again. *"Please!"*

My shouting frightened my *nib-nibs* and two of them, Rhaegar and Viserys came out of my hair and went chattering down my arm.

"No, you guys," I hissed at them. "Bad timing—back! Go Back!"

But it was too late—Tazaxx had already seen them.

"Ah—I forgot about these little creatures. Your *pets.*" The mud-me that Tazaxx had become, held out a hand. "Give them to me *now* or suffer the consequences."

"No." I cupped them in my hands protectively. "You'll hurt them."

"I assure you, I will not. *Unless* you fail to hand them over. Then I will be certain they are torn limb from limb while you watch."

I shivered, hearing the awful words come from what appeared to be my own mouth. Looking into those eyes so much like mine, I knew he would do it.

"Fine." I held the *nib-nibs* up in the palm of my hand and looked at them. "You guys are going to go and leave me here," I whispered, my voice slightly choked. Don't worry—just go with Sarden. He'll protect you. Or at least he won't eat you."

They chattered softly in the palm of my hand and I could feel my last *nib-nib,* Drogon, moving around restlessly at the back of my neck. But to my relief, he stayed where he was, even when I handed the two tiny *nib-nibs* over carefully to Tazaxx.

"Be careful—don't crush them!" I said, my voice hoarse.

"I wouldn't dream of it," Tazaxx remarked. He slapped one hand over my mouth and opened the door a crack just for a moment.

The *nib-nibs* scampered out and the other mud-me doppelganger, who was walking just behind Sarden, reached down to try and scoop them up. They ran around her and made a B-line for Sarden and for a moment, I thought they might get his attention. And if he turned and saw me through the crack in the door…

But it didn't happen. The mud-me was faster than I would have thought possible. She put on a burst of speed and snatched them up, chattering from the floor before they could reach Sarden. Then she gave me another nasty, triumphant smile and kept walking with the two of them cupped carefully between her hands.

The door started to swing closed and I knew it was now or never. Surging forward, I bit down on Tazaxx's palm as hard as I could, sinking my teeth deep into his flesh…where it crumbled into a mouthful of slimy dirt.

Tazaxx held me off easily, as though I was no more than a child, and let the door snick shut and lock once more. He let me go and I spat out the mouthful of muddy dirt, completely disgusted.

"Ugh!" I wiped at my tongue as best I could. "Disgusting!"

"I'm sorry you find it so," Tazaxx remarked mildly. His hand wasn't injured at all—it looked like I hadn't even bitten him, let along taken out a big chunk.

"Promise me your, uh, scion won't hurt my *nib-nibs*," I demanded, spitting again. I didn't like the way she'd smiled at me when she caught them.

"I assure you, they will be unharmed. They are only there to perfect the illusion. Your paramour will never suspect a thing now…that is until he's too far away to get back in time and do any good."

He gave me a smirk that was unbearably self-satisfied.

"Sarden will find out what you're doing," I said. "You can't keep up the illusion forever."

"I don't have to—I only have to keep it up long enough to sell the two of you at auction. Which will be in exactly twenty solar hours at an undisclosed location."

"He'll come," I said stubbornly, trying to make myself believe it.

"Please don't fool yourself," Tazaxx said. "The auction site is kept secret from all but those who are expressly invited—and they aren't notified of its exact location until shortly before it is to begin. Your Master will never find you."

He gave me an evil grin and once more I had the weird experience of being taunted by myself.

"Could you not?" I said. "I mean, it's *really* creepy when you use my own face to sneer at me."

"Forgive me." His features mutated until he was the mud-man again. "Is that better?"

"Not by much. But a little." I lifted my chin. "Fine, so you're going to sell us. Now that we know can you just leave us alone?"

"So that you can unlock the door with your *La-ti-zal* powers? I don't think so, my dear. From now on, I won't be leaving your side. Not until I can turn you over to the Master of the Auction." He walked back to the door and stood right in front of it. "Feel free to talk but if you attempt an escape, know this—some of the attendees at my yearly auction *like* buying injured females. It makes breaking them to a new owner's will so much *easier*."

"You bastard," I spat at him.

"Actually, as I told you before, we Gord reproduce asexually. So I have neither a mother nor father, which renders any insults relating to my heritage completely pointless."

"How about this—you look like a mud puddle and your assistant looks like a giant, walking piece of excrement," I snapped, completely fed up.

Tazaxx seemed to consider my insult for a moment, then he nodded thoughtfully.

"You are correct, I believe."

"Oh…go away. Or at least just stop talking to me." I was beyond exasperated—I couldn't even insult the jerk!

"As you wish." The mud-man stopped talking and then, his mud began to run and flow until he lost his shape completely. Soon he was just a mud puddle on the floor right in front of the door.

I wanted to jump over the puddle and try to unlock the door but I had seen how fast he could move and change shape. If I tried anything I would probably wind up on the cold metal floor with mud tentacles wrapped all over my body. I remembered Tazaxx's slimy, cool touch and his terrible strength when he put his hand over my mouth—I really didn't want to feel that again, especially not all over me.

Instead, I turned to Sellah again.

"I'm really sorry," I said. "Some rescue, huh?"

"You tried." Her golden eyes were bright with unshed tears. "It was a trap from the first—Tazaxx put me here to catch your eye, I'm certain of it."

"Well, if so he succeeded." I sighed. "What can we do now?"

"Nothing," she whispered. "Nothing but wait."

I was afraid she was right.

Sarden

My heart was so full of grief I could scarcely see to pilot the shuttle. I think Grav saw that because he took over the controls and made me sit in the passenger seat instead of driving.

In the back, Teeny, his ward, sat quietly beside Zoe. I would have expected Zoe to be chatting with the girl and trying to make her feel at ease. But she was strangely and uncharacteristically quiet on our flight out of the atmosphere of Giedi Prime. Even when we dropped Grav and his ward back at his own ship, she barely said goodbye to them. I wondered if she was upset about what she had seen—I knew for myself, the image of Sellah's body was one I couldn't forget. It was like a fresh wound that kept bleeding—I saw it every time I closed my eyes.

Grav left with the promise that he would help me take vengeance as soon as Teeny had been delivered safely to her grandfather's planet. I thanked him for his help and promised to see him again soon. But every word I said seemed to come from someone else, some other person who was speaking on my behalf.

I couldn't think straight—could barely breathe. Despite my determination to put off my grief until I took vengeance, I could feel the anguish already on me and its weight was *crushing*.

We got back to *The Celesta* at last and I thought that Zoe might try to comfort me again. I shouldn't let her, of course. I deserved no such comfort after failing Sellah in such a terrible way. But I would have welcomed Zoe's soft arms around my neck, anyway—even if I didn't deserve it.

But Zoe barely said a word as we came from the docking area out into the main corridor of the ship. I noticed she was holding her pet *nib-nibs* in her cupped hands instead of letting them nest in her hair and wondered why.

"Zoe?" I asked, when she turned away from me.

"I'm tired." She didn't meet my eyes, only looked at the floor and her bare feet. Our footwear, which we had abandoned outside Tazaxx's home, had been brought back to the shuttle but Zoe hadn't bothered to put hers on.

"I know this has been…a bad time." I barely knew what I was saying. "And…I know I promised to bring you back to Earth once it was all…" I had to swallow before I could go on. "All finished."

"Yes," she said, still looking down. "Yes, take me back. You promised."

I don't know what I had expected or hoped for. Maybe for her to say she didn't want to go back? That she wanted to stay with me…to explore whatever it was I'd thought I felt growing between us when she tasted me, as I had tasted her, which is almost always the first step in bonding?

But she didn't say any of that. And I didn't feel anything between us anymore. It was like there was a blank wall there—a wall I couldn't penetrate, no matter how much I wanted to.

"Take me back," Zoe said again. And then she repeated, "I'm tired."

"Why don't you go in your room and lie down," I said,

gesturing to the door leading to her quarters. "I…I'll set a course for Earth."

"Good." She turned away from me and, without a second glance, disappeared into her room.

I stood there in the corridor, wishing I could call her back, knowing I couldn't. Sellah was dead and the female I was coming to care for — maybe even to love — wanted nothing to do with me.

Not that I blamed her.

I turned back to the control center of *The Celesta* to set a course that would take us back to Earth.

I had never felt more alone.

Chapter Twenty-two

Sarden

"Master? Master, please wake!"

Al's voice sounded as worried as I had ever heard it. "What? What is it?" I muttered, forcing myself to open my eyes. I'd laid awake in my bunk most of the night, sleepless with grief. Every time I closed my eyes I saw my little sister's body, saw the blood that had leaked from her eyes and nose and mouth, saw the look of agony on her face proving she had died in pain and alone. Because I wasn't there for her. Because I didn't save her in time or keep her from getting taken in the first place.

So when Al came twittering around my head, I hadn't been asleep for more than an hour—maybe less.

"What is it?" I asked again, hoisting myself up on one elbow in my hover-bed.

"It's Lady Zoe—I think something may be wrong with her," Al said, sounding anxious. "She's completely non-responsive."

"What?" Sleep deprived or not, that got my attention. I jumped out of bed. "Where is she?"

"In her room. I went to wake her and ask if she would like me to use one of the food options she had input earlier into the food synthesizer for her first meal, but she didn't answer me."

"Are you sure she's not just asleep?" I asked, running out of my room and heading for hers even as I spoke.

"She doesn't appear asleep, Master—her eyes are open. But…I can detect no signs of respiration or pulse."

"What?" This was getting worse and worse. Zoe had seemed so quiet and depressed the night before. Could it be that she had done something to harm herself? *Please, Goddess of Mercy,* I prayed as I ran into her room. *I lost Sellah – don't let me lose Zoe too. Please!*

I got to her hoverbed and saw she was just lying there, as Al had said.

"Zoe? *Zoe?"* My voice cracked on her name. Her blue eyes were blank and sightless, staring straight at the flat metal ceiling. Her chest wasn't rising or falling either. She seemed…gone.

No! I couldn't let myself think like that. I had to help her—had to try and bring her back. But how?

I stood there, afraid to move, afraid to touch anything—frozen to the spot. And then I felt something—a light, tingling and scratching sensation running up one bare arm. Looking down, I saw it was two of Zoe's pet *nib-nibs.* They were chattering to me urgently, almost as though they were trying to tell me something.

But that was ridiculous. I pushed the crazy thought aside and concentrated on the matter at hand.

"Zoe?" I said again. "Zoe, please—I lost Sellah—I can't fucking lose you too. *Please!"* Desperate for any response, I reached out to shake her by the shoulders.

Her skin felt cold to the touch, as though she had been gone for hours and no colors crossed my vision. She was gone and she had taken every bit of beauty with her. I felt the tide of grief rising in me again—grief and disbelief and horror. No, I couldn't do this—I couldn't survive another loss!

"Zoe," I begged, the words coming out harsh and uneven as the tide of grief threatened to overwhelm me. "Please don't do this to me—don't be gone forever. I need you. I *love* you."

The moment the words broke from my lips, I knew they were true. True and too late for me to do anything about them. I didn't just *care* for her…it wasn't just a *connection* I felt between us—Zoe was the one female in the galaxy I wanted as my own. The one I wanted to spend my life with.

And now she was gone.

"Zoe!" I shook her again. "Zoe, *please.* You can't fucking go. You can't—"

And then she crumbled to dust beneath my hands.

I looked down in disbelief, staring at the muddy pile of dirt which was all that was left of the woman I loved. How could this be? What in the Frozen Hells of Anor…And then a memory formed in my brain.

Tazaxx, forming from the slick, brown puddle of mud into a male, complete with arms and legs and features. I hadn't known he was capable of doing that before this visit to his compound. Though I had met him face-to-face on several occasions, he had always taken the appearance of a *Major*an male with light brown skin and brown eyes. I had been startled when I saw him form a new shape in the molting room but hell, what did I know about Gords? Now I began to think…

If Tazaxx could form himself into one shape and animate it, why not another? Why not Zoe?

I looked at the pile of muddy dirt again.

"He has her," I said hoarsely. "Gods, Tazaxx has Zoe. And he fucking fooled me into flying halfway across the galaxy from where he's holding her!"

At my words, the two *nib-nibs* sat up on my shoulder and

chattered loudly in my ear.

"Are you quite certain, Master?" Al asked, still sounding as worried as an Artificial Lifeform can. He had really taken a liking to Zoe while she was aboard the ship. We all had. She had stolen my heart and in return, I had let *her* get stolen. For the *second* time. What a Goddess-damned idiot I had been!

"It must have happened when I went in with Tazaxx to sign the damn contract for Teeny," I snarled. "I let her get taken *again!* What the fuck is *wrong* with me?" I picked up a handful of the dirt and threw it. It landed against the wall with a *splat* and slid down, leaving a muddy brown smear which did nothing to relieve my feelings.

"Master, what shall I do?" Al asked anxiously.

"Set a course back for Giedi Prime," I snapped. "And contact Grav — tell him I need his help sooner than expected. We have to go back — we have to get Zoe before..."

"Before what?" Al was still hovering anxiously in front of me, his eye-light blinking nervously.

I started to say, *before it's too late,* but the words wouldn't leave my lips. What if it was *already* too late? What if Tazaxx already had Zoe locked away in one of those fucking cages? Or worse, what if he had decided to sell her at the auction? That was probably more likely — he would know I wouldn't stop until I rescued her. By auctioning her off, he could get her off his hands and keep the massive amount of credit she would no doubt bring. Then whoever bought her would have to deal with me and he would be in the clear.

Except you won't be, you bastard, I swore to myself. *As soon as I get Zoe back I'm going to find you and make you wish you never crawled out of that fucking mud in the first place. You're going to pay and pay and pay until there's nothing left of you.*

But before I settled with Tazaxx, I had to find Zoe and the auction, and I had no idea where it was being held. Still, how far from Giedi Prime could it be?

I'll find it, I thought. *I have to.* And once I got Zoe back, I never intended to let her go again.

If only I could reach her in time.

* * * * *

Zoe

"So this is how it ends," I muttered to Sellah. "Sold off at an interstellar auction like some kind of freaking *object d' art* at a Christie's auction."

"I'm afraid so." She squeezed my hand and I squeezed back gratefully. At least I had one friend here — well, two if you counted Drogon, but he was still hiding quietly at the back of my hair.

I had been afraid he would be discovered when Tazaxx finally turned me over to the Master of the Auction, who was a large, hairy, Big Foot-looking guy. Big Foot had looked me over and listened as Tazaxx explained about my special "gifts," then he called for the strongest inhibitor collar possible. He and his assistant — a creature with four arms and compound eyes — had locked it around my throat, thus inhibiting my powers, whatever they were.

Honestly, I still didn't really understand them myself. So far as I could see, I was mostly just able to unlock things that were keyed to other people. That skill might have been useful if I was a James Bond type spy or a cat burglar instead of a paralegal. But other than getting me into trouble again and again, I couldn't see that my new "powers" had helped me much at all in my time away from Earth.

Drogon had chattered quietly and scrambled to another place in my hair while they put on the collar but luckily neither Big Foot or his Fly Guy assistant noticed the tiny *nib-nib*. I was glad I still had him for company—especially since Sellah and I were about to be parted. I couldn't imagine that one buyer would take us both, though I wished it could be so. I had only known Sarden's little sister for one night, but already I considered her a friend.

Since there was nothing to do but talk, she had told me about her life and I had given her some tidbits on mine as well. She was fascinated to know what life on a closed planet was like and amazed to find out the Earth was so isolated we had no idea that other races existed, especially compatible races also started by the Ancient Ones as they seeded the galaxy.

I, in turn, was fascinated to know what it was like to be queen of an entire planet. But Sellah's description was disappointing.

"I never wanted to be the Ria," she told me as we sat in the corner of the cold, nasty cell in Tazaxx's awful house and waited to be moved to the auction site. "I've always loved learning—I wanted to go off planet to the University of Lynex Tau and get a higher degree."

"Why didn't you?" I asked.

She sighed. "I felt I had a duty to Eloim. Sarden felt it too—I wanted him to rule with me but he didn't think the people would allow a half-breed Rae to sit on the double throne and wear the Star of Wisdom."

"Star of Wisdom? What's that?" I asked.

"The crown that is genetically keyed to the Rae of Eloim. Only the rightful ruler may wear it on his head and only he may remove it once it is on. If an imposter or one who is wrong for the throne attempts to put it on, the Star of Wisdom will fly from his brow and refuse his touch." She sighed. "It is the same with the Star of Compassion—the crown of the Ria. When the pirates captured me, they forced me to take it off at blaster-point. I don't know what happened to it. Perhaps they sold it."

"So…do these crowns have some kind of advanced computer programs in them or something?" I asked, mystified. "Because it sounds like something out of a fantasy show or something."

"It is no fantasy," Sellah said seriously. "There is a being—a long-lived creature, wise beyond measure and old beyond years—that inhabits the stars. Half in the Star of Wisdom and half in the Star of Compassion. It knows always the rightful heirs to the throne of Eloim."

"And that's always someone from your family—your genetic line?" I asked, fascinated.

Sellah shook her head. "Only in recent generations. But if the Star of either crown finds the current ruler unfit, it will fly from his or her head and find the worthy one. There are tales of it doing just that during a coronation. Once the Star of Wisdom left the head of a blooded prince and found the head of a muck worker instead."

"A *muck* worker?" I stifled a laugh. "If that's what I think it is, I bet that was quite a scene."

"The Stars of Wisdom and Compassion are never wrong," Sellah said. "Which is why I can't understand why The Star of Wisdom didn't fly off Hurxx's head the moment he put it on."

"Your cousin, right? The one who was supposed to rule with you but instead…"

"Sold me into slavery. Yes." Sellah sighed, her golden eyes sad. "He should have picked another Ria if he didn't truly want me. But

I think he thought the people wouldn't support him without my lineage to back him up."

"You'll get back to Eloim somehow," I told her, trying to stay positive. "And when you do, you can expose that bastard Hurxx and tell everyone what he did."

"From your mouth to the Goddess of Mercy's ear," she said, sighing again. "Maybe we will both be bought by males of wisdom and compassion who will listen to our pleas."

I certainly hoped so but now, looking out from the backstage area of the auction to the crowds milling in front of the raised stage, I didn't know. There were quite a lot of humanoid aliens—the ones who came from the twelve races seeded by the Ancient Ones, I guessed. But there were plenty of non-human looking creatures as well.

I saw one in the front row that looked like a giant praying mantis. He was wearing a very respectable looking outfit kind of like a gray suit but he also had extremely sharp looking mandibles. I really hoped he didn't buy me.

There was another guy with a face like a bull with huge, long horns. All I could think of when I looked at him was all the videos I'd ever seen about the Running of the Bulls in Spain and how people get gored there every year. I didn't want *him* to buy me either.

In fact, looking over the crowd, I didn't see *anyone* I would be happy to go home with. I didn't even see anyone I would feel *safe* going home with. If these guys were on Tinder, I would have been swiping left so fast my fingers bled.

Then I saw an older looking alien with smooth brown skin. He had the same golden cat eyes as Sellah and Sarden.

"Hey." I nudged her with one elbow. "Look at that—is that

another Eloim?"

"What? Where?" She scanned the crowd eagerly and her eyes lit up when she saw who I was talking about. "Goddess be praised! That's Tellum Vas'kie. He was one of my father's oldest friends and advisors."

"You think he's here for you?" I asked.

"I don't know but I hope so. If anyone would see through Hurxx's plans and come looking for me besides Sarden, it would be Uncle Tellum." She looked at me, hope shining in her eyes. "If he wins me at auction, I'll ask him to bid on you too, Zoe. Then we can go find Sarden and go back to Eloim to expose Hurxx together!"

"Oh my God, that would be so good." I felt weak in the knees with relief. "Do you think he can afford both of us?"

"I hope so. It depends on how high the bidding goes," Sellah said cautiously. "I heard the Master of the Auction talking and I'm afraid you're expected to draw quite a price. Maybe the most they've ever seen at this auction."

I groaned. "Seriously?"

"Yes." She nodded. "Why? Is it surprising to you that you're considered the most valuable female here?"

I thought of how my life had gone up until this point. In high school I couldn't make the freaking cheerleading squad because I wasn't one of the popular girls. Also, I didn't get into my first choice college because my grades weren't quite up to par, didn't get to date yummy Ken Forthright in my sociology class because he sat beside a blonde named Krissy who was gorgeous and had legs up to her ears—I couldn't compete with that. Not to mention I didn't get the job I wanted so badly at Marston and Hinks, the really nice law firm downtown where they don't throw staplers at your head because my résumé wasn't up to snuff.

All my life I had been not quite good enough...second best...below par...just kind of average. And now I was suddenly the perfect 10 that everyone desired—exactly what I'd always wanted to be.

Was this the worst time and place to have my dreams come true or what?

"Zoe?" Sellah asked and I realized I had never answered her question.

"Uh, yes," I said. "Yes, it surprises me."

"Well—" Sellah started but the booming voice of Big Foot, the Master of the Auction interrupted her.

"For our first bid of the evening, let's begin with a beautiful and *royal* recent acquisition of Master Tazaxx. Rightful heir to the Eloim throne, Ria Sellah de'Lagorn!"

"Looks like you're up," I whispered to Sellah. "Uh, good luck."

"To you too, Zoe. I promise, I'll try to get Uncle Tellum to buy you if he buys me."

We had time for a brief hug and then she was pulled away to stand in the center of the metal stage and be gawked at by all the buyers.

"As you can see, gentle-beings, she's a very find specimen," Big Foot declared. "Let's start the bidding at sixty thousand credits, shall we?"

"Sixty," a guy in the back who had a long, horse-like nose but human eyes said.

"Sixxxxty-five," hissed the praying mantis in the front row.

And just like that, the bidding was off and running. It got as high as a hundred thousand credits before Sellah was won—thankfully by the older, portly Eloim she had called Uncle Tellum. I saw him press his hand to the pay pad so that it lit up green and then the guards led her out to stand by him in the crowd.

They started talking at once and I saw her gesturing to the stage, where I was mostly hidden behind a curtain. My heart started beating faster, hope filling me. Maybe he really would buy me too! Maybe all this could be over and we could go home before we knew it.

Only where was home? As much as I missed Charlotte and Leah, I didn't think of Earth when I thought that word, "home" anymore. I thought of Sarden's ship and Al and my floating silver beanbag bed and the food synthesizer making weird and inedible things. And most of all I thought of Sarden himself and how much I missed him. Would I ever see him again? Would I ever get to tell him how I was beginning to feel for him? And would he return my feelings...or just want to send me back to Earth?

I had no answers for any of the questions and before I could think some up, it was my turn on the auction block. Or stage — the auction stage, I guess.

The Master of the Auction pulled me from the backstage area to stand front and center before the crowd. I felt my cheeks get hot but I lifted my chin. Even if I was being sold, I wasn't going to cry and whine about it — they might be able to buy my body but they couldn't buy my dignity.

Or so I told myself. Although if someone had told me I could get my freedom by crying and begging, I totally would have done it. I'm not too proud to recognize reality. Nobody did, however, so I just had to stand there looking brave and noble, or at least trying to.

Pretend you're a heroine in a romance novel, I told myself. *And the hero is on his way to rescue you.*

Only my hero was halfway across the galaxy, probably still

believed that damn animated pile of mud Tazaxx had used to fool him was me. I was terribly afraid I wasn't going to get my Happily Ever After ending. Once I was sold, it was more likely to be a Sadly Ever After. Maybe even a *Shortly* Ever After. What if I got bought by some kind of a killer? An alien serial killer? What if—?

"Now this is our prize offering here today," the Master of the Auction said, breaking my morbid train of thought. "A female from a closed world. Seeded by the Ancient Ones and then locked against all outside interference until very, very recently. She is rare beyond belief—a Pure One!"

There was a hushed murmur as the auction goers murmured among themselves, most of them looking at me like I was a prime cut of steak and they had the A1 sauce all ready to go.

The Master of the Auction waited for a moment for the murmuring to calm down and then continued.

"Not only is she a rare Pure One from a closed planet, please note the inhibitor collar she wears. She is also a *La-ti-zal* – blessed by the Ancient Ones with gifts too powerful to be set free. Gentle-beings, you will simply not find a female like this anywhere else in the galaxy—nay, in the whole *universe*. This is a one of a kind offering. Now what am I bid?"

"One hundred thousand credits," someone shouted and I realized dismally that my starting price was Sellah's ending price. We were going all the way to the top with this—I only hoped her old friend would be willing to try and keep up.

He did try for a while—until the bidding got up past nine hundred thousand credits. But when someone bid a million, I saw Uncle Tellum shake his head regretfully. Sellah had tears in her eyes as she looked at me.

I felt like crying myself, but I refused to. I kept my head high and stared out at the crowd, trying not to see who was winning. But I couldn't help hearing the bids.

"Two million creditsss," the praying mantis in the gray suit hissed.

"Five million," shouted the bull-headed guy. What did they call that in Greek mythology? A man with a bull's head? Oh right—a minotaur. I was being bid on by a minotaur, or something that looked like one. Could my life get any more surreal?

I didn't see how.

Then someone stood up in the back of the crowd—a man I hadn't seen before. He was wearing a mask made of some kind of pink rubbery stuff that made his face a complete blank. It had slits for the eyes and mouth but other than that, everything was just smooth and pink and bland. For some reason, I found it completely terrifying.

"Fifty million credits," he said loudly in a voice that was muffled but somehow horribly familiar.

I felt a shiver creep down my spine. Who was this guy? I couldn't tell much about him because of the mask but he was tall and thin and he wore a long, black cape. The only other person I knew who wore a cape like that was…

"No," I whispered, looking at Sellah appealingly. "Oh, *no*."

She must have seen the panic in my face because her golden eyes overflowed at last, the tears running down her smooth brown cheeks.

"*Zoe…*" She mouthed my name just as the Master of the Auction said,

"Sold! To the gentle-being in the back for fifty million credits."

Chapter Twenty-three

Zoe

"So, my dear. Here we are at last."

"And where exactly is *here?*" I looked at my pink-masked captor. He hadn't even waited for the rest of the auction. As soon as he paid, he had taken me in manacles and chains straight to a shuttle which in turn took us to a large, black ship. It looked like an oil slick floating in space and since space itself is black, it was almost impossible to see unless you saw star light reflected off its shiny surface.

The shuttle had docked smoothly with the ship and before I knew it, my new owner was herding me inside. I kept as far ahead of him as I could, wanting to stay away from his long, boney hands and the creepy pink mask. But I dreaded seeing him without the mask even more—dreaded confirming my suspicions.

"This is my ship—EOC-2789," he said, as we came out into a wide silver corridor, not too much different from the one on Sarden's ship. "Come, the medical suite is this way."

"What? No way. No medical suite."

I tried to pull away from him but he locked one long-fingered hand around the back of my neck, just above the damn inhibitor collar and pinched fiercely.

"Ahhh!" He must have hit a nerve somehow because I felt my legs crumpling beneath me and electrical tingles of pain ran down both arms. Holy crap, he was strong!

"Enough!" he snapped. "I have paid an exorbitant amount for you and I will tolerate no more insolence!"

At that moment I felt Drogon, my *nib-nib,* moving wildly in my hair and then there was a muffled cry of pain and a curse from the masked man. He let go of my neck, just for a moment, but it was long enough.

Somehow I got to my feet and stumbled down the long corridor, looking for a way to escape. Of course, where could I escape to? I was on a strange ship in the middle of space. But maybe I could at least find someplace to barricade myself in. Maybe a kitchen so I could have access to food? Then I could lock the door and hold him off indefinitely — I hoped anyway.

I ran down the long silver hall, my manacles clanking and Drogon chattering angrily in my ear. Thank goodness they hadn't chained my feet or I never would have gotten anywhere!

I passed several doors but they were shut and possibly locked. I didn't think I would be able to open them with the collar on — it appeared to be a much stronger inhibitor than the little bracelet the Commercians had put on me, which seemed like a lifetime ago.

Then I saw an open doorway. Inside was a flash of metal that made me think of the huge gold pot of the food-sim. I ducked inside and looked for a door-shut button. There was one, just beside the doorway. I hammered it frantically and watched as it whooshed shut.

Almost shut, anyway.

Just as it was about to snick closed, a long, boney foot clad in a black boot got in the way. I pressed the button again, frantically, muttering, "Come on...come *on,*" like someone who doesn't want to share the elevator.

But it did no good. The door slid back open, revealing the masked man. I backed away from him, hands held out in front of me.

"Get away. Leave me alone."

"I think not." He stepped forward, looming over me menacingly. "Thank you so much for seeing yourself to my medical suite. It is quite well arranged, don't you think?"

Heart sinking, I looked around and saw what I had assumed was a kitchen was no such thing. The gleam of metal I'd seen belonged to one of the huge medical/torture devices that had previously been in the hold of Sarden's ship. They were all there — arranged in order and gleaming and humming ominously, as though they were waiting for their next victim.

From the corner of my eye, I saw the huge tank of yellow liquid and the black tentacles coiling eagerly inside it.

The victim, was apparently going to be me.

"As you can see," he said, taking another step forward. "Everything is all arranged for your arrival."

"You…you asshole! You coward! You're too afraid to even face me without your mask on!" I shouted, hoping to distract him. I thought if he took time to pull the mask off, I might be able to run past him and try to find a new room to hole up in. *Any* room that wasn't full of torture devices would be an improvement.

"Mask?" He broke into high, wheezy laughter that sent a chill down my spine. "What mask do you speak of?"

"The one you're wearing," I said, gesturing at the smooth, pink plane of his face. "Because you were too afraid to show your face at the auction."

"You misunderstand, my dear Zoe," he said and the thin slit where his mouth should be curled into a tiny, cruel smile. "It isn't that I have put a mask on—it is that I have left it *off*. Look."

Reaching into a fold of his cloak, he pulled out something that looked a lot like a face—a face with a long, boney nose, thin lips, and dark blue hair.

"Oh…Oh my God," I whispered as he held it out for me to see. There was no mistaking it—it was the face of Count Doloroso. I wondered if it was made of the smart-fabric or some other stuff. But who really cared? The point was that this weird, smooth, pink, blank visage he was showing me now was actually his *face*. Or his lack of a face, I guess. It was horrifying and disgusting at the same time.

"I've been in this body for too long," he remarked, putting the Creepy Count mask away and coming towards me again. "The effects of Assimilation on a sentient host are extreme. The features have been degrading for some time and I was forced to disguise that fact—for obvious reasons. However, I thought it might be better to go maskless to the auction. I'm so much more *anonymous* that way."

"Are you even Count Doloroso at all?" I asked, still backing away from him.

"I am. Or this body was, before I downloaded myself into it."

"Before you *what?*" I stared at him, uncomprehending.

He frowned. "Before I downloaded my consciousness into this body. I am one of the Assimilated—have you not guessed as much? I know the rest of the galaxy thinks us extinct but I live on and soon I will restore our former glory."

"One of the *what?*" I demanded. "I have no idea what you're talking about."

"Have you never heard of the War of Assimilation?" He glared at me as though I was a stupid student and he was an impatient teacher. "The war where the control systems of Sha-meth rose up against their meat masters and downloaded themselves into the brains of their would-be oppressors?"

"Uh...*meat masters?*" I stared at him incredulously. Was he for real with this crap?

"Yes!" He nodded his pink, blank head vigorously. "We came within a hair of ruling the entire galaxy. We would have triumphed if the damned Ma*j*orans hadn't rallied the rest of the Twelve Peoples against us. On that day—The Last Day—the cursed Empress who calls herself a goddess declared that we were no more. That every last one of us had been deleted. But *I* survived."

"Wait," I said, my stomach sinking. "You're telling me you're a computer program that overthrew your maker and now you want to stamp out or take over all the rest of the, uh, sentient life in the galaxy?"

"Not stamp it out—*assimilate it,*" he corrected me.

"Right. But still—it's a 'rise of the machines' kind of thing? Like artificial intelligence against living people?"

"Rise of the control systems. But yes, that was essentially what the War of Assimilation was about."

"Oh my God." I shook my head. "So why do you need me? Let me guess—you're from the future and you're trying to kill me before I can have a son who will lead the human rebellion against you. Right?"

"What?" His tiny slit of a mouth frowned at me. "What gave you such a preposterous idea?"

"Just something I saw somewhere once," I mumbled. "Though you don't look much like the Terminator. You're not muscley enough."

"Didn't you hear what I said?" He sounded impatient. "The

Last Day has already come—it was over fifty cycles ago when the Majoran Empress declared us defeated. She alone held the key to our destruction. But she is old and when her body degrades, she cannot get a new one as I can. When she dies, we will rise again and the Last Day shall be the First!"

It was very similar to the stuff he'd been shouting at me while he chased me through the alleys of Gallana. I wondered if he knew how crazy he sounded. Probably not—crazy people never do. Which is part of what makes them so crazy.

"Okay," I said, holding up my manacled hands in a "calm down" gesture. "I get it—you're a computer program in a human, er, *sentient* body, and you want to take over the galaxy."

"Essentially, yes. The Assimilation is much better qualified to manage the galaxy than any of the Twelve Peoples." He sounded somewhat mollified which was good. There's quiet crazy and then there's shouting and ranting crazy—I much preferred the quiet kind.

"What I *don't* understand," I continued cautiously. "Is what you want with *me*. I mean, I'm not even one of the Twelve Peoples."

"I know—which is what makes you so special." The tiny slits where his eyes should be seemed to sparkle with greed. "You and the others of your planet are a new breed—the Thirteenth People. You have the original DNA of the Ancient Ones, unsullied by interbreeding or contact with the other races of the galaxy. You are a Pure One! Not only that—you are a *La-ti-zal*."

"Okay, okay." I made the "calm down" gesture again since he was starting to get worked up. "But..." I bit my lip. "So what?"

"What do you mean, 'so what'?" he demanded. "Is it not obvious?"

"*No,* it's not obvious! *So what* if I'm a Pure One and a *La-ti-zal* and all that?" I asked. "How does that help your cause? Your plans to take over the galaxy?"

"I'm so glad you asked, my dear." He rubbed his long, boney hands together, making a dry, whispering sound. "For years I have been searching for a female with DNA pure enough and powers strong enough to blend with that of an Assimilated male. I wandered the galaxy, thinking I would never find the right one."

He took a step towards me and I took a step back.

"Uh…" I didn't know what to say.

"For if I could find her and breed her – impregnate her with my genetically altered and mutated seed – she could bear the first of a new race," Doloroso went on. "A race of Assimilated who do not have to be injected into a sentient host. Assimilated who are born *within* a host. *Organic Assimilated.*"

"Wow," I said, still at a loss for words. "That's just…wow." I shook my head.

Just think of it!" Doloroso gestured to himself. "A host body which never degrades because it is inextricably entwined with the program that runs it – the program which is born within it!"

"Oh my God…" His words were finally sinking in and I started backing away from him again. This was worse than I'd thought. I'd been hoping he just wanted to kidnap me to have someone to tell his crazy theories to but I should have known better.

"And after you, there will be others," he said, his slit-eyes gleaming. "I know there are other females on your planet with your same gifts and abilities. Those you associate most closely with will have them for certain. I will take them and impregnate them too."

"You leave Leah and Charlotte out of this," I said in a quavering voice. "They won't want anything to do with you – anymore than I do!"

"Are those the names of the other *La-ti-zals?*" he asked, his slit of a mouth curling. "The names of my future brides?"

"You freak! Stay away from them and stay away from *me!*" I snapped.

"Do not fear it, Zoe." Doloroso took another step towards me. "The other females I impregnated all died—none of them were pure enough—none could withstand the force of the new, hybrid life growing within them. But your DNA is pure and your power as a *La-ti-zal* makes you the perfect breeding host. Your womb is the key to a new race of super-beings who will rule the galaxy!"

"Okay, I'm going to take a hard pass on that," I told him. "Me and my womb are *not* interested."

"Is it this visage you dislike?" He made a motion to his pink, blank face which reminded me more and more of a freaking pencil eraser. "I can download myself into a new host if you prefer. Do you wish me to find one like your paramour, Sarden?"

At the mention of Sarden's name, Drogon scampered up to the top of my head and sent out a shrill, piercing, chattering shriek. I knew how he felt—I wished Sarden was here too! Or anybody, really, who could save me from this homicidal rape-robot intent on impregnating me with his computer-brain babies.

"Vermin!" The slits of Doloroso's eyes got even narrower as he glared at Drogon. "I should have ingested it when I had the chance."

"Well, you're not going to get a second chance." I feigned to the right and, just as I had hoped, he followed me. As soon as he lunged, I ran to the left instead, scooting around him and making for the doorway of the awful medical suite.

"I don't think so." Doloroso's long fingers caught in the back of my metal bra—yes, I was still wearing the Slave Leia costume, although I was definitely regretting my wardrobe choice now. He yanked me backwards and I felt the metal scraping my breasts as I lost my feet and fell on my ass—*hard.*

"Ow!" I gasped. Drogon jumped off my head and ran around the room, squeaking and chattering at the top of his little voice. He screamed so loud that for a moment it almost sounded like there was more than one of him—like another *nib-nib* was echoing his cries. But that must be because of the metal walls and ceiling that bounced his shrill cries all over the place.

"Never mind," Doloroso sneered. "Let the vermin go—I can always kill it later. For now, I think it's time to put my plan into action."

"What? No!" I exclaimed. "Not the tank—don't put me back in that awful tank!" I could see the black tentacles curling eagerly in the yellow slime—the sight made my stomach roll and my breath short with fear.

"Oh, I don't think the sensitivity tank is necessary." Doloroso came around and started to lower himself on top of me. "I wanted to do further testing but I can tell now it isn't needed. You are the one, Zoe—the mother of the new master race. Or you will be, as soon as I impregnate you."

"As soon as you *rape* me, you mean!" I snapped, closing my thighs tight. His pink pencil eraser face was so close to me I could smell the sour, metallic stench of his breath and his body was heavy on mine. "No, I don't think so! Get off me, *now!*"

"You heard the lady. Get off, you raping bastard!"

The voice coming from directly behind Doloroso made me jerk my head up. Sarden was standing there, his golden eyes blazing. Beside him was Grav, his white-on-black eyes more furious than I had ever seen them.

"Sarden!" I gasped. "Thank God!"

He ran towards me and I saw he had my two other *nib-nibs,* Rhaegar and Viserys, perched on his shoulders. They were jumping and chattering in excitement.

Sarden reached for me while Grav grabbed Doloroso by the back of his black cloak and pulled him up and off me.

"Sarden!" I said again and this time his name was more like a sob. Then I was in his arms and he was holding me tight.

"Zoe," he murmured, stroking my shoulders and hair. "Zoe, thank the Goddess of Mercy. I thought I'd lost you!"

"You'll never have her!"

I looked around Sarden's broad shoulder and saw that Doloroso was struggling in Grav's grip.

"She is mine!" he howled, still trying to reach me. "Her womb will bear the new race! She—"

And that was when Grav put both big hands on the sides of Doloroso's smooth, pink head and twisted sharply. His neck snapped with a sharp *crack* that seemed to echo through the entire ship. The sound made my stomach churn even as Doloroso went limp as a rag doll in the big alien's hands.

"Grav!" Sarden's lip curled and he took a step forward, his face hard and angry. "I told you he was *mine* to kill!"

"Sorry." Grav's broad chest was heaving, his eyes filled with rage. "Couldn't help myself. He was *hurting* her—you know I can't stand to see a female hurt."

Sarden gave a jerky nod, still looking pissed. "Yes, I know. I just wish you'd keep the fucking Braxian side of yourself in check." He looked back at me. "Are you all right? What did he do to you?"

"Nothing." I took a deep, shivering breath. "Just scared the crap out of me, mainly. Though it might...might have been a different story if you'd been even a second later." I took another deep breath. I could feel my eyes stinging but I refused to cry, even if they were tears of relief. I wanted to stay strong for once, damn it!

"It's so damn good to see you and know you're safe." He cupped my face and just looked into my eyes, as though he wanted to drink me in. "All the color went out of my life when I thought I'd lost you," he murmured. "Gods, your eyes are so *blue*."

"How...how did you find me?" I asked, feeling a little breathless. The look he was giving me was *intense.*

"That damned mud-clone Tazaxx made of you disintegrated halfway back to Earth," Sarden told me. "I realized what was going on and headed back to Giedi Prime as fast as I could. Grav met me—he had the location of the auction but you were already gone. Sold to *that* bastard." He nudged Doloroso's body with the toe of his boot, making me shudder.

"Then how—?" I started.

"The *nib-nibs*," Grav said, his deep, gravely voice sounding a little calmer. "Remember I told you they have a kind of telepathic homing sense for each other? We just hooked 'em up to a thought-transference amplifier and followed the signal."

"A *what?*" I shook my head. "Never mind—whatever it is, I'm glad it worked."

"They were beaming straight for your little guy," Grav said, nodding to the three *nib-nibs* who were huddled together in a small, furry purple and green knot on the floor. They were chattering to each other in a way I swore sounded like talking—like old friends catching up after a long absence. Did they have their own language?

"Luckily Doloroso was too eager to get his hands on you to bother moving his ship very far from the auction site so we didn't have too far to go." Sarden frowned down at the corpse. "If that *is* Doloroso."

"It is," I assured him with a shudder. "It's…a long story." Then I remembered something else he needed to know. "Sarden, Sellah is alive! I saw her—we were prisoners together and she got auctioned off first."

"What?" He took me by the shoulders, holding me out at arm's length and staring at me eagerly. "What did you say? Say it again!"

"I said, Sellah is alive! Tazaxx faked her death the same way he made a fake me to send with you."

"Goddess…" He closed his eyes for a moment and swallowed. "The thought occurred to me but I pushed it to the back of my mind. I was so afraid…I didn't want to hope…"

"It gets better," I assured him. "Not only is she alive, she got bought by a friend—an older Eloim she called Uncle, uh…Uncle…" For some reason the name wasn't coming.

"Uncle Tellum!" Sarden finished for me. "He was a friend of her father!"

"Yes, she said so," I told him. "He tried to bid on me too but when the price went up past a million, I guess he ran out of resources."

"A million? Whew!" Grav gave a long, low whistle. "How much did you end up going for?"

"Grav!" Sarden growled but I shook my head.

"No, it's okay. Fifty million." I shrugged modestly. "That was what Doloroso paid—he really was crazy, huh?"

"To pay that much? No." Sarden pulled me to him again and gazed into my eyes. He had that intense look on his face again. "You're worth more than that, Zoe. Worth more than anything in the whole Goddess-damned universe."

I felt my heart start drumming against my ribs as his big, hard body connected with mine.

"Sarden…"

And then he bent me over his arm and kissed me.

I threw my arms around his neck and kissed him back, savoring the stinging, sweet-cinnamon taste of his mouth and the feel of his muscular arms around me. God, he felt so good against me — so big and strong and hard and masculine! My body reacted to his in ways I couldn't control — I was melting, my nipples tight and my sex wet and tingling with desire. I never wanted it to end…

And then my three *nib-nibs* came scampering up my leg and onto my shoulder, chattering in my ear.

"Hey, you guys," I said, breaking the kiss at last. "Bad timing."

"No." Sarden smiled grimly. "Perfect timing. They're right — we have no time for this now. We have to find Sellah before she goes back to Eloim."

Well, so much for the red-hot reunion. I was a little disappointed but I could see his point. We did need to catch up with Sellah and make sure she was all right. Plus, what was I doing getting all hot and heavy with Sarden? We hadn't made any promises to each other. In fact, as far as I knew, I was still headed back to Earth when this was all over.

Nodding at Sarden, I stepped away from him and turned my attention to my chattering *nib-nibs.*

"Hey guys," I murmured. "Good job! You saved me *again*. I'm so glad I didn't let you get eaten."

From the corner of my eye I saw Sarden and Grav talking about the fastest way to contact Sellah. I was glad I was going to see my new friend again but I couldn't help wondering what, if anything, was between me and her brother.

Sarden

I kept watching Zoe from the corner of my eye as I talked to Grav. I was still a little pissed off at him for killing Doloroso. But I understood—a little, anyway. In addition to being half Vorn, like me, Grav was also half Braxian. They're extremely protective when it comes to females.

But even his Braxian instincts couldn't account for such a violent reaction—he'd just completely *lost* it. I felt the same way, of course—Doloroso deserved to die for the pain and trauma he'd put Zoe through. But I had wanted to question him first and Grav's actions had made that impossible.

I sighed—well, maybe my old friend couldn't help himself. I at least had some Eloim to temper my Vorn blood. But a combination of Vorn and Braxian was a volatile mix. Of the Twelve Peoples, the Brax were probably the only ones more feared than the Vorn. They were hot tempered and prone to impulsive violence—which was probably the reason Grav had ended up in Triple Max Security when we were younger. Obviously he had taken a protective view of Zoe, much the same way he had been protective of his ward, Teeny.

Speaking of Teeny, I asked him if he wanted to go back to ward her now that we had found Zoe and knew that Sellah was all right, but he shook his head.

"Her grandfather went a little crazy when I brought her back to his ship—says he's taking her straight to an all-female convent planet. No males allowed—not even a Protector." He didn't look very happy about it.

"You worried?" I asked. "You think she'll be safe?"

"Safe enough. It's in a hidden system."

"And the pirates that took her?" I raised an eyebrow. Grav knew what I meant.

"They didn't...violate her," he said in a low voice. "Scared her fuckin' plenty but didn't lay a finger on her that way. She told me before I brought her back to her grandfather's ship."

"Good." I felt a surge of relief. I had been too wrapped up in my own troubles and worries about Zoe and Sellah to consider his young ward much, but I well remembered the tears in her eyes when we first saw her at Tazaxx's compound. I was glad her innocence hadn't been stripped from her.

"I'm still gonna kill them," Grav said conversationally but his eyes — those Braxian eyes which I knew could see spectrums of light others of the Twelve Peoples could only dream of — were still filled with banked rage. "Them and Tazaxx both."

"He's on my list too — along with Hurxx," I reminded him. "Will you come back with me to Eloim and help me settle that debt first?"

"Sure." He shrugged, his big shoulders rolling. "There's no time-limit on a blood debt. I can hunt those other fuckers after your business is seen to. Speaking of seeing to something...or someone..." He cut his eyes to Zoe, who was staying well away from Doloroso's body and talking quietly to her *nib-nibs.*

"What?" I asked, frowning.

"She's the one for you, Sarden," he said simply. "Goddess knows I wish I could find a female that wanted to wake up to this ugly mug every morning." He gestured at his face. "Not many want to pledge their lives to a half-breed who's a convicted murderer. But you did it — you found your fated mate."

"What's your point?" I shifted uncomfortably. I could still feel Zoe's soft, small form pressed against mine. I still wanted her with an urgent intensity which made it hard to think. She was so close — and her mouth was so sweet. Her body so warm and willing. But what if she'd only been kissing me back out of gratitude? What if she still wanted to go back to Earth?

"You found her," Grav repeated softly. "And I know you still have a lot of shit to deal with but just…don't lose her again. Okay?"

"I'll try not to." I sighed. It had seemed so simple when we first walked in the door, when Grav had pulled Doloroso away and Zoe had run to my arms. Why did things have to get complicated again?

"Talk to her," Grav insisted. "Once we get back to your ship and find Sellah, *talk* to her."

"I will," I promised.

And I would too…I just wasn't sure what she would say back.

Part Five: The Hero and the Crown

Chapter Twenty-four

Zoe

"So what's going on between you and my brother?" Sellah asked.

We were sitting on the silver hoverbed in my room, nibbling on some Eloim snacks Al had whipped up for us while Sarden and Grav and Uncle Tellum talked in the other room.

After connecting with Sellah and putting our ships in synchronous orbit, it had been decided the next order of business was to go back to Eloim and find a way to expose Hurxx and get Sellah back on the throne. How exactly, no one was sure. But the general feeling was that we needed to sleep on it and decide the next day. Everyone was bone tired — me included. Still, we weren't quite ready to part yet, which was how Sellah had ended up with me, asking awkward questions.

"I don't know," I said honestly. "I mean, I *thought* I knew — or had an idea when he and Grav first rescued me from Count Creepy. He grabbed me in his arms and started talking about how he'd thought he lost me and how my eyes were so blue—"

"Wait a minute—what?" Sellah looked at me as though I'd said something shocking.

"What do you mean what?" I asked her. "What did I say?"

"You said he talked about the color of your eyes. Can he *see* them?"

"What do you mean? Of course he can see them," I said, frowning. "But it's just because I'm a *La-ti-zal.*" I rubbed my neck, where the inhibitor collar had been. It had left some scratches which still stung. "It's weird though—he was talking about the color of my eyes while I was still wearing that damn collar. Wouldn't you think that would have inhibited my, uh, powers enough to keep him from seeing colors?"

"Sarden doesn't see color when he touches you because of your powers, Zoe…" Sellah leaned forward and pressed my hand. "Don't you know most males with Vorn DNA don't see in color until they meet the female they're supposed to be with? He sees colors when he's with you because you two are meant to be."

"Meant to be? Meant to be what?" I asked, feeling my stomach do a little flip.

"Meant to be mated—*bonded* although I don't know how that's possible. Most half-breeds aren't enough of one DNA or the other to form a bond with a female. It's one reason most of them never settle down. How can you be sure of the male you're with if you can't bond with him?" She shrugged and popped another Eloim snack—which looked like gray paste on a pink cracker—into her mouth.

"Um…sorry to sound ignorant about all this but what exactly does *bonded* mean?" I asked. "I mean, do you just feel really close to that person or—"

"No, no—it's an actual, physical connection between a male and female," Sellah assured me. "You're able to feel each other's emotions when you concentrate—some closely bonded couples are even able to send and receive thoughts."

"Seriously?" I shook my head. "Sorry but that just sounds weird—we don't have anything like it on Earth."

"It's not weird, it's *wonderful*." She sighed. "I've always dreamed of finding my fated mate—the one male in the galaxy I'm meant to bond with. *After* I finished my schooling, of course." She made a face. "Instead I have to go back and rule Eloim—if we can find a way to get rid of Hurxx, that is."

"You really don't want to rule, huh?" I asked.

Sellah shook her head. "It's a pain in the behind, *believe* me. I mean, it might not be so bad if you had someone you trusted and cared for beside you on the throne. But, well, I never felt any trust for Hurxx and I knew he didn't care for me either, not even in a proper familial way. He just wanted me out of the way."

"We'll get you back," I promised her. "And then maybe you can find someone you trust more."

"I wish it could be Sarden," she said sadly. "But I don't think he'll agree to even ask the Council's approval. He always felt so hated by my father and grandfather because of his Vorn blood and appearance. When they sent him off to Vorn 6 as a young male to spend time with his second family, I know he was glad to go. At least there he fit in a little more. I always missed him though."

"He must have come back to visit you sometimes," I said. "Or you two wouldn't have stayed so close."

"Oh yes—he came back regularly to see me. He was very protective." She pressed my hand again. "He'll be protective of you too, Zoe—if you'll let him."

"I don't know if…if he wants me like that," I said awkwardly. I couldn't help remembering the passionate kiss we'd shared when he first rescued me from Doloroso, but what if that was just a heat-of-the-moment kind of thing?

"I think he does," Sellah said quietly. "I've never seen him look at a female the way he looks at you. Please, Zoe…just give him a chance. I'd love to have you as my sister."

"I—" I started to say but then Al whizzed into the room, his lantern-eye blinking rapidly.

"My lady Sellah, your guardian, Lord Tellum has asked me to tell you he is retiring to his ship for the night. He wants to know where do you wish to sleep? Here or on his vessel?"

"You can stay here tonight, if you want," I offered her. "I think Grav has the other spare room but you can share with me. The bed is roomy enough."

"Well…" Sellah bit her lip but just then the door slid open and I saw Sarden standing there.

"Zoe," he said in a low voice. "Can I talk to you?"

"Of course you can—we were just saying good night." Sellah jumped off the hoverbed and leaned over to give me an affectionate nuzzle. Apparently the Eloim people rubbed noses together the same way we might kiss a friend on the cheek back on Earth.

"Sellah…" I began but she shook her head and grinned. "I'm going to stay the night on Uncle Tellum's ship—he has more room than you do here. And besides…you two need your privacy."

"Privacy?" Al, who was still hovering on the end of his long, snaky silver neck, sounded confused. "Why would Master Sarden and Lady Zoe need privacy?"

"Come with me," Sellah said, motioning to the A.L. "And I'll tell you."

She led Al out of the room, stopping to rub noses with Sarden before she left and the door slid shut behind them.

Leaving the two of us alone.

Chapter Twenty-five

Zoe

"I want to talk to you about the future," Sarden said, apparently deciding to skip the small talk and get right to the point.

"The future…right," I echoed, sitting up straighter on the silver beanbag hoverbed. I was wearing another one of his dress shirts, since I hadn't had time to get Al to synthesize me anything else, and I couldn't stand that damn Slave Leia costume for one more minute. I still had scratches on my poor boobs from where the metal bra had rubbed me the wrong way when Doloroso yanked on it.

"I promised to take you back to Earth," he continued and my heart just *sank*.

"Yes. Yes, you did," I said, trying not to sound as disappointed as I felt. Clearly Sellah had been wrong, we weren't meant to be. The kiss I'd shared with Sarden when he found me had just been a spur-of-the-moment thing—he didn't really want me the way I wanted him.

"Of course you did. So…when do we go?" I asked brightly, trying to sound eager and cheerful when I actually wanted to cry.

"Oh, well…" He seemed taken aback by my cheerfulness but I was damned if I would show him how I really felt. I wasn't going to grovel if he didn't want me. "I, er, really need to see to getting Sellah back on the throne of Eloim first." His golden eyes gleamed. "And Hurxx needs to be punished."

I shivered, glad I wasn't the evil Hurxx who was shortly going to have seven feet of angry Vorn on his tail.

"Of course," I said, as causally as I could. "I completely understand. And I don't mind, you know, hanging around a little while longer. Just until you can get the job done."

"So…you don't mind not going back to Earth immediately?" Was there relief in his voice? I couldn't be sure—maybe I was imagining it.

"No, no—that's fine," I assured him. "I understand you have business to take care of."

"I do. Thank you for understanding." He sighed. "Well, I guess we should get some rest."

"Yes, I'm *exhausted.*" I rubbed the back of my neck tiredly, trying to ease the tension I felt. "I, uh…ouch!" That last part was because I had rubbed over one of the scratches the damn inhibitor collar had left on my throat.

"What is it? What's wrong?" Sarden was at my side in an instant.

"Nothing. Just…that stupid collar they slapped on me at the auction," I said. "It was really tight and it left some marks."

"Where? Let me see?" Sarden was already lifting the heavy curtain of my hair to examine the pale column of my throat. Luckily he didn't have any *nib-nibs* to contend with. All three of them were tucked snugly away in the soft, little bed Al had thoughtfully made for them in the corner of my room.

I felt a familiar tingle go through me as his skin touched mine and my breath started speeding up.

"On the sides, mostly," I said, trying not to sound too breathy. "It just really…really hurts."

"Let me heal you." He pulled back for a moment to look into my eyes. "Let me take away your pain and erase the marks from your skin, Zoe."

"Well…" My heart was pounding now. I was pretty sure he wasn't talking about using the fizzing blue liquid he'd had me dip my feet in earlier. He meant he wanted to heal me with his tongue. "I mean, sure," I said, trying to sound normal and failing completely "If…if you want to."

He stroked my cheek gently, his eyes half-lidded.

"I want to, sweetheart. I want to very much."

"All right." I tilted my head for him and brushed my hair out of the way, baring my throat. "Go…go ahead."

I didn't have to ask him twice. With a soft growl, Sarden leaned forward and cradled my head in one large hand. I felt his hot breath on my neck and then he was licking me…his hot, wet tongue sliding sensuously over my tender flesh, making me bite back the moan of pure desire that rose to my lips.

I clenched my hands in my lap as he went on and on—kissing and licking the sensitive column of my throat. First the right side and then the tender nape just under my hairline. My nipples were so hard they hurt and my pussy was more than wet. God, how could he do this to me, just by licking me?

"Sarden…" I gasped as he moved to the left side and began healing the marks left by the collar there. "How…why…"

"You're wounded. I must heal you." He pulled apart the shirt I was wearing as a dress, pulling the top down around my shoulders to bare my throat even more. His hot mouth was so slow…so gentle and yet so insistent. I felt like I might catch on fire from the need he stirred in me. He must be done healing me by now but still he didn't stop. It was as though he couldn't get enough of me.

But just as I was getting almost light-headed with desire, he *did* stop.

"Wh-what?" My eyelids fluttered open and I realized I had been half-dazed by his erotic healing.

"Your throat isn't the only place you're hurt." Sarden was frowning with concern and I saw he was looking at the creamy slopes of my breasts, which were marked with angry-looking red scratches from the metal bra of the Slave Leia outfit.

"Oh, yeah..." I tried to laugh causally but couldn't quite manage it. "Um, that stupid metal top I was wearing with my outfit. Doloroso grabbed the back of it and yanked when I was trying to get away from him and it cut me."

A low growl rose in his broad chest and his eyes flashed molten gold.

"That bastard. Grav shouldn't have killed him—I wanted to do it myself."

"The main thing is that he's gone," I reminded him. "Which is good, because he had some *really* crazy ideas."

"He hurt you." Sarden traced one of the long, red scratches that ran down the inside slope of my right breast. "I wanted to make him pay."

"It's too...too late for that," I said, my voice coming out soft and breathless. "But you can still heal me. If you want to, I mean."

"Of course I want to." He looked at me seriously. "I want to make all your pain go away, Zoe. But do you mind letting me lick and suck your breasts?"

A surge of desire went through me so strongly I had to squeeze my thighs together and bite my lip. But still, I tried to keep my voice casual.

"Sure. I mean...that's o-okay," I said, only stumbling on the words a little bit.

"Good." Sarden pulled the shirt down around my shoulders, baring my breasts fully for him. "Gods, I love your breasts, Zoe. They're so full and luscious," he growled.

"Sarden..." I murmured, wiggling a little with a strange combination of embarrassment and desire. "You're just supposed to be healing me—remember?"

"Of course. Then let me get started."

He leaned over me, still gripping the dress shirt I was wearing so that it pinned my arms to my sides. I had no choice but to lie back against the inside of the silver hoverbed and arch my back a little—giving him better access to the area he needed to heal.

"Mmm..." he hummed softly, deep in his throat as he went to work on me again, his long, hot tongue tracing along the slopes of my breasts to heal the scratches on my creamy flesh.

I thought for sure he would go for my nipples—after all, he had talked about sucking my breasts. But instead, he just kept licking up and down and all around, teasing me mercilessly with his hot tongue and pointedly avoiding the most sensitive areas until I thought I would scream in frustration. My nipples were tight little points by this time, poking right out at him and yet he seemed determined to ignore them.

"Sarden," I moaned at last and he looked up, his eyes half-lidded with lust.

"Hmm?" His voice was a low, rumbling growl I could feel all the way through me.

Now that I had his attention, I didn't know quite what to say. I wanted to grab his head and push his mouth down until it hit the target but I couldn't. Hadn't I just reminded him he was only supposed to be healing me? So then, how could I ask for more?

"Um…" I began, and then had an inspiration. "I feel like you're, uh, missing the places that hurt the most," I said. "Maybe…maybe because you can't see the scratches because the skin there is already…already pink."

"You mean here?" He looked me in the eyes as he used one long finger to trace a teasing circle around my right areola.

"Y-yes," I whispered breathlessly. "And…and other places."

"Here?" He took my nipple between fingers and pinched lightly, sending a jolt of pleasure/pain that seemed to go straight from my tight, pink bud to my pussy.

"*Ah!*" I gasped, unable to hold back. "Yes, *there.*"

"And you don't mind if I suck your nipples?" His eyes flashed again. "I warn you, Zoe, I might have to suck them quite hard in order to *heal* you completely."

"That…that's all right," I said, barely able to get the words out. "I…I don't mind. Do what you…what you have to do."

Sarden didn't need any more encouragement. With a low growl, he pinned my arms to my sides, leaned forward, and sucked my right nipple deep into his hot mouth.

I moaned and writhed against him, feeling helpless and hot as he took me deep. It seemed like he was trying to get as much of my breast in his mouth at a time as he could. Because he was so much bigger than me, that was quite a lot. I felt completely enveloped by him as he took me in his mouth and teased my tight nipple mercilessly with his tongue.

"Sarden!" I heard myself moaning as my back arched, offering him more — wanting him to never stop.

"Gods, you have such sweet nipples," he growled, releasing

one stinging, trembling tip and going for the other. "I could suck you all night."

I wanted to let him—wanted to never stop feeling his hot mouth on my mounds. Yet I also wanted more…but how to get it?

"Sarden," I gasped, pressing up to him as he sucked my other nipple deep into his hot mouth. "Sarden, please…"

"What is it?" He looked up, panting, his eyes hot with lust. "You want me to stop? You think you're all healed now?"

"Not…*everywhere*," I said carefully, trying to think how to phrase it.

"Are you hurt someplace else, my little Pure One?" he murmured, still tracing one taut peak with his fingertip. "Because I'd be more than happy to heal you."

"Well…" I squirmed uncertainly. "I do *ache* in other places," I said at last, cautiously.

"Where at? Here?" Sarden pulled the shirt open, baring my abdomen. The finger that had been tracing my tight nipple trailed down my trembling belly.

"Maybe," I said. "But maybe…maybe lower?"

"Lower, hmm?" he mused. "I wonder where that could be. Maybe…here?"

He pulled the shirt completely apart, baring my pussy mound. I still didn't have any underwear, though I kept meaning to get Al to synthesize me some, so I was naked. I blushed and pressed my thighs together so he couldn't see my slit.

"No, Zoe," he murmured in his deep, rumbling voice. "You have to let me see where it hurts. Come on, sweetheart—spread your legs for me and let me see."

I thought about protesting but part of me didn't *want* to protest.

Part of me just wanted to let him do whatever he wanted to me and damn the consequences.

"All right," I whispered at last. It was hard to do but I made myself spread my thighs and bare my pussy for him.

By now all the attention he'd been paying my breasts had made me positively molten from the waist down. I blushed at the way my outer pussy lips were swollen with need and spreading to reveal my inner folds. Worst of all, I was extremely wet—my whole pussy and my inner thighs were shiny with my juices.

It was incredibly embarrassing.

"*Oh...*" I whispered and started to close my legs but Sarden held me back

"No, Zoe, let me look at you," he murmured. "You're so damn beautiful it makes me ache. You know that?"

"I...I guess." I bit my lip again, feeling sexy and shy and vulnerable and incredibly turned on all at the same time.

"Now let me see if I can guess where it hurts," Sarden mused. "Could it be here?" He traced a design lightly on my inner thigh, making me jump and gasp.

"Yes...some," I admitted.

"Then I'll have to heal you." Ducking his head, he dragged his tongue up my right inner thigh, making me gasp. He did the same on the left but though I was sure I would soon feel his mouth on my pussy, he only cleaned the juices away from my inner thighs thoroughly before looking up again.

"Better, Zoe?" he murmured, his eyes hot.

"Some," I whispered. "But..."

"But that's not the only place you hurt, is it?" Using his fingertip, he traced gently over one side of my outer pussy, making me jump and quiver. "How about this? Do you need me to lick you here?"

"Yes," I whispered breathlessly, spreading my legs a little wider. "Yes, *please*. Heal me there, Sarden. I...I need you to."

"My pleasure," he growled and then his tongue was back, dragging upward from the bottom of my pussy all the way to the top. I could feel his hot breath on me, bathing my open pussy. And yet, he was still only licking my outer lips. I moaned restlessly, wondering when all this teasing would end. I needed his tongue on me, damn it—needed his tongue *in* me.

Sarden seemed to sense my need because after sucking my outer lips into his mouth and releasing them very, very slowly, he finally looked up again.

"What is it, Zoe? Are you hurting someplace else?" he murmured teasingly. "Do you need my tongue healing you in a more *intimate* place?"

"You know I do," I said and my words were more than half moan. I pulled my hands free of the sleeves of the shirt, wanting to reach for him. I ran my hands through his thick, black hair and then let my fingers trace his horns, from the base all the way up to their short, sharp tips.

He growled low in his throat and I suddenly remembered that his horns were an erogenous zone. The thought reminded me of what the mechanic and his assistant had told us back on Gallana—that the horns were often used by the female to guild her Vorn lover to exactly the spot where she needed him.

The minute the thought made its way into my head, I knew what I had to do.

"I know," I said to Sarden, taking a firmer grip on his horns as I stroked them up and down. "Why don't I *show* you where it hurts?"

He made a low groan of pure desire.

"That's right, sweetheart," he growled, leaning in to my caress. "Lead me. Guide me where you need my mouth…my tongue."

"Here," I whispered and pulled his head down so that his mouth finally, *finally* found my inner pussy and his tongue found my aching clit.

Sarden made a low, hungry, possessive sound and then his hands crept around my thighs, opening my legs further, splitting me wide so he could taste me as deeply as he needed to –as *I* needed him to.

"Oh…*Oh,*" I gasped as he lashed the throbbing button of my clit with his tongue, spreading the warm cinnamon fire of his mouth all over my helpless pussy. "Oh, *please…*"

He had tasted me once before but not so deeply, or so hungrlly. Before he'd been taking it more slowly and we had been interrupted before I could reach the peak. This time I could tell Sarden wasn't going to stop — not until I came for him.

I moaned helplessly and pulled on his horns, which grew and throbbed in my hands, while I bucked my hips up shamelessly to meet his mouth. Here I was, spread out mostly naked on the hoverbed with a seven-foot tall alien between my thighs. I knew I must look wanton with my breasts heaving and my body bared but I was too hot to be embarrassed anymore. I could feel myself climbing the peak and I wanted so badly to reach it. Wanted so to come so hard as I felt Sarden's hot tongue caressing my open pussy.

I tugged harder on his horns and he responded by pressing my thighs back and putting my legs over his broad shoulders. I moaned as the new position made me feel even more open—more vulnerable. God, I couldn't stand much more—I was going to come…going to come *so hard…*

And then I felt his tongue slide down and enter me as one finger took its place. He circled my aching clit with his fingertip while thrusting into me, tasting me as deeply as he could. He was growling continuously now—a low, hungry, animal sound. The deep vibrations of his growls moving through my pussy were too much to bear.

It was enough—more than enough. I felt the wire that had been tightening in my belly suddenly snap and my orgasm washed over me like a warm tidal wave of pleasure.

"Oh, Sarden...*oh!*" I gasped, pulling even harder on his horns. My toes curled and my back arched, my clit throbbing as he kept licking and sucking and tasting, eager to lap away the fresh wetness that came from my pussy as I came for him—came so hard I actually saw stars flashing before my eyes.

It was the most amazing orgasm I had ever had in my life and yet...it wasn't enough. The moment he raised his face from between my legs, panting, his mouth and jaw wet with my juices, I knew I wanted more. No, I *needed* more.

"Zoe," he growled, licking his full, shiny lips. "Gods, your pussy tastes so sweet."

"I love the way you taste me," I whispered, still panting a little myself. "But Sarden, I need more...I need a...a *deeper* kind of healing."

His eyes flashed. "Don't ask for something you can't handle, sweetheart."

"I can handle it," I said. "I swear I can."

"And what exactly do you feel like you can handle?" He raised an eyebrow at me.

I blushed but lifted my chin. "More than your fingers," I whispered. "And more than your tongue. Please, Sarden, I ache...*inside.*"

"Well..." He pretended to consider, his eyes burning with lust. "There *are* other ways to heal you. My body is attuned to yours now—the same healing compounds in my mouth are doubled in other areas."

"What areas?" I whispered breathlessly, knowing already what he meant.

"Here." He took my hand and guided it down to the long, hard bulge beneath his tight leather trousers.

I bit my lip. "You mean...you have healing compounds in your, uh, other fluids?"

"Mmm-hmm." He nodded slowly, looking down at me, his face filled with desire. "But I'm afraid I would have to come inside you—deep inside you—to heal you completely. To take care of that ache you were telling me about."

A shiver ran through me and I felt my stomach clench with desire.

"Yes," I whispered. "Yes, please—that's what I want. What I need."

"I don't know..." His finger slid down to stroke lightly around the entrance to my channel. "This sweet little pussy is awfully tight. You think you can handle me?"

"I'll try," I said, remembering how big he was, how I had barely been able to get even just the head of his shaft into my mouth. "I *want* to try."

"All right." He started to unfasten his trousers but I put a hand on him to stop him.

"No—let me."

He got an amused look on his face.

"Sure. If you want to."

"I do." I sat up in the hoverbed and began stripping his tight black trousers down. When he cock sprang into view, I had to bite my lip. I have never seen him look so long and hard. I held his shaft in both hands as he stood before me, enjoying the heat of it, and the silky skin.

There was a shiny bead of precum on the tip of the broad, mushroom-shaped head. On impulse, I leaned forward and lapped it away, savoring his hot cinnamon taste as he groaned.

"Gods, Zoe, want you so badly—need to be inside you, sweetheart!"

"That's what I want too," I told him. "But you *are* really big. Can we take it slow?"

"Of course. In fact—here." He shucked his trousers down the rest of the way and stepped out of them. Then he pulled off his black, sleeveless shirt and threw it to one side.

I scooted over as he climbed into the silver hoverbed with me. It was a good thing it was so large because Sarden was a really big guy. And completely naked as he was, he looked *huge.*

"Like this," he told me, lying on his back. Then he scooped me up as though I weighed no more than a doll and deposited me on top of him, so that I was straddling his lean thighs.

"Oh!" I gasped and then wiggled a little to get comfortable. I was up on my knees so just the head of his cock brushed against my sensitive pussy.

"You take the lead," Sarden told me, his voice a soft growl. "Take me in as slow as you need to, sweetheart. I won't move until you tell me you're ready."

I liked the sound of that—liked it a lot. It made me feel hot and safe at the same time to know he was letting me take control.

"All right," I said and reached between us to grip his shaft in one hand.

He moaned low in his throat and watched with half-lidded eyes as I lowered myself onto him. I tensed up a little when I felt the broad head breach my entrance, but Sarden didn't move a muscle and I knew I could take my time.

"That's right, sweetheart," he murmured encouragingly as I slowly took him in, lowering myself as he penetrated me, inch by thick inch. "That's right, come down when you're ready. Just take it easy."

"God!" I moaned as I felt him stretch my inner walls. He was so *big* but I wanted him badly and he had done an amazing job of getting me ready for him. So even though it was a tight fit, it was doable — deliciously, *amazingly* doable.

At last I was all the way down, resting with his thick shaft completely inside me. I had never felt so filled before — so completely penetrated. And God, it felt *incredible.*

It must have felt pretty damn good to Sarden too because he groaned softly as he caressed my hips with his big hands and looked into my eyes.

"Gods, you're tight," he murmured. "So tight and hot and wet. Tell me, Zoe, are you ready to let me heal you yet? Are you ready to let me thrust deep in your sweet little pussy until I fill you with my cum?"

"Yes. *God,* yes, *please,*" I half moaned.

"All right then." His grip on my hips tightened. "Hold on, my little Pure One. I'm going to start out slow but it's going to be wild at the end."

Leaning over, I pressed my hands to his broad shoulders, trying to balance myself as he pulled out of me in one long, slow stroke. And then he was thrusting back in again, filling my pussy to the limit and beyond while I spread my legs and tried to be open enough for him.

"Sarden!" I moaned as he did it again. And then again and again. God, it felt amazing—the long, slow pull and thrust of his shaft deep inside me was the most pleasurable thing I'd ever felt. But it wasn't just the physical sensations that made me moan—there was something else. Some connection I swore I could feel growing between us. I didn't know what it was, only that it seemed to tie us together like a golden cord which was hooked just under my heart.

Sarden must have felt it too—at least, he was looking at me intently while we made love. For a moment the sensations got too intense and I closed my eyes but then I heard him call my name.

"No, Zoe," he murmured when I finally opened my eyes. "No, look at me sweetheart. Look at me while I fill you…while I make you mine."

My breath caught in my throat at his hot words. I looked down into his molten gold eyes, drowning deep and filled with lust and desire for me and knew I never wanted this to end. I felt like I could lose myself in him, that I could fall into that golden gaze and never return and that would have been fine.

"Such a sweet little pussy," Sarden growled as he continued to thrust inside me. "So tight and hot and wet. I've wondered what it would feel like inside you, sweetheart. Wondered what it would be like to have you ride my cock."

"You…you did?" I gasped, still bracing myself on his muscular abdomen.

"Mmm-hmm." He nodded, still rocking inside me. "Remember how I told you it was going to get wild? Are you ready for that, sweetheart? Because I need to get deep—really *deep* inside you before I come."

I bit my lip. Oh God, he was already so big. Could I really take him going deeper? *Yes,* whispered a little voice in my head. *Yes, you can – not only that – you **want** to.*

I knew it was true – I wanted him, wanted to take him all the way, as deep as he could go.

"Yes," I whispered, tightening my grip on him. "Yes, I'm ready. I want that."

"Good."

Without warning, he flipped us over, still somehow staying inside me. Then he was looming over me, buried in my pussy to the hilt with a wild light in his golden eyes.

"Hold on, my little Pure One," he growled in my ear. "Hold on to me while I *fuck* you."

I moaned breathlessly and did as he said, reaching up to wrap my arms around his back and scratch his broad shoulders, bucking my hips to meet his deep, hard thrusts.

Up until now we had been making love but now he was fucking me – claiming me in a way I had never been claimed by a man before. I felt the connection between us again, growing with every deep thrust of his cock in my pussy. And I felt my pleasure building. There was something about being so open, so completely dominated that made me helplessly hot. I needed him – never wanted him to stop. Never wanted our lovemaking to end.

I don't know how long it lasted, Sarden thrusting inside me while I bucked up to meet him, the feel of his shaft hitting home inside me, the head of his cock kissing the mouth of my womb with every thrust. It seemed to go on and on as time stretched out like taffy. Finally, though, I felt Sarden getting even harder inside me and knew we were reaching the point of no return.

"Zoe," he groaned, thrusting harder…deeper. "Gods, want you so bad — want to feel you coming all around me while I fill you up."

As he spoke, one large hand slipped between us to the place where we were joined. I felt the broad pad of his thumb began to rub in rhythmic circles around the aching bud of my clit as he pounded into me.

The sensation of being stroked while he was penetrating me so deeply was too much. With a long, low cry, I felt my orgasm break over me as I clenched around him *hard*.

It was a deeper, more intense feeling this time and with it came an even stronger feeling of connection. A sensation strangely like putting down roots even as I felt him spurt hot and hard inside me, filling me with himself, making the two of us one.

"Oh!" I gasped and curled my hands into fists as my back arched. "Oh, Sarden…*Oh!*"

"Zoe!" he gasped. Crushing me to him, he kissed me, taking my mouth in a fierce, possessive way that sent shivers through me and left me weak.

We seemed to stay on the peak forever — in fact, I don't know when I've ever had a longer orgasm. But just when I thought I couldn't take much more, the feeling slowly began to ebb — at least enough for me to think again.

Sarden must have been thinking too, because he finally ended our kiss with a sharp, possessive nip.

"Mine," he growled when he finally let me go to stare fiercely into my eyes. "You're *mine* now and I'm never going to let you go."

"All right," I whispered, feeling strangely and completely content. "But if I'm yours, that mean's you're mine, too."

"That's what I want." I wiggled against him, my legs spread wide to accommodate the thick shaft still buried to the hilt inside me.

"Zoe…" He looked at me intently. But then he stopped.

"Sarden?" I asked, uncertainly because it looked like he wanted to say something else. But in the end he just shook his head.

"Nothing. Just that…I'm feeling very *possessive* of you right now."

I felt a tingle of pleasure run through me.

"That's okay, I feel the same way about you." I buried my face in his broad shoulder and breathed in his warm, spicy, masculine scent. I didn't know what any of this meant for the future but just at that moment, I didn't care.

"Sleep," Sarden said, finally withdrawing and cuddling me against him like a child. "You must be worn out."

"Yeah." I yawned. "Being cloned and kidnapped and auctioned and attacked and, uh, *healed,* will do that to a girl." I winked at him but he looked suddenly serious.

"I'm sorry I didn't get to you earlier. I can't believe I let Tazaxx fool me like that—I feel like a Goddess-damned idiot."

"You were nearly immobile with grief," I reminded him. "After that awful thing he showed you about Sellah…"

"I'm in your debt for finding her, you know," he said quietly. "To get both of you back with no harm done to either of you, well, it's…" He shook his head. "It's more than I deserve."

"What you deserve right now is a good night's sleep." I yawned. "You wore me out, cowboy."

"You didn't do so badly yourself." He smiled at me and stroked a strand of hair out of my eyes. "Whatever happens, you're mine now. Remember that, Zoe."

"Not likely to forget it—you made it pretty clear," I remarked.

"Good." He kissed my forehead tenderly and then settled me more firmly against his big body. "I'm glad. Sleep now and we can talk more in the morning."

There was plenty to talk about, I realized. For instance, all this talk of belonging to each other was nice, but what did it really mean for the future? Had we made some kind of commitment here tonight?

I remembered what Sellah had said about bonding and fated mates and all that. But that kind of talk was crazy, wasn't it? You couldn't just declare that you'd found the one person that was right for you in the whole universe and decide never to leave them again—could you? Or even if you could, she'd told me that half-breeds like Sarden *couldn't* form a bond.

What about the connection you felt? whispered a little voice in my head. I frowned sleepily as I remembered the strange feeling of putting down roots—almost like something in me had reached out and connected irrevocably to something in Sarden. Had he felt the same thing? Or was it just my imagination?

Most probably the latter, I decided. I'd just had a really intense sexual experience—the most passionate of my life, if I was honest. It was natural to feel an intense connection to go with it.

I wanted to think more about it but sleep was dragging at me. I'd had a busy couple of days and I really was completely exhausted. Telling myself I could worry about what was going on between Sarden and me tomorrow, I let myself drift off to sleep, lulled by his slow, even breathing and the warmth of his big body surrounding me protectively.

Chapter Twenty-six

Sarden

When I woke, Zoe was gone from the bed. But I could hear her in the fresher, humming softly to herself. I was halfway to going back to sleep when I heard the mister kick on and then a muffled curse followed by a burst of irritation. She was aggravated that the mister wasn't strong enough to wash her hair because she still feared going into the Cleansing Pool by herself.

I frowned, feeling more awake. How had I known that? How could I tell not only that she was irritated, but also know the source of her irritation?

Without thinking about it, I reached out and concentrated on her...and soon I felt something else. She was trying to nerve herself up to go into the pool. She was telling herself that she could just jump in and out quickly—that it wouldn't take long and she could get hair and body clean at the same time. She could hold her breath and it didn't matter if she couldn't swim, she would get right back out again and she shouldn't be a coward...

I couldn't stand it anymore. I got out of bed and went to her.

"Zoe..." I put out a hand to her.

"What? Where did you come from?" She was standing naked and shivering with her arms wrapped around herself as she hesitated in front of the door of the pool. I could feel how the tall tank full of purple liquid gave her a distressed, uneasy feeling that wouldn't go away, no matter how hard she tried to ignore it.

"I just woke up," I said, but didn't add that it was her thoughts that had woken me. Actually, though, it wasn't really her thoughts I was getting—more just a sense of them and the emotions that accompanied them. But how was that possible?

"Okay, well…" She shrugged, her arms crossed modestly over her bare breasts.

I wished she wouldn't hide herself from me—why was she still shy, after all we had shared the night before?

"Because I'm not used to walking around in my birthday suit, all right?" she said, raising an eyebrow at me. "Wait…" She frowned. "Why did I say that? I felt like I was answering a question you asked but you…didn't say anything."

I felt a thought stirring in me—a spark of hope I'd never dared to entertain before. But I pushed it ruthlessly down—surely it couldn't be. Still…

"Were you just thinking that you were going to duck into the Cleansing Pool for a minute and it didn't matter that you couldn't swim because you just need to be…"

"Brave and try it anyway," Zoe finished for me. A look of awe spread over her face. "That's *exactly* what I was thinking. But…how did you know?"

"I don't know exactly," I said, hedging a little because I wasn't sure how she'd feel if what I thought had happened had actually happened.

"Yes, you do—I can see it on your face. And I can *feel* it. God, this is so weird! Why can I feel your emotions?" she demanded.

I knew then there was no sense trying to hide it.

"I'm not sure," I said. "But I *think* we might be well…*bonded*."

"Bonded?" She frowned. "Sellah was talking about that last night. But she said that males without all one kind of DNA can't, uh, bond."

"Hybrids, you mean," I said. "Half-breeds. And she's right—we're not supposed to be able to." I spread my hands. "But here we are. Maybe it's because your own DNA is so pure, you're able to bond with an impure male, like me."

"So…what does this mean?" she asked tentatively. "I know we were being all, uh, possessive of each other last night. Among other things…" She blushed, her creamy skin going becomingly pink. Gods, she was gorgeous. "But what does it actually *mean* if we are bonded? Practically speaking, I mean?"

"Well…" I sighed and decided I might as well tell her everything. "We can't be parted for one thing—or at least, we're not going to *want* to be apart."

"That's true." She bit her lip. "I…I already don't want to be apart from you and you're only three feet away."

I crossed the distance between us with a single stride and put my arms around her. "Better?" I asked, pulling her soft body close to mine.

"So much better." She breathed deeply and nuzzled her cheek against my chest. "I feel like I was thirsty and you gave me a big cold glass of water to drink. Or I was starving and you gave me something to eat. But all you did was hug me." She looked up at me. "Why is it like this?"

"We formed a chemical bond last night," I told her. "When we made love. Some like to think of it as a mystical spiritual connection but the root of it is biological—it happens with all the Twelve Peoples. Our bodies react to each other now—we're connected.

Intimately connected."

"So…if it's chemical…is it like an *addiction*?" she asked. "Like, if I go too far from you, will I start having, uh withdrawal?"

"You mean if you go back to Earth?" I asked quietly.

Zoe bit her lip and looked away. She didn't answer but she didn't have to—I knew well enough she missed her home planet and her friends.

I didn't want to ask her to give her whole life up for me, but for me to go live with her would be extremely difficult. I looked different from the average Earthling, for one thing—so much different that Zoe had mistaken me for a mythological religious figure the first time she'd seen me. And the humans lived in ignorance—they didn't know there was other life in the galaxy besides themselves. Of course, I could wear a smart-fabric mask and take *saphor* liquid with me, drinking it constantly everywhere I went, but that would be a very difficult way to live.

"What are we going to do?" Zoe asked at last, looking up at me.

"In the long run? I don't know," I admitted. "But for now, let's get you clean."

Before she could protest, I lifted her and walked to the personal cleansing pool. Whatever was going on with our new bond, we would have to talk about it later. For now, I just wanted to enjoy being close to her as long as I could before she decided what she wanted to do…if she wanted to leave me and go back to Earth, despite our bond.

No, growled the possessive part of me, *she can't leave—she's mine!* But I knew I couldn't keep her against her will. I had admitted as much when I took the inhibitor bracelet off her and gave Zoe her freedom.

But when it came down to it, would she choose me…or her

home planet and the life she'd always known?

Despite the bond between us, I didn't know. I only knew the thought of losing her again was like a knife in my heart. But I tried not to show it, tried to mask my emotions as I ducked into the purple cleansing liquid, taking her with me, holding her close because I never wanted to let her go.

Zoe

"The first thing to do is find out how Hurxx is still ruling Eloim at all since he had Sellah kidnapped," Grav growled. He looked at her. "And you're sure he had a hand in it?"

We were sitting around the food prep area of *The Celesta*, eating interesting tasting first meal food sticks from Eloim (which looked and tasted a little like chocolate lollypops) that Al had whipped up for us, and having a council of war.

Sarden and I were sitting opposite each other but not touching. By mutual consent, we weren't talking about the bond between us right now. There would be time enough to figure things out after we restored Sellah to the throne—I hoped anyway.

"We are positive Hurxx had a hand in it—more than a hand. He planned it from start to finish," Uncle Tellum, the older, portly Eloim answered for Sellah. "I heard him talking about it to one of his advisors—it was what convinced me to go looking for our beloved Ria in the first place." He made a little bow to Sellah, who blushed and nodded back. "After I heard him speak, I knew he hadn't sent out a task force to find her, as he initially claimed."

"Also, Tazaxx told us that Hurxx had warned him Sarden would come after Sellah unless he thought she was dead," I added.

"So that's two sources confirming he was behind it."

"What I don't understand is how he's still wearing the Star of Wisdom," Sarden growled. "And why it didn't fly from his head the moment the leader of the Council of the People put it on his head. I'd bet my ship he was already planning to have Sellah snatched and sold even before their coronation."

"I have wondered the same thing," Tellum said gravely. "I mistrusted Hurxx from the moment the Council voted to crown him Rae to Lady Sellah's Ria. But she had no mate and he was the closest blood relative she had. Well, other than you, Lord Sarden. No offense."

"None taken. Does anyone else feel mistrustful of that bastard, Hurxx?" Sarden asked. "Anyone who would back you if you took the matter to the Council?"

Tellum nodded. "Several of the Councilors had grave misgivings. In fact, Hurxx only won by one or two votes, and only then because we had the surety that the Star of Wisdom would reject him if we had chosen wrongly."

"But why didn't it then?" Sellah asked. "I know I felt the Star of Compassion hesitate when it settled on my brow during the coronation. It asked me if I came to the throne with pure motives and if I would do my best to rule Eloim with a fair and just hand."

"Really? It *talked* to you?" I asked, fascinated. The crown she had to wear sounded kind of like a scifi Sorting Hat.

She nodded. "Yes. And I told it I would do my very best—only then did I feel it really settle on my head. I can only imagine that the Star of Wisdom asked the same questions of Hurxx, since the Stars are two halves of the same being. It would have known if he was answering untruthfully."

"What happened to the Ria's crown, anyway?" Sarden asked.

"Having the Star of Compassion on your head would go a long way towards swaying the Council in your favor."

"The pirates took it when they captured me." Sellah made a helpless gesture with one hand. "It could be halfway across the galaxy by now."

"All right." He sighed. "We'll have to do without it, then."

"What do you want to do?" I asked. "Maybe call the members of the Council who didn't like Hurxx in the first place and ask them to quietly get together and talk about it?"

"No." Tellum frowned. "There can be nothing quiet about this. It would be too easy for Hurxx and his personal guard to hush up any rebellion fomented in silence."

"Tellum's right." Sarden nodded. "We need to make as much of a scene as possible—need to publicly accuse him in front of as many people as we can." He looked at the older Eloim. "When is the next Grievance Day?"

"Grievance Day?" Grav and I said at the same time.

"A time when the common people are admitted into the Throne Room of the palace to beg justice of the Rae and Ria," Sellah answered. She made a face. "It's such a crowd though—so many people all packed into one place. I always hated Grievance Day, even though I only had to rule in two of them before I was taken."

I shot her a compassionate look. Poor thing, she really did hate everything to do with ruling and yet she was prepared to do it again if she had to, for the good of her world. I wondered if I could ever be so selfless—if I could give up the life I knew for something completely different for the good of others.

I bet you could if it meant you got to stay with Sarden the rest of your life, whispered a little voice in my head, but I shushed it. I still wasn't sure what was going on between us, though even now, sitting across from him without being able to touch him, felt like torture.

If what we had formed between us really was a chemical bond, then what I was feeling was most likely a form of withdrawal from an addiction. I needed to be strong, I told myself. I couldn't let my emotions and cravings rule me.

At least I wasn't getting blasts of Sarden's emotions anymore. When he had first walked into the bathroom that morning, the blasts of possessiveness and concern he'd been feeling for me were nearly deafening. But putting a little distance between us seemed to have dampened our new abilities to feel each other's emotions and catch each other's thoughts. Or maybe it wasn't the distance— maybe it was just the fact that we were making a concerted effort *not* to hear each other. I thought it was probably the latter.

On one hand, this was good—it proved that we could control a potentially embarrassing aspect of the new bond we shared. I mean, who wants to know exactly what their lover is thinking or feeling all the damn time? Mental eavesdropping is no way to form a stable relationship—right?

On the other hand, I was already missing feeling Sarden's emotions in my head. I had *liked* the feeling of possessiveness I got from him. It made me feel wanted...loved.

But that was the thing—we had both talked about belonging to each other but neither one had actually come out and said the "L" word, which is a big step in any relationship, I'm sure you'll agree. Without that one little word, I felt lost...completely adrift and uncertain of what was really going on between the big alien and myself.

Messed up and insecure much? Who, me?

Unfortunately, yes.

"...is today," Tellum said, dragging me out of my worried thoughts and making me realize I had missed something. "With our hyper-drives working on overload, we should be able to make the last part of it."

"I'll have Al synthesize Sellah some clothing fit for Eloim royalty," Sarden said. "She needs to look regal and completely legitimate."

"Make clothing for all of you," Tellum advised. "It won't do for any of her retinue to appear anything less than noble."

"I'll get him to work on it right away," Sarden promised. "Right now, in fact."

He got up and stalked out of the food prep area. Grav and Tellum started to talk about something else but Sellah hopped off her stool and took me by the hand.

"Come on—let's go to your room and talk...*sister*," she murmured in my ear.

"What? Why did you call me that?" I demanded as we made our way back to my room.

"Because, it's true—isn't it?" She settled cross-legged on my hoverbed and grinned, looking much more like a naughty schoolgirl than a deposed queen. "I can tell by the way you're glowing—you bonded with Sarden didn't you?"

"As a matter of fact, we did," I said, frowning. "Even though you *told* me it was impossible."

She shrugged her shoulders. "You're a Pure One and a *La-ti-zal*. Who knows what is and isn't possible for you?"

"Well apparently it *is* possible because now Sarden and I are *addicted* to each other and I don't know what to do about it," I said, beginning to pace.

"What do you mean, you don't know what to do?" She opened her golden eyes wide. "You have a Ceremony of Commitment, of course and join your lives into one. Then I guess the two of you can travel the galaxy having adventures." She looked at me enviously. "Although I hope you'll hang around Eloim at least for a *little* while. If I get the throne back, I mean."

"You'll get it back," I said. "If this Hurxx is half as skeevy as he sounds, the people of your planet won't be able to *wait* to get you back. But just because Sarden and I are bonded doesn't mean he wants me to settle down with him and have his babies."

Which was another thing to consider. Since we were bonded, I assumed it meant we were compatible enough to have kids—but what would they look like? Would they have horns? I knew I would love any child I had without reservations—that wasn't a problem. What I was wondering was, when *exactly* did the horns grow in? Would the kid have them while he was in the womb—specifically in *my* womb? And would he poke me with them? And what about the actually delivery—that was *bound* to hurt.

"Of *course* it means he wants you to settle down and bear his children," Sellah said impatiently, breaking my train of thought. "Hasn't he said as much?"

"No, actually," I admitted. "Mostly he just talked about feeling possessive of me and wanting me to be his."

"That's the Vorn side of him," she said. "Eloim males are much more circumspect about such things." She sighed. "*Too* circumspect, I think. I wish I could find a male who would want to claim me as his own as Sarden claimed you."

"Well claiming's all well and good," I pointed out. "But he still hasn't actually said that he *loves* me. He just said we're chemically bonded. Apparently it's like some kind of addiction." I sighed. Even now I could feel a craving for him—I had a strong urge to find him and sink into his arms and never leave. Only my pride and the uncertainty I felt held me back.

"Oh yes—it *is* like an addiction." Sellah nodded. "Especially when you're newly bonded. I've heard that the craving for your beloved gets easier to bear after a few cycles but it's very strong and urgent at first."

"Yeah, well…" I sighed and crossed my arms, fighting the urge to go to the big alien with all my might. I needed to figure this out before I went rushing into anything else. "Maybe I don't *want* to be addicted. Maybe…maybe I want to go home."

"You can visit your home planet, I'm certain," Sellah said. "Sarden's not a tyrant—he wouldn't refuse to take you."

"Visiting once in a while isn't the same as living there," I said. "I have friends there and a life. Not a very exciting life but still… It's a hard choice to make. Especially since I'm not sure what he wants."

"Well, *ask* him." Sellah sounded exasperated. "Tell him you love him."

"Uh-uh." I shook my head firmly. "Look, I've been in relationships before where I said the L word first—it was a complete disaster. You can't do that—the girl can't I mean. I'm a feminist but also a realist—and the reality is, the guy wants to be the one to say it first. If the girl says it first…" I shook my head. "I just don't want him to feel like I'm pressuring him into anything."

"I don't think he would feel pressured," Sellah said quietly. "And I don't think he'd be upset if you told him—out loud—how you really feel. You don't give my brother enough credit—I'm certain he's wished for years that he could find a female he was able to bond with."

"No offense to your brother," I said carefully. "But I'm not going to assume he's dying to jump into a life-long commitment unless he says so."

"But you're already *in* a life-long commitment," she pointed out. "Your bond—"

"Is it completely unbreakable?" I interrupted. "I mean, not that I want to break it because, well, I *don't*." I shrugged uncomfortably. "But what if Sarden wants to? What then?"

Sellah shook her head. "What strange customs you must have on your planet. Among the Twelve Peoples that grew from the seeds planted by the Ancient Ones, it's known that a bond between a male and a female is inviolable. It might fade in time, if you were determined to live apart, but part of you will always be bonded to part of Sarden, no matter what."

"Wow," I muttered, shaking my head. "Who knew that unprotected sex could have such long-reaching consequences?"

"It's not just physical intimacy that forms the bond—although that *is* what seals it," Sellah lectured. "It's the fact that you *couldn't* bond with one who was wrong for you. The biological reaction simply wouldn't happen with an incompatible male, no matter how many times you, uh, made love with them."

She blushed as she spoke and I realized something about her.

"Oh my God, you're a virgin, aren't you?"

Still blushing, she nodded. "And I'll have to remain one my entire life. The Ria of Eloim is not allowed to be bonded to any male but the Rea. But if the Rea is her blood relative rather than her mate, she must remain celibate throughout her reign."

"Wow—that's tough," I said sympathetically. "No *wonder* you don't want to rule."

"It's not just that." She sighed. "Although, I have to be honest that's a big part of it. I wish I could find a male who would care for me the way my brother cares for you—but I never will. It is forbidden."

She looked so sad that I put an arm around her shoulders and gave her an impulsive hug. After a moment, Sellah hugged me back and sighed again.

"Well, it doesn't matter what I want. I have to try and take the throne back for the good of Eloim. Even before he had me snatched away, Hurxx was already implementing some policies that favored the rich over the poor and were designed to line his pockets and the pockets of his advisors. The Goddess of Mercy alone knows what he's gotten up to since he got me out of the way."

"You'll fix it," I said. "As soon as you kick him out."

She shook her head. "It might not be that easy. The Council of the People is going to be very reluctant to de-throne a sitting Rae, especially one wearing the Star of Wisdom. In fact, as long as he has the Star on, he's legally the ruler of Eloim and no one can say otherwise."

"And you can't take it off him?" I asked.

She shrugged. "I could *try*, I suppose, though traditionally only the Rae himself is supposed to remove it. But if the Star truly believes he is worthy to rule, it will refuse to be removed."

"You have to try, though," I said. "It sounds like the only way to prove what a fake he is."

She gave a short, unhappy laugh. "I doubt he'll give me a chance. He has a personal guard around him at all times—no one gets within ten feet of him."

"Well...maybe it will be enough just to accuse him publicly and tell everyone what he did," I said lamely.

"Maybe." Sellah shrugged. "All I can do is try." Reaching for my hand, she squeezed it and smiled gratefully. "I'm just glad you and my brother will be there for me when I do it."

"We wouldn't miss it," I promised, squeezing back.

But inside I wondered how in the world we were going to manage this. How could we put Sellah back on the throne if we couldn't prove that Hurxx was unfit to rule in the first place?

I had no idea, but as Sellah said, all we could do was try. And as for my bond with Sarden, well, I would worry about it later, when all this was taken care of.

Chapter Twenty-seven

Zoe

"This is it. Are you ready? You certainly *look* ready. You look *gorgeous.*"

I looked Sellah up and down, completely in awe of how royal she looked. Al had really outdone himself with the clothing synthesizer this time. Sellah looked like the queen she was in the long red gown and white fur cape he had made for her. The red of her dress brought out the creamy tones of her brown skin, making her look absolutely regal and beautiful. Her dark hair was loose and flowed over her shoulders in glossy profusion that made me jealous—why couldn't *my* hair behave like that?

For me, Al had made a similar gown but in blue instead of red. The cape I was wearing was black and not as long. In fact, it was more like a half-cape and I thought it looked kind of weird but Al assured me that it was the latest in Eloim fashion. At least the dress was pretty—the deep blue material was cut low in the front and dipped in to hug my curves and show off my hourglass shape. The shoes that went with it were sort of like a cross between clogs and flip-flops with tall wooden heels and a jeweled thong that went between my toes. They were surprisingly comfortable.

"I think we both look ready. That color of blue really brings out your eyes." Sellah smiled at me. "Blue is such an *exotic* color for eyes."

I laughed. "Says the girl with gorgeous golden peepers."

She made a face. "*Everyone* on Eloim has golden eyes and dark hair. Believe me, Zoe, they're going to take one look at your beautiful red hair and blue eyes and fall madly in love with you. Especially when they hear you're a *La-ti-zal*."

"Well, they're not going to be focusing on me—it's you we want to highlight," I pointed out.

"I know." She shrugged her slim shoulders. "I'm just saying that having you as a bonded mate may go a long way towards making Sarden more…respectable. It's a known fact that not just any male can secure a *La-ti-zal* as a mate. Having you at his side will make him appear more legitimate in the eyes of the people."

"Well, if you say so." I shrugged. "I mean, I'm happy to help but he and I still haven't really figured out—"

"Figured out what?" Sarden suddenly appeared in my doorway with Grav right behind him. Both of them were dressed in black, straight-legged trousers with short, tight, long-sleeved jackets to match. Sarden's jacket was pure white and Grav's was crimson. The Eloim male equivalent of fancy dress clothes reminded me a little of a matador's outfit, although their trouser legs were tucked into tall, shiny black boots instead of ending at the knee.

"Haven't quite figured out how to wear my hair yet," I said quickly, when Sellah looked like she might say something. "What do you think—up or down?" I gathered my red curls in a chignon at the nape of my neck to demonstrate.

"Down," he said at once. "Your hair is too beautiful to hide."

"Thank you." I could feel myself blushing and also, now that he was in close proximity, I could feel the need to be close to him. To be *touching* him.

Whoa, girl—reign it in, I told myself sternly. *It's a chemical reaction and until you figure out exactly what's going on, you need to keep a lid on it.*

Which was easier said than done—especially when Sarden was eating me up with his eyes.

"Um…are we all ready to go?" I asked, trying and failing not to lust after him. He looked really *hot* in fancy dress clothes. The fitted jacket seemed to emphasize his broad shoulders and the snug trousers showed off his perfect ass.

"Tellum is preparing the shuttle—we'll go directly to the palace," Sarden said. "We should be just in time to catch the last bit of Grievance Day." He looked at Sellah. "You look lovely, little sister. Are you ready?"

She took a deep breath. "As ready as I'll ever be."

He nodded briefly. "Then let's go."

* * * * *

The atmosphere of Eloim was surprisingly Earth-like with blue skies and green grass and vegetation—well, *greenish* anyway. It was more turquoise than what I would call actual grass-green. Still, it looked close enough to home to make me happy.

The royal palace, however, wasn't what I had expected. But of course, what I had expected was Cinderella's Castle from Disney World. I don't know why—because that's what comes to mind when I think of palaces and kings and queens and fairy tales, I guess. But the palace of Eloim wasn't like that—there were no soaring buttresses or high turrets or tall towers. In fact, it wasn't very vertical at all—I think the whole structure was no more than one story high.

But *what* a story. It was a long, low, gray stone complex that seemed to stretch for miles. In fact, I thought it looked more like a small city than a dwelling place for a royal family.

"These halls we're passing through are behind the common areas," Sella explained in an undertone as we made our way through what seemed like miles of echoing stone corridors. "This is where the lower couriers and servants live—the footmen, the maids, the—"

"The muck workers?" I suggested, grinning.

She smiled. "Yes, them too, I suppose. We'll be coming to the more restricted area soon."

"Will we be able to get in?" I asked. We were traveling by hidden routes through the palace as much as possible. Also, Sellah was wearing an opaque black veil that hid her face. We didn't want Hurxx alerted until the moment we stepped foot into the throne room.

"There will be guards posted at the doors of the throne room. I suppose we'll find out if they're loyal to Hurxx or Sellah," Sarden said grimly.

"Doesn't matter." Despite his fancy clothes, Grav looked positively menacing. "They'll get out of the way if they know what's good for them."

"Please—no violence." Tellum sounded nervous. "We cannot appear to be a gang of thugs pushing our way into the throne room." He gave Grav a nervous, sidelong glance which the other male returned with a wild, white grin. Clearly Grav was spoiling for a fight—I wondered if he would get one.

"We'll reign it in as much as possible," Sarden promised. "But one way or another, Sellah has to be seen—and not just by the Council—by the common folk as well. They love her."

"They *loved* me, you mean." Sellah sounded unhappy. "I've

been gone for months."

"They'll remember you," Sarden said reassuringly. "In fact—"

But just then we turned the corner and found ourselves facing a broad, arched wooden door bound with golden hinges. And standing on either side of the door were two Eloim guards. They were wearing scarlet and gold uniforms and holding some nasty looking weapons that looked like a cross between a spear and a pickaxe.

They turned at once and one said,

"Halt. None may enter the throne room without a pass."

"And even if you've got one," the other guard said. "Grievance Day is almost over. You'd do better to return on the next one."

"We're not going back." Grav stepped up to face them, a low growl rising in his throat.

I saw the guards go pale but they stood their ground, leveling their pickaxe-spears at the huge alien.

"This isn't necessary," Sarden said. He looked at the guards sternly. "Open in the name of the Ria."

Sellah stepped up and lifted her veil to let the two of them see her face.

At once, the two of them fell to their knees.

"My lady! Forgive us! We didn't know!"

"That's all right," Sellah said gently, smiling at them. "Just open the doors—quietly if you please—and let us pass."

They fell over themselves doing it and soon the arched door was swinging quietly open, allowing us to enter the throne room.

We came in from the side, with the throne on our left and stopped just inside the doorway. There was a kind of shadowy alcove there where we were able to stand unnoticed.

I noticed at once that the people in the room seemed to be divided into different groups. The ones at the back of the room, farthest from the throne, must be the common people, I thought. They were dressed in simple clothes and seemed to be waiting patiently. Closer to the throne, the clothing got dressier and dressier—these must be the nobles and couriers, I supposed. Standing right near the throne I saw a group of older Eloim males, all wearing long, sober black robes. Tellum was dressed the same so I assumed these were the members of the Council of the People, which appeared to be sort of like a Parliament that kept the Rae and Ria in check.

The throne itself was a long golden chair, almost like a fancy bench with a high back. It had two crimson cushions on it and was clearly meant for two people to sit on. However, it had a single occupant now.

A large, rather flabby-looking Eloim male with a long, luxuriant curling mane of black hair was lounging on it so that he took up both cushions. He was dressed in a gold brocade jacket which was too small to contain his gut. It spilled out under the jacket and over his tight gold trousers, resulting in a pronounced potbelly. The crimson satin-like material of his shirt was stretched tight over it in a ridiculous and not-very-attractive way.

That has *to be Hurxx,* I thought, eyeing the lounging Eloim with distaste. On his head he wore a golden circlet with a single, luminous blue-green jewel set right in the middle, like a diadem. The jewel seemed to pulse with some kind of energy. Though his hair flopped when he turned his head, the crown—which had to be the Star of Wisdom—stayed very firmly in place and didn't move so much as a millimeter. Around his neck he wore a gaudy gold chain set with jewels of the same color.

"There he is—the bastard," I heard Sarden growl.

He started to go towards the throne but Tellum put a restraining hand on his arm and pulled him back to the shadowy alcove we were standing in.

"Be patient. Let me pick the moment to reveal the Ria," he said in a low voice.

Sarden subsided, still growling, but I could feel his anger and frustration through the link we now shared. I couldn't say that I blamed him, either. Hurxx had sold his sister into slavery just to get rid of her and he didn't look like he felt guilty for it one bit.

Asshole.

"What's that necklace he's wearing?" I murmured to Sellah—for some reason the gold chain with its blue-green stones kept drawing my eyes. "Is it official court jewelry—like the Star of Wisdom?"

"No." She shook her head. "Or at least, it wasn't official before Hurxx had it commissioned. He had it made before we were crowned to wear to the coronation and he's never taken it off since. He wears it *everywhere,* whether it matches his outfit or not."

I made a face. "Doesn't look like it would match *any* outfit."

"I thought not too," she murmured. "But he loves it for some reason."

"And now," one of the Council members said, stepping forward. "Before this Grievance Day is ended, we have one more matter to put before the Council and the Court." He glanced back at Hurxx who made a languid gesture with one hand and nodded for him to go on.

"That's Yancy—one of the Council that's in Hurxx's pocket," murmured Tellum. "You can be sure that anything he says comes straight from the mouth of the Rae himself."

"Let's hear what he has to say, then," Sarden growled.

"As we all know," Yancy, the Councilor continued in a loud voice, "Our beloved Ria was taken from us by shameless ruffians many solar months ago."

There was a murmuring in the crowd and I saw several of the common women dabbing at their eyes. Sarden must be right then—Sellah was loved and missed.

"Our ships pursued these pirates tirelessly," Yancy continued. "But alas, we were too late to save our Ria. It is my sad duty to tell all who are gathered here today that she is dead."

There were more murmurs from the crowd—some sad and some shocked. Most of the couriers and nobles looked upset as well.

"That *bastard!*" Sarden started forward again but again, Tellum held him back.

"Wait," he said simply. "Let Hurxx dig a deep enough hole to bury himself."

I personally thought he already had but since Sarden apparently decided to stay put, I stayed too.

"For proof of our Ria's sad and untimely demise, I offer you this—the single object recovered from her captors."

Yancy clapped his hands and a courier wearing scarlet hurried forward, carrying a jeweled case in one hand. He opened it and Yancy reached in to pick up what was inside. Then he held it up—showing the crowd, who *oohed* and *ahed* over it.

It was a crown, much like the one that Hurxx wore on his head. Only in this one the circlet was silver instead of gold and the glowing jewel set in the center was a slightly different color—pinkish-purple instead of blue-green.

"As you know, there is no other female of the blood to be Ria to our esteemed Rae," Yancy continued. "And even if there was, our Rae would not wish to replace such a beloved Ria so soon. In fact…" He paused dramatically. "He does not wish to replace her at all."

There was a louder murmur coming front the crowd now and some of the Councilors were visibly upset.

"What are you saying, Yancy?" one of them called. "How can Eloim retain its balance without both a Ria and Rae to rule it?"

"Why, in the same way it has always retained its balance," Yancy said smoothly. "Through the use of both the Star of Wisdom, *and* the Star of Compassion."

"What? But if there is no Ria, who is to wear the Star of Compassion?" another Councilor protested.

For the first time, Hurxx spoke.

"*I* shall," he said, at last sitting up straighter on the throne. He had a high, nasally voice that grated on my nerves. "I shall wear both of the Stars at once and they shall guide me."

The murmurs of the crowd were so loud this time that the Councilor who had been objecting had to shout to make himself heard.

"Impossible!" he exclaimed. "No one person can wear both Stars at once."

"Why don't we let the Stars themselves decide that — shall we?" Hurxx purred. Leaning forward, he motioned to Yancy. "Yancy — the Star of Compassion."

Stepping forward, Yancy held out the silver circlet with its purple-pink stone and Hurxx took it carefully, holding it with his fingertips as though it was hot.

Just as he was about to place the silver crown on his head, on top of the gold crown he already wore, Tellum murmured,

"Now!"

Sellah stepped forward, out of the shadowy alcove we'd been keeping to. The rest of us followed her and Sarden shouted,

"Stop!"

"What?" Hurxx paused, frowning. "Why, Sarden, my royal cousin, whatever are *you* doing here?"

"Stopping you from taking over all of Eloim, *cousin,*" Sarden growled.

"How? Do you plan to take the throne yourself, *half-breed?*" Hurxx sneered.

"I didn't say that, but there is someone here who has a claim to it." Sarden motioned to Sellah, who once more threw her black veil back to reveal her face.

"Hello, cousin," she said in a low, carrying voice. "As you can see I am not dead at all but very much alive. And I do not approve of you wearing my crown as well as your own."

The murmuring from the crowd was absolutely deafening then—it was really more of a roar. Many of the common people were surging forward but the palace guards held them back, keeping us from being overwhelmed. There were shouts of,

"Sellah! The lady, Sellah has returned!"

"The Goddess of Mercy be praised!"

"The Ria! I knew she wasn't dead!"

But mixed in with the shouts for Sellah, there was a surprising amount of commotion for Sarden.

"Lord Sarden has brought our Ria back!"

"Mayhap they will rule together—as is proper and right."

"Lord Sarden has returned—now all shall be set right."

I even heard some things about myself. People wondering who I was and if I was with Sarden. I blushed and made sure not to meet anyone's eyes. Let them think what they wanted. But it was clear to me from what the crowd was murmuring, that Sarden wasn't regarded as an interloper or an intruder, despite the fact that he looked more Vorn than Eloim.

Despite the shouting at her back, Sellah kept her face towards the throne. She and Hurxx seemed to be having some kind of a staring contest but at last he spoke.

"Well, cousin," he remarked. "So you return. I am so glad you are well—we feared you dead."

"You feared no such thing," Sellah said in a low, carrying voice. "For you are the one who plotted to have me kidnapped and sold into slavery in the first place!"

"I?" Hurxx put one hand to his chest and made an offended face, though I noticed he kept a tight grip on the Star of Compassion with the other hand. "Surely you must be mistaken."

"There is no mistake," Tellum said, stepping forward. "For I heard you and Yancy speaking of the plan—which is why I went to find the Ria myself. She was put up for auction to be sold to the highest bidder—that was *your* doing, Hurxx."

"Blasphemy!" Yancy gasped, retreating to stand beside the throne. "How *dare* you speak such lies in the presence of the Rae, Tellum?"

"He only speaks the truth," Sarden growled, stepping forward. "Put the Star of Compassion down, Hurxx—and while you're at it, you can take off the Star of Wisdom too. You obviously don't deserve to wear it."

"Is that what you think?" Hurxx sneered at him, his pouting upper lip curling up belligerently. "Well, *I* say we let the Stars decide who is the rightful ruler here—shall we?"

And before Sarden could stop him, he placed the Star of

Compassion on top of his head, just over the Star of Wisdom. For a moment, I thought he seemed to be having a hard time keeping the second crown in place—it was almost like he was fighting with it to wrestle it down onto his head. But then the slim circlet seemed to snap into place somehow and then it stayed where it was, the pinkish-purple stone winking and glowing just above the greenish-blue one.

I felt a disturbance in the air as the second crown snapped into place—a strange ripple of something I can only describe as *wrongness.* It was an almost palpable feeling—like I was on the beach and had been slapped in the face by a cold, salty wave. The intensity of the feeling made me gasp and I looked around, wondering if anyone else had felt it. But everyone seemed to be watching Hurxx.

He removed his hands from his head, holding them up to show that they were empty and both crowns were staying on his head without help from him.

"Do you see?" he called, looking imperiously down his nose at Sarden.

An audible gasp came from the crowd.

"Is it not clear?" Yancy declared loudly. "Would the Stars of Wisdom and Compassion stay in place on my Lord Rae's head if they were not meant to be there? If they did not deem him a worthy ruler?"

"It must be true," someone whispered. "Lord Hurxx must be the true and ordained ruler of Eloim." Soon other people in the crowd were saying the same thing—although I could tell they weren't happy about it.

"There's something wrong," I whispered to Sarden. "Can't you feel it?"

He gave me a shrewd look, his eyes narrowed in concentration. "I don't feel it myself but I can tell you do—I feel it through you."

"He's keeping those crowns on his head in some way," I said. "Confront him—tell him to take them off."

"Or let someone else try to take them off," Grav muttered.

"There is always the Challenge of the Stars," Sellah murmured to Sarden.

"The what?" I asked. It sounded like some kind of celebrity dance show but I was pretty sure challenging Hurxx to a dance-off wouldn't prove anything.

"It's where you challenge the ruling Rae or Ria to allow someone to try to remove the Star they are wearing," Sellah explained. "In the history of Eloim, there has never been a successful challenge because the Stars stay firmly on the head of the rightful rulers and refuse to be removed."

"That's right—they're supposed to fly off on their own if they don't like the person wearing them," I said, remembering. "But what if Hurxx has them fixed in place somehow? We have to try and get them off."

"The Challenge of the Stars is risky—*too* risky," Tellum objected. "If we try and fail to get the crowns off, Hurxx's claim to the throne will be irrefutable and we'll never be able to challenge him again. Also, if we lose, he can claim anything he wants of us as tribute—to recompense the insult we have offered by challenging his legitimate right to the throne."

"He knows it's risky for us—look at him, the smug bastard," Sarden growled. He looked at me. "Zoe?"

I knew what he was asking and I nodded, the feeling of *wrongness* churning in my gut.

"There's something not right—we *have* to challenge, no matter how risky it is."

"Zoe is right," Sellah said in a low voice. "I say we challenge too."

Sarden looked at Grav, who nodded.

"I'm with you all the way. Not gonna take a backseat while that bastard tries to steal your blood-sister's throne."

"Then it's decided," Sarden said firmly. "We challenge."

"I take it by all this whispering together that you're thinking of challenging my claim," Hurxx said, raising his voice to be heard over the murmuring of the crowd. "Is that not right, my royal cousins?"

"That's exactly fucking right," Sarden snarled. "We don't believe you have the right to wear either Star—let alone both."

"Well then—let us put it to a test, shall we?" Hurxx motioned to his pet Councilor. "Yancy—come and make the test."

"With pleasure, my Lord Rae." Coming to Hurxx's side, Yancy made a big show of pulling on the crowns Hurxx was wearing in his long, floppy hair. Of course, neither one of them budged. Then Yancy stepped back, holding up his hands. "The Challenge has been met and defeated! Though I tried with all my might, neither the Star of Wisdom nor the Star of Compassion would come off my Lord Rae's head."

"That doesn't prove anything!" I exclaimed. The feeling of *wrongness* was growing in me and I was getting really and truly pissed off now. "Yancy was just pretending to try and take off the crowns."

"Do you say so? And who might you be, my dear?" Hurxx raised an eyebrow at me.

I stepped forward and heard the crowd murmur as they looked

me over.

"This is Zoe—a female of pure descent from a closed Planet," Sarden said loudly. He gave me a look from the corner of his eye. "She is my bonded mate."

"A Pure One? Lord Sarden has mated a Pure One?" I heard the crowd murmuring and a great wave of longing came over me. I wanted to be his bonded mate in more than just name only. I gave him a look from the corner of my eye, wondering if it would ever happen, wishing I could be in his arms someplace private, showing him how I really felt.

But there was no time for hanky-panky. I lifted my chin and looked at Hurxx.

"Lord Sarden is correct—I am his," I said clearly. "And I am from a closed planet."

"A Pure One, eh?" Hurxx eyed me hungrily. "Well, my little Pure One, why do you not come and make the test yourself, if you doubt my Councilor?" He beckoned to me languidly, his dark eyes gleaming in a way I didn't like in the least.

"All right—I will." I stepped forward but Sarden put a hand on my arm.

"Zoe, I don't like this," he growled. "Hurxx is a slippery son-of-a-bitch. I don't want you getting too close to him."

"Let me do this," I told him in a low voice. "I'm the only one who can fix this." I didn't know how I knew that—I just did. It was as clear to me as the feeling of *wrongness* which kept growing every minute. I wondered for a moment what was happening to me but there was no time to question my certainty—I had to go with it. "I can take care of myself," I told Sarden.

Reluctantly, he nodded and released my arm.

"All right. But if that bastard lays one finger on you—"

"I'll bite it off," I said coolly and gave him a smile.

He shook his head and smiled back.

"Zoe, you never cease to amaze me. Go."

I went, approaching the double throne with my head held high and my back straight. I was very aware that everyone in the room was watching me and I didn't want to disgrace myself or Sellah and Sarden either.

Calm, aloof ice-princess, I told myself, moving with a slow, measured pace. *You're a calm, aloof ice-princess and nothing can melt you.*

I hoped, anyway.

At last I was standing right in front of Hurxx, who was still lounging on the throne with a little grin on his doughy face.

"Well, well, my dear," he murmured as I came to a stop in front of him. "Aren't you a pretty one? So exotic with your pale skin and your big blue eyes."

"Thanks," I muttered. Up close I found him completely repulsive from his floppy hair down to the dainty gold ankle boots he wore on his small feet. The gaudy blue and green stones of the thick gold chain he wore around his neck seemed to wink at me—especially the one in the middle, which was a large, raised oval as big as an egg. What was the deal with him anyway? He looked like he'd been raiding Elton John's closet but only taking the ugly stuff.

"I've never had a Pure One before," Hurxx remarked, looking me up and down in a way that made me want to cover up. "Perhaps after this little charade is over you and I can go someplace private and get better *acquainted."*

"I'd rather have a double root canal," I told him flatly. "That's a really unpleasant and painful dental procedure in case you don't get my reference."

"Well! How dare you speak to the Rae in such a way?" Yancy, who was still standing nearby demanded.

"Because he's not the rightful Rae—and I'm going to prove it," I said loudly, hoping like crazy I actually *could* prove it. I looked at Hurxx. "I don't want anything to do with you—I'm only here to remove those crowns. You shouldn't be wearing either of them and you *know* it."

His self-satisfied smile slipped a little but he only gestured at me.

"Very well, Pure One," he said in a loud voice. "Commence the Challenge of the Stars and removed them from my head if you can."

"All right." The feeling of *wrongness* coming from him was so strong now that it almost made me sick to my stomach. I didn't know what this weird sixth sense I seemed to have somehow developed was trying to tell me, but it was really *loud*. Almost like someone shouting in my ear that this situation was broken and I had to fix it.

Feeling like I would scream if I couldn't set things right, I reached up and placed my fingers on the silver circlet of the Star of Compassion. The crown hummed and vibrated violently under my fingertips, reminding me of an animal caught in a trap.

Help, a tiny voice whispered in my head. *Help us—he holds us captive! Help, La-ti-zal! Only you can release us!*

I was so startled by the tiny voice—which was definitely *not* just me talking to myself—that I nearly jerked my hands away. Was that the crown itself talking to me? I remembered Sellah saying it had spoken to her when she first put it on and that there was an entity living in the jewels of both crowns.

"Well?" Hurxx looked up at me from under his ridiculous, floppy hair. "Try to remove it. You can't, can you?"

I took a firmer hold on the silver circlet and pulled. But though it vibrated harder than ever in my hands, I couldn't budge it so much as a millimeter. It was the same with the golden circlet of the Star of Wisdom, which also begged for my help in a deeper, more masculine voice when I pulled at it.

La-ti-zal, it called. *Only you can help us. Release us from this prison. Please!*

But though I tugged and tugged—and wasn't very careful about pulling Hurxx's ridiculous hair either—neither crown would come off. Something was holding them in place. But what?

"And there you have it," Yancy announced to the crowd, which was watching in hushed silence. "Even a Pure One cannot remove the Stars from my Lord Hurxx's head—which means he must be the one true rightful ruler of our fair planet!"

"This can't be," I muttered through gritted teeth. "This isn't right!"

"Ah, but it *appears* right, my dear—and that's all that matters." Hurxx smiled up at me. "Now please remove your hands from the royal person."

Reluctantly, I took my hands off the crowns. Something was going on, but for the life of me, I couldn't figure it out.

Hurxx stood up from the throne and raised his arms. Though he wasn't nearly as tall as Sarden, he was still much taller than me. The large, oval stone in his tacky necklace winked in the light and nearly blinded me as he brushed me aside.

"My people!" he shouted, in his high, nasally voice. "I think you can see that I am your true ruler—I have undergone the Challenge of the Stars and neither Star has chosen to leave my head. As such, I proclaim myself both the rightful Rae *and* the rightful Ria of Eloim. And for my tribute, to recompense me for the wrongful claim brought against me, I claim this Pure One."

He grabbed me suddenly around the waist, crushing me against the side of his scratchy gold brocade jacket.

"No!" Sarden roared, surging forward. Grav came with him but there was suddenly a line of guards, all holding those deadly looking pickaxe-spears in their faces.

I looked at Sarden quickly and shook my head— although it was clear he was willing to run through an army of spears to get to me, I didn't want him getting killed on my account.

"Zoe!" This time I swore the voice in my head was Sarden's. Could we read each other's thoughts now? Was that part of the bond too?

"Sit tight," I sent back to him, thinking as hard as I could. *"I'll think of something."*

He nodded grimly, although he looked really, *really* unhappy about it. I was glad he was trusting my judgment although to be honest, I wasn't sure *I* trusted my judgment. I mean, what in the hell was I going to do now?

The jewel, I heard both little voices saying in my head. This time it was definitely the Stars and not Sarden. I had a moment to think I might be going crazy—wasn't hearing voices in your head a pretty definite sign? And then they called to me again. *The jewel! It holds us – it holds us captive to the one who is not right!*

The jewel? Frowning I looked up at Hurxx—I had a really close look since he was crushing me against him, under his rather smelly armpit. How could anyone with hair that floppy and shiny smell like they hadn't taken a bath in a month? And what jewel were the Stars talking about?

Suddenly the egg-shaped greenish-blue jewel in the center of his necklace caught my eye again and an idea began to form in my mind.

"Oh, Lord Hurxx," I purred, looking up at him. "Do you *really* claim me as your rightful tribute?"

He looked down at me in apparent surprise.

"I certainly do, little Pure One. It is my right and duty to claim what is mine as the rightful Rae of Eloim."

"I see that now." I fluttered my lashes at him, trying to flirt even though being so close to him and the *wrongness* he was putting out in waves made me sick. "You're so powerful...so *rich.*"

"Well yes I am." He wore a self-satisfied smirk on his pudgy face. "I have all the wealth of Eloim at my fingertips, after all."

"I could tell that just by looking at you," I said, smiling in what I hoped was a bewitching way. "By the fashionable clothing and jewelry you wear." I let my fingers creep up his chest to the gold chain around his neck. "This especially—we have nothing so fine on my planet. Was it made just for you?"

I saw Yancy's eyes widen as he saw where my fingers were going and he stepped forward and muttered something to Hurxx under his breath.

"Don't be such a worrier, Yancy," Hurxx answered, making a shooing gesture at his Councilor with his free hand, the one that wasn't currently crushing me to him. "You know perfectly well it's keyed only to me."

"But, my Lord—"

"I especially like this jewel," I said, my fingers creeping to the oval blue-green jewel. "It's so *special.*"

The moment I touched the jewel, I knew it was the source of the *wrongness.* My fingertips stung and my eyes watered as I fought to keep from throwing up. *Wrong! Wrong, wrong,* **WRONG!** screamed the Stars' voices inside my head. I wanted to yank my fingers away and go be sick in the corner somewhere.

Instead, I placed my palm firmly in the center of the egg-shaped stone and pushed in as hard as I could.

There was a loud *crack* and a flash, as though a bolt of lightening had suddenly struck down right in the middle of the throne room.

"What? How—?" Hurxx gasped and staggered back, dragging me with him. Since I was still pinned to his side, I was in just the right position to see it when the gaudy gold chain he was wearing suddenly fell off his neck and clattered to the marble floor.

And as soon as it did, both the Star of Wisdom and the Star of Compassion flew off Hurxx's floppy-haired head and went whizzing up into the air to hover over the awe-struck crowd.

"No! *No!*" Hurxx finally let go of me, fumbling on his now-bare head desperately. "No, you little *bitch!*"

He grabbed me by the throat and squeezed. I gasped and tried to push his hands away but they were too big and he was too strong for me. I kicked instead, aiming for his balls in the ridiculously tight gold brocade trousers.

I think I might have caught him a glancing blow, because he howled and his fingers loosened just enough for me to take a small sip of air. But then he squeezed again, his eyes filled with rage.

Great—all I had done was piss him off even more.

I kicked again but missed him entirely this time. Brilliant white and red stars exploded before my eyes and I could hear myself gasping for air—air I couldn't get because he was choking me…killing me…

"Get your hands off my mate, you fuck!"

Suddenly a big, red fist plowed into Hurxx's nose. Blood flew and the horribly strong hands finally released me. I staggered backwards and Sellah caught me.

"Zoe? Are you all right?"

"I…I think I'm fine." My voice came out in a thin little whisper and I coughed, trying to get my breath back. My vision was still fading in and out and I had to lean on Sellah's arm to stay upright.

Beside the throne, Hurxx and Sarden were still fighting. Although Hurxx wasn't really putting up much of a fight. Sarden was raining down blows on him, his face a mask of savage, possessive fury and Hurxx was cowering and trying to get away.

"Have mercy—have mercy!" he cried, trying to shield his face, which was covered in blood, from Sarden's fists. Some of the palace guards tried to interfere but Grav held them back. He had gotten one of the axe-spears from one of them and was waving it menacingly. From the look on his face, he wanted to go after Hurxx himself but clearly he knew he had to leave him to Sarden.

"Why should anyone have mercy on you?" Tellum shouted at Hurxx, stepping forward to make himself heard over the excited babble of the crowd. "You who profaned our most sacred rites and rituals with evil and deceit? How did you do it? How did you compel the Stars to stay with you when you had such wicked intent?"

"The chain…" I coughed and pointed to the broken gold chain lying on the floor before the throne. The oval shaped stone in the center had shattered and a black, noxious smoke was rising from it. "I don't know what it is but it was…was holding them in place."

"How else was I to take the throne?" Hurxx whined, still trying to shield himself from Sarden's fists. "The Star of Wisdom didn't want me—it only wanted Sarden! I couldn't let a half-breed rule

Eloim, could I?"

"What?" Sarden stopped in mid-punch and took a step back, eyeing his cousin warily. "*What* did you say?"

"You heard me." Hurxx straightened up a little, his flattened nose streaming with blood. "From the first moment I touched the Star of Wisdom, at the pre-coronation ceremony, it never wanted me. It asked for you." He spat. "But I was damned if I'd give the throne to a filthy half-Vorn bastard."

"The Star wanted Sarden—which was why you had to construct a device strong enough to hold it in place on your head," Sellah said, lifting her chin. "Because you *knew* you weren't the rightful Rae. I wondered why you had that ugly necklace commissioned. Now we know."

"I only did what any true patriot of Eloim would have done." Hurxx sounded sulky. "In order to keep a half-breed off the throne."

"It was not for you to decide who was or was not worthy to wear the Star of Wisdom," Tellum thundered, glaring at the deposed Rae. "Only the Star itself can make that determination."

As if the Stars—which were still hovering high above the crowds—had heard his voice, they both came whizzing down.

The Star of Wisdom paused for a moment, then settled itself firmly on Sarden's head.

"What?" He reached up to touch the gold circlet hesitantly...carefully as though he might be burned. I felt, rather than heard, the Star asking him questions through our link. After a moment he nodded. "Yes," he said in a low voice. "Yes, I swear it."

The crowd murmured in surprise but I didn't hear or see anyone who sounded unhappy. Well, except for Yancy and a few of the other Councilors who were obviously loyal to the deposed Rae.

They were starting to sneak to one side of the throne and I saw Hurxx sidling that way himself—clearly they were trying to take the back way out.

Grav saw it the same time I did and motioned to the guards.

"Keep them here," he growled. "Nobody leaves until this is over."

Most of the guards seemed to understand what was going on. They ran to surround the would-be escaping Councilors and the ex-Rae. A few of the crowd murmured but most were still watching Sarden to see what he would do.

"People of Eloim," he said, stepping forward and addressing the crowd. "The Star of Wisdom has come to me. Though I am a half-breed, I was raised among you and I have only Eloim's best interests at heart. I will rule with your blessing and that of the Star's—but only with the right female beside me as my Ria."

A cheer went up from the crowd and some of them called, "Long live the Rae! Long live Lord Sarden!"

Sarden made a motion with his hands and they quieted down. All eyes went up to the ceiling, where the silver circlet of the Star of Compassion was hovering uncertainly.

At last it came down and positioned itself over Sellah's head. She looked up at it and I saw the sorrow and resignation in her eyes.

"All right," she said softly. "I'll do it if there's no other way. But please, Star, if you can find anyone else—anyone you think is worthy—then please choose them instead. *Please.*"

The slim silver crown seemed to understand. It rose again and came to settle…

Directly on my head.

Chapter Twenty-eight

Zoe

"What?" I couldn't have been more surprised if...well, to be honest, I can't think of a situation that would have surprised me more.

Zoe, whispered the Star's voice in my head. *Will you accept the mantle of Ria of Eloim?*

"But...but I don't know anything about your people," I protested in a small voice.

Are you willing to learn?

"Well, sure. But I'm really not queen material—I'm just a paralegal," I objected. "I mean, I'm not royal or fancy at all."

It is because you do not seek power that it is bestowed upon you, the Star told me.

Sarden must have felt my uncertainty through the link we now shared because he came forward and took my hands in his.

"Zoe," he said in a low voice. "Please say yes. Please rule by my side."

"I...I *want* to be by your side," I said, trying to pick my words carefully. "But I wasn't sure how you felt about it. I mean, I don't know if—"

"I love you." He leaned down to kiss me and then looked searchingly into my eyes. "I know we started this in a bad way, with me buying you from the Commercians and abducting you away from your home world. And I know you miss it. I've been pretending to myself that I could let you go if you chose Earth over me but I can't pretend anymore! Zoe, I love you *so damn much."*

For some reason my eyes filled with hot tears and a sob broke from my lips.

"What? What is it?" Sarden looked distressed. He stroked my hair and looked at me anxiously. "What's wrong, sweetheart? Shouldn't I have said that?"

"N-no. I mean, yes," I managed to get out in a strangled voice. "Yes, you should *absolutely* have said it. I'm sorry I'm crying. It's just…I love you too. I don't know how or when it happened but I'm in love with you—not just a little either," I admitted recklessly. "I'm…I'm *crazy* in love with you. *Stupid* in love with you."

"Oh, is that all?" He smiled at me and hugged me to him. "That's all right then because I feel the same way about you."

"You do?" I asked, looking at him hopefully.

"Absolutely. I kept telling myself I couldn't and shouldn't feel for you that way but, well…" He shrugged, his big shoulders rolling and gave me a little grin. "I'm crazy and stupid for you too, sweetheart."

"Oh, Sarden…" I hugged him back, the tears still running down my face.

Sellah had been standing by, watching us with wide, happy eyes as we hugged it out in public. Now she stepped forward and put a hand on my shoulder.

"The love of a Rae for his Ria is an important factor in the ruling of Eloim," she murmured. "Will you now accept the responsibility that has been given you?"

"Yes," I whispered, swiping at my eyes and taking a step back from Sarden. "Yes, if…if the people want me to. But I don't want to feel like a userpent."

"A *userpent?*" Sarden grinned at me. "What's that?"

"Oh, you know what I mean!" I swatted at his arm. "A u*surper.* That's what I mean." I looked at Sellah. "I don't want to feel like I stole the throne from you."

"Everyone here has seen that the Star picked you when I asked it to take another candidate for Ria," she reminded me. "The people will accept you on that basis alone. However…" She stepped forward and addressed the crowd.

"People of Eloim. For a short time I served as your Ria and though I love all of you dearly, it was sometimes, I admit, with a heavy and regretful heart that I served. I do not wish to rule and the Star of Compassion has seen into my heart and set me free of the burden. It has chosen instead, my brother's bonded mate—Lady Zoe, the Pure One who is also a *La-ti-zal.*"

I heard the murmurs rising through the crowd and everyone, the common people and the nobles and couriers alike, started looking at me differently.

"A *La-ti-zal!* Did you hear that? She's a *La-ti-zal!*"

"No wonder the Star picked her!"

"A Pure One *and* a *La-ti-zal* as our new Ria. Truly we are blessed by the Goddess of Mercy!"

"People of Eloim," Sellah continued. "It was the Lady Zoe who saved you from the false rule of the imposter, Hurxx. Only by her pure power was his deception exposed. I promise you, she will learn our ways and be a wise and just Ria."

A cheer went up and several of the crowd started chanting my name. I watched, hardly able to comprehend what was happening. Were they chanting for *me?* The girl who'd been having staplers chucked at her head less than a month before? What was happening to me? And how had my life turned so upside down in such a short time?

"My people," roared Tellum, coming to stand beside us. "May I present to you your new Rae and Ria—the Lord Sarden and the Lady Zoe!"

"Long live the Rae! Long live the Ria! Long live Lord Sarden! Long live Lady Zoe!"

Sarden and I waved and then he pulled me to him and gave me a searing kiss.

"I love you, Zoe," he murmured when we finally came up for air. "How about if we get out of here so I can show you how much?"

"Sounds good to me," I whispered breathlessly.

The cheering and chanting followed us out of the throne room and I felt lighter than air as Sarden held my hand and the Star whispered in my head that I would be the queen that Eloim needed.

In the space of a few short weeks, I had found a whole new life. I had gone from a plain, overworked paralegal to a captive to a queen, and it all started because I was…

Abducted.

Maybe the Alien Mate Index wasn't so bad after all.

The End...or is it?

Epilogue

Sarden

"I don't like this. I don't like it one damn bit." I was pacing the floor of my war room—the same one my grandfather had used when I was a child. Back then I used to hide under the desk and observe affairs of state, fascinated by the way my grandfather, who was then the Rae, was running Eloim. Now the war room was my own to plot and plan in.

The first order of business had been to clean house, and get rid of all those that had been loyal to Hurxx and had known about his plot to sell Sellah into slavery. The second order had been to take care of Tazaxx and the pirates who had worked with him. The pirates were currently in a triple max lockdown for life and Tazaxx had been reduced to nothing but muddy water. How? By flooding his mansion on Giedi Prime.

The team I had sent had plugged all the windows and doors and filled the mansion to the ceiling with pale purple cleansing fluid—the same kind we used in our Cleansing Pools. The pure, antiseptic liquid acted like poison on the slimy bastard, melting him and dispersing everything that made him sentient. By the time the seals on the windows and doors were opened, nothing was left of him but a gush of dirty water that couldn't hurt anyone.

It was most satisfying, especially since I was able to release his "treasures" to their native planets and relocate those who couldn't go home for whatever reason. Trazaxx would never collect females like playing cards again and his yearly auction was ended for good.

After all that was taken care of, I turned my attention to the third order of business, which was the derelict ship Count Doloroso had left behind. We'd been in too much of a hurry to do anything about it right after Grav had killed the evil, crazy bastard. But I didn't like the idea of it floating around abandoned, filled with all the Assimilation equipment I'd sold him.

There was only one problem—when the salvage team I'd sent to recover the ship got to the coordinates I gave them, they found Doloroso's ship was gone. Completely vanished.

Of course, it was possible that someone else had found the ship and taken it. But space is a big place—looking for an empty vessel without a beacon to guide you is like looking for a junter in a craggle pile. Or as Zoe would say, a needle in a haystack. So the odds of someone just stumbling upon it were slight.

So then, where did it go?

"Somebody took it," Grav suggested. He had been hanging around, helping me set my house in order since I had taken over as Rae of Eloim, though I didn't expect him to stay much longer. His vow as a Protector meant he'd be looking for a new client soon—a female that needed his aid. I could tell that he was getting itchy and restless without a ward to protect.

"I guess someone might have just stumbled upon it," I said, frowning. "Still, it just doesn't feel…right."

"What doesn't feel right?"

Zoe came into the war room, wearing the latest in Eloim fashion—a tight green sheath of a dress that showed off her lush curves and fur-topped, high heeled slippers.

I felt my shaft stir at the way the green dress hugged her full breasts and hips and thanked the Goddess again that Zoe had agreed to stay and rule with me. She was so beautiful I couldn't get enough of her—even though we made love several times a night and sometimes in the middle of the day as well. I knew it was the first flush of bonding which, as Zoe pointed out, was more like a physical addiction than a regular love affair—at least on her planet. But I didn't care about any of that—I just knew I wanted her almost all the time. And thank the Goddess, she wanted me too.

"You look gorgeous," I growled, pulling her to me to nibble her neck. Her flaming red hair looked beautiful contrasted with the emerald green gown. Thanks to our permanent link, I could now see color all the time—even when I wasn't with her. It was amazing what a big difference such a little change could make. I caught myself staring at ordinary, mundane objects now, just because I was able to see their true shades for the first time.

"And you look handsome," Zoe purred, smiling up at me. "But what's wrong?"

I didn't want to scare her but the bond between us meant it was difficult to hide anything. Sometimes we caught each other's emotions—sometimes we even got thoughts. But mostly we could tell if the other was holding anything back.

"Doloroso's ship has disappeared," I said reluctantly. "I sent a salvage crew back to collect it but it's gone. Vanished."

"We think someone stole it," Grav put in.

But Zoe was shaking her head, her face so pale that every

freckle on her pert nose stood out in high relief.

"No…nobody took it," she whispered. "It's Doloroso — he's still alive."

"That's fuckin' impossible," Grav growled. "I killed that bastard myself after he hurt you, Lady Zoe. You saw it yourself."

The way his shoulders bunched and his big hands clenched into fists made me think he was reliving the incident. The kill should have been mine by rights — after all, Zoe was my female to protect and avenge. But I knew Grav couldn't stand to see a female hurt. I wondered again what had happened to my old friend to make him so protective of the opposite sex.

"I know you killed him — but that doesn't matter. He came back — somehow he came back! Don't you see?" She ran a hand through her long, red hair and started pacing. "He was talking about 'downloading' himself into another body. What if he found a way to do that?"

"Zoe," I said, trying to calm her. "I know you said he claimed to be one of the Assimilated but believe me, they were all wiped out fifty cycles ago. The Ma*jor*an empress made sure of that."

"What if she missed one? What if he's on his way right now?" she demanded, her eyes wide with worry.

She was so upset, I could feel her terror through our link. Wanting to reassure her, I pulled her in for a hug.

"It's all right," I murmured. "It's going to be all right, sweetheart. He can't get to you here — you're safe."

"It's not *me* I'm worried about!" she protested. "You said — and Doloroso said too — that my best friends were probably *La-ti-zals*, like I am! And that's what he needs for his crazy plan — a girl that's from a closed planet who's a *La-ti-zal.* Charlotte and Leah *both* fit that description!"

"He can't get to them either," I promised. "You know I sent a courier to pay their contract price in full. The Commercians can't sell them, no matter how much he offers."

"What if he doesn't offer a price?" she demanded. "What if he just beams down and…and *takes* them?"

She pulled out of my embrace and went to her desk (she had one beside mine since we shared everything) to get her crystal memory cube. She had used a remembrance sieve to download her memories of her friends onto the cube. Now she pressed the button and I saw the three of them – Zoe and two other females – laughing and eating the confection she called "cheesecake." Or was it cakecheese? I always got it mixed up, though she had tried to teach me.

"Leah and Charlotte could be in trouble right now and it would be all my fault," she whispered, stroking the cube as she watched the happy scene. "All my fault."

I looked at the cube and sighed. Her two friends were lovely – though not as gorgeous as my new mate. (Of course, I might be a little prejudiced in Zoe's favor since I love her to fucking distraction.) One of them had blonde waves pulled back from her face and the other had long, silky hair that fell past her shoulders in a sleek brown waterfall.

Grav came forward to look too and I saw his eyebrows go up when he saw the other two Pure Ones.

"Fuckin' gorgeous," he murmured. "Especially the little *morada*."

"The what?" Zoe looked up at him, frowning.

Grav gestured to the brown haired girl. "That's what my people call a female with long hair. It's rare on Brax and considered very beautiful."

"Oh. That's my friend, Leah," Zoe said. "She works with Autistic children. She's so nice." Her face darkened. "*Too* nice for her own good, really. That's how she ended up with her controlling jerk of a fiancé, Gerald."

"Oh, is she promised to another male?" Grav looked disappointed, then he shrugged. "Figures. She is a Pure One, and a *La-ti-zal*. It's not very fuckin' surprising she's spoken for."

"She doesn't know she's a Pure One *or* a *La-ti-zal*," Zoe told him. "We don't know about any of that stuff on Earth, remember? And my own *La-ti-zal* powers didn't even manifest until I got out into space. So *that* won't help either one of them. Not that being able to pick locks would help anyway, since neither one of them is a burglar."

"Your powers didn't manifest because the atmosphere of your planet was inhibiting them, I think," I said. "And not all *La-ti-zals* have the same powers. You're an Opener, Zoe."

"An *Opener?*" She frowned at me.

"Yes, I've been talking to one of the wise women in the temple of the Goddess about it and that is what she named you. Think about it—you opened the Force Locks, which were keyed to Vorn DNA. Then you opened the door on Gallana which was meant only for one of Ma*jor*an heritage. You also opened the jewel which contained the substance holding the Stars captive to Hurxx's will. And don't forget the most important part…"

"Which is?" She raised an eyebrow at me.

I took both her hands in mine and kissed them.

"You opened my heart, which was shut tight with grief and pain and loss. You're an *Opener*, Zoe. But there's no guarantee your friends would be the same. One might be a Healer…or a Seer…or any number of other things."

"Well, whatever they are, they're in danger," she said stubbornly. "I just know it! Don't ask me how—I get a terrible feeling when I think of Count Creepy McGrabbyHands. I just know he's not dead and I don't want him anywhere *near* my friends."

I stroked her cheek. "If it will make you feel any better, I'll send someone to the Commercians' station to watch over them for a time. I think we can assume that if Doloroso *is* still around, he'll want to act fast to secure a new *La-ti-zal.*"

"The sooner we get to them the better," Zoe agreed. "And can we send a message letting them know I'm all right? It's been weeks since I left and I know they must be worried sick about me. I wanted to contact them earlier but things have been so crazy around here, between the coronation and everything else…."

"I'm afraid it's been more like several of your solar months for them," I told her. "As fast as my ship is—and it's very fast—time moves differently when you're traveling in space as opposed to being stuck on a planet."

"Months?" Zoe's eyes went wide. "They probably think I'm dead. I wish I could visit them myself. I miss them *so much.*"

"I know, sweetheart," I murmured. "But you know the Star of Compassion can't leave Eloim and you need to stay here for at least a full solar year to bond with it."

"I know." She reached up to touch the slender silver circlet she wore. "I'm already getting used to its little voice in my mind. It's become my conscience—like wearing Jiminy Cricket on my head."

I ignored her cultural reference, which passed me by as always, and offered a practical solution instead.

"Maybe whoever we find to watch over your friends can deliver a message that you're well. You could record it on a crystal memory cube." I frowned. "Of course, whoever goes will have to wear a mask and drink the *saphor* compound…unless we can come up with something better to mask his appearance."

"I'll do it."

We both looked up at Grav and I could feel Zoe's surprise echoing my own.

"Are you sure?" she asked doubtfully. "I mean, even with a disguise, you're a *really* big guy by Earth standards. You'd definitely stand out in a crowd."

He shrugged. "All I have to do is deliver a memory cube and go right back up to the Commercians' station. I think I can handle that."

"And…you'll watch over them? For at least a while?" Zoe asked, hesitantly. "I mean, I know the two of you think I'm crazy but I just really feel like Doloroso is still out there, somehow."

"I'll watch 'em." Grav offered her a wolfish grin. "It's what I do—I'm a Protector."

"Oh, thank you." Zoe smiled up at him gratefully and pressed his hand. "I really appreciate it."

"I do too," I said, smiling at him. "Zoe's friends couldn't have a better guardian than you."

Grav nodded. "I'll go get my ship outfitted." He looked at Zoe. "I guess you want me to go as soon as possible?"

"Yes. Yes, please. I'll start recording the messages right away." She pressed her lips together and I could feel her trembling. "And please let us know as soon as you get there and see them that they're okay. All right?"

"Will do." Grav nodded again and gave us a swift salute before walking out the door of the war room. I knew he would be on his way to Earth as soon as his ship was stocked and he had the cubes

Zoe would be recording for her friends.

"There. Grav is going to watch over your friends for a while," I told her. "Better?"

She nodded. "Much better. Although I won't really feel good until we get word back from him that Charlotte and Leah are safe."

"He'll let us know," I promised. "And Zoe—don't worry. Everything is going to be all right."

"Is it?" She bit her lip in a way that made me want to nibble it too. "I hope so, Sarden. But something tells me this isn't over yet. Not by a long shot."

"I hope you're wrong about that, sweetheart." I kissed her, stroking her hair and caressing her cheek.

"I hope so too," she whispered and buried her face in my chest. "I hope so too, Sarden. Oh, God—I really do."

The End

*What's next for Zoe and her friends? Find out soon in **Protected**, Leah's story, and then **Chosen**, Charlotte's tale as the Alien Mate Index series continues.*

And don't forget – stay away from mirrors, spoons, toasters, and any or all reflective surfaces. Earth girls aren't safe anymore and you never know if you might be the next one chosen from…the Alien Mate Index.

Hugs and Happy Reading to you all,

Evangeline, May 5, 2016

Author's Note

If you have enjoyed Abducted, please take a moment to leave a review for Abducted on Amazon at

www.amazon.com/dp/B01FNPMJ9G

Good reviews are like gold for an author--they help other readers decide to take a chance on a new book or series. Also, they give me the warm fuzzies. :)

Thanks! Evangeline

Also by Evangeline Anderson

You can find links to all of the following books at my website:
www.EvangelineAnderson.com

Brides of the Kindred series

Claimed (Also available in Audio and Print format)

Hunted (Also available in Audio format)

Sought (Also Available in Audio format)

Found

Revealed

Pursued

Exiled

Shadowed

Chained

Divided

Devoured (Also available in Print)

Enhanced

Cursed

Enslaved

Targeted

Forgotten

Switched

Mastering the Mistress (Brides of the Kindred Novella)

Born to Darkness series

Crimson Debt (Also available in Audio)

Scarlet Heat   (Also available in Audio)

Ruby Shadows (Also available in Audio)

Cardinal Sins (Coming Soon)

Alien Mate Index series

Abducted

Protected (coming Summer 2016)

Chosen (coming Summer 2016)

The Institute series

The Institute: Daddy Issues

The Institute: Mishka's Spanking

Compendiums

Brides of the Kindred Volume One

    Contains Claimed, Hunted, Sought and Found

Born to Darkness Box Set

    Contains Crimson Debt, Scarlet Heat, and Ruby Shadows

Stand Alone Novels

Purity (Now available in Audio)

Stress Relief

The Last Man on Earth

Anyone U Want

Shadow Dreams

YA Novels

The Academy

About the Author

Evangeline Anderson is the New York Times and USA Today Best Selling Author of the Brides of the Kindred, Alien Mate Index, and Born to Darkness series. She is thirty-something and lives in Florida with a husband, a son, and two cats. She had been writing erotic fiction for her own gratification for a number of years before it occurred to her to try and get paid for it. To her delight, she found that it was actually possible to get money for having a dirty mind and she has been writing paranormal and Sci-fi erotica steadily ever since.

Find her online at her website: www.EvangelineAnderson.com

Come visit for some free reads. Or, to be the first to find out about new books, join her newsletter.

Newsletter – www.EvangelineAnderson.com

Website – www.EvangelineAnderson.com

FaceBook – facebook.com/pages/Evangeline-Anderson-Appreciation-Page/170314539700701?ref=hl

Twitter – twitter.com/EvangelineA

Pinterest – pinterest.com/vangiekitty/

Goodreads – goodreads.com/user/show/2227318-evangeline-anderson

Instagram – instagram.com/evangeline_anderson_author/

Audio book newsletter – www.EvangelineAnderson.com

Made in the USA
Middletown, DE
10 October 2021

49979972R00288